TOMAR

THE EVIL SORCERER

S.L. Reel

Published by Hemingway Publishers

Cover design by Hemingway Publishers

ISBN: Printed in the United States

Edited by: Laurine Mangels

slreel@yahoo.com

Dedication

In remembrance of my cousin, Thomas Rohn. Tom was a kind-hearted individual who always brought joy and laughter into my life.

About the Author

Sandra lives in a quaint community in Nevada. She is the proud mother of a daughter and adores her four grandchildren. Known for her optimism and sociability, she enjoys befriending new people. In her youth, she had the opportunity to drive a semi-truck, which allowed her to explore various parts of the country. Among her favorite places are Aspen, Colorado; Kenai, Alaska; and the Black Hills of South Dakota. She has a love for all animals, and her favorite food is Mexican Cuisine.

Her remarkable teacher, Phyllis Ihly, who gave her the confidence to express her thoughts on paper, served as the inspiration for her writing passion. Fantasy is her preferred genre, filled with mythical creatures, epic battles, and grand adventures. Her second debut novel, **Tomar, The Evil Sorcerer**, captivates readers from the start and is now available in hardcover, paperback, and eBook formats. She is diligently crafting the sequel, **The Zundar Dragon**, aiming to deliver an even more enthralling and action-filled experience. Her aspiration is to motivate others with her words and craft a realm where readers can transcend the mundane and delve into her imaginative world.

Table of Content

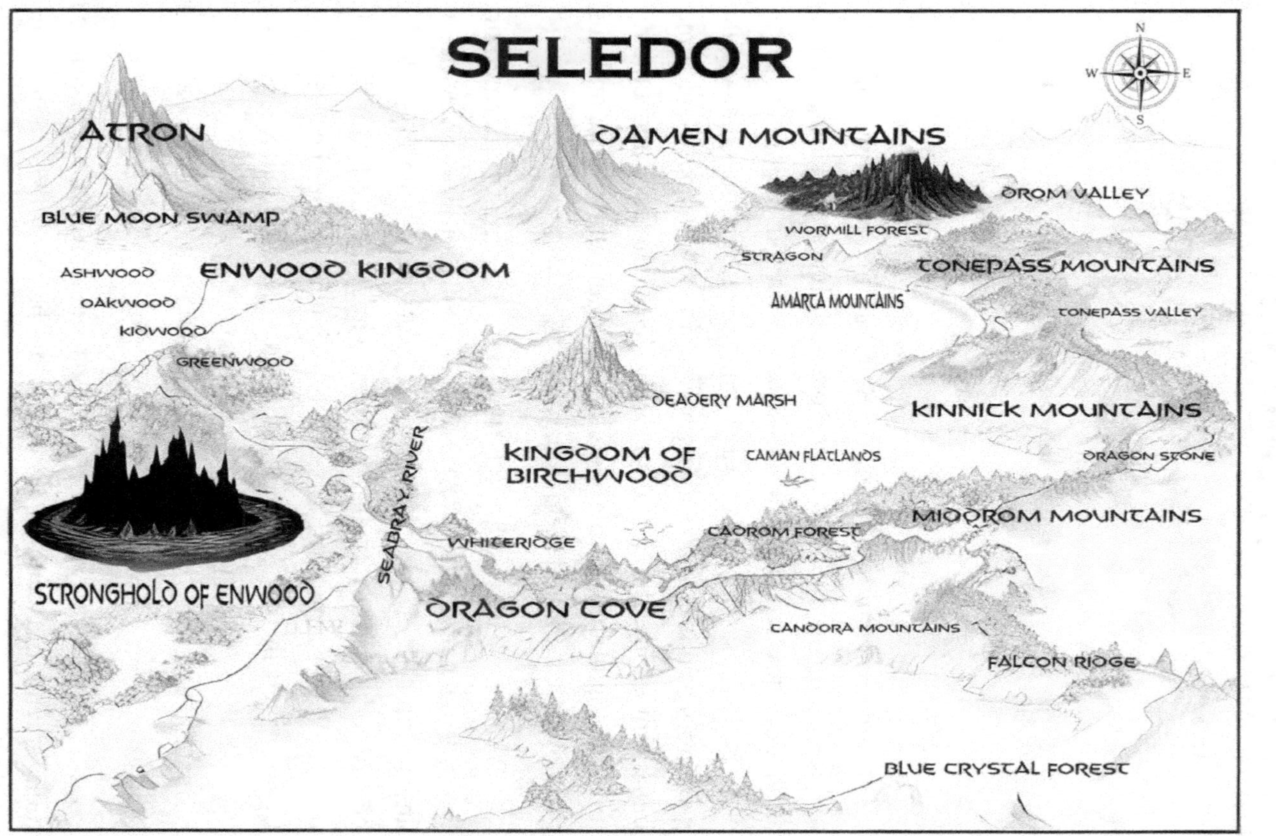
SELEDOR
N E S W
ATRON
DAMEN MOUNTAINS
DROM VALLEY
BLUE MOON SWAMP
WORMILL FOREST
STRAGON
TONEPASS MOUNTAINS
ASHWOOD
ENWOOD KINGDOM
AMARTA MOUNTAINS
TONEPASS VALLEY
OAKWOOD
KIDWOOD
GREENWOOD
DEADERY MARSH
KINNICK MOUNTAINS
KINGDOM OF BIRCHWOOD
CAMAN FLATLANDS
DRAGON STONE
SEABRAY RIVER
CADROM FOREST
MIDDROM MOUNTAINS
WHITERIDGE
STRONGHOLD OF ENWOOD
DRAGON COVE
CANDORA MOUNTAINS
FALCON RIDGE
BLUE CRYSTAL FOREST

Prologue
In the Beginning

In the enchanting realm of Seledor, the brilliance of white magic and sorcery held dominion over all. Its fertile lands, rich and abundant, nurtured crops that reached skyward in their quest for the sun. Noble dragons and brave zundars served as the vigilant protectors of this domain, living harmoniously alongside the human inhabitants. Graceful whitetail deer, sleek antelope, and untamed mustangs galloped freely across the undulating hills and lush meadows that cradled the ancient forests.

Birdsongs wove through the air, weaving a mesmerizing tapestry that captured the very essence of Seledor. Enchanted beings and mortals flourished side by side, reveling in the myriad gifts bestowed by this mystical land. Deep within the mountain thickets, timber wolves remained cloaked in mystery, while the grand oak trees thrived in the Tonepass and Middrom Mountains. Towering woodlands, with their stout and enduring trunks, stood as a testament to nature's steadfast spirit amidst the rugged beauty of Seledor.

In the majestic Kinnick Mountains, titanic redwoods flourished, their splendor ascending towards the heavens. These towering sentinels cast a protective canopy, draping the forest floor in a mosaic of gentle shadows. Their mighty trunks, symbols of enduring strength, served as a sanctuary for countless creatures of the wild.

To the northwest, the Atron Mountains cradled ancient pines that thrived in their embrace. Their lush, aromatic needles prospered in the rich soil of the Mountains. Their sprawling branches extended outward, crafting a lush canopy that sheltered a diverse array of birds and small animals. The sight of these noble pines stood as a profound emblem of the deep bond between the natural world and the essence of life itself.

Those who ventured into the western marshes and wetlands did so at great risk to their lives. This part of Seledor was fraught with peril and uncertainty. Treacherous sinkholes and deceptive quicksand lay in wait for the unwary traveler. The waterways teemed with venomous water serpents and fearsome alligators. The grasses and reeds of the wetlands created a perilous boundary between land and water, encircling the lakes and streams. The thick foliage, coupled with the unpredictable depths, rendered navigation a daunting task, and lurking predators only heightened the dangers. Only the most intrepid and skilled adventurers dared to tread upon these hazardous grounds, seeking to unveil the secrets hidden within.

A river marked the border of the Enwood territory. The stronghold of Pildar, the Potentate, stood majestically upon a notable hill to the west of the Seabray River, which formed the northern limit of Enwood. To the east, the land blossomed into a lush forest, teeming with diverse creatures and ancient trees that seemed to whisper their hidden tales. Dotted across the expanse, scattered towns and hamlets breathed life into the landscape, each carrying its own stories and traditions.

In the distant northern reaches, the Damen Mountains towered with grandeur. To the northeast, the mysterious Drom Valley awaits, cloaked in secrets, beckoning only the most daring souls. Further south, Black Wormill Forest stood as a foreboding sentinel, guarding the shadowy stronghold of the wicked sorcerers, Tomar and Nadora.

As one steps into this malevolent forest, the radiant sunlight is devoured by the darkness, while a chilling fog dances among the twisted trunks of ancient trees. The ghostly silhouettes of fallen warriors flitted through the shadows, casting an unsettling presence upon the woodland. Jagged thorns of black and brown encircled the western edge, forming a foreboding barrier. The land undulated and contorted, heavy with the foul scents of smoke, decay, and rot.

Within the tangled underbrush, monstrous ebony serpents and gigantic scarlet spiders lurked. The fearsome Ice Cat and the elusive Nightshade Fire Wolf, summoned by the sorceress Nadora, patrolled the Black Wormill Forest, ever watchful in their guardianship of the dark palace. Other creatures, shaped by the harshness of their surroundings, flourished in this perilous realm, their predatory instincts honed to perfection. Whispers of legends spoke of a mythical beast hidden deep within the mountains, safeguarding a treasure that bestows unimaginable power upon its wielder. In the northern lands, Giant Mountain Trolls and the fearsome Gilzdars, with their flat visages and reptilian hides of black and gray, roamed. These formidable creatures, renowned for their immense strength, presented a grave danger to any who dared to traverse their territory, adding yet another layer of peril to this unforgiving land.

In a realm shrouded in mystery, Tomar and his wife, Nadora, etched their mightiest enchantments into a shadowy tome, forging a vessel of sinister power. They christened this formidable volume the "Sormara", a grimoire designed to uncover vile curses and expose those who conspired against them. Its gilded edges gleamed as it revealed secrets, granting them dominion over minds and mastery of the elements, solidifying their reign of terror.

As the seasons turned, the Sormara's might burgeoned, birthing increasingly perilous spells. Clad in the strength of this dread artifact, they became nearly invincible, instilling fear in the hearts of all who dared to oppose them. The wicked sorcerers would scour the tome's pages beneath the ascendant moon. In the gentle embrace of moonlight, they convened in their hidden refuge, encircled by flickering azure flames and the musty scent of ancient scrolls. With each page turned, they delved deeper into the arcane knowledge of the Sormara, unearthing new incantations and dark secrets that heightened their nefarious powers. As they chanted in unison, their eyes glimmered with a wicked light, fully aware that their dominion over the mystical arts was growing ever more formidable.

On a chill night, bathed in the silvery glow of the full moon, they gently unfurled the ancient manuscript. A disquieting silence cloaked the chamber as the pages of the Sormara fluttered with eager anticipation, charged with electric energy. The tome unveiled the alliance—a bold pact between Cadar, the Sorcerer of Light, and Masar, the Dragon King, forged in defiance of tyranny. Together, they embarked on a noble quest to dismantle the oppressive rule that darkened their land. Fully aware of the dangers ahead, Cadar and Masar stood steadfast in their resolve, driven by an unyielding pursuit of balance and justice. Yet, unbeknownst to them, their valiant undertaking would summon forth trials beyond imagination—challenges that would stretch their endurance to its very limits.

Knowing the peril his family would face should their endeavor fail, Cadar concealed his expectant wife and their unborn child within the protective embrace of the Middrom Mountains. His heart was heavy with sorrow at the thought of parting from them, yet he grasped the necessity of shielding them from the looming turmoil. With a sorrowful farewell, he pressed a tender kiss upon his wife and vowed to return triumphant, fervently hoping that their sacrifice would not be in vain.

Beneath the vast expanse of a star-studded sky, Cadar and Masar set forth on their treacherous quest. Shadows stretched ominously, obscuring their path as they pressed onward, spurred by an urgent sense of purpose. The wind howled like a banshee, a chilling reminder of the perils that lurked nearby. They recognized that their triumph was vital, not solely for their own kin, but for the tranquility of the entire realm. The valiant defenders of Seledor stood firm, determined to eradicate the malevolence once and for all.

With each step, their resolve deepened, fortified by an unwavering belief in their abilities and the grim truth that failure was not an option. The weight of responsibility bore down upon them, yet they were resolute in their willingness to bear it for the sake of their beloved. As they ventured deeper into the treacherous night, Cadar and Masar's determination remained unyielding, prepared to face whatever trials lay ahead. Alas, disaster struck, and they soon fell prey to a cunning trap set by the sorcerers, and the Sormara unleashed their dreaded black-ice demons. These fiends emerged with a ferocity that chilled the very marrow of Cadar and Masar, their razor-sharp claws and glowing crimson eyes instilling a paralyzing fear. Yet, they refused to succumb to despair; instead, they summoned their inner fortitude and crafted a plan to escape this dire predicament. They fought valiantly against the encroaching darkness—but ultimately, the sinister forces triumphed. Without the guardians of Seledor, the realm descended into chaos and despair. Once a land of vibrancy and harmony, it now lay in ruins, its people ensnared in an unending cycle of fear and uncertainty.

Tomar and Nadora ruled with an iron grip, casting a pall of dread and subjugation over the land's denizens. Their ironclad hold on power brooked no dissent, as they mercilessly snuffed out any flicker of rebellion that dared to challenge their supremacy. The land, once vibrant and alive, now lay ravaged by cruelty and death, leaving its people in desperate longing for liberation from their tyrannical reign. The once-bountiful forests withered, disrupting the sacred harmony of nature.

Yet, from the depths of despair, the zundars and dragons rose against the encroaching darkness, their spirits unbroken. Defying the odds, they forged a formidable alliance, their valor igniting a spark of hope among the oppressed. With daring assaults upon the oppressors' stronghold, they fought valiantly to restore justice and freedom to their cherished homeland. However, as the dragons and zundars found solace in their lofty mountain abodes, a cataclysmic explosion rent the night, obliterating their empires and heralding the demise of the Dragon Dynasty. Only three zundars emerged from the ashes, burdened by profound grief as they mourned their fallen kin and comrades. Their once-mighty coalition lay in tatters. Yet, in sorrow, the zundars vowed to honor the memory of those they had lost and to rekindle the flame of hope in a world cloaked in shadow

The woodlands, once lush, fell prey to wickedness. Birds silenced their songs. A fierce blaze raged uncontrollably, casting a pall of smoke and ash that veiled the sun's warm embrace. As the leaves of the barren trees drifted to the ground, the landscape became a stark wasteland. In the depths of tangled thickets, thriving in the shadows, spiders and serpents found their dominion, armyworms feasting upon rotting bark. Once a land of abundance, Seledor now languished in dire drought and famine, its soil stripped of vitality by dark forces. A grave scarcity of water and sustenance reigned, for the rivers and lakes had vanished into arid nothingness. Here, its denizens now battled for survival, clinging to the last remnants of hope.

Synopsis

A sorrowful raven, steeped in the spirit of Tomar and Nadora, embarks on a treacherous journey to the north, fraught with peril at every turn. Their path leads them to a hidden cave, the lair of a mysterious sorceress yet to unveil her true nature.

The Sorceress of Light watches intently as the skies to the northeast grow dark and foreboding. With a swift motion, she sends forth Lundar, the resplendent white eagle, to survey the rugged mountains ahead. Yet, in a twist of fate, Tomar seizes the eagle, and in a moment of peril, Lundar urgently conveys a desperate message to Suhzar, his cries echoing with urgency through the winds.

Upon receiving this urgent call, Suhzar transforms into a mighty dragon and soars to the eagle's aid. Upon his arrival in the Valley of Drom, he encounters a fearsome army gathering under Tomar's command. Realizing the dire threat posed to Seledor, he swiftly warns Easha, who comprehends the pressing need to eradicate this sinister force before it shrouds the realm in shadow. Without delay, she assembles a diverse coalition to fight for this vital quest.

A quintet of brave warrior factions embarked upon a daring journey to the fabled Valley of Tonepass, encountering a myriad of trials, including ferocious creatures' intent on thwarting their advance. United by a common purpose, they endure the perils of mortality and turmoil as they traverse unknown territories. Upon arriving at their sought-after haven, they gather to devise a plan for the impending clash. Faced with peril and the ever-present specter of death, they stand firm, prepared to confront the malevolent forces in a pivotal showdown that promises to demand a steep toll.

1st Chapter

A mournful black raven cried out, his voice echoing through the air. In its beak, it bore the tormented spirits of Seledor's once-mighty dark lords, Tomar and Nadora. The raven grasped the weight of its mission: to transport these malevolent souls to safety, shielding them from the encroaching light.

Above the notorious Fortress of Doom, a foreboding sky loomed, thick with lingering dark enchantments. The sinister stronghold quaked as if seized by a fierce tremor. Clouds of dust whirled chaotically, cloaking the area in a shroud of uncertainty. The walls emitted a mournful groan, and cracks in the stonework widened ominously. The sorrowful cries of black vultures echoed as they circled above their sovereign's domain. A chilling wind swept through Wormill Forest, causing the air to grow frigid.

"I must seek a way to escape from this crumbling bastion before I lose the very essence of Tomar and Nadora," the raven murmured, his heart racing with trepidation. "The chill that envelops me is unlike any I have ever encountered; it seeps into my very being. Could it be that the dust has transformed into ice? The horror that has befallen the sorcerers is beyond my comprehension. I must tread lightly, for the assassins may return."

With his keen, obsidian eyes surveying the area around him, the raven beheld the scattered remnants swirling in disarray. A palpable sense of danger hung thick in the air. The eastern wall exuded foul vapors, poisoning the air with unseen malice. Aware of the dire situation, the raven knew he must act with haste to protect himself from the deadly mists that enveloped the atmosphere. He knew hesitation meant death. Time was slipping—its escape had to be swift. Drawing a deep breath through his nostrils, he focused on finding a route to liberation from the crumbling stronghold ere time slipped through his grasp.

The air was oppressive and suffocating, rendering each breath a daunting task. "I must find a way to flee this place before all crumbles to ruin," the raven rasped, flitting anxiously through the wreckage. His heart raced as he desperately sought an escape. His wings fought against the toxin-laced wind, their frantic beats stirring the dust into choking clouds. With every tick of the clock, the palace fell further into decay, amplifying the urgency of his flight.

Then—pain. A jagged stone struck his left wing, jolting through bone and muscle. The sharp pang of agony sent him spiraling towards the floor. I must master my descent or perish, he pondered, flipping over mid-air and clenching his beak tightly as he braced against the inevitable descent. The collision came hard, and he awkwardly landed upon a mound of tattered robes. Striving to regain his footing, the raven understood he must flee with haste ere it was too late. A fierce determination to survive ignited within him.

"Fortune favored me this day, yet I cannot rely on such whims again. I must seek a sanctuary," he whispered, grimacing as his wounded form protested while he sought out an exit. Trembling with trepidation, his gaze swept the surroundings until it fell upon a window.

"A passage to the north! That shall be my route to freedom."

Fueled by the fire of adrenaline, the raven propelled himself forward, disregarding the pain that coursed through him. The vision of liberty and safety urged him onward, racing toward the open window, his sole beacon of hope for survival.

To regain his composure, he inhaled deeply, centering his thoughts on the gravity of his quest. As he neared the open window, the palace trembled around him, its stonework cracking under unseen forces. Yet his gaze remained fixed upon the wooden frame. The quaking walls only strengthened his determination. He recognized that this very opening was his gateway to liberation. With a final surge of determination coursing through his veins, he leapt towards the aperture just as the edifice shuddered once more, unleashing a torrent of debris. His heart thundered fiercely within his chest.

"The window frame has shattered. I must seek another path to freedom. The crumbling ceiling poses a deadly peril."

He quickly surveyed the chamber for another means of escape, his mind racing with options. His eyes fell upon a narrow staircase, once concealed behind a tapestry, urging him to hasten towards it. As he descended, the din of chaos intensified, growing ever more ominous.

The air thickened with dread as he comprehended that any hesitation could lead to calamity in this perilous and life-threatening predicament.

Descending into the shadowy depths of the fortress to regain his steadiness, he fought to pierce through the haze of tears that blurred his vision. The flickering crimson beams of light twisted the ruined halls, warping their surroundings. His breath hitched in his throat, and he gasped and coughed.

"I know these phantoms arise from the noxious fumes I have inhaled; I am losing my grip," he whispered hoarsely. Struggling to clear his mind, the raven understood the pressing need to banish the disarray and discover a path to safety. With each fleeting moment, the urgency and despair of his plight grew, shrouded by the effects of the toxins.

Meanwhile, hidden in the shadows, the sorcerer crept silently behind Nadora, blinking twice as he siphoned her magical essence, placing her in dire jeopardy.

Feeling her powers diminish, Nadora turned in shock, locking eyes with Tomar's wicked grin. Realizing the necessity for swift action to prevent him from further depleting her magic, she summoned the remnants of her power to conjure a protective barrier around herself, prepared to withstand Tomar's treachery.

Yet, it was too late. The sorcerer erupted into a victorious cackle, reveling in the exhilarating surge of power that coursed through his veins after he had consumed Nadora's magical essence.

The sorceress let out a heart-rending wail, "Nooo!" From the raven's beak came a low, grief-stricken grunt, and at that moment, Nadora's spirit was violently expelled—cast into the abyss.

A tidal wave of sorrow and regret engulfed him as he lamented the extinguishing of Nadora's life force, his tears cascading down his cheeks. Overwhelmed by despair, he collapsed to the ground, his breath trembling with anguish, "Though my vision is clouded by tears," he whispered. "I must press on. I sense a concealed portal that promises freedom, yet where might it be?" Drawing a deep breath, he used his wings to brush away the tears and staggered forth through the dust-laden chamber, steadfast in his resolve, knowing that beyond this chamber lay its only path to salvation.

Tomar's heavy spirit wrapped around him like a dense shroud, urging him to continue his quest. He surveyed his surroundings, searching for an escape route. A soft breeze brushed against his face, easing the tension gripping his chest. Then, his gaze flickered to the left, and his voice rang out in sudden recognition.

"I see dirt swirling on the ground!"

A narrow crack caught his eye—an opening just large enough to offer a chance at freedom. Fueled by a surge of adrenaline, the raven tapped into his final reserves of strength and propelled himself toward the gap in the wall.

As he maneuvered through the tiny aperture, a suffocating atmosphere surrounded him, the air thick and unrelenting. A rush of dizziness washed over him. "What's going on?" he murmured, his body trembling from exhaustion before he fell to the ground, succumbing to the void of unconsciousness.

A storm gathered on the horizon, its heavy pall casting an eerie shadow over the fallen raven. The wind started to whip around him, carrying the scent of impending rain and the distant rumble of thunder.

Meanwhile, a growing sense of urgency enveloped Tomar as he pondered his dire predicament. The sands of time slipped swiftly through his fingers, compelling him to act without delay. Harnessing the depths of his dark sorcery, he unleashed the possession incantation. Brilliant crimson rays burst forth from his being, his eyes igniting with an eerie glow that pierced the very essence of the raven. As the enchantment took root, he seized dominion over the creature. In a heartbeat, the raven blinked open its eyes, regaining a semblance of awareness, and staggered toward a nearby tree as if guided by an unseen force. Its cries echoed with a blend of despair and frustration. A wave of confusion washed over him as he whispered, "Could it be that the toxins I have inhaled are clouding my mind? I must reach the tree ere I succumb to darkness once more."

The frigid wind wailed as he lay beneath the blackened tree, the fallen leaves shrouding him from view. After five long hours, the withered foliage disintegrated; the icy gusts whisked them away, unveiling Tomar, the Black Raven. His heart surged with a rush of exhilaration.

"Freedom!" The sorcerer was engulfed by a wave of joyous elation. With wide eyes, he beheld his slender limbs and feathered form. "I stand on the brink of reclaiming my true form," he murmured, his voice tinged with unshakable confidence. Yet caution tampered his thoughts. "But first, I must find sanctuary."

A distant rumble carried across the land—low and insistent.

"A squall approaches," he mused. As lightning danced across the East Middrom Mountains, he watched, transfixed, caught in the thrilling mix of dread and wonder at nature's raw and untamed.

"Verily, the art of flight cannot be so daunting," the sorcerer mused, casting a cautious glance at the shadowy boughs that swayed about him. Lost in contemplation, Tomar pondered his next endeavor. Then, with a burst of resolve, he dashed forth and unfurled his wings, only to stumble over his own limbs and tumble face-first into the ground.

Grumbling, he muttered, "Well, that did not unfold as I had envisioned."

Drawing a deep breath of the muggy air and pushing past his frustration, he proclaimed, "This time, I shall ascend from this place." With resolve gleaming in his gaze, he spread his wings anew and charged forth, only to crash to the ground yet again, the impact echoing in his ears. He exhaled a weary sigh but remained resolute in his pursuit of refuge before the squall descended.

The foreboding clouds drew nearer, and the wind began to howl. With haste, he scanned the surroundings for any haven that might protect him from the impending storm.

With a breath filled with determination, Tomar reflected, *the gusting wind hinders my escape, and the rain is closing in fast.* "Raven, I know you can hear my call. I need your assistance. We must unite to find shelter before the tempest strikes. Decide quickly; the storm is racing toward us." His heart raced as he reached out to raven, longing for a response. The dark clouds hovered ominously above, ready to engulf him.

"If you set my spirit free, I could carry us away from the storm's wrath."

"I cannot do that, but I promise to free you once I regain my physical form."

Silence hung for a beat. Then came a reluctant reply:

"I have no choice but to offer you my help. You need to assist me by managing my right wing while I handle the left. Our movements must be in perfect harmony; we need to coordinate our wing beats, or we'll remain grounded."

Taking a deep breath, the raven announced, "When I say 'go,' you need to begin flapping your wing. Do you understand?"

"Yes," came the confident reply from within.

A pause. Then—

"Go."

Tomar bolted forward, feet pushing against the ground.

"Stop, sorcerer! Why did you make me run?" the raven squawked, frustration crackling in its voice. "Birds don't run; we rise by flapping our wings. Let's try this again."

This time, there was no hesitation. Together, they unfurled their wings and ascended into the sky.

Tomar gazed in awe at the enchanting, shadowy landscape beneath them, the world stretching far below as they climbed higher. A surge of exhilaration and freedom enveloped him. The sorcerer directed, "We must journey northward across the Damen Mountains. There lies our sanctuary," all the while scanning the terrain, taken aback by the diminutive stature of the fortress trees.

"Focus on the path we are taking, sorcerer," the raven scolded, irritation laced in its voice. "I grow tired of your unpredictable movements,"

Tomar ignored the bird's complaints, captivated by the mesmerizing and ominous scenery that stretched out below.

"Sorcerer, you must grant me control over my body. If you do not, we will fall from the sky," the raven pleaded.

Finally, Tomar tore his gaze from the enchanting vista and focused on their quest, proclaiming, "It is within our grasp; I vow to remain vigilant, yet the exhilaration of soaring is a potent distraction." He inhaled deeply, reminding himself of the significance of their undertaking.

"I offer you one final chance," the raven warned. "Traveling with you has drained my strength."

"Do not let your fatigue cast a shadow over me," the sorcerer retorted sharply. "I am committed to my responsibilities. Your lack of stamina is irrelevant to me."

The raven bristled. "I have plenty of strength. I am powerful. Sorcerer, you have disrespected me, and I will not tolerate it. Do not speak to me again."

"So be it!" the sorcerer shot back, his fury ignited by the raven's mockery.

Their quarrel faded into the wind as they soared above the majestic four peaks of Damen. Below them, the perilous landscape stretched far and wide. The thick, fog-laden air invigorated their spirits, igniting a thrilling sense of adventure and danger within.

As they neared the top of Damen, the raven cawed, "Tomar, stay sharp! We are close to the summit. Remember, we must work together, or we risk bringing disaster upon ourselves."

The warning came too late. The raven landed awkwardly, tumbling head over heels across the desolate mountaintop. He skidded through the dust and rock until a sturdy bush broke its fall.

For a moment, silence hung between them. The sudden stop had left them both momentarily dazed, but Tomar quickly collected himself and groaned, "Is this how birds usually land?" he muttered, pressing a wing against his aching body. "My head is spinning, and my body is sore."

"No, sorcerer! You have nearly led us to our doom. You disregarded my warnings," the raven cawed, his eye trembling with anger.

Tomar met his stare with a defiant glare, his voice unwavering and icy, "I'm not to blame for this," he shot back, frustration lacing his tone. "The winds were too fierce and threw me off balance." With a resolute attempt to ignore the enraged bird, he turned his focus to the right. "Is there a threat coming our way?" he inquired, scanning his surroundings as his senses prickled. Then, his breath hitched, zeroing in on the impending danger. "Raven, a red spider is charging toward us. We need to take flight!"

They ascended into the sky, but not before the predator seized their tail feathers in a ruthless grip. The sorcerer and the raven twisted and turned through the air, desperately attempting to dislodge the relentless attacker, who held on with fierce determination.

The raven exclaimed, "Sorcerer, this weight is too much! We can't keep flying like this," struggling to maintain altitude. "What should I do? I can feel the spider creeping up my feathers. Soon, it will be able to inject its venom into us."

The seriousness of their situation sent the sorcerer's mind racing as he searched for a solution. A strategy began to take shape in his thoughts, and he concentrated on steering them toward safety.

"Raven, head towards those boulders ahead," he commanded. "As we approach, ascend higher. If luck is on our side, the spider will release its hold before we crash into them."

The raven acknowledged the sorcerer's strategy with a nod. The boulders grew nearer, and they prepared for the daring maneuver ahead.

The world snapped into focus as they raced forward, driven by the desire for their plan to succeed. The venomous fangs of the spider inched closer, its grip unyielding as they approached the rocky outcrop. Finally, they arrived at the boulders, where the raven and the sorcerer expertly started their ascent. As they climbed higher, the spider's grip began to falter, giving them the chance to escape just in time and avoid a collision with the rocks.

The spider, relinquishing its hold, dropped onto a lower boulder and scurried away into the shadows.

Tomar and the raven erupted in joyous celebration. The sorcerer felt a wave of relief wash over him, grateful for their narrow escape. The raven cawed triumphantly, his wings spread wide, unscathed.

As the sorcerer relished the refreshing breeze brushing against his face, he felt an unsettling shift in the atmosphere. "Something feels amiss," he whispered, his instincts on high alert. Glancing over his shoulder, his pulse quickened.

"What are those feathers I see?" Tomar's gaze widened as recognition flashed in his eye. "They belong to an eagle!" He knew what the eagle's arrival meant—it was an omen, a harbinger of death.

"Raven, a menacing eagle, is on our tail! It's getting closer!" They turned to the left, spotting the enormous bird, its expansive wings casting a dark shadow over the ground as it hurtled toward them.

With an expression of fierce hunger and unwavering resolve, the eagle's sharp, penetrating gaze locked on its target. Its piercing cry sliced through the air, announcing a victorious herald of impending doom.

Tomar realized that the Harpy Eagle before him was not just any foe; it was a mythical predator renowned for its unmatched accuracy and terrifying claws.

Urgency tightened his voice, and Tomar asked, "What plan can we devise to escape this relentless creature? It's closing in!" He urged his companion to quicken their pace to evade the relentless hunter. His heartbeat thundered in his ear as he focused on their next move, acutely aware that a single error could spell disaster.

"It's bleak, my friend. Once a harpy eagle sets its sights on a prey, it won't back down. I've witnessed one crush a coyote's skull. The enormous bird gouged out its eyes and, with its formidable talons, tore through flesh as it devoured the raw meat," he recounted, his voice quaking.

As Tomar listened intently to the eerie story told by the raven, he resolutely proclaimed, "I've made it this far, and I won't let a monstrous bird bring me down." Realizing that his only chance of survival lay in outsmarting this persistent predator, he searched the terrain beneath him for a place to hide. In a flash, he spotted the dense undergrowth to the north, offering the cover he desperately needed.

At that moment, the raven gasped for air, his heart pounding with fear. The shock of fear coursing through him only strengthened his determination to flee before the eagle could close in. With every labored breath, he pushed forward, fully aware that his very life depended on his swiftness.

As the tempest unleashed its fury upon the Northeast Mountains, Tomar pondered that perhaps remaining dry may not be the wisest of choices. Observing the unyielding deluge, he understood that he must craft a more cunning strategy to outsmart the relentless predator and ensure his safety. "Raven, though it may seem mad, we ought to retreat and soar into the heart of the storm. If my instincts serve me right, the rain shall bewilder the eagle, granting us the opportunity to navigate through the lesser trees and seek refuge."

Raven hesitated, "I am confused by what you say. The storm poses a threat to us too."

Tomar's determination flared, "We must have faith, for this is our greatest chance to escape. We need to confront this danger if we are to survive. The rain may be a fierce adversary, but if we stay on our current course, the eagle will dominate us. We must take this calculated risk to improve our odds of survival."

His voice steadied as he laid out their grim reality. "You have two choices: let the beast tear us apart and feast on our remains, or face the storm with bravery. What will you choose?" he asked, a trace of exasperation in his tone.

Raven nodded thoughtfully and replied, "I choose to face the storm. I refuse to accept being its prey. How can we slip past the eagle without falling into its trap?" He recognized that daring to confront the danger was crucial for any hope of escaping the eagle's grasp.

Tomar exhaled sharply, his mind already set on their course.

"We will confront the eagle directly," he announced. "The moment we meet its intense gaze, we'll swiftly shift to the right and plunge into the downpour. This maneuver will compel the eagle to pivot and pursue us, granting us a fleeting opportunity to reach the storm. Once enveloped by the torrential rain, we can leverage the strong winds and unyielding rain to our benefit. The eagle will find it difficult to maintain its focus, increasing our odds of making a successful escape."

Raven swallowed hard. "Looking into the eagle's eyes sends a shiver down my spine," he confessed, quaking slightly. "But we have no other options."

"I sense your fear, but you must find your bravery. Our destinies hang in the balance," Tomar asserted with unwavering conviction. "Are you prepared to confront the eagle directly and seize our chance for freedom?"

Summoning his resolve for the challenges ahead, Raven took a deep breath and announced, "I am ready. Let's begin this quest."

The two advanced, their resolve igniting their bravery as they faced the imminent danger posed by the eagle. They realized that their survival hinged on outsmarting the powerful bird. As they initiated their strategy, a pulse of raw instinct coursed through their bodies. With each strong flap of their wings, they closed in on the eagle.

Then, as one, they turned to confront their foe. The eagle let out a piercing cry, its talons ready to strike as Raven stood firm. Harnessing his magic, the sorcerer blinked three times, momentarily disorienting the eagle. Seizing the moment, Raven and Tomar veered to the right, heading toward the cloudburst, then swiftly darted left, vanishing into the thick foliage.

Silence swallowed them. Tomar and his companion took a moment to rest, concealed within the thick foliage, fully aware that they had eluded the eagle's relentless pursuit. They breathed a sigh of relief, having cleverly outwitted their formidable adversary.

As they observed the magnificent bird gliding above, the duo remained perfectly still, understanding that even the slightest movement could reveal their hiding spot to the fierce raptor. With great caution, they inched further into the verdant underbrush, hoping to evade the eagle's keen eyesight.

The hungry eagle quickly caught sight of a small boar and dove down with impressive speed.

Feeling thankful for its survival, the bird murmured, "We have succeeded."

Tomar, still riding the high of their escape, smirked, "Only because you have the strength of a powerful sorcerer at your side," he replied, pride shining through his words.

Grateful for their unexpected escape, Tomar and his ally Raven emerged from the foliage just as the eagle shifted its focus to a new target. A burst of vigor coursed through them, invigorated by their encounter with such a daunting foe and their hard-earned victory. Relief washed over them as they hurried away, eager to distance themselves from the threatening predator.

2nd Chapter

As the sun sank behind the majestic Atron Mountains, its fading light cast long, jagged shadows across the rugged terrain. A fierce northern wind swept across the landscape, whipping dust and brittle leaves into the air while carrying with it the scent of damp soil and ancient stone.

Tomar and the raven reached the Valley of Drom, where a thick, foreboding fog curled around their ankles. Navigating through the murky haze, they spotted enormous boulders guarding the entrance of a cave.

"What's troubling you, Tomar?"

"I'm weary. I'll feel much more at ease once we find a place to rest."

"You are wise, sorcerer."

The duo ventured into the cold, dim cave, their senses sharpened as they examined the damp walls for any signs of danger. The unsettling atmosphere surrounded them, enhanced by the soft sound of water trickling nearby. A faint shimmer called to them from the depths, enticing them to draw closer. With each step, the air thickened with an ancient energy, igniting their curiosity and heightening their anticipation.

"I don't sense any immediate threats. That's a good sign. What do you think, sorcerer?"

"Yes, I agree, but the cave floor is littered with an unusual amount of debris. It's clear that some sort of explosion has shaken this mountain. We must stay alert until we uncover the truth behind this place. Raven, look over there—there's a robe leaning against the eastern wall. I can't help but wonder why it was left behind, along with remnants of past meals."

Raven nodded, deep in thought. "Tomar, it could be a trap." He ruffled its feathers and scanned the cave with sharp, calculating eyes, looking for any additional signs of danger.

A sense of curiosity enveloped them as they cautiously approached the shadowy robe, an unsettling sensation washing over them as if unseen eyes were watching. It was clear that something unusual had transpired in this eerie location.

As they trod carefully across the cave floor, they stayed alert, acutely aware of their environment while scrutinizing both the space around them and the mysterious garment they had discovered. Was it merely forgotten—or did it hold secrets that were waiting to be unraveled?

"Don't worry, Raven; fortune is on our side. We'll have a meal and rest here for the night," Tomar reassured.

"It's time to indulge, my friend." The raven seized a piece of dried rat, tilted its head back, and swallowed it in one gulp.

Tomar exclaimed, "This meat is incredible."

The raven clicked its beak, amusement flickering in its gaze. "You look surprised. In the world of birds, every morsel is a delight."

Their voices seemed small against the cave's vast emptiness. As the two friends relished their meal, an eerie silence enveloped the cave, amplifying every sound they made. It was a silence that was too perfect, as if the cave itself was listening—waiting. They continued to eat, hoping that a satisfied stomach would provide some solace before night descended.

Tomar yawned, exhaustion creeping in like a slow tide, "It's time to call it a day." They wrapped themselves in the frayed fabric of the robe and closed their eyes. The stillness spread impossibly wide, as if the walls themselves were holding their breath in anticipation. A heavy tension lingered in the air, cloaking them in darkness. Despite their full bellies, an unsettling sensation kept sleep at bay.

• • •

As dawn's first light spilled across the horizon, the stars faded, making way for a new day. The meadows and forests of Seledor stirred to life, vibrant with color and promise. Yet, deep within the cave, where shadows clung like a shroud, morning's warmth could not breach the darkness. A foreboding presence lingered. A sinister force stood pooling at the entrance, guarding, casting a dark pall that kept the sun's warmth at bay.

Tomar stirred within his borrowed body, feeling the raven's steady yet rapid heartbeat beneath layers of feathers. As he adjusted to his host's senses while filtering the world through unfamiliar perceptions, a distant sound reached him. Footsteps.

"Raven, it's time to wake up. Someone is approaching. I can hear their footsteps getting closer. If we remain silent, they might not discover us. We must be careful," Tomar whispered urgently.

The ground trembled beneath their feet, a clear warning that danger was drawing near. Anxiety gripped their hearts as they braced themselves for the unseen threat lurking within the cursed cave.

They held their breath for a moment—one mind guiding the body, another lingering beneath, wary but bound. They strained to hear every sound that became increasingly distinct with each tick of the clock. Soon, a warped figure flickered across the northern wall of the cave, distorted by the dim glow of morning's unwelcome arrival. A slow, creeping dread unfurled within Tomar.

"Raven, stop fidgeting. Your movements might give us away."

"I can't help it," Raven replied, trembling against his will.

Tomar steadied his presence, pressing calm into his borrowed muscles. The tension between them was palpable—a silent struggle between sorcerer and host, instinct and reason.

"Focus on a stone; it will help clear your mind and bring you some calm."

Taking Tomar's advice, the raven concentrated on the rough, dark stone to his left. Tomar felt the heartbeat stabilizing. His influence was molding seamlessly into his companion's instincts.

"Raven, we'll stay hidden under the cloak until we discover who resides here."

"I agree; your judgment is sound," Raven replied, and they nestled beneath the robe, ready to face whatever awaited them. Only their round, dark eyes peeked out. A surge of confidence washed over Raven; with the sorcerer by his side, he felt they could tackle any looming darkness together.

"It's a woman," Tomar gasped, his eye widening as she stepped into view.

She held a candlestick, its flames flickering in shades of blue and black, while her tattered black gown hung loosely around her. Her long, wild, dark hair, tangled and unkempt, framed her face like woven shadows and appeared as if it had never known a comb.

As she drew closer, Tomar scrutinized her cold brown eyes, which betrayed no emotion. It was clear she had endured something deeply tragic. Without thinking, Tomar urged Raven forward. Emerging from the shadows, he took a step toward her. "What are you doing?" Raven's voice cut through his thoughts, his tone laced with warning. "You're putting us both at risk. She could be dangerous." He hesitated before adding, "I don't want to abandon the cloak."

With determination, the sorcerer moved forward, tightening his grip on the raven's instincts and declaring, "Raven, whether you like it or not, we're closing in on the mortal."

As the raven confronted the sorcerer, Raven's right foot struck the ground with steadfast determination. The struggle between sorcerer and vessel was brief, and it quickly became clear that Tomar's might had overwhelmed him, compelling him to push onward.

Mirra stood frozen at the sound of movement, her senses on high alert. She scanned her surroundings, but everything seemed normal.

"Who dares to invade my cave?" Her voice trembled with fear, her brows knitting together in a fierce warning. "Reveal yourself, or face your end." She strained to hear, but the oppressive silence weighed heavily on her, making her own breath sound unnaturally loud in her ears. As she concentrated, her heart raced, yearning for any sign of the hidden intruder. Ready for action, her left hand instinctively reached for the dagger resting on the rocky ledge. Taking a deep breath, she declared, "I seek no conflict, but I will strike if you threaten me," her voice brimming with fierce intensity. The lingering quiet only heightened her anxiety, amplifying the sensation that unseen eyes were tracking her every movement. Then, a voice answered.

"It's just me and my companion, Raven," Tomar said, locking eyes with her. His deep voice reached Mirra, causing her heart to race. A wave of relief washed over her, though a trace of concern remained. As the raven approached, she instinctively stepped back, her gaze flitting through the dim light as she focused intently on the raven.

"You are a bird. How can I understand your words?" she asked, lowering her eyes, her expression a mix of disbelief and astonishment. The woman's clay-colored, oval features reflected her unease. Mirra gently caressed her left arm, grounding herself and then ran her tongue along her dark bottom lip, an unconscious attempt to steady herself in the face of uncertainty.

"Though I am a bird, I can communicate. It's quite a tale, but I assure you, I mean no harm," Tomar replied in a soothing tone.

Silence stretched between them as Mirra pondered over his words; her skepticism began to wane, replaced by curiosity.

Perched on a stone next to the enigmatic woman, the sorcerer asked, "What name do you go by?"

The woman hesitated, contemplating whether to reveal her identity to this captivating, talking raven. After a brief moment of introspection, she decided to trust her instincts and responded, "I am Mirra. Now, share your name and the reason for your presence here."

"My name is Tomar, as I mentioned earlier, and this is my companion, Raven," he replied.

Mirra inhaled sharply, recognition sparkling in her eyes. "Tomar, I've heard stories about you and Nadora. You're the notorious sorcerers trapped within your tome. My husband, Aldar, spoke with you before you fell silent. Why have you taken on the form of a bird?"

"Mirra, I sense your uncertainty and fear. Let me clarify. Easha, the Sorceress of Light and the Key, performed a powerful ritual that reduced the book imprisoning us to ashes. As the Fortress of Doom crumbled, the raven absorbed our very essences and escaped."

"What has become of Nadora?"

"She didn't make it. Once I reclaim my physical form, I will seek vengeance on the people of Seledor. But tell me, what brings you to this cave all alone?" he inquired.

With a gentle smile, Mirra reminisced about her solitude and replied, "Many years ago, fierce warriors arrived with a dragon. My husband lost his life when the creature collapsed the cave entrance. After the attackers left, I unleashed a powerful explosive potion. I wasn't fast enough to escape. The blast threw me against the wall, and I lost my unborn child. Sometimes, I wish I had perished that day."

Silence thickened, swallowing the space between them as Tomar listened closely to Mirra's tragic tale, his desire for revenge intensifying.

"Life is always filled with purpose," he murmured. "Just look at me; I stand here, destined to one day envelop this land in darkness."

Mirra took in Tomar's electrifying words, realizing that their quest for justice had reached a critical turning point.

"I am a sorceress. I can help free you from this form," she declared, her face lighting up with excitement.

Tomar's gaze sharpened. "You must also be a vengeful dark sorceress."

"Yes, and I have a collection of potions hidden deep within the cavern. We can brew a tonic that will restore you to your true self." Her gaze remained fixed on the raven, a blend of curiosity and determination washing over her as a shiver ran down her spine.

Tomar's tone carried a mix of enthusiasm and caution as he replied, "Creating a transformation potion is complex and requires time for proper brewing and maturing."

She rubbed her grimy hands together, her eyes sparkling with anticipation. "The sooner we begin, the faster you'll regain your freedom. I thrive on a good challenge," she said, offering a playful grin.

The sorcerer interjected, "I need to concentrate. Precision is crucial for this potion. Mistakes cannot happen."

Tomar and the raven closed their eyes, entering a deep meditative state. They understood that the outcome of this potion would ultimately determine the success of their journey.

Mirra, watching, gently lifted the unconscious bird and ventured deeper into the cold, shadowy cave. She carefully placed him on a makeshift bed made from tattered clothing, a smile spreading across her face as she pondered the mysterious future that lay ahead.

• • •

Stepping out of the bedroom, Mirra's gaze was immediately captured by the fireplace, where an old cauldron sat—a symbol of her history. A wave of memories associated with the pot's past brews surged through her, evoking a profound sadness that welled up in her eyes, twisting her expression into a frown. Swiftly, she dried her tears and inhaled deeply, determined to focus on her mission.

"I must let go of my past burdens and concentrate on aiding Tomar in regaining his physical form. Only then can I seek my revenge," she promised herself.

She leaned closer, her fingers gliding over the cauldron's rough surface, its texture grounding her. Her eyes drifted downward and caught sight of a tattered piece of cloth discarded on the floor. With a sharp exhale, she bent down and picked it up.

"I will scrub this dark vessel until my reflection shines through," she proclaimed, working the cloth in slow, deliberate circles. As the grime gave way, the cauldron gleamed, revealing her face on its polished surface.

She studied her own reflection—faint, distorted, and unfamiliar. "I can hardly recognize how grimy I look, and my hair is such a dull brown. I need to freshen up, but first, I must gather my potions." A small, reassuring thought surfaced. "It's comforting to know I'm not alone in this.

Her gaze swept across the dimly lit room until it landed on an empty crate positioned to the west of the hearth.

This will do perfectly. She quickly grabbed the box without hesitation and hoisted it onto her shoulder, making her way to the potion chamber. One by one, Mirra filled the crate with the ingredients—her fingers brushing against dried herbs, vials of strange liquids, and powders clinging to the edges of glass she believed Tomar would need.

"I can't believe how weak I've become," she whispered, adjusting the box's weight as she navigated the winding cave corridors. Upon returning to the bedroom and setting the crate down beside the bed—where the bird lay still—she couldn't help but smile.

A haunting tune, learned from a childhood friend, surfaced in her mind. Without thinking, she whistled softly, the melody wrapping around the silence.

"I wonder if I can speed up the transformation potion," she mused.

As the faint sounds of vampire bats echoed in the distance, she made her way to the main chamber, her breath growing slower, heavier. Leaning against the eastern wall, she took a moment to catch her breath. A quiet sense of fulfillment enveloped her—this was progress, no matter how gradual.

Mirra watched as twilight settled around her. She ran a hand through her tangled hair, brushing it away from her tired eyes. Reaching into the food storage, she retrieved a piece of dried rat and then retreated to her sleeping quarters.

• • •

With the arrival of dawn, the bats returned to their resting places, their silent departure marking the beginning of a new day.

Mirra stirred awake to the gentle sounds that signaled the start of a new day. Stretching her arms high above her head, she turned to admire the still raven perched beside her.

"Today is going to be amazing," she whispered, breathing in the fresh, musty scent of the morning air. Rising from her bed, she adjusted her robe and headed to the front room, her fingers grazing the rough walls as she moved. She picked up a pitcher, carrying it into the western chamber, where water dripped softly from a crack in the stone wall.

She exchanged her empty container for a full jug and peered into the bucket, pondering, "It's intriguing how water seeps from the rocks." As her gaze drifted downward, something caught her attention. To her astonishment, she noticed a small, shimmering crystal resting at the bottom of the bucket. Enchanted, Mirra examined it closely, wondering if it held the secret of the water's origin. Shaking off the thought, she set the crystal aside and turned her attention back to the bucket.

"There's enough here for a bath," she noted before walking ten paces to a patch of dark stones to cleanse herself.

An hour later, fresh and invigorated, she ran her fingers through her damp hair and exhaled with satisfaction. "I feel rejuvenated."

With a burst of energy, she headed toward the cave's entrance. Yet, as she approached, a hesitation settled within her.

Drawing in a deep breath, she reassured herself, "I can do this. Just one step at a time." A soft sigh escaped her lips as she stepped out of the cave for the first time since her husband's untimely passing. The wind struck her instantly, howling violently through the valley. A chill coursed through her, and goosebumps prickled her arms. Around her, the dark soil stirred, whispering the echoes of her past. Boulders stood like silent sentinels, bearing witness to the memories buried deep inside her, while the skeletal branches of lifeless trees clashed together and brittle leaves danced around her feet.

Taking another deep breath, she crouched down and began to sift through the rich, dark soil in search of worms. Mirra recognized that facing her past was essential for her healing process.

"Eight worms should ease their hunger," she mused, a wave of satisfaction washing over her as the wriggling creatures brushed against her palms. Gathering them carefully, she stood and made her way back to the cave with her catch, "Tomar and Raven will be thrilled with these. I can only imagine how hungry they must be." At that moment, as she made her way back, she realized that it was Tomar's unwavering support that had empowered her to confront the pain that had long confined her. And now, she had truly begun her journey toward healing.

3rd Chapter

A brisk gust of wind swept into the cave as it traversed the Valley of Drom, scattering dust and leaves in its wake.

Shivering at the cold's sudden bite, Mirra rubbed her arms in a futile attempt to generate some warmth. Steeling herself, she stepped into a dimly lit chamber where a small stack of firewood leaned against the northern wall.

"I have less firewood than I anticipated, but it should be enough for the transformation potion," she reflected.

With unwavering resolve, she knelt beside the pile and began gathering the logs in her arms. She precariously balanced them against her chin while navigating toward the hearth. Pushing aside a stubborn strand of hair, she meticulously arranged the firewood into a sturdy pentagon shape.

"Now, to get the cauldron ready so we can start brewing the tonic. Where did I leave that steel bar?"

As she explored the eastern part of the cave, her eyes landed on a steel pole carelessly lying on the ground.

"Got it!" she shouted, grabbing the pole and dragging it toward the fireplace. "All I need to do is slide this under the pot's handle and secure it. It seemed so simple when Aldar did it for me, but now it's my turn to figure it out."

The thought of Aldar tugged at her heart. She blinked quickly, brushing away a tear as she recalled how effortlessly Aldar had managed such tasks. Yet, a spark of determination ignited within her as she prepared to slide the steel pole under the pot's handle and lift it.

"This pot is far too heavy for me to lift. I need to remove the wood from the firebox," she thought, quickly tossing the logs onto the floor beside her. "Now, for the other side," she whispered, attempting to raise the bar. "It's too heavy." She gritted her teeth and lifted one end of the steel bar, maneuvering it to the opening. "For the other side, I guess I'll have to use my shoulder. There's no other way to lift this rod."

Taking a deep breath, Mirra, grunting with exertion, crouched down and struggled with the urn's rod until she finally stood tall, securing the pole in place. Sweat trickled down her forehead, and she winced as she rubbed her sore shoulder from the weight of the steel. A surge of triumph washed over her as she carefully returned the wood to the firebox.

Turning to face the fireplace, she declared with quiet pride, "We are now ready to brew the transformation potion."

From the shadows, Tomar approached and stood beside her, commenting, "Sorceress, your efforts are truly impressive."

Startled by his sudden presence, Mirra gasped, but her surprise quickly melted into delight as she exclaimed, "What a wonderful surprise to see you!" Then, scooping him in her hands, she added with a mysterious smile, "I have something special for you." She carried him to the ancient stone table at the center of the room. With a flourish, she lifted the black lid, revealing a wriggling mass of black worms.

The raven's eye widened in shock as he gazed at the squirming delicacy before him.

Tomar gasped, filled with alarm. "I won't allow you to eat them." He declared, his voice thick with disapproval.

"I intend to relish this delicacy," the raven replied, undeterred. "You have no authority to stop me." He plucked the plumpest black worm from the heap, lifted its head in victory, and swallowed it in a swift gulp.

"Don't even think about having another!" Tomar shouted, his eyes wide with disbelief.

"Just watch me!" the bird chirped back, eagerly devouring three more wriggling worms, completely disregarding Tomar's furious command.

"I can't believe you're ignoring me," he yelled, his frustration clear in his tone.

With a playful glint in its eye, the raven retorted, "You can't dictate my actions; I'll do what I want."

Mirra, exasperated by their bizarre quarrel, stepped between them. With a swift motion, the sorceress placed her hands on her hips and shook her head. "This squabbling is ridiculous. A bird arguing with itself is the strangest thing I've ever seen—and it will haunt my dreams. But we must focus on the potion," Mirra interjected, cutting through the tension between the sorcerer and the raven, steering their attention back to the task at hand.

"I want to show you my potions," she said, gently lifting the bird from the table and settling it on her shoulder. "I've kept them in the bedroom while you were resting." Mirra's voice quivered with excitement.

Together, the three of them stepped into a room where shelves lined the walls, brimming with glistening vials, dried herbs, and mysterious concoctions. Tomar scrutinized each potion alongside the spread of ingredients laid out before him.

As they delved into the possible uses and effects of the potions, Tomar nodded thoughtfully, examining the varied selection of components.

Mirra beamed with pride, her heart swelling with gratitude for the sorcerer's approval.

"Let me see what you've got," he said, rummaging through the collection of small jars scattered across the floor. His eye darted between labels as he spoke, "We'll need six black roaches, the lethal root of the castor plant, and six weasel eyeballs."

He curiously looked at each and scanned some more, not sparing a glance at the sorceress. "Additionally, we need three leaves from the poison antery plant, four centipedes, eight fangs from green spiders, and a toenail from a black vulture." Tomar recited, scanning the ingredients.

When he was done, he looked toward the sorceress, who seemed happy at the commendation. "You have everything except the green spider fangs. Before we can brew the potion, I need eight of those. Mirra, you'll need to catch four spiders. They're clever and dangerous, so this will be quite a risky endeavor," Tomar cautioned.

"I'll start as soon as the bats return to their roost. I promise I won't let you down," she replied, feeling honored to assist. "Since we have some time, let me show you around my home." She settled the raven on her shoulder and guided him through the various chambers of the cave. Tunnels opened into hidden rooms where roots hung from the ceiling like ancient chandeliers, and glowing moss shimmered faintly beneath their feet.

Before long, they reached the main chamber and sat down at the weathered stone table that bore the grooves of countless meals and magical experiments to chat.

Tomar looked up and said, "You should have seen my attempt at flying! I charged forward with all my strength and ended up face-first in the dirt."

The sorceress burst out laughing, her eyes twinkling with amusement.

"I tried again," he continued, "convinced it would be easy, and if that storm hadn't rolled in, I would have soared through the clouds."

The raven chimed in, "No, you would have just kept running, just like you made me do."

Mirra giggled harder, her face glowing with joy. "I can totally picture it," she giggled, her cheerful sound filling the room as the sorcerer shared his exaggerated and funny tales about the enormous spider and the gigantic bird.

"I can't forget our thrilling adventure; it rattled me to my core. I genuinely thought I was going to die. Yet, we wouldn't have succeeded without you, sorcerer."

As dusk settled in, the bats took flight from their cave, and a wave of sleepiness washed over her. "Today was truly wonderful; I'm grateful for it, but now it's time to say goodnight." She rubbed her eyes, stifled a yawn, and reached her arms skyward, her limbs heavy with fatigue. "It seems tomorrow will be quite a long day," she announced as she rose to her feet.

Raven chimed in, "You could use the bats to keep track of time." He tilted his head, curiosity evident in his voice. "That seems a bit strange."

"I find it strange that you're debating with yourself. I'll always remember that," Mirra replied with a playful smile.

He returned her smile and playfully challenged her, "I bet I can reach the room before you!" With that, he dashed off in a flash.

"You'll definitely win since you have wings!" she laughed, calling after him as he flew from view.

As Mirra stepped into the chamber, her gaze softened. There, perched in the bedroom where Aldar had once rested, was the raven—silent, watchful. "Sleep well tonight," she whispered, taking a deep breath as a sigh escaped her lips. A wave of sorrow enveloped her as memories of her late husband bloomed like shadows on the wall. "I'll see you when the bats return," she murmured softly.

A soothing tranquility enveloped her as she closed her eyes, finding solace in the image of the raven as her protector, a reminder of Aldar's enduring presence.

• • •

Despite the sun having risen, it remained hidden behind the gloomy clouds. The sky hung low and brooding.

"Tomar, it's time to get up. We have a long day ahead of us," Mirra called gently.

He stretched his wings and slowly opened his eyes, suppressing a yawn. His one eye blinked sleepily before he ruffled his feathers and shuffled toward the cave's entrance.

"Are you hungry?" she asked.

"No, I'll eat when we return," Tomar replied, moving toward the cave's entrance.

The cool, damp air of the morning enveloped them as they stepped outside, and Mirra inhaled deeply, her heart racing with anticipation for the day ahead. The sorcerer scanned the landscape and commented, "The fog has lifted."

"What fog? I've never noticed mist in this valley," she frowned.

The raven chimed in, agreeing with Tomar, "Perhaps that's because you've never ventured out to see it for yourself."

Before she could answer, Tomar turned, now fully alert. "We don't have time for debates; we have crucial tasks to tackle. Mirra, you must ascend the West Mountainside," Tomar instructed, pointing his wing toward the path. "About halfway up, you'll find a meadow with a small rock formation at its northern edge. This area is home to the perilous green spiders, so proceed with caution; the trail can be treacherous. We will lead you to the spiders' lair and assist you as much as we can."

A fierce determination sparkled in her eyes as she nodded, took a deep breath, tilted her head back, and let her long black hair flow around her like a battle banner. With renewed resolve, Mirra proclaimed, "I can do this." After another steadying breath, she began her ascent up the mountainside. The rugged and intimidating landscape challenged her, thorns scraping at her arms and slick stones threatening every step, yet her unwavering spirit propelled her onward.

The soft breeze rustled through the branches, but Mirra remained undeterred. Driven by a fierce determination to conquer the mountain and overcome every challenge, she skillfully navigated through the trees that blocked her way. With each step, her confidence grew, sharpening her focus. Suddenly, she felt the ground tremble beneath her. She froze.

"The source of this trembling fills me with unease. I must gather my strength, for I can feel something enormous drawing near."

Mirra waved her arms wildly at Tomar, signaling the impending arrival of gigantic creatures. The ground trembled violently beneath her feet, the resounding thud of enormous footsteps reverberating through the air, stirring a mix of fear and excitement within her. She crouched low, hiding behind a robust tree trunk, her eyes flicking nervously from side to side as she prepared for the looming threat of the colossal beasts.

Taking a deep breath to steady her racing heart, the sorceress fought to keep her composure. Clamping her hands against her chest, she steadied her breath. Her body felt like a coiled spring, her heart racing as adrenaline coursed through her veins, heightening her awareness of the approaching danger.

The ground quaked under the weight of the beasts' thunderous strides, and her gaze was drawn to a narrow crack in the rocky terrain nearby. A wave of dread washed over her as she spotted two massive trolls crashing through the thick underbrush of the western forest, their heavy footfalls echoing ominously as they advanced. Their breath came in rasping huffs, and their eyes burned with cruel hunger as they stomped forward. Her mind raced, frantically searching for a clever way to escape their path of destruction.

In a moment of sheer terror, a sneeze escaped her lips, "Achoo!" Her sneeze burst forth uncontrollably. She quickly clamped her hand over her mouth, freezing in place, eyes widening in horror, and hoping the monsters hadn't noticed her. Holding her breath, she watched as they halted, their enormous eyes scanning the area for any sign of movement. Seizing this brief opportunity, Mirra began to retreat slowly, slipping silently behind a wide tree trunk like a wisp of smoke in the fading light.

A low, rumbling growl emanated from one of the giants. "Oug thre whos?" the largest troll bellowed, causing the other towering creature to freeze, their ears perked for any sign of movement. The surrounding silence wrapped around them like a heavy blanket. Mirra held her breath, her heart pounding as she watched the trolls scan the area with eyes that flickered like wild flames. She mentally berated herself for her rashness, desperately hoping her hiding spot would remain hidden from their sight.

Suddenly, the colossal beast unleashed a thunderous roar that sent nearby bushes crashing to the ground, flattened beneath its fury. A wave of terror washed over her. If only the trolls could overlook her presence, perhaps they would eventually move on. The thought of darting to the safety of the rock's crevice crossed her mind, but the distance loomed like an insurmountable wall, ready to betray her. Mirra bit her lip. *Don't move. Don't move.*

At that moment, Raven and Tomar swooped down, their sharp cries slicing through the stillness and diverting the trolls' attention.

The trolls' faces contorted in irritation as they shifted their massive forms southward, granting Mirra a fleeting chance to escape. One swiped at the air in irritation. The giants snarled and lumbered south, their frustration echoing behind them.

As she breathed a sigh of relief, curiosity began to stir within her. "What could have drawn the trolls to this part of the forest? It's unusual for them to stray so far from their typical territories," she mused, brushing off her gown.

"A more significant threat must have driven these trolls from their homeland," the raven observed. "They will go to great lengths to seek a new sanctuary."

Mirra nodded, taking in the weight of the raven's wisdom as she reflected on the trolls' unyielding pursuit and the enigmatic forces encroaching upon their realm. She understood the importance of staying alert while traversing this treacherous terrain. Whatever was coming, it would not wait for readiness, it would not pause for us to be prepared. "Mirra, you're just a hundred feet from the spiders' territory," Tomar called out from above, his voice crisp.

"Thanks for the warning," she murmured, pressing forward. "I'm not sure I can push on much longer," she confessed, her voice filled with fatigue, as she skillfully weaved through the trees as she neared the rocky outcrop, casting a curious glance at the raven.

Feeling drained, she sank onto a log not far off and remarked, "I can hardly believe I've made it this far. The climb and the warm afternoon sun have really taken it out of me." She gasped and huffed. "I need a moment to rest," she added, leaning against a boulder to ease her tired muscles. As she closed her eyes, the sounds of tiny creatures scurrying around her filled the atmosphere.

"You can relax, sorceress," Tomar reassured her. "We'll be on the lookout for any threats." Then he settled onto a nearby branch, his protective gaze fixed on Mirra.

"Thank you," she whispered, "I'm worn out from the journey." Her voice faded as she gently shut her eyes, surrendering to sleep. The sorceress felt a sense of comfort under the raven's watchful eye as the sun dipped toward the Atron Mountains, casting a warm glow over the rugged cliff where the hunters stood, poised for the arrival of twilight.

4th Chapter

A s dusk settled in, the hunters felt the night creeping closer, the light around them fading into a soft, smoky haze. In contrast, the sorceress remained unfazed by the cooling rays of the late afternoon sun, lounging comfortably among the rugged stones. Shadows stretched long across the landscape, painting it in vibrant hues as the sun sank below the horizon.

"Awaken, Sorceress," the raven urged, its voice sharp and filled with urgency. "Dusk has come, and the time for the venomous creatures to surface is at hand." Perched on a jagged rock beside the young sorceress, he cast a worried glance at the dark clouds swirling ominously over the East Kinnick Mountains, his heart racing with a silent hope that they would remain at bay.

The sorceress stirred, her sharp eyes scanning the terrain when a subtle rustle caught her attention.

"A hunter is disturbing the grass," she murmured, her gaze fixed on the movement.

"Be cautious, sorceress! Step back, or you might get bitten," the raven warned.

From the shadows, a large green spider emerged, its legs moving with eerie grace. The sorceress rose to her feet slowly, captivated by the creature's graceful movements.

"It's enormous," she whispered, eyes gleaming. "What's your strategy for capturing it without harm?"

The raven recoiled at the sight of the formidable arachnid, its alarm evident. "Surely you're not thinking—"

But she was already moving. A sly smile spread across as she retrieved a small rawhide pouch from her pocket. Taking a moment to study the spider's deliberate actions, she crouched just inches behind it, a thrill coursing through her. Sensing the urgency, she lunged forward, seizing the creature in her grasp. Then, standing tall, she forcefully struck the pouch against a nearby rock, swiftly ending the spider's life.

A beat of silence followed—then a voice broke through, startled by the sudden turn of events, "Well, that was unexpected!" Tomar exclaimed, his eye lingering on the pouch, and then shifting to the gathering shadows.

The scent of the deceased spider drifted through the air, subtle at first, then stronger, drawing in others from their hiding places. Creatures stirred, awakened by their hunger and instinct.

Time passed quickly. Within just an hour, the sorceress had gathered all the essential ingredients required for their potion. The urgency that had once hung in the air now gave way to a sense of grim purpose.

"Place the pouch down, and we'll carry it back to the cave while we assess your path. We can't afford any further delays," Tomar growled, gripping the bag tightly with his claw as he headed toward the cave.

As they began their return, the last light of day slipped away. Night fell quickly, and with it, the temperature dropped noticeably.

With a playful smile, Mirra looked up at the sky, where swirling gray clouds danced like spirits across heaven. She glanced at the raven, and for a moment, an unexplainable connection seemed to blossom between them as the cool breeze ruffled her hair. "From my vantage point, the moon is shrouded in darkness. Life is truly extraordinary," she said softly, then turned her attention back to the trail ahead, whistling merrily as she descended the mountainside into the Drom Valley. The shadows of the mountains stretched behind her like a forgotten dream.

As she strolled through the valley, the moon's distorted shadows appeared to share secrets with her, stirring memories long buried. Her steps slowed as she passed the stones that had once claimed her husband's life.

"That was a long time ago. I must focus on what lies ahead," Mirra murmured, tossing her hair over her shoulders, and gently caressing her left arm. With a steadying breath, she stepped into the cave.

Inside, the air was thick with the scent of soil and ash. The raven, perched near the entrance, tilted his head. "Why did you take so long? We've been waiting for you for quite a while," he asked, his tone half-teasing, half-concerned.

Mirra shook her head, a small smirk tugging at her lips. "No, you haven't. I spotted you perched on that tree branch the moment I started my walk through the valley. You love to tease me, but I can't let myself get distracted right now. I need to light a fire and prepare the potion," she replied.

She moved with purpose, igniting a fire beneath the cauldron. The flickering flames cast eerie shadows that danced across the rough stone surfaces. The enchanting flicker of blue and black flames held her mesmerized, but when she caught sight of Aldar's face, she froze in place.

"Is everything okay, Sorceress?" Tomar asked, worry etched across his features. "You look as if you've seen a ghost."

She subtly brushed away the tears with her sleeve and replied, "I'm okay; I was just waiting for the pot to warm up." However, her heart raced wildly in her chest.

"We've got the roaches you requested and set them on the table for you," he said, sensing her unease and trying to divert her thoughts from the past.

"Thanks," she replied, her voice steadier now. She turned to the task at hand, swiftly chopping off the heads of six weasels and sending them flying into the steaming cauldron.

The trio listened intently as a sizzling sound filled the air. Their eyes widened in shock as they watched the weasels' eyes turn a deep, inky black, swirling like ink in the water.

"It's time for the roaches," she declared, methodically decapitating them and letting their heads fall into the frothing pot, one after another.

Tomar leaned in closer, his gaze fixed on the scene, and cautioned, "Raven, I can sense the drool gathering at the corners of your mouth. Try to resist the urge to eat them!"

"Don't tell me what to do," the raven snapped, plunging his beak into the remnants, rearranging the pieces as he searched for the tastiest organs and tissues before devouring them with relish.

"I can't believe you ignored my orders and ate them." The two began to argue, causing Tomar's wing to quiver with irritation.

Meanwhile, as the debate raged on, Mirra emptied the contents of the spider bag onto the table, absentmindedly prodding at them with a stick, her mind already shifting to the next step. She then moved to the mantle, retrieved three black cloth rags, and folded them neatly to shield her skin from the venom.

With practiced precision, the sorceress extracted the venomous fangs from the spider and let them fall into the bubbling cauldron.

The argument behind her faded into silence as Tomar and the raven halted, entranced by Mirra as she deftly mixed the ingredients with a wooden spoon. Each gentle stir ensured that the components melded perfectly, while the sorcerer's eyes remained fixed on her.

Suddenly, a sharp breeze swept through the underground chamber, ruffling the air around the simmering potion.

"Is it common for the potion to create such an abrupt gust of wind?" inquired Tomar.

Mirra didn't look up. "Yes, I've heard that can happen depending on the tonic being brewed. However, this is the first time I've experienced it myself."

The potion shimmered, casting strange reflections on the cave walls.

"This concoction is not only fragrant but also visually captivating. It simply needs to shimmer for three days and nights. My lady, your guidance has been essential in this endeavor. Your potion-making abilities are truly remarkable," Tomar praised.

Mirra's heart swelled with gratitude at his kind words. She offered a small nod, her eyes softening.

As the trio wrapped up their lengthy day, the cave glowed with the light of the enchanted fire. The sorceress, surrounded by her companions and the fruits of her craft, radiated a rare and quiet happiness.

* * *

At dawn's first light, brilliant flashes of lightning lit up the nearby mountains.

"No!" Mirra cried out, a tear trailing down her cheek. Once again, she found herself trapped in the chilling nightmare that plagued her thoughts. Sweat trickled down her forehead, dampening her hair as her breath came in shallow gasps. In an instant, she was jolted awake, her eyes scanning the room in panic.

"You just had a nightmare; the storm outside heightened your dream," Tomar comforted her, standing beside the frightened woman on the bed.

His voice grounded her. She swiftly gathered her hair, pulling it back from her face, and wiped the sweat from her brow before sitting up. Taking a deep breath, she attempted to dispel the lingering fear that clung to her. After a yawn, she swung her legs over the side of the bed, her feet hovering just above the floor, and murmured, "I'm so relieved you're here with me." Her voice was still tinged with sleep. Rising to her feet, she adjusted her robe and added, "I'm feeling better now, and I'm thankful not to be alone. I have some dry rat if you're hungry."

"Yes!" Tomar exclaimed, "I can't remember the last time I had a proper meal!" and hurried to the table with the enthusiasm of someone long deprived.

While he busied himself, the sorceress quietly slipped into a small nook to the east of the main living area. Her gaze landed on the pendant Aldar had made for her, a timeless red-eye charm still resting on the second shelf. Her throat tightened. She fought back tears, cleared her throat, and took three quick, calming breaths. Then, with practiced hands, she grabbed two pieces of bark from the stone ledge and began piling up dried meat on top.

"Two rats should be enough to satisfy our hunger," Mirra reflected, a wave of nostalgia washing over her as she recalled the grand feasts she once enjoyed with Aldar.

In the next room, Tomar stirred. "I can hear footsteps, Raven. Mirra is about to arrive."

Moments later, the sorceress entered the chamber, expertly balancing two plates in her hands.

The rat's stickiness, preserved from being dried for twenty moons, clung to her fingers. She placed the bark on the table, tore the rat into pieces, and offered some to the bird.

The trio shared their humble meal in quietude, the storm's distant rumble their only companion.

"This is the finest meal I've had since becoming a spirit," Tomar proclaimed. "Sorceress, how may I assist you?" His heartfelt words warmed Mirra, bringing a grateful smile to her lips.

"I have only one rat left," she said, glancing toward the dwindling stores. "It's time to seek more food. I've been subsisting on rats for far too long."

"We would gladly assist," the raven replied, his feathers ruffling with purpose. "Catching young rabbits is simpler, but the sorcerer enhances my skills, enabling me to capture larger ones. How many do you need?"

"Three will suffice," she answered, her tone resolute.

"We'll gather the food you require," Tomar promised. "Just keep an eye on the potion while we're away." The raven flew toward the cave's entrance, calling over his shoulder, "We must ensure nothing disturbs the tonic in our absence."

As the bird ascended into the sky, Mirra followed him to the threshold. She paused, inhaling deeply, relishing the moment before retreating back into the cave. A rare feeling of companionship enveloped her, dispelling the loneliness that had lingered for so long.

This gives me time to return the ingredients and potions to their rightful places within the chamber, the sorceress thought as she moved toward the bedroom, her eyes scanning the area, contemplating potential future uses for them.

I wonder when the hunters will return, she mused. After retrieving the container from the northern wall, she carefully transported it to the back chamber, organizing her potions with precision. When she made her way back to the main area, she noticed a rabbit resting on the table.

"Tomar must have come back with the meat. I can't believe they didn't let me know." She said aloud, surprised.

In one smooth motion, the sorceress grabbed the rabbit, binding its legs with twine before hanging it near the cave's entrance. She positioned a deep crimson and black bowl beneath the suspended carcass.

"Every drop of blood will be collected in this bowl. I'm not entirely sure how I'll use it yet, but I have a feeling it will be essential for brewing a potion. Perhaps I could concoct a new elixir to preserve my youth. Yes, that sounds like a fantastic idea." A mischievous smile spread across her face as she gazed at the bowl, excitement bubbling within her at the thought of using the rabbit's blood for her own ends.

With a swift cut, she opened its belly, allowing the rich red liquid to flow into the bowl. Mirra dashed into the pantry and grabbed a bag of curing salt, her heart racing with anticipation. She returned just in time to witness the last drop of blood fall into the vessel. After expertly skinning the rabbit, the sorceress coated the meat in black salt and wrapped it tightly in aged cloth.

As the sorcerer approached the cave, his eyes fell on the bowl brimming with rabbit blood, curiosity igniting in his mind about Mirra's intentions. The bird's claw deftly dropped the meat onto the cold stone table.

"I'll be back soon with the last rabbit," Tomar said, offering a reassuring nod before disappearing once more into the dim morning light.

Mirra dipped her finger into the blood, savoring the taste as she brought it to her lips.

"The blood has an intriguing salty flavor. Now I see why predators prefer their meals fresh." She mused. After removing the second rabbit from the table and performing her ritual again, she turned to find the raven swooping in low through the entrance and landing gracefully on the table.

"I appreciate this," she said warmly. "This rabbit will make for a delightful dinner tonight. Do you like it cooked or raw?"

The raven responded without hesitation, "I prefer it raw."

Tomar chimed in, "Cooked is far more delicious. You'll truly enjoy the rich flavor of the exquisite meat, I assure you."

Mirra smiled at their banter. After expertly draining the rabbit's blood and skinning it, she took the meat to the fire, placing it on a metal plate. The air was filled with the mouthwatering scent of roasting meat, accompanied by the crackling of the flames.

A surge of excitement washed over her, but a hint of curiosity remained—would she truly enjoy the raw delicacy as much as the raven claimed?

"I can't wait to taste raw rabbit someday, feeling the blood run down my chin." The alluring aroma intensified, making her mouth water as she moved closer to the rabbit sizzling over the fire.

"It's time for dinner." Mirra alerted the raven. She set the warm meat on the table and began slicing it. A generous portion of rabbit was placed in front of the raven, and she watched as its claws eagerly sank into the meat, diving into its feast.

The three of them enjoyed their meal in silence.

"Am I correct, Raven? The meat tastes better cooked," Tomar inquired.

"Absolutely, it was one-of-a-kind and quite delicious," he admitted.

The sorceress glowed with pride, a wave of accomplishment washing over her.

Mirra commented, "The potion will be ready by tomorrow. I can hardly believe how quickly these three days have passed. It's time to wrap up the day." She placed the bird on her shoulder, rose to her feet, stifled a yawn, and covered her mouth. "Today was wonderful and filled me with joy." She spread her robe across the bed and settled in. "I'll see you at dawn."

"Why do you always lay a robe in the middle of the bed, Sorceress? I promise I won't harm you," Tomar said, looking at her earnestly.

"I'm just worried I might accidentally roll over onto you," she replied, her expression revealing her concern.

"I'll cast a spell on the bed to keep us safe."

"Can you really cast spells while in bird form?" she asked, her eyes sparkling with curiosity.

"Not exactly," he admitted. "But I can channel my magic toward you if you're receptive. It won't hurt you. Do you have a shiny object in sight? If so, I can focus my magic on it. Are you ready to see if it works?"

The raven interjected, clearly anxious, "I genuinely believe this is a risky endeavor," his feathers bristling with unease.

"Yes, I would love to give it a try! I have a shiny object hidden away. If you perch on my shoulder, I can take you to it."

With a gentle flutter of his wings, Tomar perched on her shoulder, his eyes glimmering with excitement.

Together, the three of them made their way to the spot on the floor where a shiny metal plate lay in wait.

"Let me clean this up. When Aldar gifted it to me all those years ago, it was radiant." She pulled a black cloth from her robe, gave it a quick shake, and started to buff the metal.

"Take a look in the mirror, Sorceress," Tomar urged, locking his gaze with hers as he silently recited the incantation.

"BAQUE!" Mirra echoed the spell, her voice steady. A shimmer passed through the room.

"Now the raven and I are protected while we rest." Tomar declared. The trio returned to their bedroom and climbed into bed. After draping her robe at the foot of the bed, the sorceress closed her eyes and drifted off into a peaceful slumber.

5th Chapter

A s the first rays of sunlight began to spill over the horizon, a sharp frost lingered in the atmosphere, creating a crystalline sheen across the ground. The air hung unusually still, enveloped in a serene quiet that felt almost sacred, as if nature itself was holding its breath in anticipation. However, casting a shadow over this tranquil scene, dark and foreboding clouds began to amass in the sky, their heavy presence signaling the approach of an impending storm.

Inside the cave, vampire bats flitted around, rousing Mirra from her deep slumber. As she blinked awake, the chill of the morning brushed against her skin, and a wave of anticipation for the day washed over her. With a swift motion, she brushed her hair back, stretched her arms high, yawned broadly, and focused on the raven still lost in dreams.

"Tomar, it's time to rise. The potion is ready," she called out, leaping from her bed and running her fingers through her tangled hair in a flurry. But the raven remained unresponsive, nestled in his sleep. Tenderly, she reached out and stroked his feathers, feeling a comforting warmth radiate from him. A sigh of relief escaped her lips as he slowly began to awaken.

"We need to head to the fireplace, Sorcerer," she declared, placing the bird on her shoulder and quickly moving toward the hearth, her voice weaving an unsettling melody.

"That's the creepiest tune I've ever heard," Tomar muttered, blinking groggily.

Mirra paid no attention to his comment. Instead, she whistled even louder, the eerie tune echoing off the cave walls as they approached the fireplace. Shadows danced along the cave's edges, flickering in rhythm with her steps.

In a swift motion, she grabbed the rod, lowered one end of the steel bar, and gently placed the gleaming cauldron on the ground. The metal clinked softly against the stone floor.

As they gazed into the pot, the trio marveled at the successful tonic. "It looks amazing, Mirra. You've done an outstanding job," Tomar said, inspecting the texture of the thick, dark concoction.

"The odor is revolting," Mirra said, wrinkling her nose. "Now I understand why the cave has such a delightful scent." The raven cawed in agreement, clearly sharing her aversion.

"Not everything has a foul smell. Once the potion cools down, it will be ready to drink," Tomar reassured her.

Still uneasy, Mirra stepped outside. Her foot sank slightly into the dark soil as she took on a formidable stance, letting the cold air bite at her skin. The sky above churned with heavy clouds, and the scent of rain lingered on the breeze. After a moment, she turned and reentered the cave, her steps quick and restless. She began pacing anxiously in front of the cauldron, the raven still perched on her shoulder, his eyes following her movements with mild amusement.

"Cease your pacing. It won't speed up the potion's cooling," the sorcerer remarked, remaining comfortably perched on her shoulder.

"I know, but it's consuming my thoughts," she said, stepping out of the cave only to quickly return, her expression unchanged.

Then she paused and noticed a softer scent wafting from the potion, no longer acrid and sharp, but faintly floral, like crushed violets under moonlight. Curious, she moved closer to the cauldron, reached out, and touched the cold metal surface. The chill of the steel sent a shiver down her spine, but she didn't pull away.

Drawn in by the transformation, the potion piqued her curiosity. She picked up a sturdy stick from the cave floor, its bark rough beneath her fingers, and pierced the ominous black orb floating at the center of the brew. A thick, glistening liquid oozed out, dark as ink, yet shimmering faintly with violent hues. "Here it is; soon you'll return to your true self," she said, her voice low and reverent, as she perched on a stone beside the sorcerer. He nodded, his eyes brimming with eager anticipation.

The raven, however, was less convinced. He shifted uneasily on the stone, feathers ruffling.

The raven's beak twitched. "You don't plan to eat that, do you?" Then, in a voice that did not belong to the bird —a voice deeper and older —Tomar spoke.

"Yes, my friend," he said from within, his tone calm and resolute. "And soon your spirit will be liberated, and I will regain my physical form. If not, it will make us ill."

The raven's feathers bristled. His body stiffened, resisting the pull of the sorcerer's will. Though they shared one vessel, the raven still had a mind of his own—and he understood all too well what was at stake. He understood that once Tomar swallowed the tonic, there would be no turning back. Tomar pushed forward, attempting to force the beak open, but the raven clenched it shut with stubborn strength.

"Raven," Tomar said, his voice tightening with frustration, "I need your assistance. I can't seem to open your beak. How did you manage to open your mouth to eat the worms and roaches without my help?"

"You never had control over my beak," the raven retorted, its eye glinting with defiance.

Tomar paused for a moment. "If you give me control over your beak, I promise to cast an eternity spell on you, granting you life as long as I exist." The raven tilted its head, considering the sorcerer's proposition. The weight of the moment pressed down on them all.

"You would grant me immortality! I accept your terms. I will relinquish full control of my body to you. Just don't betray my trust," the raven replied.

With the pact sealed, the sorcerer opened his beak wide and took a generous bite of the thick concoction. The potion clung to his tongue like tar, bitter and electric. As the sticky substance adhered to his beak, Tomar felt a thrilling surge of energy course through him, ancient and wild.

"Stop eating, or I—" the raven's voice tried to rise again, but it was already fading.

Before he could finish its warning, Tomar gulped down the remainder of the potion.

The bird quivered violently, its wings thrashing in a wild uproar and feathers scattering like ash. It plummeted to the ground, feet pointing upwards, its form limp and lifeless.

"Tomar!" Mirra cried out in alarm. She dropped to her knees and pressed her hand against the raven's chest, but felt no pulse. Panic surged through her. In a frantic attempt, she moved her fingers back and forth, whispering spells under her breath, hoping the potion hadn't taken his life.

Suddenly, dark ash erupted from his abdomen. The air thickened, charged with magic. In a heartbeat, a tall figure materialized before her, rising from the smoke like a shadow reborn. Mirra gasped.

The sorceress recognized the cobalt-black hair cascading to his shoulders, framing his pale, elongated face. His eyes, as dark as the midnight sky, resembled Aldar's, highlighting his sharply defined cheekbones. Tomar's intense gaze sparkled with a playful glint, enveloping him in an aura of enigma. He exuded confidence and authority, leaving no doubt about his formidable magical prowess. The sorcerer's fitted black robe clung to his muscular frame, runes etched into the fabric pulsing faintly with power.

She caught a brief glimpse of Tomar's physique, gasped again, and quickly covered her face with her hands.

"What's wrong? You look as if you've seen a ghost," he asked, his voice deeper now, edged with a blend of concern and confusion.

Mirra lowered her hands slowly. "You look strikingly like my late husband, Aldar. He often recounted stories of the powerful dark sorcerers who once ruled Seledor, expressing his longing to possess power akin to that of the notorious dark sorcerer. It was only when I saw you that the connection hit me. You must be his descendant."

In that instant, Tomar felt the weight of her words, absorbing the truth. Then his cheeks flushed a deep crimson.

"Fear not; they will pay for the loss of your husband and my great-grandson. We will exact our revenge," he declared with fierce resolve. Raising his arms, he summoned his magic, conjuring a lightning bolt that struck the Tonepass Mountains. The ground trembled violently as the bolt hit, releasing a thunderous roar that reverberated through the valley. A fierce spark ignited in Tomar's eyes, his expression resolute. "Together, we will ensure they regret the day they dared to confront our lineage," he proclaimed, his voice brimming with righteous anger.

Mirra stepped forward, her brow furrowed. "Did you and Nadora have a child? Where is the baby now?"

Tomar's expression shifted, shadowed by memory. "Before Nadora came into my life, I was already enchanted by a powerful witch named Circe. Together, we welcomed our beloved daughter, Agnes, into our shadowy existence. Tragically, not long after, Circe fell gravely ill, and death loomed over us. She took our precious girl to the Witches' Realm, where Agnes ultimately met her fate. I suspect Circe kept my identity hidden from them, as I had agreed it was the safest option for our child. Now, thanks to Aldar, I find comfort in knowing my daughter was surrounded by love." He turned away, his voice firm. "But enough of the past; gather your things. It's time to leave this place of memories and boldly embrace our future."

Without hesitation, Mirra slung her belongings—wrapped in Aldar's robe—over her shoulder. "I need nothing more," she stated as she moved closer to the sorcerer.

Together, the three of them exited the cave and headed west. The sky had begun to clear, but the air remained heavy with magic. The wind carried the scent of pine and distant fire. Suddenly, a sharp squawk pierced the air. The raven—now separate once more—halted in midair, reminding the sorcerer of the promise he had yet to keep.

Tomar stopped. "You are right," he acknowledged, gesturing toward the bird while quietly reciting an incantation that went unheard. The raven trembled, enveloped in a swirling crimson mist that soon dissipated.

"My vow to you is fulfilled. We must press on with our journey."

Observing the unfolding scene with quiet awe, "Come here, Raven; I'll look after you well," she said softly as she gently placed him on her shoulder.

"He's merely a bird, Mirra. Let him fly free," Tomar countered, continuing their journey.

The sorceress paid no heed to his words; her attention was fixed entirely on the raven.

"You deserve a name that captures your elegance," she pondered, a smile lighting up her face as she admired the splendid creature. "I've got it! I'll name you Derail."

"Mirra, we must stay concealed until the time is right," he reminded her, leading them up the eastern slopes of the Damen Mountains.

As she trailed behind, the sorceress couldn't suppress a giggle. Leaning closer to Derail, she whispered, "Striking the Tonepass Mountains with a lightning bolt on a clear day is a clever way to remain unnoticed."

The raven let out a soft chuckle at Mirra's humor, his eyes twinkling with mischief. "Yes," he agreed, and they continued on with renewed determination.

• • •

As noon approached, the trio traversed the mountaintop, surrounded by dense, charred trees, moving quietly toward a hopeful future. The air was thin and cool, and the silence of the highlands pressed around them like a secret.

Mirra and Derail shared an unbreakable bond. She held deep admiration for the brave raven who had saved Tomar's life.

As they continued their journey, Derail reflected on his astonishing fortune. *It's hard to believe how lucky I am. Tomar has bestowed upon me immortality, and I now have a family. The solitude that once plagued me feels like a memory fading away. This realization brings me a deep sense of peace.*

In a tender gesture, the raven gently nuzzled Mirra's cheek.

Mirra beamed, a warmth blossoming in her heart that she hadn't felt in years. With Derail and Tomar by her side, she felt prepared to confront any obstacles that might come their way.

• • •

Later that day, Mirra and Tomar made their way through the eastern mountain range. Their dialogue flowed effortlessly, much like the soft breeze that surrounded them.

"Before I met Aldar," Mirra began, her voice quiet but steady, "my adoptive parents performed a ritual that suppressed the magic within my twin sister and me. They knew the darkness that resided within us. We had to learn to live without our powers. Despite losing our abilities, we adapted and thrived. Then came the day Aldar invited us to his lavish eighteenth birthday celebration, a truly magnificent event. From the moment we met, an undeniable connection sparked between us. That day marked the revival of my magic. I believe his overwhelming darkness broke the spell my parents had cast. Aldar and I became inseparable until his tragic death. I haven't seen my sister since my marriage, but I have a strong intuition that she is still out there, alive." She deeply inhaled before continuing.

"We assembled a formidable army of beings, commanding the massive trolls and the fierce gilzdars; yet, our most extraordinary creation was the annicks. Our potion transformed ordinary army ants into daring mutants. Aldar's plan for revenge against Pildar for the murder of his parents was on the brink of fruition. We had just four days left before we embarked on our journey across Seledor. How they uncovered our intentions remains a mystery."

Tomar asserted, "This time, we will remain resolute. We will utilize spies to alert us of any intruders." he paused, turning to meet the sorceress's gaze.

"We are journeying into the Wormill Forest, a realm filled with dangerous creatures. We must proceed with caution to avoid provoking them," he cautioned her.

The sorceress nodded solemnly, fully understanding the gravity of their task. "I will remain vigilant and ensure that we go unnoticed," she vowed to the sorcerer.

Tomar then led them into the foreboding Wormill Forest. As they ventured deeper into the thicket, an eerie silence enveloped them, swallowing even the sound of their footsteps.

The gnarled branches of the trees creaked softly, creating a disquieting sound that reminded Mirra of the rustling made by army ants as they morphed into fierce warriors.

Around them, the forest hummed with strange, dissonant sounds—whispers in the wind, distant rustles, the occasional snap of unseen movement, each noise heightening her anticipation. She contemplated the possibility of other mutated creatures lurking in the shadows, ready to pounce on unsuspecting prey.

The ground beneath her felt brittle, like walking on a bed of fragile bones. A profound stillness blanketed the area, as if nature itself was holding its breath in suspense. With each step, her footsteps echoed in the quiet, intensifying her exhilaration. It seemed as though the woods were watching, harboring secrets just beyond her grasp, and soon, those mysteries would be unveiled.

"Derail, I can sense the spirits of fallen warriors wandering this land. This place fills me with immense joy, as it is the most daunting and shadowy landscape I have ever encountered. It's truly thrilling," she whispered while gazing at the darkened trees. The raven nodded, his eyes darting nervously from one shadow to another. The sorceress's words sent a chill down the raven's spine, yet he couldn't shake the thrill of excitement. The allure of the unknown was too strong to resist, and his curiosity about the secrets hidden within this eerie forest intensified.

Suddenly, Tomar halted and raised a hand. "Quiet!" he hissed urgently, placing a finger against his lips. His eyes narrowed as he pointed toward a sizable group of rats lounging in a small, desolate meadow surrounded by dense underbrush. Without a word, Tomar slipped behind a cluster of trees that hid them from view.

The sorceress crouched low, her curiosity piqued. She paused to observe the mutant rats, and the sight of these bizarre creatures sent a shiver down Mirra's spine.

They were as large as bobcats, with pig-like snouts and no visible ears. Their dark brown fur allowed them to blend seamlessly into their environment. The rats' long tails twisted in a spiral.

Mirra couldn't shake the eerie feeling that these mutated rats were merely a glimpse into the strange and dangerous world that lay hidden within the forest.

Derail nudged her ear, as if urging her to continue onward. She looked ahead and saw that Tomar was about fifty feet in front of her, already moving deeper into the forest.

"Hold on; we need to move quickly." She whispered, raising to her feet and racing forward to catch up with him, her voice hushed but breathless. "Derail, it was astonishing to see such rats."

But before Derail could respond, the trees parted—and they stumbled upon a campsite occupied by enormous creatures.

Mirra froze. Her eyes widened, and her brow furrowed with worry as she took in the sight of the beasts. Their towering forms filled her with dread. She could feel their raw power radiating, and her breath caught as a cold weight settled over her.

"Derail, those creatures look like a hybrid of a gilzdar and a troll," she whispered.

The creatures towered over typical trolls, their heads and hands a dark gray, reminiscent of a gilzdar's features. Their robust forms were adorned with growths that resembled tumors. Their roars reverberated through the air, sending fresh shivers down Mirra's spine. She understood that underestimating these beings would be a serious error, as their distinct characteristics rendered them an unpredictable and formidable threat.

The sorceress traced her fingers over the goosebumps that prickled her arms, her mind racing with inquiries about the origins of these powerful entities and the source of their strength. What were these things? How had they come to possess such a terrifying array of attributes? They were unlike anything she had seen before. Beside her, the raven quivered—not with fear, but with a strange, eager anticipation.

A thunderous roar erupted from the largest of the giants, who advanced, blocking their path. Each of his massive steps sent tremors through the ground, dislodging pebbles and shaking the underbrush.

"I fear you not!" the malevolent sorcerer bellowed.

Mirra stood resolutely beside Tomar, feeling a surge of potent energy coursing through her veins.

Together, they conjured fireballs, launching them fiercely at the mutant's feet. Flames burst against the ground, sending sparks into the air.

The creature responded with a deafening roar, baring its jagged black teeth. "If you desire a fight, then step forward; if not, retreat or prepare for your demise!" Tomar declared with unwavering confidence.

The two sorcerers summoned another fireball, bracing for the impending confrontation with the giants.

The colony leader grunted, his upper lip curling in contempt as he stepped aside, his fury palpable in the air.

Mirra and Tomar exchanged a significant glance, one of shared relief and sharpened resolve, their spirits lifted by the leader's retreat.

With a fresh sense of purpose, the sorcerers moved forward, their fireballs casting a fierce glow that pierced the surrounding darkness.

As they skillfully navigated through the beast's encampment, Mirra adjusted her stance to avoid any hidden traps. The creatures watched in silence, their eyes following every step.

Before long, they ascended another slope, reaching the summit.

Tomar paused again, turning to the sorceress. "We are about to enter the veranda, an illusion I created long ago. Though the dark soil may seem innocuous, it conceals treacherous quicksand beneath, ready to ensnare anyone who steps on it. You must follow my lead," he warned.

Mirra nodded and carefully shifted Derail from her shoulder to Tomar's. "You'll be safe now," she murmured. Tomar moved forward confidently, with Mirra following close behind. The sorceress scanned her surroundings, but her focus remained on the ground beneath her. The alluring black soil appeared both inviting and secure. She glanced at the raven, who seemed to sense her unvoiced concern.

Derail shook his head, a glimmer of caution flickering in his eyes. Mirra hesitated, sensing the hidden danger below. Trusting Derail's instincts, she resisted the temptation of the enticing black soil. Taking a deep breath, she pressed on, carefully mirroring each of his steps until they exited the veranda.

As the sun dipped toward the western horizon, its golden light bathed the landscape in a soft amber glow. The sorcerers reached their destination and found themselves perched at the edge of a vast valley. A place that held the promise of becoming their future kingdom, a realm where their dreams could flourish.

A surge of achievement filled them, fueled by the trials they had overcome. The journey had been perilous, but they had arrived. The vast landscape unfolded before them, teeming with limitless opportunities and adventures.

A brisk wind swept through the valley as the sun continued its descent.

"Dusk is approaching. We need to find shelter. Raven, scout for a cave we can use temporarily. We'll wait for you here," Tomar instructed, leaning against a sturdy tree trunk.

"It will be my honor," Derail responded, spreading his wings and soaring northeast in search of a suitable cave for the dark lord.

As the wind settled, Mirra reached into her satchel. "Are you hungry? I have some dried meat. Would you like a piece?" she inquired, offering a piece of dried rabbit.

"No, I'm not hungry," he replied, closing his eyes and drifting into slumber.

Moments later, Derail returned, his voice carrying a note of promise. The sun was vanishing behind the jagged mountain peaks, and twilight had begun to drape the valley in dusky hues.

"I found a cave to the east of here. Come, follow me; I'll guide you," he called out.

Mirra looked up, her voice tinged with fatigue. "I appreciate your efforts, but I'm feeling quite weary. Can we stay here on the mountaintop and head to the cave in the morning?"

"It's only a short distance away," the raven reassured her. With its glossy black feathers shimmering in the dappled sunlight, it leaned closer to her, its sharp eyes glinting with reassuring wisdom. "It's just over the hill," it croaked, the words lingering like a whisper in the air.

Mirra's gaze drifted to the sorcerer, who exuded an air of authority and sophistication that was impossible to ignore.

Tomar's intense expression, marked by piercing eyes, seemed to see through the very fabric of reality. They held her captive, making her wonder what secrets lay hidden behind that enigmatic facade. In that moment, she felt an undeniable pull towards him.

Tomar stirred, slowly opening his eyes. "The sky is clear. I don't see any reason we can't rest here for the night."

Rising to his feet, he turned toward the north and lifted his arm skyward. His fingers danced elegantly, akin to a pianist's gentle performance, while he whispered hushed incantations. Bright red sparks burst forth from his fingertips as he pivoted to the east, then south, and ultimately west—each turn igniting a flame that flickered momentarily in the air before disappearing. "Now we can finally rest. The protective barrier surrounding us is impenetrable," he declared, his voice steady and reassuring.

A profound wave of admiration surged through her, enveloping her like a warm embrace.

With that, the trio nestled into their chosen spot, the hush of evening settling around them like a blanket. The vast expanse of stars twinkled above them, casting a gentle, shadowy glow over the landscape.

6th Chapter

After a night of deep, restorative sleep, Derail awoke to the sharp, chilly winds sweeping through Stragon Valley. The raven stretched his wings and soared toward the nearest tree, the wind rustling through his feathers. From his perch, he cast a fond glance at his sleeping family below, his heart swelling with joy.

My life has reached incredible new heights. It still astonishes me that I have a family. This is the realization of a desire I've cherished for as long as I can remember. My dream has finally come true

Mirra's eyes sprang open, sparkling with enthusiasm. She jumped to her feet, arms raised high, playfully swaying as she shook off her old robe. The gloomy morning sun kissed her skin, and a wave of gratitude washed over her for the companionship she had found, for the raven who had become her friend, and for the sorcerer who had stood beside her in battle. She no longer had to face the world alone. She looked up and beamed at Derail, appreciating his presence and the sense of belonging he brought into her life.

He circled once, then descended. As he drew near, she playfully tapped her shoulder with a grin, inviting him to join her. He landed gently, nuzzling her cheek in greeting as her heart fluttered with happiness.

In tranquil silence, the two gazed out over their valley home. The shadowy light of dawn spilled across the hills, painting the landscape in hues of brown and gray.

"Today marks the beginning of a new adventure. Derail, our future is filled with possibilities." Mirra said softly.

Behind them, Tomar stirred awake. He sat up slowly, rubbing his eyes and savoring the joy of being alive.

He rose to his feet, taking in his surroundings. He spotted the sorceress and the raven resting at the edge of the valley.

"What has captured your attention?" the sorcerer asked, stepping forward with curiosity etched on his face.

"My new home," she replied, her face brightening with a joyful smile.

Tomar nodded, a rare softness in his eyes. "Raven, guide us to the cave." Without hesitation, Derail took flight, gliding low over the slope. Mirra followed closely behind Tomar as they eagerly trailed the raven down the steep mountainside, their footsteps crunching over loose gravel.

Tomar squinted into the distance, scanning the terrain. The valley was vast, but no cave was in sight.

"How much longer until we get there?" Mirra asked, her excitement bubbling over.

Derail circled once, then called out, "Your new home is in front of you."

The dark sorcerers slowed, exchanging puzzled glances. They turned their eyes to the landscape ahead.

Tomar's brow furrowed. He stepped forward, peering into the shadows of the hillside. Still, he saw nothing. With a frustrated shout, he stomped his foot and proclaimed, "I don't see any cave!"

"It's just a few feet ahead, my lord. The entrance may be small, but once you crawl through, it opens into a vast cavern," Derail explained.

Tomar recoiled at the suggestion. "I refuse to crawl like some animal," he roared, crossing his arms with regal defiance.

"My lord, I have no other way to access the cave," the raven replied calmly.

"Then I will never enter," Tomar thundered. "I'll stay above ground until I can construct a temporary shelter. After that, I will build a grand palace worthy of a sorcerer as I."

Mirra stepped forward, her patience thinning. "If we stay out here, we'll be at the mercy of the rain," the sorceress countered, her hands firmly on her hips. "You are no longer a spirit; you will need food and water."

Tomar lifted his gaze, his expression shifting. He tilted his head slightly, straining to hear a sound that seemed just out of reach.

"I can hear the gentle flow of water. Just beyond those trees to the north, there's a brook. We'll find plenty of food and fresh water there," he said, and without waiting for a reply, turned and began to follow the enticing sound that beckoned him from the north. His strides were long and purposeful, drawn by the promise of sustenance and control.

Derail remained behind, wings drooping. The raven felt the weight of his master's disappointment and lowered his head in sorrow. It was engulfed in deep sadness, acutely aware of his shortcomings. The cave had been his offering, and it had been rejected.

Mirra knelt beside him. "Don't be too hard on yourself; you did your best," she reassured him, gently stroking his head to soothe his troubled spirit. "It's not your fault that this valley lacks a mountain cave." Derail gave a faint nod, though his eyes remained downcast. Spotting Tomar a hundred feet ahead, Mirra rose and carefully placed the raven on her shoulder.

"Derail, hold on tight; we need to hurry to catch up with him," she urged, dashing over a small rise.

As they approached the valley's edge, the travelers entered a dense grove of trees, with the sun casting long shadows to the west. Suddenly, a narrow creek emerged, winding its way out from the depths of the woods like a silver thread.

Mirra's eyes were locked onto the serene beauty that surrounded the river. The vibrant blossoms, the glistening water, the golden light—it all felt too bright, too alive.

"Tomar, is there truly no dark, damp sanctuary where we can find refuge?" she asked, her contempt for the vibrant blossoms clear.

"Have patience. This bright sky won't last forever under the weight of our shadowy desires. Soon, a thick curtain of clouds will obscure the sun, I assure you. The trees and lush grass will soon be cloaked in darkness. In this clearing, I will construct a small hut for us, offering a temporary shelter from the elements."

The sorceress's eyes sparkled with excitement as she imagined her new dwelling taking form in the clearing. She was certain that the darkness and moisture she longed for would soon envelop them, creating the ideal backdrop for their sinister plans to unfold.

Tomar turned his gaze to the north. He began to recite ancient incantations, and the wind responded, swirling around him as if acknowledging his call.

"BEVA INSATO!" he bellowed, his voice echoing through the air as the ground quaked beneath him, a surge of energy enveloping him, heralding an impending transformation.

From the shadows, beavers emerged from the woods, hurrying toward him with unnatural urgency.

The sorcerer stood resolute, planting his left foot on a large rock. He took a deep breath, preparing to issue his command.

"You will build a timber structure tall enough for me to enter," he declared. "Now, swiftly gather the necessary wood." With that, he settled onto a massive stone, chin held high, arms crossed, observing the beavers as they hurried away.

"Sorceress, we will stay here until a grand palace is constructed," he said, casting a cautious glance at the ominous sky. "The clouds are dry; rain is not imminent."

Mirra lifted her gaze, skeptical of Tomar's forecast. But before she could respond, a thunderous crash of falling trees echoed from every direction, shattering her concentration. Trees fell like dominoes, their trunks splintering as they hit the ground.

Both the sorceress and the raven flinched as the noise intensified, the ground trembling beneath them.

As the uproar faded, the sun began to rise over the West Mountains, casting a golden glow over the chaos.

Something feels off, Mirra thought. There's movement in the woods. I suspect it's the beavers. We should steer clear of them.

She rubbed the tension from her arms, her mouth slightly agape in disbelief. They all stared in astonishment as the peculiar beavers appeared, walking upright like humans.

The strange beings approached the campsite, leaving a trail of uprooted trees in their wake.

Standing at five feet tall, they walked upright like men. Their frog-like faces were twisted in grotesque expressions, their glaring red eyes unblinking. They had no visible ears and their arms dangled low, brushing against their knobby knees, while long, flat tails ended in wiry tufts of hair.

Mirra's breath caught. She realized that Tomar had cast a split spell to control them—one that had warped them into something else entirely.

Tomar rose to his feet.

"Gather around so everyone can hear me clearly. In this clearing, surrounded by trees, we will build the hut. You will work diligently until it is finished." With a commanding look, he ordered, "Now go and follow my instructions."

From her vantage point, Mirra watched the creatures closely and noticed one of the mutants displaying aggressive behavior. Its tail whipped against the ground, kicking up clouds of dust. Then, with a guttural snarl, it charged toward the sorcerer.

Mirra reacted instantly. She conjured a blazing fireball and hurled it at the mutant.

The beaver ignited in flames, its anguished screams piercing the air as it writhed in pain, ultimately succumbing to the blaze. Tomar rushed toward the workers, his mind racing with the shocking realization of what had just occurred.

"This behavior will not be accepted. If you dare to come near Mirra or me again, you will face relentless suffering!" he thundered, his fury evident in the throbbing veins on his neck. "In death, you will find no solace. Now, go and execute my commands!" he shouted. The remaining creatures scattered, scrambling to obey.

"Thank you, sorceress, but it's wise to steer clear of the beavers. They can be erratic and genuinely perilous. I'll remain here to keep watch over them until the shelter is complete," he remarked, a mischievous grin playing on his lips.

A wave of warmth washed over Mirra as she moved closer to him, her face glowing with happiness. "Derail and I will gather firewood. I promise to avoid those creatures. Just the thought of them sends shivers down my spine," she said with a laugh, then turned and walked away.

As time passed and the sun climbed high, and then began its descent across the Atron Mountains. At last, the hut was finished.

Tomar rose and ordered, "Stay put until I inspect your work." He stepped inside the hut, ducking slightly beneath the low beams. His fingers brushed through the rough timber walls as he muttered, "You could have made it taller, but it will do for now." He paused, then added, "Now, I will free you from my spell." His lips moved in silence, weaving the final spell.

The beavers trembled, lifted into the air by invisible threads of magic. Their bodies twisted and turned midair, then gently floated back down, resuming their usual spots on the forest floor.

Tomar observed as the creatures made their way into the western part of the forest, their forms fading into the trees, before he approached the sorceress.

"Our temporary shelter is secure until our palace is constructed." He said while brushing dust from his robe.

They entered the room together and soon drifted off to sleep.

• • •

Morning broke, cloaked in a dense, shadowy mist that clung to the valley like a veil.

Mirra awoke later than usual and turned her head to the left, only to discover that the sorcerer was missing.

The sorcerer must have risen early, she mused. I wonder what he's up to. She got up from her resting spot and stretched her arms. She stepped outside, blinking against the light. To her astonishment, she found him tending to a lively bonfire, with the remnants of their meal scattered around him.

"Tomar, you never cease to amaze me! You warmed up the rabbit meat for us. What plans do you have for today?" she called out with a grin.

"I'll begin formulating a plan to handle the trolls. They'll build our palace and forge our weapons. While that's underway, we'll focus on gathering a powerful army of beasts," he replied, finishing the last bite of his meal. He then stood and moved beneath a charred tree, his expression thoughtful.

"I can brew a potion to command both the crows and the trolls. But first, we need to collect supplies for tonight," she offered, walking beside him as she sharpened a branch's tip. "Have you ever tried fishing?"

"No," he replied curtly, leaning against a tree with his eyes tightly shut.

"Have you ever tasted trout?"

"No, and I have no interest in it," he retorted, irritation flashing in his eyes. "I'd much rather savor a perfectly aged deer steak."

"Have you spotted any deer around here?"

"When dawn arrives, I will feast," he answered.

"Feast on what?"

"I can summon whatever I wish. If I desire a deer steak, I'll simply conjure it. That's the magic we possess."

Mirra smirked. "Come on, let me show you how it works. It's so much fun!" She reached out her hand excitedly, adding, "You get to torment them and watch them struggle as they meet their fate."

Tomar arched an eyebrow, a spark of curiosity igniting within him. "I must admit, you are the most remarkable sorceress I have ever met. There is a unique energy that envelops you, something I have never felt before." With a sense of determination, he accepted her challenge, gently taking Mirra's hand in his own as he rose to his feet. Together, they strode purposefully toward the nearby brook, their footsteps echoing softly on the ground. As they approached, the scene transformed into a tapestry of nature, where dark, limp flowers unfurled along the water's edge, their deep hues contrasting beautifully with the murky surface of the stream.

As she stepped into the cool water, she gestured toward the shimmering fish that flitted around her legs, their scales glinting in the dim sunlight. Mirra's eyes sparkled with excitement as she swiftly plunged the pole beneath the surface, emerging triumphantly with a wriggling trout that fought fiercely for its life. With a practiced flick of her wrist, she tossed the fish onto the sandy bank, where it flopped helplessly, gasping for breath. "Look at it struggle," she remarked, a hint of satisfaction in her voice. "It won't survive much longer, and soon it will be part of our meal." Turning to the sorcerer beside her, she handed him the spear, urging him to take his turn and join in the hunt, the thrill of the chase palpable in the air around them.

With a firm grip on the spear, he tossed his hair back with a confident flair, declaring, "This doesn't look too difficult. There's nothing I can't accomplish." As he entered the stream, water splashed around him, and he added, "I'm sure even a child could do this."

Mirra chuckled softly. "It's not as easy as it seems. You're scaring them off," she pointed out.

The sorcerer dismissed her words, his gaze locked on the shimmering black trout as he raised a finger. In an instant, a large fish leaped from the water, crashing onto the dark foliage with a thud.

"It's a piece of cake; no skill required," he boasted, his chin held high with pride.

"You can't catch a trout with magic. That's just not how it works," she said firmly, her eyes narrowing as she surveyed the scene with disapproval. Her voice was firm, slicing through the atmosphere with a hint of command.

Tomar stood resolute, a fire igniting in his eyes as he embraced the challenge laid before him. With a determined nod, he accepted the task of showcasing his fishing prowess without the aid of magic, a feat he was eager to accomplish. Grasping the spear firmly, he stepped into the cool, flowing stream, the water swirling around his legs as he focused intently on the darting fish beneath the surface. With a swift and practiced motion, he thrust the spear into the water, only to emerge with an empty rod, the fish having eluded his grasp. Undeterred, he tossed his hair back with a confident flick, his voice ringing out with conviction as he declared, "I can do this; nothing is beyond my reach." The challenge only fueled his determination, and he prepared to try again, the thrill of the hunt coursing through him.

The sorceress moved with an ethereal grace, her presence a whisper against Tomar's sturdy frame as she pressed herself against him. Her breath, cool and delicate, brushed against his ear, carrying a message of encouragement. "I believe in you, Tomar. Remember, success isn't solely dependent on magic," she murmured softly, her words wrapping around him like a gentle embrace. As she gently guided his arms, their bodies moved in a synchronized dance, igniting an unspoken connection between them. Despite the warmth of the moment, she quickly shook off the burgeoning feelings, her focus shifting back to the task at hand. "You need to watch where the fish are swimming and learn to move in harmony with them," she instructed, her voice steady, yet laced with an undercurrent of intimacy that lingered in the space between them.

Tomar took a deep breath, feeling a rush of emotions, he hadn't experienced in ages, thanks to her presence.

"Focus on the fish's movements," she urged again, her voice a tether pulling him toward clarity.

The sorcerer's sharp gaze locked onto the glimmering surface of the stream. The flowing current, a sensation of the stream's rush against his skin. Suddenly, he caught a glimpse of darkness as a trout elegantly darted through the murky water. With a swift and practiced motion, he thrust the spear into the cool depths, reeling in a hefty fish. Its scales sparkled like dark jewels under the gentle dim sunlight. The exhilaration of the catch coursed through him.

"You did wonderful! We can enjoy a delicious dinner tonight," she cheered. Mirra glanced at the rippling water, dipped her hands into the cool, dirty brook, and playfully splashed Tomar.

"Wow, I can't believe you actually splashed me! That's a first!" he said, astonished.

"You've just experienced something new for the first time," Mirra teased, her smile wide.

Tomar chuckled as he wiped the water from his face. "I suppose I should have anticipated that," he remarked, his grin growing even wider

The sorceress laughed, pleased by his playful nature.

"This is all for you, since you love exploring new experiences." In a quick movement, Tomar lifted her and playfully tossed her into the stream.

Mirra let out a joyful squeal as she splashed into the water, sending waves cascading around her.

Tomar's laughter echoed, celebrating the carefree spirit of their playful moment

As she emerged from the water, her hair glistening and her clothes clinging to her form, Mirra shook her head vigorously, sending droplets scattering in every direction.

With a laugh, Tomar reached out to assist her. "I suppose I need to be more cautious around you," he teased as they made their way back to the bank.

"That was such an exhilarating experience! It was my first time being fully immersed in the water, and it felt incredible. Thank you, Tomar. I've never seen you this joyful before; your smile is truly something special." She adjusted her damp robe, cradled the fish, and headed home.

Tomar felt a warm glow of contentment from the unexpected bond they had formed, her radiant smile etched in his memory.

The sorcerer followed closely behind, captivated by her presence as she led the way.

Once they reached home, Mirra struck two stones together, creating a spark that ignited a lively fire.

"Why didn't you just use your magic to light it?" Tomar asked, puzzled.

"We can only stay hidden if we avoid using magic; that's how the white sorceress found us," she clarified, expertly skewering the unclean fish with a sharp stick before placing them on a spindle. She turned the rod every few minutes, ensuring the fish cooked evenly over the flames.

Tomar found himself enchanted by the sorceress's remarkable cooking skills as she prepared their meal, realizing that her practical talents were as impressive as her magical prowess. The mouthwatering aroma of the fish sizzling over the flames made his stomach rumble, heightening their appetite.

She removed the meal from the fire and approached Tomar.

"Watch out, it's hot," she warned, pressing the trout on a smooth stone with her fingers before popping her fingers in her mouth to cool them down. In one seamless motion, she handed a fish to Derail, gripping it by the tail.

The raven's eyes widened in astonishment at the size of the fish, and he accepted it with wide eyes and a grateful smile.

"Tomar, are you ready to enjoy some delicious food?" she inquired, skillfully slicing the largest trout in half with a sharp stone and presenting the larger portion to the sorcerer.

With a playful wink at the captivating sorceress, Tomar took a bite.

He exclaimed with delight, relishing the exquisite taste of the fish. Rising to his feet, he adjusted the folds of his robe with a graceful motion before bowing deeply, his gesture brimming with theatrical appreciation.

Mirra couldn't help but chuckle softly at his enthusiasm, a warm blush creeping across her cheeks as she watched him. She absentmindedly tucked a damp strand of hair behind her ear, her gaze lingering on him a moment longer than intended, as if captivated by the sincerity of his enjoyment. The atmosphere between them crackled with an unspoken connection, the simple act of sharing a meal transforming into a moment of shared intimacy. Firelight danced across their features, illuminating fleeting expressions and unguarded moments.

As the warmth between them settled into a contemplative hush, Mirra's gaze drifted to the embers and then back to Tomar, her voice barely louder than the breeze.

"Tomar, do you think we can exact our revenge?" she asked.

He didn't answer immediately. Instead, he stared into the fire, the reflection of the flames dancing in his dark eyes. Then he turned to her, his expression hardening with purpose.

"Absolutely, I am a force to be reckoned with. No one can stand against me. The local cowards will be begging for mercy," he replied, locking eyes with her in steadfast determination. "We will make them pay for their actions," he asserted confidently. With a spark in his eyes, he began to devise their plan to conquer Seledor as the sun dipped behind the West Mountains. And beneath that shadowed sky, blissfully unaware of the storm gathering in silence, the world slept—never suspecting what was coming.

7th Chapter

Mirra slowly opened her eyes, squinting against the faint light that spilled across the ominous clouds swirling above Stragon Valley. Her gaze lingered on the churning sky before turning to the sorcerer beside her. "Tomar is missing," she said quietly, her voice tinged with concern. "Derail, what do you think has happened to him? Is it possible he has abandoned us?" Rising to her feet, with a raven perched on her shoulder, she stepped outside. Her eyes scanned the valley until she spotted the sorcerer emerging from the dense underbrush.

She narrowed her eyes, observing, "He's carrying an old cauldron, but I can't quite make out what's in his other hand."

As he approached, a smile blossomed on her face, washing over her with a sense of relief.

Derail and Mirra observed intently as he finally positioned himself in front of them. Wind tousled his dark hair as he placed the cauldron down.

"Would you like some delicious fruit? Take a bite; they are tasty. I found them while searching for the troll colony. Once we cast a control spell on those creatures, they'll help us build a magnificent palace." Settling onto a nearby large rock, Tomar bit into his fruit, his expression melting into quiet enjoyment. He savored the flavors before glancing at the sorceress, who was examining the vibrant orange and yellow fruit before taking a bite.

"This fruit is strange to me. It has a sharp tang," she said with a wrinkle of her nose.

Tomar nodded, enjoying the fruit's unique flavor. "Yes, it's been ages since I last tasted this," he remarked, noticing the juice running down the sorceress's chin. "Let me help you," he offered, gently wiping her chin.

His touch was tender, and as she drew closer, her fingers found his—tightening with quiet intent.

"Have you ever tried squirrel meat?" she asked suddenly.

Tomar pulled back slightly, surprised. "No, and I have no plans to," he replied, amused.

"I know you would like the tender meat. I'll be back after I catch one. You're in for a delightful surprise."

Tomar raised an eyebrow, intrigued. "Catch one? What do you mean? Use your magic and get as many as you want?"

Mirra's playful mood softened into a serious one. She looked out across the valley, her voice low.

"No! If we rely less on magic, we can stay hidden longer. I suspect the Sorceress of Light can detect dark magic. That's how the warriors found us without us even knowing."

Tomar gazed at her, taken aback by her resolute demeanor. Before he could speak, she leaned in, pressed a kiss to his cheek, and straightened with purpose, "I'm off to hunt; I'll return before night falls." As she headed south with the raven perched on her shoulder, she continued, "Derail, I need to find some long branches to make a snare. I'll need at least ten of them."

The raven scanned the landscape before him. "To the left, beneath that tree, you'll find plenty of branches," he said, gesturing with his wing.

Mirra approached the pile of sticks, kneeling to examine each piece. "They look sturdy enough. Now, I need you to watch for any threats. I want to avoid any unexpected surprises."

"I would go to any lengths for you, sorceress," Derail cawed as he glided into the northern sky with a shimmer of loyalty.

As Mirra rummaged through the woodpile, she selected the sturdiest branches. The sound of soft wing beats returned her focus as she spotted her friend approaching from the north.

"I didn't sense any threats," Derail reported, settling comfortably on her shoulder.

"That's a relief. I intend to conceal my trap behind this tree to keep it hidden."

The sorceress meticulously laid out four branches on the ground, expertly binding them together with twine. With a vine in hand, she carefully measured each twig, arranging them to create a flawless square.

"Derail, it feels like forever since I made one of these. Do you think it resembles a trap?"

"I can't really tell. I've never encountered one like it. Do you think it will work?" he replied.

"Yes, I made plenty of these in my younger days, and they all worked great."

She tucked the seed from her breakfast into the rear of the crate, fastening the door with a stick bound by twine.

Then, as if summoned by fate, the northern wind stirred the underbrush. A ravenous squirrel emerged from the forest, shattering the stillness that enveloped them.

Derail shifted uneasily. "Is this the feeling you often experience, Sorceress? Why does my heart race as I watch the creature come closer?"

"It's exhilarating, isn't it? My heart races too." Mirra whispered.

The squirrel paused, sniffing the air and scanning its environment before quickly jumping into the crate.

With a swift tug on the string, Mirra ensnared the animal inside.

The squirrel thrashed wildly, desperately trying to escape the confines of the makeshift cage. Its tiny frame ramming against the twine and splinters with desperate energy.

As the sorceress observed the frantic little creature, a wave of sorrow washed over her; she saw something she hadn't expected— she recognized it as a mum. Thoughts of her waiting young filled her with deep sadness, followed by a heaviness she couldn't quite shake.

Turning to Derail, she managed a soft smile. "Derail, you know, I think we should have fish for dinner again tonight since I really enjoyed our meal last night."

With steady hands, she opened the cage and watched as the mum hurried away with the seed. A smile spread across her face as she crushed the trap beneath her foot and declared, "Derail, I couldn't save my own child, but at least I had the chance to save hers. Let's go home now."

The raven let out a gentle croak, circling once overhead before resting on her shoulder. As the sorceress and the raven approached the campsite, a playful grin appeared on Tomar's face as he remarked, "It looks like your trapping attempts didn't go as planned."

Mirra returned the grin and replied smoothly, "I loved the fish so much last night that I thought we'd have it again tonight," opting to keep the earlier events to herself.

With the raven perched on her shoulder, they walked along the narrow path toward the brook while scanning the deep gray flowers swaying in rhythm with the wind. Thunder rolled far off in the distance, and mist curled up from the stream like breath from the land itself.

"What a beautiful day! Derail, would you like to join me? The water is deepening in color, yet it feels so refreshing," she said aloud as she stepped into the brook, skillfully catching three fish. "Have you seen how the trout have taken on the stream's dark hue? I think their vibrant color will enhance the flavor."

Once satisfied, Mirra gathered the fish and nudged her raven companion. "It's time to head back."

Upon their return, the burning scent of pine met them. A fire crackled, already waiting for her.

Her face brightened as she conveyed her appreciation, saying, "Thank you."

Tomar acknowledged her with a nod and raised his left arm.

"Derail, we need to get dinner ready; the sun is going down," Mirra called, lifting the catch.

She speared the muddy fish and arranged them on the spindle she had crafted the previous night. "When dusk breaks, I'll cook the meat so Tomar can enjoy a warm meal." They waited patiently, and as the first light kissed the West Atron Mountains, Mirra set their meal over the flames.

As the aroma began to rise, she stood and called toward the flickering light, "Sorcerer, it's time to eat! I hope you've worked up a good appetite!"

Tomar approached the fire pit, his shoulder-length black hair dancing in the cool breeze, like ink caught in motion. The flickering flames cast amber reflections across his chiseled features, making him look more like a painting than a man.

As he settled beside the crackling fire, the sorceress couldn't help but admire his strong build, a smile spreading across her face.

"This meal is fantastic," Tomar said, chewing thoughtfully as he savored the crisp, smoky flavor.

Mirra turned toward the raven, eyebrows raised. "Wow, Derail, I can't believe how quickly you finished that fish! Are you still hungry?" she exclaimed, surprised.

Derail nodded, ruffling his feathers sheepishly.

"I'll share a piece of mine with you," she offered warmly, placing a small fish on the stone next to him. The raven pecked at it with gratitude.

Tomar brushed the crumbs from his fingers and rose, extending a hand. "Mirra, the meal was delightful, but we should end our day."

She accepted his hand and stood. Together, they entered the wooden shelter and lay out their bedding five feet apart.

Derail nestled closely against the sorceress for the night, wings folding in for the night, a soft rasp escaping him like a sigh.

• • •

As dawn broke, a biting wind swept through the valley. A thick fog enveloped Stragon Valley, casting a shadow over the once-vibrant landscape. The vibrant wildflowers that once colored the campsite had withered into muted gray petals, strangled by a malevolent force creeping in the unseen.

Derail fluttered to the open window, feathers puffed against the chill. "I had a fantastic night's sleep," he said brightly, gazing out at the courtyard.

"What do I see?" The raven squinted, trying to discern the movement. "Is that a beaver?" His voice rose in surprise, completely unaware of Mirra standing right beside him.

"What are you looking at, Derail?"

"I can't see it now, but I'm sure I spotted a beaver darting behind the tree to the left before it disappeared."

"Maybe it was just the shadows playing tricks in the faint morning light."

She adjusted her cloak and lowered her voice. "Hop onto my shoulder, and let's go see what is lurking around our home."

They stepped outside and headed north toward the mist-laced woods, unaware that the sorcerer was watching them. Tomar was watching from the shadows of the shelter. Concern etched across his face; he finally called out.

"What are you doing now? This isn't the time for games. We need to devise a plan for the trolls."

As Tomar lingered in place, the sorceress approached him with purpose

"I can brew a potion. Tomorrow, we can enter the trolls' territory and distribute it among their foliage. It proved effective for Aldar and me."

Tomar scoffed, folding his arms with visible disdain. "I refuse to use a potion. I am a sorcerer, a master of magic," he replied. "That's not our way; potions are beneath us."

"I beg to differ. We created a mixture that turned red army ants into fierce warriors. Thanks to a potion, you regained your true form. Without it, you would still be a bird."

She stepped back, putting distance between them.

"You cannot dictate my choices," she declared, pivoting on her heel and walking away.

"I am the sorcerer, and you will obey my commands," he insisted with authority.

She spun around, locking eyes with Tomar's fierce gaze, and stated, "No, I don't care who you think you are; we are either partners or not at all."

Tomar paused, reflecting on her words.

"You've made your position clear; I won't dismiss the notion of potions, but you will be the one to craft them. Do we have an agreement?" he asked, his tone softening.

Mirra beamed and replied, "Yes, we have a deal." Without a word, she entered the hut nestled along the west wall, where she kept her potions and raw ingredients. "It seems I have everything I need to create a control potion," she said, laying out the items on a cloak and carrying them outside to the fire pit.

Kneeling beside the fire, she carefully arranged the ingredients around the ancient cauldron suspended above the flames. Mirra struck two stones together, producing a spark that ignited the fire. She then picked up three black moss roots, brushing her fingers across their soft texture before tossing them into the bubbling pot. One by one, she added ingredients, scrutinizing each for freshness and magical potency.

Tomar approached quietly, leaning in for a closer look.

"How's your potion coming along?" he inquired, eyeing the mostly empty cauldron.

"Don't worry; I've got this," Mirra replied, gesturing for him to step back. Taking a deep breath, she returned to her work, her focus unwavering.

Nearby, the raven perched on a flat rock, its sharp gaze fixed on the swirling concoction.

"Derail, by daylight, the potion will be ready," she stated confidently, adding, "Tomar will have no reason to resist using it."

As the sorceress added the final ingredient to the brew, a crimson glow appeared over the pot.

"Don't worry, Derail, it's normal. Soon it will vanish," she added as the raven shifted nervously.

Then she turned abruptly, "Watch over my potion. I need to fetch a jug. I'll return shortly." Mirra rushed toward the southern wall of the house, retrieving an empty container and a metal lid. When she returned to the fire pit, she peered into the bubbling cauldron and gave a satisfied nod.

"Thank you, my friend," she remarked.

"It's time to put out the fire," she declared, tossing dirt over the flames and then firmly placing the steel lid on the cauldron to trap any escaping steam.

Derail fluttered to her shoulder and suggested, "Let's search for Tomar. He's by the eastern trees."

Mirra's gaze drifted toward the wooded edge. "Tomar seems to be burying something along the edge of the trees. I can't shake this uneasy feeling about what he might be hiding," she replied warily. Although she felt a strong pull to approach Tomar, a persistent sense of distrust nagged at her.

The sorcerer turned to the sound of her footsteps.

"I've finished the control potion, and it will be ready by dawn. If you'd like, I can assist you right now," she offered, keeping her tone neutral.

She adjusted her stance, deep in thought. Perhaps she could uncover his secret. Her eyes widened as she absentmindedly caressed her left arm.

"No, this isn't your concern. Return to the hut. I'll come to you when I'm finished here," Tomar ordered.

"Why do you think I can't be trusted with what you're doing?" she shot back, eyes narrowed.

"It's for your own protection, I promise," he said, trying to soften his tone.

"I won't take orders from you. I'm not a child!" she shouted, turning and striding away.

Once inside the shelter, Mirra whispered to the raven, "Derail, we will uncover what he's hiding before dawn." Then she sank onto her bed, lost in thought.

As the sun dipped behind the West Mountains, the sorcerer completed his work and made his way back to the hut. Upon entering, he found Mirra fast asleep. Tomar murmured to himself, "She needs to rest; she must be worn out," as he lay down beside her, drifting off while thinking, "Tomorrow will be a long day." His gaze lingered on Mirra's peaceful face, the firelight flickering across her features. A quiet warmth spread through him. Gently, he covered her with a blanket, his fingers brushing lightly against her hair. Then, with the moon climbing high above the canopy, its silver light spilling through the shutters, Tomar closed his eyes and let sleep carry him into the hush of night.

8th Chapter

The stroke of midnight enveloped Stragon Valley in a chilling mist. As Derail awoke from his dreams, his wings grazed the sorceress Mirra's arm. She opened her eyes and offered a warm smile before rising elegantly to her feet. With a gentle gesture, she signaled that it was time to leave. Stealthily, Derail and Mirra slipped out the door, careful not to disturb Tomar's peaceful slumber, stepping into the moonlit haze with only the rustling of leaves to guide them.

The moon's pale light cast eerie shadows that danced around them, igniting a sense of unease. Mirra listened intently to the soft rustling of nocturnal creatures in the nearby woods. A chill ran through her as she wrapped her arms around herself, inhaling the crisp night air. The rustling leaves and distant calls sent a shiver down her spine. They quickened their steps, driven by a desire to uncover the secrets hidden in the dark underbrush, when the raven cawed, "It seems we're approaching the spot where Tomar hid something."

"Derail, do you hear that strange growl or see anything moving?" The raven shook its head in response.

"No," he replied as they arrived at the grave.

Mirra knelt to inspect the disturbed topsoil, plunging her hands into the soil until she encountered something solid. With a sharp breath, she began to clear away the dirt, murmuring, "This must be what Tomar buried."

Derail leaned in closer. "Sorceress, what do you perceive?"

Mirra pulled back layers of soil to reveal a creature—small and grotesque. "It's a mutant beaver, still in its altered form. Tomar shielded me from the knowledge of this frightening creature, ensuring I wouldn't have to face any fear," she clarified as they made their way home.

The raven cawed softly in agreement, and together they turned back to camp.

• • •

The fog had lifted, revealing the stunning splendor of dawn. Morning had arrived while the sorcerer remained soundly asleep.

Mirra rushed to gather her potion. Lifting the lid of the steel kettle, she observed the red and black particles swirling inside. Satisfied, she poured the concoction into a container and placed it by the door.

"Tomar has no reason to refuse the potion." As the sorcerer stepped out of the cottage, Mirra slipped inside. "You're up early," he remarked, stretching.

With a mischievous grin, the sorceress responded, "I have a surprise for you. It's a powerful elixir to control the trolls."

"Oh, how delightful!" he replied, dripping with sarcasm.

"I know you're not fond of potions, but there's no need to be rude," she said, grasping the vial and heading into the forest.

"I apologize; I was just joking. You caught me off guard. I'll join you and assist with distributing the potion," Tomar said, his brow furrowing as he accepted the vial from the sorceress, placing a gentle kiss on her hand while contemplating the swirling red and black flakes within.

Mirra's eyes sparkled as she released the container.

Tomar turned to Derail. "Raven, scout the northern region. I want to avoid any unexpected encounters," Tomar commanded.

"Your wish will be granted," the raven replied, taking flight toward the towering peaks of the distant mountain range as the sorcerers began their ascent.

As the sun rose in the east, the group arrived at the edge of the troll's territory. Tomar turned to Mirra and said, "You should remain here where it's safe. I'll spread the potion among the trees."

"Tomar, why can't I accompany you? Does that mean it's safer for you?" she questioned, worry evident on her face.

"Not at all, but it gives me peace of mind knowing you're out of danger," he replied, gently kissing her forehead before venturing into the forest. Once she was out of sight, Tomar poured the potion into the dark underbrush. He raised his arms, closed his eyes, and focused on the troll camp to the north. With a decisive twist of his wrist, he pronounced the word "COSER," casting the spell toward the west, south, and east. Afterward, he retrieved the empty bucket and returned to where Mirra awaited.

"In the morning, you'll witness the effects of my control potion," Mirra said with quiet confidence, blissfully unaware that he had discarded her tonic.

As the first light of dawn filtered through the trees, the sorcerers emerged from their shelter. Tomar positioned himself behind Mirra, wrapping his arms around her waist. The brisk morning air playfully tousled their hair as they gazed at the enormous trolls standing in the center of the fortress.

"My potion is as potent as any spell," she asserted proudly.

With a commanding presence, Tomar approached the giants. "Pay attention and follow my orders without delay. This is the site where you will construct the grand stone palace. Once that task is complete, you will turn your efforts to crafting siege weaponry. Now, hurry and collect the stones needed for the palace," he instructed, urging the trolls to move swiftly toward the rocky outcrop to the south.

Mirra moved closer to Tomar, standing beside him. "What gives you such confidence that the creatures will return?" she inquired, her gaze resting on him for a fleeting moment.

"They're under a spell, so there will be no delays," he replied smoothly.

"Are you suggesting they've been enchanted by a potion?" Mirra sought clarification.

"Precisely!" he said, a grin spreading across his face.

By midmorning, the creatures returned, hauling stones as large as houses.

Tomar observed with growing satisfaction as the trolls adeptly handled the massive rocks, setting the stage for the palace's construction.

• • •

Five days later, the courtyard was filled with towering boulders, each one meticulously arranged like sentinels awaiting their purpose.

Tomar sat atop a large rock, surveying the giants for any signs of dissatisfaction, but found none. Their faces were unreadable but calm—no trace of restlessness or resistance in their demeanor. Satisfied, he stood and addressed them with steady authority, "At dawn tomorrow, you will commence building the palace. You will remain within the fortress grounds until the work is complete. The two largest trolls may venture out to gather your meals, and one can fetch water from the creek."

Without protest, the trolls established their camp at the western edge of the estate. Tomar was impressed by their immense strength and skill, noting their unwavering dedication and productivity each day. Under their capable hands, the palace began to take form, filling Tomar with a deep sense of satisfaction.

• • •

The sorcerers had been vigilantly observing the trolls for several months. Each day, Tomar silently wrestled with the same question: how long could he truly maintain control over these towering beasts?

While Mirra wasn't convinced that caution was still necessary. "Why is it necessary to keep such a close eye on the trolls? I've already demonstrated how effective my potion is, haven't I? Only a spell can shatter its influence," she shot him a piercing look, daring a response.

Tomar rubbed his temples warily. "Let's talk about this at dawn; I'm too exhausted right now." With that, Tomar turned away and slipped into the shelter, leaving the conversation hanging in the cool night air.

Later, as the camp fell silent, Mirra and Derail made sure the trolls were soundly asleep before concluding their day.

• • •

As the months rolled by, the sorcerers closely monitored the progress of their formidable fortress. Yet even as the palace neared completion, it wasn't just the structure taking shape.

Tomar and Mirra found themselves entangled in something deeper than they had anticipated. It began with shared glances and fleeting touches, an unspoken connection that drew them together in quiet moments. Their attraction intensified with each passing sunrise, threading itself into the fabric of their days.

• • •

Three full moons later, the trolls finished building the stone palace. A magnificent structure loomed to the east of the valley, its grand entrance crowned by a towering spire that reached defiantly toward the sky. The ominous mansion glimmered with fireballs suspended from a thirty-foot ceiling, casting a haunting red and black glow. To the south of the main hall, a room brimmed with potions, their glass containers shimmering in the dim light. A welcoming hearth crackled nearby while the sorcerers' sleeping quarters, perched on the upper level, offered a sweeping view from the spacious balcony that faced the valley. Meals were served in the galley to the north, where enchanted cookware performed its duties without a single whisper.

The malevolent sorcerer had also fashioned rooms for the townsfolk destined for enslavement. Below, in the cold, dark recesses, narrow, damp stone corridors led to a dungeon designed for those peasants who dared to resist. Stone steps ascended to the main living area, adorned with wicked artifacts and sinister tapestries that sparked unease and unsettling curiosity in equal measure. The oppressive presence of the evil sorcerer permeated the estate, instilling dread in all who ventured inside. Four concealed corridors provided the sorcerers with easy access, while a stash of weapons lay in wait on the western side of the fortress grounds.

Mirra stirred from her slumber, her senses perfectly attuned to the world around her. Stepping onto the balcony, she breathed in the cool, smoky air that wafted over the valley, enjoying the day's dreary atmosphere. "What a splendid day, Derail!" she called out, her laughter echoing as she observed the parched dust stirring up little dust devils across the basin. Her eyes drifted toward the serene expanse of Black Wormill Forest. Though it seemed peaceful, she was acutely aware that anyone daring enough to venture into those treacherous woods might never return.

As Tomar approached the enchanting woman, he set his hand on her shoulder and spoke with purpose, "Now is the moment to assemble our army." He locked eyes with her striking, icy-brown gaze and pressed his lips to hers, slow and deliberate, as dark and deep as the night.

Mirra's smile widened, her mind racing with visions of their future dominance. With Tomar at her side, she felt invincible, ready to confront any challenges that lay ahead. The sorceress was captivated by the sorcerer's formidable power. Taking his hand, she gazed into his deep, brooding brown eyes and asked, "What is your strategy for summoning this unstoppable army, my lord?"

"We will recruit the mightiest beings from every corner of the realm, uniting them to our cause through the strength of our combined magic." As he spoke, the intensity in the sorcerer's gaze softened as it met hers.

Mirra nodded slowly, her imagination vividly painting the unbreakable bond they had forged together.

"Do you recall the gigantic creatures and the mutated rodents we encountered on our journey here?" he asked, a playful grin tugging at his lips. "They'll be fierce adversaries. First, we'll use a control potion on the rats, and then I'll cast a spell to transform them into our allies. We'll need a powerful potion and a strong incantation to tame those hybrids."

"Tomar, I need to head back to the Valley of Drom to gather the essential ingredients for my potion. I've noted my potion recipes on the cave's back wall," she said, leaning against the balcony railing. "I can't quite remember all the components required for the hybrid potion," she confessed.

Tomar's brow furrowed. "Going to Drom by yourself is dangerous; I should go with you," he urged.

She shook her head, her voice firm. "I can handle myself, believe me."

He exhaled sharply, a flicker of frustration surfacing. "You're infuriating," he muttered.

"You need to safeguard our home and keep an eye on the trolls. Distract them, and I'll navigate around the perilous creatures and traps hidden in Wormill Forest." She countered.

"How do you plan to do that?" he inquired.

"I'll avoid the path we took to arrive here. I know another route to the Valley of Drom. I've traversed the Highlands many times with Aldar," she assured him. "His parents taught him how to navigate the treacherous landscape, and he shared that knowledge with me."

Tomar hesitated and then nodded. "You're right. I need to ensure everything runs smoothly here. We can't afford any delays," the sorcerer said, placing a gentle kiss on her cheek.

Later that evening, Tomar walked among the siege engines, watching the trolls at work. He rubbed his chin, pondering how long it would take the trolls to finish crafting their assault weapons. Stealthily, he maneuvered around the catapult, avoiding the attention of the busy creatures. With both hands, he grasped the main beam and gave it a firm shake, impressed by the trolls' impressive craftsmanship. As twilight began to blanket the sky and the day drew to a close, he turned his gaze toward the west.

Upon returning to the palace, he opened the door to the potion room. There, he was captivated by the sight of the barefoot sorceress, diligently tending to the four cauldrons she had set up. The room shimmered with magic. He crossed to her, took her hand, and led her quietly to the bedroom.

Mirra glowed with joy, excited to make her first vow to another man.

As they entered the bedroom, the sorcerer sensed the powerful energy radiating from her, creating an atmosphere charged with passionate anticipation. When the first light of dawn began to chase away the shadows, they lay entwined in each other's arms.

"Time to rise!" Derail called out to his family.

Mirra nodded, stretching her arms wide. "You're right, my friend—the sooner we depart, the sooner we'll return."

Tomar gently pulled her back down, his voice firm. "No, you can't leave."

"Please, let me go. I promise I will return to you." She stood and pressed her lips to his once more.

"Sorceress, I'll free the trolls and accompany you," he replied, though the uncertainty in his voice betrayed his growing fear of what her return might mean.

"That won't be necessary. I swear I'll be back in three days. Derail will keep you informed if anything goes awry."

Tomar enveloped her in a warm embrace, his lips brushing against her neck as he whispered softly, "Always remember that my love for you is steadfast, and I will be here, waiting for your return."

After the sorceress and the raven departed from the palace, Mirra slung a bag of supplies over her shoulder and followed Derail as they journeyed northwest through Stragon Valley. She paused briefly, looked back, and blew Tomar a kiss as a farewell gesture.

As the sorcerer watched her silhouette fade into the horizon, a surge of unease enveloped him. He worried over the perils that lay ahead for her in the valley—the hidden traps, the lurking beasts, the unknown. With a heavy heart and furrowed brow, Tomar turned and made his way to the armory, the echo of her farewell lingering in the air behind him.

In the quiet folds of the valley, Mirra drew her cloak closer and shivered, "Derail, I hoped the sorcerer wouldn't fully understand the risks of this journey. We must move carefully." She whispered, the solemnity in her voice unmistakable. The raven cocked its head, its beady eyes indicating it understood the gravity of the situation.

9th Chapter

Mirra and the raven reached the outskirts of Stragon Valley as the morning mist curled around the gnarled trees. She settled on an ancient log, yearning for a moment of tranquility. The cool water she sipped helped soothe her frayed nerves.

"Derail, could you check the surroundings for us? I'll wait here until you return," she asked softly.

"Of course, I'd be glad to," he replied, taking to the skies. He flew east, skillfully navigating through the trees, but the dense foliage limited his sight. After a comprehensive search, he came back to the place where the sorceress was waiting.

"Did you spot any threats?"

"No, the underbrush was too thick; it blocked my view," he answered, landing gracefully beside her.

Mirra scanned the woods and took a deep breath. "It feels safe here."

"Thank you for your efforts," she added, rising and adjusting her backpack. Without further delay, they ventured deeper into the woods, their footsteps muffled by moss and fallen leaves. The trees loomed above, ancient and watchful. But as they walked, a sudden unease stirred within her.

"I can't shake the feeling that we're being watched," she murmured, a shiver running down her spine as the branches rustled. "Maybe it's just an animal moving through the leaves…" The sorceress paused mid-step, her instincts prickling, and signaled for the raven to scout ahead. It darted forward, wings slicing through the still air.

"I can sense a dark presence nearby, but the trees conceal everything," she said, eyes narrowing as she scanned the shadowed trunks.

Suddenly, a deafening flutter broke the silence as a flock of crows burst skyward from the southern treetops, their shrill cries echoing through the forest.

"It must have been those blackbirds I heard. They were likely startled by Derail," she sighed, feeling a wave of relief wash over her.

Unbeknownst to Mirra, a monkey-like creature was watching her from the branches above, cloaked by leaves and shadows.

In a swift motion, it descended and snatched her pack.

She looked up just in time to catch a fleeting glimpse of the thief before it disappeared with her possessions.

Derail swooped down, wings brushing the air as he landed next to her.

"Did you see which way it went? I really hope we can catch up," he asked eagerly.

"No," she replied, shaking her head in disappointment.

"It's not your fault that creature took our things," she added, gently smoothing his back feathers to ease his worries.

"We can't go much further without food or water. We need to find a stream to replenish our supplies," she continued, lowering herself onto a sun-warmed rock. Beads of sweat dotted her brow as she pulled her hair back.

Without hesitation, the raven spread its wings and soared eastward, determined to retrace its previous route.

"I really hope Derail returns; I just want him to be safe," she murmured, eyes fixed on the sky. As if summoned by her wish, Derail returned from the southern edge of the clearing.

"I'm so glad you're back; I was really worried about you," she said, tilting her head to meet his gaze and giving him a reassuring pat on his head.

The raven surveyed the ominous terrain ahead, scanning the shadows and sensing something amiss. Tension rippled through the air. In a flash, he darted to Mirra's side, wings slicing through the quiet like a warning. Mirra squinted into the gloom, but the dense canopy made visibility almost impossible. Her heart pounded as the air grew heavier.

The ground rustled nearby.

"Leave now, or face your doom," she declared into the dark, voice steady despite the tremor in her chest. But the creature didn't answer.

"I could conjure a fireball, but that would set the entire forest ablaze. I could lift the creature, but the dense canopy would hinder that. Let me think this through." The creature remained unseen, cloaked in shadow, but its presence clawed at her senses.

Mirra steadied herself. Her breaths came slow and deliberate. Then, with a surge of resolve, the sorceress raised her arms high, palms facing the ground. A subtle hum stirred the ground. Then, with a whisper of ancient command, she lowered her hands. The forest answered. Branches cracked and fell, plummeting like thunder from the canopy. A sharp, startled growl erupted from the dark. The predator, whatever it was, had been caught in a cage of fallen timber.

In the stillness of the night, Derail shifted his wings and sensed a rare moment of deep tranquility. The creature, for now, had been dealt with. After a long and tiring day, rest was essential. The fire would serve as their guardian. When dawn broke, they would uncover the secrets hidden beneath the foliage.

Mirra gathered a mound of leaves to fashion her resting place.

Derail settled beside her, but the sorceress was restless, unable to find peace as thoughts of the enigmatic creature troubled her. He found it difficult to drift off, acutely aware of her agitation. Finally, he moved a few feet away, allowing space for her restless energy. And with one last glance, he closed his eyes and surrendered to sleep.

As the first rays of sunlight painted the sky, the travelers welcomed the new day. Mirra blinked away sleep, rose to her feet, and stretched her arms skyward before moving toward the tangled woodpile.

"Well, my friend, it seems all is calm. Let's uncover the beast we defeated," she said, gently parting the branches. But the trap was empty. "I'm not sure what I buried, but it looks like it has slipped away. Let's hope it doesn't cross our path again. We must continue; finding water is crucial. I'm quite thirsty."

With heightened awareness, the sorceress and Derail moved forward cautiously, alert for any concealed dangers among the trees.

"Sorceress, I'll go ahead to search for water," he offered, wings poised for flight.

"Be careful; it's been a long time since I've navigated these mountains. I'll wait here for your return," Mirra replied, leaning against a lifeless tree. She moistened her dry lips, rubbed her left eye, and absentmindedly traced a dark symbol in the dirt with her finger.

Her voice was barely audible: "I sincerely wish for Derail's swift return. I can't imagine life without him."

As the sun climbed over the jagged peaks of the Kinnick Mountains, the raven appeared on the horizon, gliding low and fast.

"I've found water; come with me!" he called out.

Mirra followed as he led her through a stretch of clustered trees to a rugged outcrop. Clear water trickled through the massive stones, glinting like jewels in the morning light.

"I'm right here, sorceress!" Derail crowed proudly.

"You're amazing, Derail. Honestly, I can't picture how I'd manage without you," she responded, climbing the towering stone formation with practiced ease.

Clear water trickled gently through the crevices of the massive rocks.

"You've done a fantastic job; I'm truly proud of you." The sorceress cupped her hands to drink deeply. The water soothed her parched throat, its coolness refreshing after the morning's tension. As she turned her head, something small darted in her peripheral vision—a green lizard sunning itself nearby. Without hesitation, Mirra picked up a stone and tossed it, sending the lizard tumbling to the ground.

"Now I have a meal," she declared with a smirk, grabbing it and biting off its head in one swift motion. "Want a taste?" she offered, holding out the headless creature.

"No, it's too small; go ahead and enjoy it," Derail replied, his tone dry but amused.

She savored the lizard, wiped her lips, and then cupped her hands to gather more water.

"This water might taste even better with a bit of dirt," she laughed. "We should move on."

Derail let out a low caw of amusement, and the pair pressed forward. The raven soared northeast above the treetops while the sorceress followed closely from below, their shadows stretching long beneath the dwindling light. As dusk settled across the mountains, the familiar outline of Mirra's old home appeared on the horizon. Her breath caught.

Atop the mountain, she paused to gaze across the sprawling Valley of Drom. Its vastness felt both familiar and haunting.

"I see a dragon!" Mirra cried suddenly, her eyes locked onto the dark shape curling in the clouds. The mere idea of such a creature sent a chill down her spine. She paused, briefly closing her eyes, then reopened them to survey the landscape once more.

I can't see or hear a dragon. It must be the shadows from the dark clouds playing tricks on my mind. That's what I believe, she reassured herself, as her heartbeat began to calm, enveloped in a soothing wave of tranquility.

Derail and Mirra made their way down the mountainside into the Valley of Drom. As she approached the cave's entrance, her steps faltered. Her attention was drawn to the enormous boulders that had taken her loved ones from her.

The sorceress stepped closer to the final resting place of Aldar and her son, kneeling down in reverence.

"I will always carry you in my heart. I hope you can forgive me for needing to move on," she whispered, tears streaming down her face as she rose to her feet.

"Derail, we must act now," she breathed, her voice thick with emotion. "Together, we will begin our journey."

As they entered the cave, a wave of memories engulfed her, leaving her momentarily frozen in place.

"I can't bear to continue," she murmured, wiping the tears from her cheeks.

Derail glided down and landed on the old stone perch where he and Tomar had once found comfort. He confidently strode to the center, lifted his beak, and let out a loud, echoing caw.

Mirra turned at the sound, recognizing her friend. A deep breath filled her lungs, and the weight of her sorrow lightened slightly, replaced by the warmth of companionship.

"Derail, are you hungry?" she asked gently, lifting him with care and carrying him to the remnants of dried rabbit and water. She settled onto the cave floor, crossing her legs in front of her.

The raven settled beside her as they shared the aged meat.

"The sooner we start, the quicker we can return home," she declared. Rising to her feet, she picked up two stones and struck them together, igniting the candle. "This will give us some light," she added, her eyes dimming with sorrow as she watched the flickering blue-black flames dance.

"It will be alright," the raven reassured her, sensing her unease. He fluttered briefly and landed on her shoulder, and together they ventured into the second chamber.

"There must have been an intruder in the cave. I'm sure I didn't leave my tree bark on the ground," she observed warily, eyes scanning the shadows. They listened closely, scanning the shadows for any signs of movement.

Bending down, she picked up a piece of wood.

We need to stay alert. The intruder could still be lurking nearby, and we can't afford any delays.

With determination, they pressed deeper into the cave's hidden recesses. The sorceress reached into a narrow crevice along the eastern wall and pulled out a small piece of coal—its rough texture familiar, grounding her.

They continued onward, the air growing colder until they reached the back chamber. At its threshold, they paused to assess the surroundings before stepping inside. The left wall was lined with a collection of handwritten recipes, spells, and notes, many of which she had committed to memory. Mirra carefully sifted through the extensive array of layered scrolls until she found the specific potions she needed to replicate.

I've documented the first and second potions, and if I stay focused, I should be able to finish by midnight. Once that's done, we can return home, she thought.

But before she could turn back to her work, a loud crash echoed through the chamber.

Mirra snapped upright. "Derail, I think I heard something fall near the entrance," she murmured, her voice low. The raven landed beside her, and they both stood frozen. The flickering candlelight stretched the corridor, unveiling a shocking sight.

A piercing scream shattered the silence.

"It's a mutant beaver that has escaped from the fortress."

The creature snarled, stepping into view. Its jagged teeth gleamed under the trembling flame, menace woven into every movement.

The raven darted at the beast, wings wide, aiming for its eyes. But the beaver ducked, twisted its body, and retaliated with a powerful swing of its tail, sending the bird crashing against the rocky wall.

"Derail!" Mirra cried out, her heart pounding as she saw him lying motionless.

The creature advanced with a threatening stance; its intent, clear.

Mirra backed away, her heart pounding. "I have no choice but to resort to magic for protection. I can't cast a fireball; I fear it might harm Derail."

The beaver approached her menacingly.

She pressed herself against the wall, raising her arms to shoulder height and turning her palms upward. Magic surged through her fingers.

With a commanding breath, she lifted the mutant off the ground, pinning it against the ceiling.

The grotesque beaver shrieked and thrashed about, desperately trying to break free from its restraint.

Mirra gazed at the scarred creature, recognizing it as the companion of the one she had previously set ablaze.

"It seeks revenge," she mused, enticing the beast to come closer until she could duck beneath it. In a fluid motion, she dropped her arms, sending the creature crashing to the ground.

Channeling her magic, she lifted the beaver once more and hurled it against the wall. Then, breath quickening, she hurried to Derail and enveloped him in her arms, seeking refuge behind the table.

As she scanned the tabletop, she noticed the creature had moved. Rising gracefully, she conjured a fireball and launched it at the beaver, incinerating it entirely.

She dropped to her knees beside Derail, cradling him gently. "Derail, are you okay? Do any of your bones feel broken?"

"No, I just feel a bit dizzy, but it will pass," he murmured.

Mirra nodded and gently carried him into the bedroom.

"Rest here," she said, laying him down. "I'll be back after I gather the potions." Her voice was laced with concern as she left the room.

Time slipped away unnoticed, and soon midnight had come and gone.

"I have the recipes I need," she announced upon her return, noticing her friend still deep in slumber.

"I'll take a quick nap until morning, and then we can begin our journey home," Mirra yawned, placing a robe beside Derail before drifting off.

The rustling of vampire bats roused both the raven and the sorceress from their sleep.

She hurried to the southern corner, retrieved a hollow log, and filled it with the ancient potions and formulas she had left behind. Grabbing food and water, she placed them on top. Quickly, she rushed back to Derail. "I'm ready to head home. Would you like to ride on the sled?"

"Yes, but only for a little while," he chirped with enthusiasm.

Together, they stepped out of the cave and took in their surroundings.

The sorceress took a deep breath of the crisp, fog-laden morning air, noticing the boulders surrounding the cave's entrance were completely covered in a thick layer of black moss.

Mirra drew in a deep breath and looked toward Derail.

"Derail, do you understand that we might never come back here again?"

"I do, but we'll be living in a palace instead of a cave, with a powerful sorceress to protect us," he responded, landing at the front of the sled.

"I'm really eager to go home," Derail insisted.

As they ascended, the raven noticed the sorceress struggling with the sled, beads of sweat glistening on her forehead.

He soared into the overcast sky, hoping to lighten her burden with his watchful eyes and presence.

Mirra pressed forward, pulling the hollow log up the incline step by step. At last, they reached the summit. Together, they paused and took one final glance at the valley below.

"It's time to return home," she said softly. "I've packed my explosive potions in case we encounter any creatures along the way."

With no hesitation, they moved forward through the dimly lit forest, the light behind them fading.

The sun sank behind the jagged silhouette of the Atron Mountains as they reached the edge of Stragon Valley.

"Our journey has reached its conclusion," she said aloud, her voice soft with wariness. "I'm genuinely proud of you, Derail, and I'm grateful for your help. I'm feeling quite tired. Let's rest here for the night and cross the valley at dawn."

The raven nestled close to the sorceress, tucking his head beneath a wing.

Soon, sleep embraced them both, silent and complete beneath the watching stars.

10th Chapter

Mirra jolted awake, her eyes wide with surprise. She sprang to her feet, brushing off the leaves that clung to her robe, and shook her stiff left arm to restore some feeling. Above her, the branches of the trees clashed together, creating a chaotic melody that mirrored the frantic beat of her heart. Rubbing her eyes, she gazed up through the tangled limbs, only to find a heavy shroud of gray clouds looming ominously overhead. A sudden gust of wind swept by, sending a chill down her spine. It dawned on her that she slept longer than she wanted to. With urgency rising in her chest, she sat up, scanning her surroundings for any signs of danger.

"Pulling this sled has taken us twice as long to get here due to the weight of this carrier. I'll leave the log here and take my potions and bark instead," she muttered, adjusting a rucksack filled with essentials on her shoulder. She paused to survey the forest, her lips parted in thought.

"What's causing the branches to move? There's no wind."

The sorceress looked up, wiped her lips, and concentrated on the sounds around her. A deep growl echoed somewhere beyond the clearing, raising goosebumps along her arms. Instinctively, she reached for her explosive potion, ready to confront whatever threat might be lurking in the shadows.

"Did you hear that growl?" she called out, her voice tight. Mirra wrapped her arms around herself, pushing her hair back as she peered into the dense tree line to the east, but the shadows remained still. A chill coursed through her, her heart racing as she tried to pinpoint the source of the unsettling sound. An instinctive fear enveloped her, as if unseen eyes were watching her every move.

She cautiously took a step forward when a pair of luminous eyes ignited in the darkness, sending a surge of fear coursing through her. Mirra tightened her grip on the explosion potion, steeling herself against the unseen danger lurking in the woods.

"Derail, that creature watching us resembles the one I buried. It's the source of the rustling in the underbrush. If it dares to attack, it will meet its demise." She spoke through clenched teeth.

Drawing in a long, steady breath, Mirra summoned her courage and confronted the shadowy figure. "I'll obliterate you if you come any closer!" she shouted, her left hand firmly planted on her hip while the other clutched the potion.

"You can have whatever you desire once we're gone," she declared, her voice brimming with determination.

She cast one last wary glance at the menacing silhouette lurking in the shadows. "Derail, let's head home. The forest and my supplies are theirs for the taking."

With excitement bubbling within her, the sorceress and the raven set off on their journey through Stragon Valley. Mirra felt a swell of pride for her accomplishments, her head held high as anticipation surged through her veins. With the raven perched on her shoulder, she knew they were a formidable pair, ready to tackle any challenges ahead. "Do you think Tomar is worried about us?" she asked, wiping the sweat from her brow.

The raven tilted its head in contemplation. "I sense the sorcerer trusts your abilities. He recognizes the strength and wisdom you embody as a sorceress. Whenever you're away, he will always be concerned for you. You mentioned you'd return by evening; if we're not back by dawn, he'll come searching for us. He has never seemed more at ease than he does right now. I believe he cares for you more than you realize."

Mirra felt a comforting wave wash over her as she smiled at the raven's words, ready to prove her worth with each passing moment. "I find him difficult to comprehend. I cherish him, yet how can I fully trust him?" she admitted.

Derail cawed softly, his eyes shining with understanding as he replied, "Trust is a journey, but love will light the path. In time, you will come to know the sorcerer. He may appear enigmatic now, but let your love guide you to uncover his true essence," the raven murmured. His words ignited a spark of hope and resolve within the sorceress. A gentle warmth enveloped her heart, assuring her that her feelings for Tomar would help her navigate the uncertainties ahead.

They walked in silence for a while, the forest around them hushed. As Mirra paused to catch her breath, she noticed the sun had passed its zenith. "Derail, we've reached the midpoint of the valley, and I need to rest," she said, settling onto a rock, stretching her legs, and wiping the sweat from her brow with her sleeve. "The light is fading as the sun sinks toward the West Mountains. I welcome the coming of night," she continued, gathering her hair back. "This truly is the most enchanting time of day."

"Can you use your magic to take us home, Sorceress?" the raven inquired, standing beside her.

She shook her head and replied, "To my knowledge, there isn't a spell for transportation. Perhaps the sorcerer possesses such knowledge and will one day share his magic with me. I can't fathom why he keeps his abilities hidden; it feels as though he doesn't trust me."

The raven tilted its head, contemplating her words. "Tomar has his reasons for concealing his magic. Perhaps one day, he will choose to share them with you. He may be hard to understand, but I believe that in time, he will unveil his impressive abilities to you."

"You're right. I, too, have my doubts about the sorcerer. It's strange—how trust can fade even when I care for someone. I never experienced this uncertainty with Aldar." She rose, adjusting her robe as her tone grew steady, "I trusted him from the very first moment we met."

The raven fluttered onto a branch nearby. "While he may be enigmatic, I truly believe his intentions are noble. Keep an open heart and see where this journey with Tomar leads you. I've known him all my life," he said gently. "And I've never seen him so joyful."

Mirra turned, her eyes catching the soft light between the trees.

"We should resume our journey home," Mirra said, her voice warm with longing. "The thought of curling up next to Tomar's cool presence in a hard bed fills me with happiness. Before you and the sorcerer came into my life, I had been convinced I would spend my days alone in that dark cave. I'm so grateful to have been mistaken."

"I felt the same way," Derail replied quietly. "Before I met you, I had no friends. For years, I longed for companionship, but my chances were limited without leaving the palace. Now you are my family, and I cherish and trust you. I'm thankful I was wrong and that you entered my life."

Mirra tilted her head, her gaze tender. "I have often wondered why you chose not to seek a partner and start a family."

"I believed my fate was to guard the dark palace of the sorcerers," the raven said, wings fluttering. "This duty has been passed down through my family for generations. We have always kept a watchful eye on the malevolent lords; just as my ancestors did, I inherited this responsibility. I had hoped that one of my children would eventually take on this role. But now, with the dark fortress gone, my purpose has come to an end."

"The grace of a raven like you is truly remarkable," the sorceress said, gently stroking the bird's neck.

Together, they continued through the winding valley, their steps steady beneath the golden light of late afternoon. The landscape began to shift, with brush thinning and the ground rising as the path curved upward toward higher ground.

After a long, reflective stretch of travel, the pair reached the summit of the gentle hill. Mirra paused, her breath catching as she gazed into the distance. The palace stood silhouetted against the fading horizon, its towers cloaked in dusky shadows.

"Derail, from this height, I can spot the palace. Our adventure is almost complete."

"Indeed, I shall go and notify the sorcerer of our arrival," the raven responded, taking flight toward the east, gliding over the landscape of barren trees and shrubs. As he neared, the sorcerer became aware of his approach. Simultaneously, Tomar's gaze was drawn to the enchanting woman advancing toward him from the hilltop.

Mirra's hair danced in the cool evening breeze, and her flowing black robe accentuated her graceful silhouette.

Feeling a surge of relief, Tomar stepped out to welcome her. She turned to him, her face brightening with a smile.

"It's so wonderful to see you; I've missed you so much." He said, his voice full and tender.

"I've missed you too," she replied softly.

Tomar smiled, then leaned in and kissed her tenderly. His arms wrapped around her, pulling her close in quiet relief.

As they parted, he reached for her backpack and slung it over his shoulder. "Did you face any challenges on your journey?" he asked gently, his eyes searching hers with quiet concern.

"No, all went as planned, and I'm so happy to be back with you," she replied with a soft smile.

He nodded, visibly relieved. "I tried not to worry, but you were always in my thoughts. I'm so relieved you made it here. Now, I want to show you what the trolls have built."

He led her to a large wooden enclosure meant for housing the mutant rats. The structure loomed with intricate beams and reinforced gates. "We'll collect the ingredients for your crow control potion at dawn," he mentioned. After planting a kiss on her cheek, he added, "The birds will alert us to any intruders in our territory."

"The pen is enormous; it can accommodate hundreds of rats," she exclaimed, her eyes shining with excitement.

Tomar kissed her once more, enchanted by the brilliance of her eyes. He felt assured of her affection for him.

"Shall we head inside for the evening?" he suggested, taking her hand and guiding her into the banquet hall.

The doors creaked open, ushering them into a space aglow with gentle magic. Mirra's attention was drawn to a candle that glowed with blue flames dancing between two vases filled with barren branches, releasing a scent that lingered in the air like damp moss after rain.

Tomar led her to the long dining table set at the room's center, then pulled out a chair with quiet care. She lowered herself gracefully, her robe gathering around her as she settled in. "I've made your favorite dish," he announced as a platter of beautifully seared golden-brown trout, paired with vibrant makic leaves, was placed in front of her. He gently tucked a loose strand of hair behind her ear and pressed a tender kiss on her neck.

Mirra's cheeks warmed, her smile blooming with gratitude. She replied, "Your effort in preparing such a delightful dinner truly moves me." The sorceress's happiness radiated, brightening the room like candlelight flickering in a long-abandoned chapel.

Tomar's eyes softened as he reached for a goblet and filled it with rich, deep red wine. "Tonight, we celebrate your return," he declared. Their glasses clinked together as their eyes locked, sharing a moment of unadulterated joy. "Enjoy your meal, my love; we are here to honor your homecoming."

Mirra took a sip and leaned back slightly, her curiosity stirred. "How did you know I would be back this evening?" she inquired, her eyes sparkling with intrigue.

"You promised to return to me this night," he reminded her, a playful smile gracing his lips.

"Tomar, no one has ever gone to such lengths for me. This is the most exquisite meal I've ever had," she said, delicately dabbing her lips with a napkin.

He stood, his chair creaking faintly, and lowered his voice as he turned toward the raven. "Raven, stay here. This night is ours." Crossing the room with slow intention, he wrapped his arms around Mirra and guided her toward the bedroom. The hallway was lined with lanterns shaped like silver blossoms, each casting subtle waves of light on stone walls veined with ivy. The floor was strewn with black rose petals, and the room glowed with candles flickering in enchanting blue flames, creating a mysterious yet inviting ambiance. Mirra inhaled, letting the scent of dark floral and old cedar settle in her chest.

"Tonight, Mirra," Tomar said, gently pulling her closer, "we are bound together for eternity." He kissed her deeply, pressing her into silken sheets, signaling the beginning of a night filled with desire, longing, and connection woven into every breath.

• • •

A jagged flash of lightning sliced through the eastern sky, heralding the arrival of dawn. The Stragon Mountains erupted with a deafening roar as the lightning struck their peaks, while the wind howled fiercely among the treetops. In that moment, the sorceress stirred awake. Her eyes snapped open, her breath catching in her throat, overwhelmed by a flood of memories from days gone by. Sitting on the edge of the bed, she turned her attention to Tomar. His presence enveloped her like a comforting embrace, instilling a sense of security. Just looking at him softened the edges of her unease. Rising with practiced elegance, she ran her fingers through her hair, shaking off the remnants of slumber. Her bare feet touched the cool stone floor as she reached for a robe, drawing it around her shoulders with a gentle sigh.

"Tomar, would you like something to eat?" she asked, her voice gentle yet welcoming.

He stirred at the sound of her voice, turned toward her, and leaned in, brushing a kiss against her cheek. "No, I'm not hungry," he replied, his voice low but sure. For a moment, he lingered there, his forehead gently resting against hers. Then, with a faint smile, he rose and made his way to the main room, his steps unhurried.

A light breeze brushed against her shoulder as she followed, delicate as a whisper. As they approached the doorway together, they were met with an unexpected downpour.

"The rain has an unusual gray hue," the sorceress observed, squinting at the peculiar sight. "This storm is unlike any I've encountered; the mountains are completely hidden."

They watched as a small stream began to form at their feet. "I wonder if this rain is responsible for the desolation around here. Such a deluge makes the valley uninhabitable," she pondered aloud.

The sorcerer stepped closer, positioning himself beside her. Mirra turned to him, her gaze fixed on his striking features. "If this rain continues, our home and the valley will surely flood. Perhaps the palace should have been built on higher ground," she commented, studying his expression intently.

Tomar's reply came with quiet certainty. "The palace serves as our sanctuary; relocating it is out of the question. The rain won't stop us from achieving our goal." The sorcerer stepped boldly into the pouring rain, lifting his arms with palms facing down until they aligned with his shoulders.

Mirra watched in silence, her breath caught as his lips moved in a low chant—inaudible against the roar of the storm. In a swift gesture, the sorcerer raised his hands, causing the ground to shudder as if struck by a quake. A thick wave of mud surged upward, engulfing the palace courtyard. Tomar snapped his fingers—once, twice, then a third time. Astonishingly, the rain halted over the palace grounds, as if an invisible shield had been erected. Droplets froze and vanished, held back by an unseen barrier. The air settled into an unnatural hush.

"There's no cause for concern. Wake me when the rain has passed." He said smoothly.

Mirra narrowed her gaze. "You've cast another spell. The white sorceress will track us down if you continue like this."

"Relax, Mirra; it was merely a small enchantment. You're exaggerating the might of the Sorceress of Light. The forces of darkness are far more powerful," he reassured her with a gentle kiss on the cheek, and amusement flickering in his eyes before adding, "I'm going back to sleep. I'll join you later."

"He's so exasperating," she muttered under her breath.

Tomar closed his eyes and crossed his arms, responding, "I heard you."

The sorceress sighed and shook her head. "We should also take a moment to rest. After the rain, we need to collect the ingredients for my control potion," she insisted.

Derail nodded, voice calm. "Yes, sorceress, a brief nap is always welcomed."

Together, they made their way to the bedroom. But sleep refused to find the sorceress.

Mirra lay beneath the silken sheets, restless while Derail snored softly in a nest of pillows nearby.

"I can't just lie here," she thought, a surge of determination sparking within her. "I'll prepare the cauldron for the potion."

With that decision made, she swung her legs off the bed and stood up. As she stepped into the room she adored, a radiant smile spread across her face. "It feels like a dream come true. I never thought I would enjoy such luxury," Mirra reflected, her gaze drifting to the flickering flames in the fireplace and then to the left side of the room.

She began gathering her containers, meticulously arranging them on the central stone table. "I'll keep myself occupied by sorting my tonics by their strength," she resolved.

Taking a moment to survey her surroundings, she mused, "Hmm, many of my potions share similar potency. I'll place them on the largest shelves."

She picked up a small vial filled with a swirling yellow and black liquid and set it in the far-left corner when she heard the raven at the door. "Derail, feel free to join me. I enjoy your company. I'm nearly finished here," She called, smiling without turning around.

The raven swooped down, wings fluttering as he landed on her shoulder.

"Mirra, it's midday, yet the gray clouds still rumble," he said, his voice edged with curiosity.

She nodded thoughtfully. "Let's step out and see if the rain has ceased."

Together, they moved to the doorway, the raven adjusting his perch as she opened the heavy wooden door. A cool breeze met them, and Mirra stepped outside, her eyes scanning the valley beyond.

"The rain has finally stopped." A wave of relief washed over her as she looked at the dark gray clouds still hanging low, but no longer spilling their endless torrent. "The wall of mud has disappeared," she added with a light laugh, remembering Tomar's remark about solving everything with a simple spell.

"I heard that," came Tomar's voice from behind, laced with amusement.

"I had no idea someone could sleep so soundly." She spoke with a teasing smile.

"My body and spirit are gradually merging. My abilities will remain feeble until they are completely united. Only through rest can I restore my physical strength. I was unaware of how close I was to the brink of death."

He paused, his eyes narrowing slightly at the memory.

"Crosoft, the Sorcerer of Light, must have known that our end was imminent. With Nadora's assistance, we used our powers to darken the golden medallion that sealed the tome. We were convinced that in seven moons, freedom would be ours. Little did we know that we were depleting ourselves by overexerting our magic. I now realize that I would have met my end if the key hadn't incinerated the tome and the raven hadn't consumed our remains."

Mirra stepped closer, her voice firm with conviction. "I'm thankful you survived. Now we can rejoice and claim our victory over Seledor. How many mutant soldiers will we need for our forces?"

Tomar's focus sharpened. "I've crafted the most effective strategy for a successful siege. We'll need at least fifty trolgilzs and five hundred mutant rats. Although my magic isn't fully restored yet, I still possess considerable strength. To cast a control spell on the enormous creatures, we must merge our magical energies. Once the trolls complete the siege weaponry, we'll be one step closer to dominating this realm. Soon, my dear, we shall reign over Seledor." He took her hands, gazing into her warm, loving eyes before continuing. "I understand your skepticism about magic, but we have no other way to achieve our goal and rule this land. You must prepare your crow control potion tomorrow. The birds will patrol the skies and alert us to any unusual activity. With the birds soaring above, we won't be caught off guard."

Mirra arched an eyebrow. "Could it be that five hundred rats are scurrying across the mountain terrain?"

Tomar hesitated, then chuckled. "I believe there are actually thousands living in that area. Enough to darken the hills if they chose to storm the valley."

"At dawn, I will gather the necessary ingredients for my potion, which requires a full day to ferment. Once it crystallizes, it will be ready for distribution," she said with a smile, clearly relishing the thought of ruling the realm not simply as its sorceress, but as its queen. She then turned, planted a kiss on his cheek, and gracefully walked away.

11th Chapter

As dawn's first light broke, Derail awoke from his dreams and glided to the sorceress's bedside.

"Mirra, it's time to rise," he cawed, lightly nudging her arm. As her eyes fluttered open, a bright smile spread across her face at the sight of the raven. She swung her legs over the side of the bed, her feet enveloped by the cozy embrace of her elk-hide slippers. "You are my dearest friend," she whispered gently. As she exited the palace, Derail soared beside her, and she affectionately stroked the feathers along the raven's neck.

"You should rouse Tomar. He'll worry if you don't," Derail advised.

Mirra shook her head. "He must remain unbothered. The forest is just a stone's throw from home, and he longs for tranquility." Outside, the muggy, crisp morning air danced among the gnarled branches of fallen trees. "That sound?" she said, pausing as winds rustled the fallen limbs. "It sends shivers down my spine every time. It's exhilarating, a reminder of my own existence."

"Not for me; I detest the sensation of fear. If I weren't immortal, it would surely shorten my life." His feathers ruffled with annoyance.

"Have you faced any fears while watching over Tomar and Nadora's palace?"

He hesitated, then spoke, "Once, a vicious white eagle graced the palace grounds, clearly in search of the hidden chamber where the all-seeing Sormara could be destroyed. Despite my efforts to confront him, he was too powerful and wounded my wing. I was engulfed by the dread that despair would follow me forever."

Mirra listened intently as he continued.

"Thirty moons later, the sorceress, a dwarf, and a girl arrived, bringing the Sormara with them. They conducted a dark ritual that turned the sorcerers to ashes. Thankfully, my wing healed, and I inhaled the remnants of their power, yet a shadow of doom hung over us. As I surveyed the destruction, the structure began to collapse. Toxic fumes filled the air as the roof caved in around us. The mournful cries of black vultures echoed in the distance. It was a terrifying time, one I long to erase from my memory."

Mirra reached for his claw. "Still, you exhibited extraordinary bravery by rescuing Tomar. From what I understand about Nadora, we probably wouldn't have agreed on much. The sorceress lacked any sense of empathy. Even if she had escaped death, Tomar would have never forgiven her for trapping them in that wicked tome. It's likely he took her powers to avoid any future confrontations with her."

Derail lowered his head, his voice more somber. "I'm still uncertain about what triggered my coughing fit that resulted in losing Nadora—was it the poison from the palace or Tomar's influence? During that chaotic moment, my sole focus was on survival."

Mirra nodded, letting his words settle over her like mist through the trees. "Let's gather what I need; maybe we can return home before the sorcerer awakens." They made their way into the southern woods. "We must find praying mantises, poison oak, centipedes, thorn rash bushes, black-tooth snails, and poison ivy. These ingredients are essential. Once I have them, I can brew my potion."

The raven soared through the sky, heading south. From his elevated position, he scanned the ground while Mirra searched through the thick underbrush below. "I see some movement to the east. I need to check if it poses a danger," he whispered.

As Derail descended closer, he spotted a pack of wolves slinking through the shadows. Mirra was their target. "I must alert her," he realized, turning back toward the sorceress. His careful descent went unnoticed as she concentrated on capturing a praying mantis, unaware of the danger creeping up behind her. "I'll create a distraction by flying over the wolves," he resolved, sweeping low across the wolves.

The raven darted toward the hunters, wings flared, yet the wolves remained unaware, stealthily drawing closer to Mirra.

In a desperate cry, the raven warned, "The wolves are nearing!"

Derail's tone turned ominous, signaling the impending danger.

Mirra looked up, brow furrowing at his alarm. Listening closely, she caught the sound of rustling leaves—heavier than any breeze. She straightened, heart quickening. "My companion warns of an imminent threat. I can hear the rustling leaves under the weight of an approaching creature." Her heart raced.

I sense danger closing in and must prepare for a confrontation, she thought.

The raven perched beside her, feathers bristling.

"Derail, what kind of peril are we facing?" she asked.

Before he could answer, menacing growls reverberated as she peered into the trees.

A black wolf stepped out from the forest's edge, howling to rally its pack for the hunt. The others slipped into view, eyes gleaming and jaws bared.

Mirra understood with grim certainty that they would meet their doom unless she harnessed her magic.

As the wolves closed in, teeth flashing and bodies low to the ground, she murmured, "The black wolf must be the alpha." Her fingers sparked with heat as a fireball bloomed in her palm.

Just as she was ready to unleash it, a brown wolf sprang at her from behind, knocking her to the ground and extinguishing the fireball.

Derail reacted instantly. With a sharp screech, he sprang toward the predator—his wings slicing through the air as he closed in on the attacker.

Fixated on the raven, the wolf lowered its head and braced for impact. As the bird approached, the predator raised its head, opened its jaws wide, and captured the bird, then forcefully slammed its body against a nearby boulder.

Mirra gasped, her heart racing with fear at the horrifying scene unfolding before her. She scrambled to her feet, her pulse quickening. Harnessing her magic, she raised her arms high, causing the attackers to flip upside down and hover above the ground.

A profound silence fell over the hunters.

"That should take care of it," Mirra announced, releasing her grip on the wolves, who then tumbled to the ground. In pain, they howled and limped away.

"Derail!" she shouted, rushing to his side. She knelt and gently lifted him into her lap. With two trembling fingers, she pressed against his chest, searching for a heartbeat. As she wiped away her tears, she tenderly stroked the feathers of the bird.

"You inspire me. You mean the world to me, and the thought of losing you is unbearable." She rocked back and forth, tears streaming down her face as her brave companion lay on her lap.

As his eyes slowly opened, the raven nuzzled her hand with the edge of his beak

"I was terrified when I saw the wolf's teeth grab you and throw you against the boulder. I feared I had lost you forever. It's a miracle you're still here. Are you okay? Did you get hurt?" Mirra breathed, relief washing over her.

Derail tilted his head. "You seem to have overlooked the fact that I am immortal. My body needed some time to recover, but I feel fantastic now. How did you manage to drive away the wolves?"

"In a moment of fear, I hurled them into the air and then brought them crashing down. They whimpered in pain and quickly retreated."

Derail chuckled weakly. "Your bravery is admirable, though I wish I could have witnessed it myself. You possess tremendous magical abilities."

"You are quite remarkable as well. Together, we could unleash a formidable darkness. I want you to rest here while I retrieve the poison ivy I noticed behind those trees to the south. I won't be long." She said softly.

Mirra gathered her supplies and set them on a bed of dry leaves beside the raven before dashing off through the bush.

"I remember seeing the poison ivy before the wolf attacked me. It's just beyond these trees." As she scanned the area around five tree trunks, the jagged leaves came into view. "I'll collect four of the large leaves. Their strength is impressive." She murmured.

Mirra pulled a rawhide pouch from her pocket, using it as a makeshift glove, and carefully plucked the toxic leaves before sealing the bag. "I need to hurry back and check on Derail," she whispered, turning swiftly.

Upon her return, she found Derail with his eyes shut. A wave of dread washed over her as she took a deep breath and rushed to his side, kneeling beside him.

"Derail, how are you feeling?" she asked, breath catching.

He opened his eyes, looking up at her in surprise. "You startled me."

"Do you think you can make it home safely?"

"Yes, I'm a bit weak, but I'll manage," he reassured her, locking eyes with her.

She smiled gently. "I'll take care of you."

She cradled the raven as if he were a child, with one hand and tightly clutched the ingredients in her other hand. As she made her way home, she spotted Tomar leaning against the palace wall, arms crossed, clearly awaiting her arrival.

"Your delay is concerning. In the future, please wake me. The forest is fraught with hidden dangers," he said, his tone serious and edged with concern.

"It took longer than I anticipated to gather the centipedes. I'm perfectly fine; I'm a strong woman and can look after myself," she replied.

Tomar softened. "I apologize for my frustration, but the forest is filled with unseen threats. I was genuinely worried for your safety. My feelings for you are deeper than I ever expected."

"I feel the same way, and I accept your apology," Mirra said, stepping close. She rose on her tiptoes and kissed him lightly.

"But why are you carrying a bird that can fly?"

"I wanted to build my arm strength, so I thought of using him as a weight. I can't let one arm be stronger than the other, can I?" Mirra answered with a shrug.

Her reasoning left Tomar utterly baffled, and he shook his head in disbelief. "Honestly, I can never quite grasp what she's saying half the time," he murmured as he watched the enchanting woman enter the palace.

Once inside, Mirra settled into a chair in the kitchen, cradling Derail on her lap. Her fingers gently examined his wings for any signs of injury. "Does this hurt?"

"My wings are a bit tender," he replied, flapping away from her lap and gliding around the room with deliberate flair.

"You made your point," she said, amused. "We should check on what the sorcerer is up to."

They made their way to the trolls' armory located to the east of the palace, where they found Tomar intently observing the craftsmen at work. "I'd rather not interrupt him. Let's go catch some frogs for dinner," Mirra whispered. "I'm sure Tomar won't even notice we're gone."

The duo headed to a nearby stream. A raven flew overhead, guiding the frogs toward Mirra, who skillfully caught eight plump ones in her bag.

As dusk approached, she glanced at the sky. "Night is descending, and he'll be back at the palace shortly." The sorceress took the live frogs and set them on a searing steel plate, listening to their cries as they cooked. "I hear footsteps," she added, just as the sorcerer strode into the room with assurance.

"All our weapons will be ready soon." He leaned in and planted a gentle kiss on her cheek, a reassuring gesture that reminded her of their combined strength, capable of toppling the walls of the Bastion Enwood.

"I bet you're feeling quite hungry. I've grilled some frogs and gathered fresh leaves from a bitter berry bush," She offered warmly.

"I've never tasted frog before. Where did you find them?" he asked, clearly intrigued.

"Derail helped me catch them while you were busy in the courtyard earlier. They live in a creek nearby. When I spotted them yesterday, they looked like a delicious treat. I can't recall the exact taste, but I remember enjoying them as a child. It was quite the adventure to catch them."

He grew serious. "Please let me know whenever you leave the palace grounds. If anything were to happen to you, I wouldn't know how to find you."

"Thank you for your concern. I did hurt my leg when I fell, but if it had been serious, Derail would have informed you."

"What if an eagle swooped down and carried him off? I wouldn't even know where to begin looking for you." His gaze held hers with intensity.

"From now on, I promise to tell you whenever Derail and I go hunting. You're absolutely right, my love." She gently squeezed his hand.

Tomar smiled gently. "I still can't understand why you're so passionate about these cooking experiences. Why not just use magic to fulfill every wish?"

"No, it's a skill I enjoy honing." She rose onto her toes, embraced him, and placed a soft kiss on his lips. "Now, have a seat and try something new."

Tomar settled into a chair, and Mirra set a plate of food in front of him, her gaze locked on him as he began to eat before she joined him at the table.

"Do you like it?" she asked, taking a hearty bite of the frog, its juices trickling down her chin. "That was unexpected," she remarked, wiping her mouth with her sleeve after savoring the taste.

"I found the dish delightful. The day has left me exhausted, and even though it's still early, I feel completely exhausted. I'll talk to you first thing in the morning." He stood, planting a gentle kiss on her head before heading to the bedroom.

"I'll join you as soon as I finish cleaning the table," Mirra called softly. As she turned, she spotted Derail and smiled at him. "Today was fantastic, and I believe even more amazing days are on the horizon." Mirra completed her table-cleaning tasks before heading to the bedroom. As the light faded, a distant rumble of thunder rolled from the East Mountains.

12th Chapter

Upon noticing the concern etched on Easha's face, Lundar paused mid-sentence.

"Sorceress, your expression betrays your worry. It appears you've encountered something unsettling."

"Look to the north. Doesn't the sky seem unusually dark?" Her nose wrinkled, and her brows furrowed in distress. "I can't shake the feeling that something is wrong." She bit her lip, wiped her mouth, and rubbed her arm, which was now covered in goosebumps.

"The skies to the north and west don't appear too different. I can see the ominous clouds gathering. A thunderstorm is certainly approaching." Lundar replied, scanning the horizon.

"You're correct. Squalls can cast a shadow over the sky," she sighed. "I'm anxious because it feels like only yesterday, we defeated dark forces. This squall must be the reason for the ominous northern sky, and it troubles me. If you have no other plans, I'd love for you to join me in harvesting melons this morning." Easha's gaze returned to the northern mountains.

"I appreciate the offer, but I must visit the elves. Lagar is expecting me today. Each meeting with him brings new revelations. I must take my leave now. I'll see you again in a few days." With that, the eagle bowed his head, spread his wings, and flew south toward the Kingdom of Elves.

The sorceress watched the magnificent white eagle soar into the heavens until it vanished from view, then shifted her focus to the garden.

"My concerns about the northern territories linger," she murmured. "I sense an impending danger; the storm clouds carry an unusual shade. When Lundar returns, I will send him to Drom to investigate whether the ominous sky is merely a storm or the result of dark forces at play. I need clarity to calm my thoughts."

Easha walked to the southern edge of her garden, where a wicker basket hung from a wooden post. She paused to inhale the musty air and knelt beside the thriving crops.

"The sight of this abundant harvest from such rich soil fills me with peace." Her lips curled into a smile. "Two beets, three potatoes, and four carrots will make a lovely stew. And I'll save this honeydew melon for dessert." After placing her treasures in the basket, she made her way to the front of her cottage, glanced once more at the frigid, deepening sky, and shivered.

"I hope Lundar is correct and that the darkness is just a storm, but I can't shake the feeling that something is off in the north. After I eat, I'll focus on honing my skills. My instincts tell me that the dark forces will continue their pursuit to conquer this land," she murmured as she stepped inside the cottage, voice low as she added, "I must prepare for the battles that lie ahead."

Easha dedicated her day to perfecting her explosive spells and enchanting lights, letting her magic flow with precision and power. As twilight descended, the sorceress stood at her doorstep, her eyes fixed on the east as the sun dipped behind the grand West Mountains.

The northern sky has now fallen under the encroaching darkness of night. It's getting late, and tomorrow will be demanding. With that thought, she retreated into her cottage, stifled a yawn, secured the windows and door, locked them tightly, extinguished the lanterns, and settled into bed.

• • •

The night gradually surrendered to dawn as the sun emerged, scattering the remnants of clouds across the pale sky. Easha's delightful cottage, with its charming brown and white cobblestone paths, was nestled in the lush embrace of Tonepass Valley, bathed in a soft, radiant light pouring in from every direction.

• • •

The sorceress awoke, her eyelids fluttering as she propped herself up in bed. "A new day filled with possibilities has arrived." She rose gracefully, cinching her flowing white robe at her slender waist, smoothing her hair back, slipping into her white slippers, and rolling her shoulders before making her way to the kitchen. She filled the teapot, placed it on the wood stove, and added a handful of dried berries.

Before long, the kettle began to whistle, steam curling upward in delicate tendrils.

"It's time to enjoy my cup of tea," she said aloud. "I wonder if anyone else shares my morning tea ritual." She peered into the cup. "The color of today's brew is especially vivid. What could have gone wrong? Perhaps the berries weren't fully ripe. That must be it."

As she watched the steam rise, she swirled her drink and let her tongue brush against the roof of her mouth.

"I can't taste any difference," she decided. "The ripeness of the berries probably doesn't matter after all." She rolled her shoulders forward to ease the tension in her back and glanced out the window. "The sun is about to rise. I need to hurry. I don't want to miss it." Exiting the cottage, she headed toward the rocking chair, noticing her white sorcerer's hat resting on the seat.

"I forgot to bring it inside. I don't see the need to wear my hat unless I'm going to the secret chamber. I'll leave it in the cottage until it's needed." She picked up the white cone hat and set it on her lap. "I'll take it inside once I finish my tea."

As she sipped and admired the vibrant green grass and wildflowers, she caught sight of two chipmunks scurrying northward.

"Beauty surrounds me from every angle, and I feel incredibly lucky to call Tonepass Valley my home. This place will forever have a special place in my heart," Easha reflected as she savored her tea.

A smile spread across her face as she inhaled the crisp morning air, her eyes drifting toward the eastern slopes of the Damen Mountains.

"The sky to the northeast is cloudless, yet it holds a certain shadow," she pondered. Easha, the Sorceress of Light, concentrated her energy, blinking as she reassessed her surroundings. Her arms quivered, and a wave of tension coursed through her muscles at the sound of leaves rustling in the warm summer breeze. She paused, clearing her throat, and examined the western sky before shifting her focus back to the east, comparing the colors.

"I can feel that darkness has returned to Seledor." As she looked toward the forest, her gaze was drawn to two majestic white eagles soaring toward her, their wings carving through the sky with grace.

"It feels like ages since your last visit, and now I see why," she exclaimed, her eyes sparkling with joy and her smile broadening.

"Easha," Lundar said as he landed, "let me introduce you to Efura. I met her on my journey to see Lagar. She descended from the sky while admiring the breathtaking mountain range. It felt like fate. We traveled through the Kinnick Mountains and entered the Elves' Kingdom. Lagar is on an important quest and won't return for five moons. I plan to visit him then."

"I held my conversations with Lagar in high regard; he is an exceptional elf and a true gentleman. Every moment spent in his presence was a treasure." Easha declared while observing the two eagles, their eyes reflecting a deep connection. "Lundar, I'm thrilled that you've found your mate. She is truly beautiful."

"Yes, we've experienced countless moments together as we've gotten to know each other. The rapid growth of our love feels nothing short of enchanting." Lundar softly brushed against her feathers.

"Lundar," Easha said softly, "if you have a moment, I'd like to ask you for a small favor."

"You know I would go to great lengths for you, sorceress. What do you need?"

"If neither of you has other obligations," Easha said, her voice tinged with concern, "Would you consider flying to Drom Valley? The basin should be uninhibited, though the sky looks ominously heavy. It seems the wind is stirring the dark soil, casting unsettling shadows above."

"Efura must depart," Lundar replied gently. "Her pa has summoned her to consult with the eagles. While she's away, I'll explore the eastern slopes of the Damen Mountains to discover the reason behind this troubling sky."

Lundar watched the sorceress as she rubbed her arms, feeling the oppressive weight of the darkened sky bearing down on her spirit.

"It has been a genuine pleasure meeting you, Easha, but I must take my leave now. I'm confident our paths will cross again soon. Lundar, I'll reconnect with you after the meeting."

Lundar and the sorceress stood side by side, their gazes fixed on the enchanting figure of Efura as she rose into the sky, her wings glinting in the sunlight before fading into the distance.

"I'll set out right away and return in two days," the eagle declared with determination.

"Lundar, you're more than welcome to stay a bit longer and visit before you leave," she offered with warmth.

"First, I'll fulfill your request. I know how important this is to you, and it will keep me occupied while Efura is away. When I return, we'll have plenty of time to catch up," he assured her.

"Yes, that thought brings me solace. I genuinely value all that you're doing for me. Please take care until you uncover the source of the darkness. If you face any challenges, reach out to Suhzar; he will keep me updated. My friend, look after yourself, and thank you once again for your support."

"You can rely on me. I will return with the answers you desire," the eagle promised with assurance before taking flight into the northern horizon.

Easha observed the magnificent creature rise, pondering, "I should find ways to occupy my time until Lundar returns. It comforts me to know he can always depend on Suhzar for help." The sorceress strolled through her charming cottage, admiring the vibrant flowers blooming along the western side of her garden. She plucked a juicy berry from a nearby bush and relished its sweetness with a satisfied bite.

"I haven't seen Jasper this morning. He must be indulging in a nice, long nap," she thought, kneeling at the garden's edge to pull up two fat beets, which she carefully set down. She stood, brushing soil from her hands. "I'll lift the fence spell around my garden until noon. That should give my friend, Jasper, plenty of time to gather his meal."

As she turned back to her garden, she drew her arms close to her chest before elegantly spreading them wide, the soft shimmer of enchantment fading from the perimeter. "There, it's done. Now that I think about it, I could use a little snack. A honey melon sandwich sounds perfect." As she approached the cottage, she paused at the entrance, looking up at the northern sky, a chill running down her spine. The northern sky had darkened

13th Chapter

Lundar's wings cut through the crisp morning air, a gentle breeze brushing against his face and amplifying the thrill of his adventure. As he soared above, his keen eyes caught sight of a brown and white rabbit darting across the ground. In a swift motion, he dove down and seized it with his talon, retreating behind a sturdy tree to savor his meal. "With my hunger satisfied, I can continue my journey," he mused. With a rustle of feathers, the magnificent white eagle ascended once more, setting his sights on the towering Damen Mountains to the north.

By midday, the sky began to darken, yet no fierce winds accompanied this somber shift. Easha had been right; shadows were indeed creeping into the valley. A sense of curiosity bubbled within him about the secrets hidden in that desolate region. The air held an eerie stillness, as if the valley itself was withholding breath.

Despite these musings, the eagle maintained his steady flight northeast, gliding over valleys and ridges as the sun dipped behind the Atron Mountains. The day's journey had taken its toll.

"It's time to find a place to rest for the night," he concluded. Spotting a nearby tree settled between two rocks, he descended and nestled into its branches. As the memory of his recent meal lingered in his stomach, he drifted into sleep beneath a sky painted in deep indigo.

As dawn broke over the majestic Kinnick Mountains, Lundar felt the gentle pull of morning beckoning him to rise.

He blinked awake, taking in the mist-kissed horizon. Stretching his neck and wings, he rolled his shoulders to shake off the remnants of sleep.

"The sooner I set off, the sooner I'll be home," he thought.

Lundar lifted his head, savoring the thick, cool air that enveloped him. But something below caught his attention.

"What could be the reason behind the crows swirling around the trees in such a meticulous formation? It sparks my intrigue—do they have a specific aim? What's unfolding here? I've never witnessed such a large congregation of crows before. Tomorrow, I will seek out the answers I crave."

He continued until he arrived at a grove of trees. Perched high in one of them, he surveyed the landscape, ensuring no one was nearby. The world seemed still, as if watching him in return.

As the sun sank behind the rugged peaks of the West Mountains, the eagle gently closed his eyes, yielding to the calming embrace of twilight. Night passed slowly, and the horizon once again began to glimmer with the promise of dawn. For a brief moment, Lundar scanned his surroundings, his sharp blue eyes vigilant for any hidden threats. A soft sigh escaped his beak.

"My fatigue has settled in, and my stomach churns with unease. Perhaps a bit more rest will soothe my troubles."

As the eagle closed his eyes, a gentle slumber wrapped around him like a cozy blanket. He felt the familiar rumble in his stomach, a lingering reminder of the delightful feast he had enjoyed the night before.

As the first light of dawn bathed the Kinnick Mountains, it beckoned Lundar to rise from his slumber.

He blinked awake, lifting his head as his feathers ruffled in the breeze. He stretched his wings wide, easing the stiffness from his limbs with practiced grace.

"The sky is clear, and home lies ahead—I must not waste the morning."

He tilted his head, breathing in the humid wind that filled his lungs with resolve. Without lingering, he took flight once more, the sky parting before him like a familiar path.

Lundar glided northeast until he reached the brink of the Damen Mountains. He hovered near the edge, wings steady, eyes scanning the quilt of trees and ridges below.

The beauty gave him pause, but his thoughts tugged elsewhere.

How will I navigate the treacherous Wormill Forest? I have traversed this land with the sorceress, and now it's time to contemplate my next move. Alone, I must trust instinct, he mused.

Without hesitation, the eagle gauged the distance to the ominous Wormill Forest from the ancient Fortress of Doom. "It's clear that I must venture further east. The once-thriving crows have vanished without a trace—what could be the cause?" Shaking off his apprehension, the white eagle ascended into the sky, making his way toward Drom Valley under the rising sun, his mind sharp and searching. Hours passed as Lundar soared across forests and peaks, the day wearing on. By the time he neared Drom Valley, the sun had already begun its descent beyond the horizon.

Perched atop a towering tree, he scanned the valley beneath him. "The courtyard remains untouched, just as the warriors left it," he remarked, observing the massive boulders that encircled the area. "The Valley of Stragon is cloaked in a dense mist. I must discover the reason." His gaze lingered, tracing the outline of shadows crawling through the grove.

Then, settling into position, he whispered, "I'll rest on this lofty branch where my view is unobstructed." As he gazed down into the valley, a wave of dread washed over him. His eyes widened in horror as he spotted a horde of fearsome creatures. His feathers bristled instinctively, and a shiver ran through him as he watched.

Unbeknownst to him, another presence stirred nearby.

On a lower branch cloaked in shadow, Derail remained concealed, eyes glinting with intent.

"It's time for me to seek justice," he breathed, and with swift, silent grace, he swept toward the palace—vanishing between the trees.

Not long after, the raven perched atop a jagged stone outcrop and turned his head toward the south. "Tomar, the white eagle known as Lundar, is concealed within a tree to our south," Derail said solemnly. "He intends to disclose our strategies to Easha, the Sorceress of Light. If we do not act now, our siege will no longer remain a secret."

Tomar—the sorcerer shrouded in power—stepped forward, robes trailing behind him like a shadow. His voice was deep and cold.

"Where is the eagle hiding?"

"Lundar was resting among the four trees to our left," Derail pointed out with his wing. Tomar scanned the treetops until his gaze landed on the horrid eagle. With a firm gesture, he directed his left index finger at the bird and declared, "You will never spy on me again."

He uttered a single word, saturated with magic: "FROAIT."

High above, Lundar remained unaware that his location had already been compromised. The sorcerer's spell took hold instantly.

Lundar's wings twitched—then froze. He tried to unfurl them but couldn't move. Panic gripped him.

"I've seen enough; it's time for me to go home," he whispered, but the words broke into a gasp. "What's happening? I can't move!"

Before he could comprehend the danger, a mysterious force pulled him from his perch. The trees blurred beneath him, and the ground seemed to vanish.

"What's going on?" he cried. "Why am I being drawn toward the dark palace?"

The air grew colder with each passing moment. As the towering structure came into view, his heartbeat quickened, thudding like drums in the depths of his chest.

"I sense dark forces at play… and I'm in grave danger."

He scrutinized the figure before him, noting the shoulder-length, raven-black hair that seemed meticulously arranged. Dressed in a flowing black cloak, the man's eyes glimmered with a sinister intensity.

Lundar hovered helplessly before him, caught in his grip.

With a mere flick of his finger, he has me completely at his mercy, Lundar thought. Why is he leading me to the summit of this palace? There's no sign of a prison. His finger keeps me hovering in place. Is he planning to let me fall and seal my doom?

Although Tomar's lips moved, no words reached him. Magic pulsed through the air like static, leaving Lundar tense and uncertain.

Fear flickered in his eyes as he drifted past the sorcerer, pulled higher and deeper into the palace's towering heights.

"I'm nearing the palace, yet there's no trace of a dungeon," he whispered, breath growing shallow.

Then, through the haze of enchantment, Lundar saw it, a dark glimmering cage suspended from a spike atop the first tower. "This must be the result of the sorcerer's malevolent magic. The door is opening. He's about to confine me within this prison, and I feel powerless to resist," Lundar thought, panic rising within him.

Drawn into the cage, Lundar tumbled against its cold iron walls. The iron gate slammed shut behind him—and in that instant, the spell fractured. He felt control return to his limbs. "The door has shut. The spell is broken. I can move again," he breathed, wings twitching with relief as he gathered himself, scanning the narrow confines of his prison. Shadows crept across the floor. The only opening revealed the grim sky—and a solitary silhouette circling above.

"It appears there's no escape from this trap. But what is that raven doing above? I'm convinced he's the one who led the sorcerer to capture me."

A piercing voice split the air.

"Eagle, do you recall our clash? In the Fortress of Doom, I fought you. Now, I have come to take my revenge." Derail sneered from above, his feathers glinting. "You will meet your demise here, starved and parched," the raven declared, before vanishing into the clouds.

But Lundar remained calm.

"I doubt his threats are sincere," he murmured. "He's just a deceitful creature. Why would the sorcerer choose to spare my life? What could his intentions be? He reminds me too much of Aldar, who fell in the Valley of Drom. It's hard to grasp."

His sharp eyes swept the courtyard beyond the cage, his eyes landing on a dark-haired woman stepping out of the palace. After a closer look, a shock rippled through him as he recognized the figure as Mirra.

"How did the sorceress manage to survive the explosion?" Lundar's thoughts buzzed with disbelief. The tension in this situation escalates with each passing moment. "I need to devise a strategy for my escape."

Lundar inhaled sharply as the noxious air invaded his lungs, triggering a violent coughing fit. With a heavy sigh, the eagle folded his wings and closed his eyes, retreating into meditation.

For Lundar, time seemed to stretch endlessly. He counted the sunrises, realizing that two grueling days had slipped by while he remained trapped, deprived of food and water.

"I'm certain Easha can feel my distress. I vowed to summon Suhzar for assistance if I ever found myself in peril. I wonder how Efura is faring. She holds a cherished place in my heart."

In his thoughts, he pictured her enchanting blue eyes and elegant white neck, a memory that sparked a flicker of warmth within his hollow chest.

As dusk fell once more, he closed his eyes, allowing his mind to drift toward the possibilities of regaining his freedom.

"I must contact Suhzar before dawn arrives. He is my sole hope for escape."

Lundar inhaled deeply and let out a series of whistles, a melody only a zundar could comprehend. The eagle's call resonated through the air. Then, a grim realization struck.

"Now I grasp why the sorcerer spared my life," he muttered bitterly. "His intention is to let me wither away slowly, and it's working. With each new day, I feel my strength waning. I can't shake the fear that he harbors more malevolent plans for me. Is there a potion that could taint my very essence and transform me into a villain? I suspect that's why he's withholding food. I would rather perish than consume anything he brews. All I can do is hope that Suhzar hears my desperate plea for help."

His breath trembled. Then, as though the final thread of strength had been cut, Lundar crumpled onto the cage floor, the world spinning around him as weakness engulfed him.

• • •

As dawn broke, it unveiled a breathtaking tapestry of purples and yellows that bathed the Middrom Mountains in a gentle glow. A brisk morning breeze danced through the rugged peaks, carrying the scent of pine and mist.

Perched at the mouth of a hidden cave, Suhzar took in the stunning panorama that unfurled before him. The view, though familiar, never failed to stir something deep within. He glanced over to see the young zundars engaged in an energetic game of tag, their joyful giggles echoing through the crisp morning air. Nestled within the Middrom Mountains, the zundars' cave was cleverly hidden behind a colossal rock formation, with towering trees and vibrant foliage guarding its entrance. A nearby waterfall cascaded down, sustaining the lively ecosystem that thrived around the zundars' sanctuary.

These zundars grew to be six times the size of an average bat. While their magical abilities were somewhat limited, they enjoyed lifespans that could stretch into the hundreds of years. Slender and elusive, these enchanting creatures displayed a striking blue and white hue, enabling them to seamlessly blend into their sunlit surroundings.

With their expansive wings, they could gracefully alight on any surface they chose. Two delicate white antennae framed the zundars' rounded azure faces, equipped with advanced sensory capabilities to detect potential threats. Their long tails allowed them to glide effortlessly through the air, while their strong legs curled their three toes against their bellies as they soared high above.

• • •

As the sun drenched the lush meadow in a warm golden glow, the two zundars, Gular and Suhzar, reveled in the beauty of the day beneath the bright sun illuminating the vibrant green grass.

"What a splendid morning, Suhzar," Gular exclaimed, inhaling deeply.

"Indeed, it's a beautiful day," Suhzar replied, beaming.

"I cherish this moment, but I can't help but worry about Stone. He has a desire for adventure, and I hope he remains safe," Gular sighed, eyes drifting into the horizon.

"Listen! I hear something," Suhzar said, his ears prickling slightly as he tuned into the harmonious blend of high and low notes that carried a message. "Lundar needs my assistance. He's trapped in Stragon Valley. I must go find him. Stay here with your family, and I'll let you know if I need your help." With that, Suhzar spread his wings and soared northward, vanishing into the open sky with purpose in his flight.

14th Chapter

Suhzar's mind raced with possibilities—perhaps a careless hunter had trapped Lundar, or a broken branch had caught him off guard during flight? As he approached the Stragon Valley, the zundar wrinkled his nose in silent dread, contemplating the grim scenarios that lay ahead. Suhzar's gaze shifted to the overcast sky, which loomed heavily over the rugged peaks of the North Mountains.

"The shadows in this perilous land have deepened," he murmured, feeling a chill burrow beneath his feathers. The air was thick with foreboding; malevolence seemed to close in from all sides. As Suhzar turned to confront the looming threat, a sudden screech snapped his focus upward, where a swarm of black crows circled ominously overhead, their cries echoing like warnings.

A biting wind howled through the Damen Northern Mountains, slicing through the air and rattling Suhzar's feathers. He cursed the fierce gusts that hindered his swift journey to Stragon Valley, where his friend awaited rescue.

When he arrived in the valley, he observed the sun hidden behind ominous clouds looming to the east. He felt a chill run down his spine at the prospect of yet another clash between light and darkness.

Perched among the shadowy branches overlooking the palace courtyard, Suhzar spotted a cloaked young woman—her raven perched loyally on her arm. His eyes narrowed. "That young woman with the raven is the sorceress we believed had perished when the mountain's entrance collapsed." He studied her movements as she strolled up to the sorcerer she called Tomar. "We were sure he had died when their tome, the Sormara, was incinerated to ash. Yet here he is, very much alive. Nadora must have fallen. The dark forces have ensnared Lundar. Our world is once again engulfed in despair."

While surveying the depths of Stragon Valley, Suhzar stumbled upon a bewildering variety of creatures. To the left of the dwelling, a stash of assault weapons lay in wait. "The sinister forces are poised to make another attempt to seize Seledor."

Suhzar caught snippets of their conversation about the impending siege of the land. As he scanned the palace courtyard, his eyes fell upon Lundar, imprisoned in a cage at the tallest tower, and he declared, "The dark forces have returned," he declared grimly.

"Lundar lies still within his prison. I must come up with a clever scheme to liberate him. Patience is essential as I plan the best approach to rescue my friend. When the sun dips behind the West Mountains, I will send him a series of signals to let him know I am on my way to free him later tonight."

With a surge of determination, Suhzar unfurled his wings and launched into the dusky sky, landing hours later at the outskirts of Tonepass—five mountains away. The frosty wind curled around him, sending a chill deep into his bones.

He pondered aloud, scanning the eerie expanse around him. "I require a strategy to save the eagle." To his left, deadened trees loomed, their bark scarred by age and decay. Lifeless shrubs clawed at the rocky ground. To his right, a strange darkness prevailed—as if an unseen barrier had blotted out the light, cloaking the land in unnatural shadow.

"It is only now that I fully grasp the sharp divide between good and evil," he murmured.

Suhzar let out a long, weary breath, a profound sigh slipping from his lips. "The resurgence of darkness weighs heavily on my heart. It seems like only yesterday we celebrated our victory over the sinister forces, but it came with a heavy toll of lives lost. And now, they reemerge, hiding in the shadows, poised to cast our land into darkness once more. I should have known that malevolence would never fully disappear." He cast his gaze downward in quiet remorse. "If I had been more watchful over the territory, I might have been able to prevent this return. But now I must focus on my purpose. I will take a moment to rest until night descends," He nestled beneath a wind-bent tree, lowering his head to rest. Silence stretched across the valley until a howling gust from the north startled him awake. Midnight had arrived.

"Midnight has come; it's time to rescue Lundar."

And then, with a burst of shimmering blue light, the zundar's form twisted and expanded—his feathers transforming into scales, his wings stretching skyward. A colossal dragon now stood where Suhzar once lay. Without hesitation, he ascended. The cold wind parted for his form, the stars above blinking through a curtain of mist. The palace emerged on the horizon, and the dragon descended, seizing the cage before soaring back into the sky. Despite the crows' ominous caws, no one stirred from their slumber.

• • •

The low rumble of thunder awakened the dark sorcerers from their dreams, signaling the arrival of a splendid day. They stepped out onto the balcony, their gazes drawn to the storm gathering on the horizon.

"Tomar, do you think the tempest will prevent the beast from crafting its weapons?" Mirra asked, her voice soft but edged with anticipation.

"Not in the slightest. I assure you, the storm will be contained by the mountains," he answered, brushing her cheek gently.

She let out a burst of laughter, light and gleaming. Excitement danced in her eyes.

"I can barely contain my excitement for our journey across the land! It fills me with such joy! I know it will be extraordinary," she proclaimed, her hands eagerly rubbing together. With a playful flick of her hair over her shoulder, she wrapped her arms around his neck and kissed him passionately. Together, they exited the palace through the grand entrance.

Tomar held Mirra's hand firmly as they approached the area where their weapons were being readied.

Suddenly, Mirra gasped, pointing to the tower. "Look, the eagle has been taken!"

Tomar's gaze followed her outstretched finger. "Yes, my love, I noticed the prison was breached the moment we stepped outside. His fellow eagles must have carried the cage away, so there's no need for worry; he'll meet his fate by nightfall. We can't afford to linger on an eagle right now. Once he's free, the cage will disappear.

We must concentrate on our mission; our siege begins in forty moons." He wrapped his left arm around Mirra's waist, drawing her close. "Don't worry, my love. I promise to protect you. I will do everything in my power to keep you safe," he reassured her, placing a tender kiss on her hand.

Mirra leaned into him as they inhaled the pungent, metallic scent of forging—a scent of war, of destiny, of rising power. Then, hand in hand, they entered the arsenal to begin preparations that would shake the land to its core.

• • •

As the zundar touched down at the foot of the Tonepass Mountains, a biting wind swirled around them.

"Lundar, it's me, Suhzar. You're safe here at the edge of Tonepass."

He shed his draconic form, feathers unfurling as his body shrank and shifted. Suhzar stood once more as a zundar, his eyes narrowing on the eagle's chest. The unsettling stillness gripped him. "I'll head south to collect some water," he announced before taking flight.

The wind tugged at his wings as he lifted off again. At a mountain stream, he found what he needed—a fragile tulip blooming defiantly among the stones. He filled its blossom with clear water and returned.

"Entering the cage is a gamble, but I must try to rouse him."

The zundar unlocked the door and stepped into the cell with the flower. He gently shook it, hoping the water would mist the eagle's face, but there was no reaction. Suddenly, he saw the eagle's right-wing twitch upward, followed by the gradual opening of its eyes and a shake of its head.

Stepping back from the cage, Suhzar declared, "I've brought you fresh water." He carefully offered the flower through the bars. "I'm uncertain how he'll respond if he thinks he's still confined. Can you hear me, Lundar?" The weight of the moment pressed down on him as he watched the eagle struggle to rise, inching the flower's stem closer to its beak in hopes it would drink.

The eagle stirred, eyes locking onto Suhzar's face, confusion painting his expression in quiet strokes.

"My friend, let me find you something to eat. It will help restore your strength," he whispered gently, before soaring into the sky once more, while avoiding the northern territory.

Soon, he returned, gliding silently with a small mouse clutched in his talon. Slipping back inside the cage, he settled beside Lundar, whose body barely reacted to the sound of his friend's voice. The eagle's eyes shut again.

"I can see you can move your head, but you don't have the strength to eat. I must take you to Easha; she can heal you before it's too late."

With a quick flick of his wing, Suhzar secured the cage door and launched skyward. Mid-flight, his form shimmered and expanded—dragon wings unfurling as he ascended toward the sunlit heights, the cage held firmly beneath him. A glance at the sun indicated it was already noon.

Concerned by Lundar's stillness, the dragon slowed his flight as he glided toward the Valley of Tonepass. Noon's light cast long shadows across the meadow where Easha waited.

Easha's heart raced when she saw the dragon descending into the meadow, clutching a cage in its talons. A surge of dread propelled her into the open field.

"Sorceress, dark forces have taken Lundar! I tried to give him food and water, but he's too weak to take anything," he shouted.

Kneeling beside the cage, she quickly unlatched the door while the eagle remained still inside.

"Lundar, it's me, Easha. Don't be afraid; I'm here to save you." With tender hands, she reached into the cage and carefully freed the eagle from his confinement. In an instant, the cage disappeared into thin air—its spell undone.

With urgency, the sorceress hurried back to her cabin, holding Lundar close to her heart. She gently set him on an oak desk by the door. Transforming back into a zundar, Suhzar rushed to Lundar's side, eager to help.

Easha pulled open the top drawer of the desk where the eagle lay and retrieved eight immaculate white satin cloths, deftly folding six of them into triangles.

"What are you making, Sorceress?" Suhzar asked, watching her every movement.

"I'm creating a serene white healing bed for Lundar; he needs a calming space to aid in his recovery."

Suhzar watched her closely, although his eyes lingered on the fragile figure of his friend. "Do you believe he will survive?"

"If he does, it will be because of you. Your timely help was crucial."

Easha focused intently on her task, spreading one piece of satin flat on the desk. She then arranged the six triangles with their tips meeting in the center, forming a perfect six-sided pentagon. Carefully, she lifted Lundar and placed him in the middle of the soft white fabric, covering him completely with the eighth piece of satin before hurrying to the kitchen. There, she opened a hidden cabinet and took out a vase with a golden lid. The sorceress grabbed a pinch of sparkling magic powder and rushed back to the eagle, sprinkling the mystical substance over him.

In an instant, the white dust disappeared. Turning to Suhzar, she softened her voice.

"Earlier today, I made a pot of beans. You must be hungry and tired. If you'd like, I can help you to the table," she suggested.

She gently patted his shoulder and moved toward the table. "Just stay here and relax while I fetch us some food."

Suhzar offered a quiet nod, watching her disappear into the kitchen once more.

Moments later, Easha returned, balancing two bowls filled with beans and berries. She set them down beside Suhzar, causing his stomach to twist with apprehension.

"Please share every detail of what happened. What circumstances led to Lundar's capture? How did you come to realize he was in danger?" she inquired, taking a spoonful of her meal and locking her gaze with him. Suhzar stared into his bowl, gathering his thoughts before speaking.

"Gular and I were enjoying the calm of the morning when I was jolted by Lundar's desperate shouts for help. I hurried to offer my aid, but what I encountered was horrifying. Once more, shadows have enveloped our realm. The young sorceress from the Valley of Drom has joined forces with Tomar. I am baffled by her survival. When the mountain erupted, we thought we had vanquished the malevolent sorcerers, yet to my astonishment, Mirra still lives."

He paused, the weight of his revelation hanging in the room.

"The sorcerers have enchanted the crows, transforming them into watchful sentinels. At the slightest hint of danger, they quickly alert their masters. They have summoned a horde of the most fearsome creatures I have ever seen, casting a pall of terror over the land. I suspect Tomar has stolen Nadora's magic; she has disappeared without a trace. As a result, he possesses more power than ever. It's likely that the sorceress has warned him of our impending attack. They are prepared for an ambush."

Easha set down her bowl with care, the urgency in her posture matching the tension in the air.

"There's nothing more we can do for Lundar. Once he regains consciousness, he'll provide us with crucial information. We need to head to Falcon Ridge to inform Rubric and the others about the malevolent army. If we travel under the cover of darkness, we can evade Pildar's forces. Our only chance of victory lies in assembling a formidable army."

She stood, brushing her hands together before glancing toward the window.

"If everything goes as planned, we'll depart tomorrow night at sunset. If Lundar is well enough, he can accompany us."

After a moment, she turned to Suhzar with a faint smile.

"I need to tend to my garden before nightfall. Would you like to join me? It won't take long."

"No, I'll stay here with Lundar."

Easha stepped out of the cottage, her mood brightening as she took in the beauty of her garden. "A melon would make a lovely breakfast," she thought to herself. Her eyes wandered to the west, where she noticed a rat, which she caught with her magic, and quickly captured into a cage. As she neared the front of the hut, she hesitated, turning to gaze at the infamous mountains. A shiver ran down her spine, urging her to retreat indoors, where she securely locked the door and window. Her eyes immediately went to Lundar, still lying motionless beneath the satin folds.

She turned to Suhzar. "Is there any news about Lundar?"

Suhzar shook his head slowly. "Sadly, no. It breaks my heart to see him engulfed in darkness. This situation is truly devastating for me."

"We'll know by morning if he still lives. For now, there's nothing more we can do. Time is running out, and we should try to rest," she replied as she made her way to her bedroom, adding, "I'll see you in the morning."

"Easha, have a peaceful night. I'll stay here with Lundar," Suhzar said, settling into the soft white satin sheets.

"I sincerely wish for your swift recovery, my friend, and I hope my magic aids in your healing." As the zundar closed his eyes, sleep quickly enveloped him.

$$\bullet \ \bullet \ \bullet$$

The sun rose brilliantly over the East Mountains, its warm rays streaming through the window where the zundar had spent the night watching over Lundar. Suhzar was stirred from his dreams as the satin beneath him shifted, revealing Lundar's feathery white head emerging.

"Good morning, my friend! It's wonderful to see you. We were all quite concerned. When we reached the Tonepass Mountains, you were unconscious. I had to take you to the white sorceress for assistance. I feared we might lose you," the zundar said with a smile.

"Where am I?" Lundar asked, looking confused.

"I brought you to Tonepass so Easha could heal you."

Lundar lowered his head with gratitude.

"I am forever indebted to you, and words cannot fully convey my appreciation. Without your swift intervention, I would have met my end. I had a feeling that Mirra was preparing a potion to take me to the dark side, but I would never have taken it."

Just then, a stir came from the sorceress's quarters. Easha, yawning and pushing her hair back, rushed into the living room.

Lundar welcomed her with a grin, saying, "Good morning. I hope you slept well."

"My dear Lundar! How are you feeling? I can only imagine how ravenous you must feel." She stepped into a room to the west, and soon after, Easha returned, clutching a brown rat she had caught in her garden. With a quick motion, she removed it from its cage, knocked it out by slamming it against the desk, and set it down in front of the eagle, which eagerly began to feast.

"I am grateful for your help," he murmured between bites. "Without your assistance, I would have surely met my end."

Easha asked, her worry evident as she anxiously rubbed her arm, "Can you please explain what occurred? What are those wicked sorcerers plotting?" Lundar took a long breath.

"I was sitting on a branch close to Stragon Valley when I caught the dark sorcerers scheming. Their plan is to launch an assault on Seledor in thirty-eight days. I attempted to flee, but my efforts were futile. Tomar cast a spell that rendered me immobile. He lifted me from the branch and drew me into the fortress, exerting complete control over me. I feared he would let me fall to my death, but instead, he conjured a magical cage, imprisoned me inside, and left me starving and parched."

Lundar recounted, taking deep breaths to calm his racing heart.

"The dark raven I battled at the Fortress of Doom betrayed my position to the wicked sorcerer. After we departed the fortress, the raven must have absorbed the remnants of Sormara. I fear that Nadora did not make it; I am convinced the sorcerer siphoned her magical essence just before her demise. Among all the sorcerers I have faced, Tomar stands out as the most perilous and cunning. His level of wickedness is unparalleled. While I doubt he aimed to kill me, his cruelty is unmistakable. He sought to drag me into despair. When I cried out for help, Suhzar came to my rescue." He took a moment to breathe in the fresh air and sip some water before continuing.

"The stronghold of Enwood will be the first to fall. We must form our defenses in order to survive the dark forces."

Easha drew herself up, determination blazing, and declared, "At dusk tomorrow, we will journey to Falcon Ridge. We must inform Rubric and the other fighters that the dark forces are on the rise. I have faith they will form an army to defend our homes. Today I'll pack the items we'll need for our trip. Since our plan is set. I want you to get plenty of rest, Lundar."

Lundar flexed his wings, resolute.

"I will, but first I must go see Efura and inform the eagles of this situation. I will be back at dusk tomorrow."

The three stepped outside into the crisp morning air. Suhzar and Easha watched as Lundar soared into the sky—his form growing smaller against the wide canvas of clouds until he disappeared from view.

15th Chapter

L undar cast his eyes upon the magnificent Amarta Mountains as he glided southwestward, the wind brushing against his feathers like a whisper of welcome.

"It's remarkable to witness how these towering fir trees thrive in such a harsh landscape. From every angle, streams and waterfalls cascade down the slopes. The interplay of light and dark greens creates a mesmerizing tapestry. This stunning vista will be etched in my memory forever," he murmured to himself.

After navigating three splendid peaks, Lundar sensed a shift in the breeze.

"I've entered the domain of the eagles, and I can feel the watchful eyes of the guardians behind me." Resting on a robust branch, a regal white eagle awaited with poise. Within moments, four brown and white eagles descended, circling gracefully before settling beside their leader. The grand eagle spoke with unwavering authority

"You have crossed into the Eagles' territory. As an outsider, you must vacate this area immediately. Your presence here violates our laws."

Lundar held his ground, speaking in the language of the eagles with respectful urgency. "I need to speak with Efura. Dark forces are amassing a vast army of beasts, poised to ravage the land and obliterate everything we hold dear."

The scouts exchanged glances, absorbing both the message and the gravity in Lundar's tone. After a brief silence, one stepped forward.

"We believe your intentions are sincere and not a ruse, but you must address the chief eagle, not Efura."

Everyone nodded in agreement, a shared resolve forming in the quiet between them.

"Let us take you on a journey through our land. Follow my lead, and I will take you to our leader." The head scout moved ahead, with the other three eagles closely following as they gracefully descended into the valley, where towering trees concealed the secrets of their realm.

Lundar was captivated by the breathtaking panorama of the extraordinary valley, lost in thought. As he flew into Amarta, he realized he had entered a world vastly different from the one he had just traversed.

The magnificent white eagle glided effortlessly above the ten lush meadows that unfurled from the valley floor. Surrounding this vibrant expanse were majestic trees, their robust trunks standing tall and dignified. To the west, a grand cliff with a wide ledge served as a natural fortress for the eagles' domain. Just south of the white eagle, a sprawling body of water caught his eye, prompting him to ponder whether it was linked to the Seabray River. Shifting his focus to the east, he spotted enormous nests nestled among the branches near the trunks, his mind racing with intrigue.

The eagles had meticulously chosen their nesting sites, balancing accessibility and sunlight in perfect harmony—a testament to their ancient wisdom and watchful care.

As the white eagle ventured further into its territory, a stunning sight emerged—thousands of brown and white eagles scattered across the landscape, a living mosaic of strength and vitality that spoke of a thriving, united community.

Continuing to follow the scout deeper into their land, Lundar noticed Efura gracefully perched on a rock beside a bubbling stream. Until that moment, he had never encountered a white eagle within the colony. A wave of warmth washed over him as he glided closer, but before he could reach her, four scouts swiftly surrounded him.

"You've come to speak with our leader, but you cannot approach the princess!" they insisted, the atmosphere thick with tension. Just then, Efura swooped in towards Lundar.

"While I appreciate your commitment to protecting our home, he is my partner. Release him at once," she commanded with a firm tone.

At her declaration, the scouts recoiled in astonishment and retreated to their assigned lookout.

"Lundar, it's so wonderful to see you! I've missed you greatly. What brings you here? Did you finish the task Easha entrusted to you?"

"You have been greatly missed, my dear. I came to speak with the eagle chief because I must warn him that dark forces are once again threatening our homes."

Efura's expression darkened, her eyes shifting toward the northern horizon. "Is that why the sky seems so much darker to the north?"

"Indeed," Lundar said gravely. "I witnessed a massive army of creatures poised to invade our land."

Her feathers trembled as she leaned forward, gently brushing her cheek against his. "This frightens me. Please, come with me to my home. Your news will surely intrigue Pa."

Efura guided Lundar to a large branch shelter near the northern cliff, where a cascading waterfall obscured the entrance to the royal family's hidden cave. The air inside was cool and reverent, touched with the scent of wild herbs and ancient moss.

"Pa," Efura called softly as they entered. "I need to introduce you to Lundar. Please listen closely to his urgent message."

"It's a pleasure to meet you, but I am curious about your reason for being here." The eagle chief fixed a sharp gaze on Lundar.

"Great beasts are on the verge of invading our territory, and I bring a grave warning. You must prepare to defend our land," the white eagle declared with steadfast resolve.

"How can I trust the truth of your words?" the chief asked, as Efura and Lundar stood in front of him.

Lundar inhaled deeply and began, his voice steady. "Easha, the Sorceress of Light, noticed an unusual darkness in the northeastern sky. She sensed evil had again entered our homeland. She asked me if I would go to Stragon Valley to investigate a looming dust storm after she observed the foreboding dark clouds amassing in the northeast. We had believed we had vanquished the sorcerer Tomar, yet I spotted him alongside a Mirra who had survived the cataclysm in Drom Valley. Their monstrous army is on the verge of unleashing havoc upon Seledor, threatening to annihilate everything virtuous in its wake."

"Tomar's plan indicates that the Stronghold of Enwood will be the first to crumble," he added, voice low and firm.

The eagle chief narrowed his eyes with intrigue.

"I thought Tomar had died ages ago."

"That's what we all believed. I was involved in the destruction of the Sormara, where he and Nadora were held captive, but we've only just learned that a raven devoured their remains and escaped from the Fortress of Doom."

A heavy silence followed his words.

"I genuinely appreciate the information you've shared. Efura, ring the council bell. A meeting must take place."

Efura gracefully landed on a robust wooden beam, her claws gripping a twisted vine as she perched above two hanging metal pieces. A loud clang resonated through the eagles' domain, summoning the male eagles to the assembly, while Lundar observed in silence. The sanctuary was enveloped in an eerie stillness.

High above the gathering, the chief raised his voice, radiating authority and dignity.

"I bring grave news. We are aware that dark forces seek to eradicate all that is good, posing a threat to our homeland. This is a situation we cannot permit. To safeguard our way of life, we must unite for this cause." The leader eagle turned to address the white eagle.

"Extend our unwavering support to your allies, Lundar, for they will have our full backing in this battle. Arrange a meeting with the Sorceress of Light for our warriors. We must prepare our defenses," he proclaimed.

Lundar bowed his head in gratitude. "Your support during these challenging times means a lot to us. I must take my leave now. Once I arrive, Easha will be prepared to head to Falcon Ridge to inform our friends. Rubric and his team will assemble a force to help us tackle Tomar's creatures."

Efura acknowledged the situation with a nod before turning to Lundar. "Wait; I'll come with you. Our strength combined will be more formidable."

Her pa nodded in approval, granting her permission to accompany Lundar.

"Follow me, and I'll guide you out of our territory. We can't afford any delays." The majestic white eagles soared into the sky, heading northwest toward the Valley of Tonepass. The air shimmered with tension, and distant thunder murmured like a warning beneath the clouds.

"Lundar, let's pause for a snack once we're clear of the Amarta Mountains. I can sense your hunger," Efura said with a knowing glance.

"Indeed, you are right," replied Lundar. "A brief pause for a snack would be perfect before we encounter Easha. She is eager to alert Rubric and the other fighters of the evil uprising, but intends to hold off on leaving until nightfall."

As they navigated through the dense underbrush of the forest, Lundar and Efura finally spotted a wild sage hen near a stream lined with silver moss. With a swift motion of his claws, he caught the bird. The two companions perched beneath a gnarled willow, sharing the meal in reflective silence. Above them, the wind whispered through the branches, as if the forest itself listened to their mission. Their strength restored, and the white eagles lifted once more into the sky, slicing through the wind with renewed purpose.

• • •

At the Sorceress's cottage nestled in the glimmering foothills of Tonepass, Easha was immersed in arranging her belongings for the journey to Falcon Ridge. Bottles of enchanted light stood on her table alongside vials of protective mist.

She glanced up at the sky, inhaled deeply, and exhaled sharply three times to quiet the thoughts swirling in her mind. Taking another deep breath, she declared, "No amount of my magic can halt the dark forces that have invaded our land." With a raised eyebrow, she continued, "Mum, Pa, I value your watchful presence. Please grant me and my allies the strength to combat the evil threatening our home."

The silence lingered like a blessing. Easha stepped into the main chamber, her thoughts momentarily grounded. On the cushion near the hearth lay her childhood friend, Suhzar, curled peacefully, a feathered cloak draped over his shoulder.

Easha called out, smiling as she approached. "Suhzar, it's time to get up." He stirred, blinking against the dim candlelight. Without hesitation, she slung her bag over her shoulder, and they both exited the cottage.

As they crossed the threshold into the clearing, a breeze stirred the leaves around them. Dark branches parted like curtains as two winged figures emerged from the forest's edge. In one graceful motion, Lundar and Efura descended from the sky, their wings folding as they landed.

Lundar puffed out his chest, his voice brimming with excitement. "I bring great news, sorceress! The Eagle Dynasty has pledged their support in our fight against darkness."

Efura's bright blue eyes glimmered with delight as she listened to Lundar's words; the sorceress could feel it—after all the searching, the eagles had at last discovered their true companions.

After a quick glance at Efura, Lundar continued passionately. "Once the warriors arrive, the chief eagle will convene here for a council. Efura will inform him when you are ready for the meeting."

"What splendid news! I am incredibly grateful for any assistance," Easha replied. "We must set off immediately if we wish to reach Falcon Ridge in three sunrises. Lundar, do you have the strength for this journey?"

"I feel well," he affirmed, "I'll explore the route with Efura."

Easha pressed her lips together, then raised her hand toward the gentle rise beyond the meadow.

"Star," she called softly.

Suddenly, a magnificent white stallion emerged from behind a gentle rise, racing ahead with incredible swiftness. His strong legs drove him forward, while his mane and tail flowed behind him like leaves dancing in the wind.

The team watched in awe as the horse raced through the colorful meadow, coming to a graceful stop beside the sorceress. Easha rested her right hand on the stallion's back, and with a flicker of her magic, a saddle appeared beneath her fingertips. The leather shimmered faintly as if stitched from moonlight.

The sorceress declared, "Our adventure is about to start." Lundar and Efura glided gracefully to the southwest, leading the way ten feet in front of the others, their silhouettes elegant and purposeful. Meanwhile, Suhzar nestled snugly in the saddle horn, his eyes flicking from shadow to sky.

As the group pressed forward, Easha lifted her gaze to the heavens. "Suhzar, am I seeing things, or does the dusk appear particularly shadowy?"

The zundar tilted his head, scanning the dimming sky. "It seems normal to me. Worry not, sorceress; we shall succeed in this mission," the zundar comforted her, assuring her of their victory over the threatening forces.

"You could be correct," she said, leaning forward to caress Star's neck softly, her hand brushing through his mane as they maneuvered around a rugged outcrop.

Easha stayed vigilant, her gaze fixed on the scattered boulders, ready to spot any concealed dangers lurking nearby. She could feel the landscape growing quieter, as if holding its breath.

"Suhzar, I can't wait for the moon to ascend and illuminate our path," she admitted, her voice barely above the hush of wind.

"Yes," he replied, "but while the moonlight may cast strange shadows, it's certainly preferable to wandering in total darkness."

A gust surged through the pass, sharp and unexpected.

Easha shivered. "I cannot believe how cold it has turned. The wind cuts through me, yet I've faced harsher conditions before."

She coiled her hair around her neck and rubbed her arms to create some warmth.

"Is the chill getting to you, Suhzar?"

"Not at all," the zundar said with a wry smile. "Your hair provides a small refuge from the cold."

As they continued their journey, a biting cold surrounded them, lingering like an unwelcome presence. Though no danger revealed itself, the group couldn't shake the eerie feeling that a malevolent force was hiding within the chilling winds. It watched, silent and patient, waiting for its moment.

16th Chapter

The rugged trail was flanked by towering trees, their branches clawing at the sky as Easha and Suhzar continued their journey. Easha narrowed her eyes, her right hand brushing against the folds of her robe, sensing the presence of an animal nearby.

"Suhzar, did you catch sight of any creature darting past us?" she inquired, her brows furrowing with intrigue.

"No, I was too busy concentrating on the branches scraping against the ground. These trees are quite unlike those in the Tonepass Mountains," the zundar replied, leaping from the saddle horn to perch on the sorceress's shoulder, inching closer to her neck. "Now I have a better view of what lies ahead and can dodge the gusts. Don't you think the rustling leaves and chirping crickets create a lovely melody?"

"Yes, since I was a child, I've often closed my eyes to immerse myself in the enchanting symphony of nature. It brings me such peace." She glanced at the zundar just as a strong gust of wind swept through the trees, striking her side and tugging at her robe.

"Grip the collar of my robe, Suhzar. The winds are picking up."

"It feels like it's trying to blow me off your shoulder! I can't wait for it to calm down. Do you think a dark force is attempting to thwart our mission to gather an army? They have numerous spies lurking in the shadows. I don't trust them at all," Suhzar grumbled, wrapping his wing around the edge of her robe's collar for added security.

Easha tilted her head, thoughtful. "I'm uncertain; perhaps the winds of the mountains are merely a natural occurrence."

"You might be onto something; certain areas definitely experience stronger winds than others. I'm not particularly fond of it; it tends to irritate my eyes," the zundar remarked as they continued onward.

As their pace slowed to navigate a patch of thorny brush, a night owl hooted softly to Easha's left, her right hand shielding her face from the cold. "I can hear the myriad sounds of the forest, yet its splendor remains just beyond my sight," she expressed.

Suhzar's reply came gently, as if not to disturb the quiet. "That's true, but the darkness conceals many threats; that's why I prefer to avoid traveling at night."

"You speak wisely," Easha responded, her eyes drifting to the twinkling stars overhead. "Dawn is approaching. The sky is starting to brighten, and soon we can take a break."

As the first hints of light began to stretch across the horizon, casting silvery silhouettes on the treetops, Easha slowed her horse. The journey had weighed heavily on her, but the sight of the majestic white eagles circling into view with wings stretching wide as they glided toward her with renewed grace offered a quiet reassurance.

"Lundar, I've calculated the distance to Falcon Ridge. If we continue until noon, we should reach it in two days. Should we forge ahead, or is it time to rest?" Easha inquired of her companions.

"I recommend we keep moving," the Eagles asserted.

Suhzar, still perched on Easha's shoulder, nodded in agreement, "If any threats arise, Lundar and Efura will warn us. It's best to reach the warriors as swiftly as possible."

"Wonderful, let's take a brief pause before continuing to Falcon Ridge. Lundar has faced quite a bit in the last few days, and I want to ensure he doesn't overexert himself."

Easha elegantly dismounted her horse and began searching through her saddlebag, retrieving a white-water jug. With her other hand, she also pulled out a mug, two pouches, and a small bowl.

Efura observed in amazement as the sorceress poured the refreshing water, her eyes widening in surprise. "How did you manage to fit all that food, containers, and water into your saddlebags, Easha?" she inquired.

Before Easha could respond, Lundar leaned closer, speaking in a hushed tone as if sharing a secret. "She harnesses white magic; you wouldn't believe the astonishing things she can accomplish."

Easha smiled as she filled a mug with refreshing cool water. "Here's some cool water, and if you feel hungry, I have dried meat and berries to share."

The eagles exchanged glances before Lundar spoke up. "Efura and I will take some water now. Later, when we're hungry, we can hunt for food. If you're interested, we could catch a rabbit for you."

As Easha placed the mug on a flat stone, she shook her head politely. "I truly appreciate the kind offer, but I've packed enough provisions for our journey. Suhzar, would you like something to eat?"

"A piece of dry elk would be wonderful," he replied, eagerly watching as she set three pieces on a leaf in front of him. Suhzar ate with delight, wiping his mouth with his wing when he was done. "Thank you, sorceress; that was delightful. I'm ready to move on. I can't wait to reunite with the warriors."

"Yes, I feel the same; it seems like ages since we last gathered with our friends," Easha said softly, carefully packing away the supplies. As she remounted her horse, adjusting her robe around the saddle and rebraiding a loose strand of hair with practiced ease, Lundar tilted his head.

"Sorceress, I spotted your white hat while you were gathering the food. Why aren't you wearing it?"

"I brought it with me in case we needed to enter the secret chamber, but I prefer to keep it hidden from prying eyes," she replied, adjusting her saddle straps. "It has a habit of flying off my head too easily. I can't recall my pa wearing his hat often unless we were setting off on an adventure," Easha added, her eyes wandering to the majestic mountains draped in forest in the distance.

With a gentle nudge of her heel, she urged her horse forward, captivated by a towering tree. "Suhzar, have you noticed how these trees soar higher than ours, with leaves that are a lighter shade of green streaked with dark green? They are truly unlike anything I've ever encountered."

"Yes, they are breathtaking," Suhzar replied, his gaze sweeping the canopy, "but I can't shake the feeling of unease that comes with the unknown here."

"The eagles gliding above offer some reassurance; I trust they will warn us of any lurking threats," Easha comforted him.

"Lundar, what did the sorceress mean by a possible relapse?" Efura asked, her face clouded with confusion.

Lundar's expression darkened. "Do you remember when Easha urged me to journey to Stragon Valley?"

"Yes, I recall."

He inhaled slowly, eyes distant. "Upon reaching the valley, I confronted the malevolent sorcerers and their sinister forces. A raven, once my foe, had betrayed my whereabouts to the sorcerer. His dark magic ensnared me, lifting me from my perch and trapping me in a cage of his making. Once the spell was broken, I regained my ability to move, but my mind remained foggy. As the days dragged on, my strength diminished. Then, one fateful morning, clarity returned, and I reached out to Suhzar. He came to my aid and brought me back to Easha. I was on the brink of death, gripped by the fear of never seeing you again. It was an incredibly harrowing experience."

"The very idea of losing you, Lundar, shatters my heart," Efura trembled. "The darkness you mention feels unyielding."

"Do not worry, my dear. I firmly believe our journey together will be long and fulfilling," he reassured her, gently caressing her wing.

As the sun bathed the east in its golden glow, the wind softened and silence stretched across the forest canopy. Majestic eagles soared effortlessly overhead, their eyes scanning the land below. Suddenly, dust rose in the distance, swirling upward in erratic bursts.

"Look! Efura, there's dust swirling in the distance. Something enigmatic is happening below," Lundar exclaimed, his gaze fixed on the churning cloud. Adjusting their flight path, the eagles circled more deliberately over the treetops.

"Lundar, Pildar's soldiers are supposed to be tracking the rebels, but they're going the wrong way. They're heading straight for us! We must warn Easha!" Efura gasped, her eyes wide.

Slicing through the canopy, the eagles dropped lower. Their sharp cries rang out, ricocheting off the trees.

Easha halted, fingertips brushing the edge of her robe as her gaze turned upward. She felt the tension in the air shift. "What danger lies ahead?" she asked, her voice steady but alert.

"The Enwood soldiers are on the move, likely chasing the Freedom Fighters, but they are lost and have taken the wrong path," Lundar noted, a trace of concern creeping into his voice. "You need to find a place to hide to avoid being seen."

Easha spotted a narrow ravine nearby. Without hesitation, she swung off Star's saddle and led him carefully down the gully, slipping behind a thicket of trees.

Within moments, the distant thrum of galloping hooves became increasingly clear as the soldiers approached from the west.

Above, the zundar had climbed to the highest branch of the tallest tree, keeping a vigilant watch on the relentless warriors as they neared the sorceress's hiding place.

Suhzar and the eagles listened intently to the soldiers' conversation as they passed by.

"Marco, we're off track; we should be going north," Bors, the second-in-command, insisted.

"How dare you question my authority? My memory is impeccable. The rebels are concealed on the eastern slopes," the commander yelled, gesturing his men to head east. "They will face their end when we locate them, as our ruler has commanded."

Bors hesitated, his eyes flicking toward the ravine. "I hear something rustling in the ravine, Marco. Should I send a few soldiers to investigate for any rebels hiding in the underbrush?"

Marco waved him off dismissively. "No, I didn't hear anything. You're just trying to delay us. Are you sure you don't want to give the rebels a chance to escape by aiding them?"

Bors stiffened. "No, I would never go against Pildar's orders. My loyalty lies with him."

"You must remain loyal to me. You are under my command. I will decide when you eat and sleep. Without my approval, you are powerless," Marco shouted, his face flushed with anger. "Now, fall in line behind my troops, or you will regret it," he warned.

The second-in-command complied with Marco's orders, waiting for the soldiers to pass before positioning himself behind them.

• • •

Suhzar and the eagles kept a vigilant watch over the riders as they vanished into the forest. Once the last hoof beat faded, the trio soared toward Easha's hiding place.

"Easha, the soldiers no longer pose a danger," Suhzar whispered, settling lightly on her shoulder. "It's safe for us to move toward Falcon Ridge."

Easha exhaled with relief. "I'm relieved the knights didn't discover us. The branch snapped loudly under my weight. I held my breath, fearing they would investigate the sound. They would have found me if it weren't for the commander. I'm thankful for his lack of insight." She scanned her surroundings and noticed the two stunning white eagles resting on a branch two trees west of her.

As if sensing her shift in mood, the eagles glided ahead of their companions, weaving skillfully through the thick forest and lush greenery. Their motion was both reassuring and urgent, guiding the path forward.

Easha watched them disappear among the trees. "Suhzar, we should take a moment here. Can you inform the eagle that we intend to stay until nightfall?"

"They're drawing near, Easha. They must be wary as well."

Without hesitation, Easha dismounted her horse. She gently released Star and laid out her bedding next to a thriving tree, ensuring she could easily spot Suhzar and the other two eagles perched on a higher branch. With her head resting on a rolled-up robe, she quickly succumbed to sleep under the silent watch of the eagles above.

• • •

As twilight began to envelop the landscape, the travelers pressed onward through the rugged terrain.

Just ten feet away, two eagles soared gracefully while the sorceress lifted her gaze to the shifting clouds above, her thoughts swirling as swiftly as the wind.

"Easha, if it's alright with you, I'll team up with Lundar. Having three of us retracing our steps feels much safer."

"I agree. Three pairs of eyes are certainly better than two," Easha replied, observing Suhzar glide elegantly on Lundar's back.

With renewed determination, the group continued their journey, aiming to reach Falcon Ridge by noon. They traversed a vibrant meadow adorned with purple wildflowers and maneuvered through a series of majestic mountain ranges.

As midday approached, a chill swept through the air as they entered Falcon Ridge territory. The eagles, along with Suhzar, circled overhead and then dropped low, sensing that the sorceress had come to an abrupt halt.

"Why have you stopped, sorceress?" the trio asked, surrounding her protectively.

"Shortly, the scout will spot me and guide me to their base. I need you to remain vigilant and hidden until you see Rubric," she instructed.

"We will follow your lead, as long as you stay safe," they replied in unison.

Easha climbed a gentle slope, feeling the weight of unseen eyes watching her. Just as tension gripped her spine, a deep voice broke the silence.

"What brings you to the mountains? Who are you searching for? Are you a spy for Pildar?" A tall, slender man with dark hair dismounted and seized Star's reins, his sharp eyes scanning her robe and expression. "You are now our captive."

"I came to speak with my friends Rolyn and Rubric. "It's urgent," she insisted.

"Rubric is someone we know well, but he has never mentioned a woman in a white robe," the man hesitated, loosening the reins of the sorceress's horse. "We'll guide you along the rocky trail."

Above her, Easha's allies soared through the air, ready to defend her at the first sign of danger.

As they maneuvered through a labyrinth of towering rock formations, a sprawling base camp emerged beyond a ridge. Tents and structures were cleverly tucked into the stone landscape, blending into the wild terrain.

The lead scout tightened his grip on Star's reins, then turned to a nearby guard. "Keep a vigilant watch on her until I understand her intentions here," he instructed before turning to leave without another word.

Easha surveyed the bustling courtyard. Her eyes landed on Rubric, Lance, and the other warriors engaged in lively sword practice. To her right, she spotted a cave where a group of women were busily preparing food, their motions confident and precise.

Notably, there was no smoke rising from the camp's exterior. Easha recognized the tactic immediately: the fires were hidden, shielded from prying eyes—just like so much else here.

Before she could take another step, a sudden blur swept through the air. Suhzar landed squarely on Rubric's shoulder, startling the warrior, and announced, "We've come to inform you of a dark uprising in Stragon Valley. We need to gather a council with you, brave warriors; Easha is here as well."

Rubric blinked, recovering from the shock. "It's great to see you, Suhzar, but where is the sorceress?"

Lance glanced up at the sky and noticed two white eagles soaring above a trio of scouts gathered around a woman in white to the west. "Rubric, the scouts are with the white sorceress," he called out.

Before long, the two warriors reached Easha, who stood resolute. "Let her go; she is our ally and will always be welcome in my home," Rubric ordered, then turned his focus to Easha.

"It's such a pleasure to see you, sorceress! We planned to visit as soon as summer ended," he said with warmth in his eyes.

Lance gestured for the guards to step back. Easha spoke softly, her tone laced with urgency.

"As Suhzar has indicated, a sinister force is gearing up to attack Seledor once more. I fear we may not emerge victorious in this battle," she said, concern evident in her blue eyes, which did not escape Rubric's notice.

"Lance, remain with the sorceress while I assemble the other fighters. We need to inform them of the situation," Rubric commanded, hurrying away.

An hour later, the sorceress watched as the men convened in the cave.

"It's time for the meeting, Easha," Lance said gently, guiding her by the arm.

As they stepped into the mountain cave, Easha was taken aback by the sight of numerous warriors gathered around a grand table. Prominent among them were Suhzar, Lundar, and Efura. The air shimmered with magical dust as the zundar flapped its wings and greeted, "It's a pleasure to see you again, Omond and Tackar," bowing respectfully.

The thirty-eight unfamiliar fighters exchanged puzzled glances, amazed that they could comprehend the zundar's words.

At the head of the table, Rubric addressed the assembly. "I would like to introduce Easha, along with Efura, Lundar, and Suhzar. They have come to alert us about an army of beasts driven by dark magic."

"If we fail to halt this encroaching darkness, our homes will be consumed by shadows. You may have heard of Tomar and Nadora. If not, they are the two malevolent sorcerers who once cast this land into despair." He paused to take a long sip of his ale, exhaling deeply before continuing.

"The mighty sorcerer Tomar has returned, accompanied by a sinister sorceress, and together they have summoned a terrifying army of malevolent creatures. A confrontation is imminent. In just thirty-five sunsets, this dark horde will descend upon Seledor. We cannot rely solely on Pildar's troops; they are likely to ignore our warnings. We must enlist the Kandoran Freedom Fighters, along with the dwarves and elves, to stand against this army of darkness. We will need brave volunteers to join our cause. At dawn, we will embark on our quest. Those who are ready to stand with us in battle should assemble here at dawn." With that, he directed his attention to the sorceress with admiration.

17th Chapter

A gentle northern breeze swept in as twilight began to cloak the scenery. Sirine and Easha gazed upward, captivated by the dazzling array of colors painting the sky.

Sirine turned to Suhzar and remarked, "Have you ever realized that every sunset is one-of-a-kind, influenced by the clouds and the way I see it?"

The zundar, snugly perched on her shoulder, nodded in agreement, "Yes, they are always changing." At that moment, a loud bell rang out, causing Easha to jump.

Rubric stepped forward, addressing the sorceress with a smile. "The dinner bell has rung; it's time for us to enjoy a meal, Easha. We would be delighted if you joined us at our camp for the night," the chief warrior kindly invited.

She nodded and said as they approached the tables, "Thank you. I think having my friends nearby will help me sleep better."

With Sirine, Rubric, and Ari by her side, she made her way to the long tables just outside the cave's entrance, three rows of timber benches and chairs were ready to welcome them with a feast of a variety of wild berries, warm, freshly baked bread, hearty stews, grilled elk, corn, and an assortment of other mouthwatering dishes.

Children raced between the adults, their laughter echoing through the twilight air as they dashed toward the feast that awaited them.

"Suhzar, the delicious scent of the food is making my stomach rumble," Sirine said eagerly, her enthusiasm evident as she waited in line. She tapped her fingers on the two brown clay bowls she carried, and her hair fluttered in the breeze, teasingly brushing against her cheeks.

"I feel the same; I'm glad the line is moving quickly." The zundar glanced at the two women ahead of them.

"Suhzar, what would you like to eat? Everything looks so delicious," Sirine inquired, her gaze locked on the bubbling pots brimming with tantalizing meals.

"I'd love some of the elk and rabbit stew, please." The zundar's mouth watered as the steam wafted from the pots, enveloping the space in delightful aromas.

With skill, Sirine poured the stew into two bowls, adding three tender pieces of elk atop the simmering concoction.

"Do you need anything else?" she asked, casting a glance at the zundar resting on her shoulder.

"No, what you have is more than enough," he replied confidently.

After serving themselves, Sirine stepped aside, waiting patiently for her friends. Rubric led the way to a sturdy wooden table, its surface decorated with jugs of ale and mulled wine, arranged with care.

"This meal is absolutely delightful," Easha said as she rose, having finished her dish. "The women who toiled to create this splendid feast truly deserve my thanks." With that, she reached for a bowl, balancing her plate, and offered to help clear the table.

"No, you are our honored guest." A young woman with brown hair gently took the plate from Easha's hands, adding, "You have traveled far to be here, and we appreciate your presence. You should rest before your journey home."

Easha nodded with quiet grace, tucking a loose strand of hair behind her ear. The warm flicker of lanterns drew her toward Ari, and she walked over, her pace unhurried, as laughter and clinking cups ebbed behind her.

As the night deepened, Rubric, walking beside Lance, said, "I think it's time to call it a night. We'll head out for the Candora Mountains tomorrow." His words drifted across the group, who began rising in gentle pairs. The walk back to camp was unhurried, winding through the once-lively trees bathed in gold and shadow. Sirine glanced up at the canopy where moonlight filtered through, then followed the others with measured steps.

At the camp's edge, Rubric offered Easha a quiet smile. "Easha, may you have a peaceful sleep," He settled down next to Sirine, while Lance and Zilar found soft patches of grass ten feet away. Ari and Rolyn soon fell asleep after he wrapped her in a gentle embrace.

The sorceress expressed her gratitude, saying, "I appreciate everyone's kindness." High in the trees, the white eagles stood silent, wings tucked and vigilant. Their stillness echoed inside her as she closed her eyes, surrendering to the calm, thinking, *their presence brings me peace,* before allowing herself a moment of bliss.

Above them, stars winked into view, scattered like flecks of silver against deep indigo.

Suddenly, a low rumble stirred the quiet—rolling across Falcon Ridge like a drumbeat from the mountains.

Flashes of lightning danced over the Candora Mountains, creating eerie shadows in the night. The booming thunder startled the fighters awake, causing them to leap to their feet and unsheathe their swords. The tension eased as quickly as it had risen when it became clear that the disturbance was merely a distant rainstorm.

"I'm glad the storm is heading east," Rolyn remarked, glancing at the scattered clouds above. "Who's in the mood for some dry elk before we set off?" He offered, reaching into the pouch with a crooked grin.

"Yes, that sounds great," Zilar replied, eagerly grabbing three pieces with a chuckle.

The others quickly joined in, relishing the tasty treats, except for Easha. From her saddlebag, she retrieved her cone-shaped hat, twisting her hair into a neat bun before tucking it beneath the white brim, a mark of her sorceress identity.

"It's going to be a long day ahead. We should get moving now." She said resolutely. Behind Rubric's horse, fifteen comrades stood ready, their faces set with determination.

"Easha, is something bothering you?" Lance asked, noticing she hadn't mounted yet.

"No, I've decided to take Suhzar and myself to the Hidden Chamber of Light. Suhzar will keep watch over the dark army. Once you reach Tonepass, you'll gain a clearer understanding of the evil sorcerers' uprising, which could help us bolster our defenses. Along your way, Lundar and Efura will act as your scouts."

Sirine glanced at her shoulder and smiled wistfully, "I'll miss you, Suhzar. Please be careful in the black mountains."

"I will miss you as well. When you arrive at Tonepass, I'll be there waiting for you," Suhzar responded, taking off from her shoulder and landing on the saddle horn of the horse.

"I'm ready, Easha." In an instant, the golden accents on her cone hat gleamed brightly. Light spilled across them in a shimmering arc—and in the blink of an eye, the trio vanished into thin air.

Grater, a young man with a mustache and brown hair, stood frozen. He blinked rapidly, mouth slightly agape as he turned to Zilar. Shock radiated from his face, as if trying to make sense of what he'd just seen.

Zilar simply shrugged and replied, "It's magic," before positioning himself behind Rubric.

"We ride," Rubric called out with quiet authority. With practiced ease, he guided his horse toward Sirine's vacated place, nodding to the others. They rode northwest in pairs, eager to recruit more volunteers.

Rubric turned and declared, "When we reach the mountain's base, we'll set up our camp. By tomorrow morning, we should have crossed into the territory of the freedom fighters. We need to tread carefully until they understand we come in peace," his tone was firm, but hopeful, as he continued his steady climb up the rugged mountainside.

Beside him, Sirine attuned her ears to the symphony of nature surrounding her. The wind whistled through the trees, mingling with the distant howls of animals and the soft rustle of leaves. The melodic songs of birds intertwined with the hoots of owls, creating a harmonious backdrop that seemed to travel with her. Beneath the symphony, she could hear the scurrying of creatures in the underbrush, accompanied by the occasional snap of a branch.

So much vitality exists in this landscape, hidden from my view, Sirine mused quietly as she journeyed eastward.

Further back, Rolyn, the elf warrior, sighed with relief, stating, "I'll finally feel more at ease once we leave this rugged landscape behind. The loose stones make it hard to keep my horse steady."

Ari nodded, saying, "I feel the same way. This slope is really dangerous."

After a lengthy ascent, the group reached the summit and dismounted, grateful for the pause. Rolyn stroked his chin thoughtfully, then leaned in and placed a gentle kiss on Ari's cheek. "I need to stretch my legs. Let's see what lies beyond the mountain," he suggested. Taking her hand, the edge led her toward the edge.

Peering down, their hopes dimmed again. They were greeted by the same rocky terrain below.

"Ari, I had hoped the descent would be easier for riding, but it appears that's not the case. Stay close to my horse. If mine stumbles, steer clear of the loose stones," he cautioned.

"Rolyn, I'll follow your lead, but please be careful. I'm eager to leave this mountain behind as well," Ari replied, their shoulders brushing against each other, a silent reassurance passing between them.

Moments later, Rubric gave a signal. "It's time for us to ride," he called out, assisting Sirine onto her horse before mounting his own.

With the group now fully assembled, they began their descent in a neat line. The slope gave way to an expansive valley lush with green. The warriors dismounted as the trees parted to welcome them.

"You, my loyal steed, can enjoy the rich green grass," the elf said, allowing his horse to roam freely.

Ari watched the herd begin to wander. "Rolyn, do you think the horses will wander off?"

"If they get frightened, he might run off, but don't worry, Ari. The eagles will warn us of any dangers," the elf reassured her, placing a gentle kiss on her hand.

Nearby, Zilar swiftly gathered some dry twigs and set them ablaze. He unwrapped bread and elk jerky, arranging them neatly on a stone warmed by the flames. "Come," he called, "let's enjoy a meal."

As the cool night air enveloped them, the warriors formed a small circle around the fire. The heat flickered against their faces as they ate quietly, savoring their food and soothed by the calm.

"I must say, you have a real talent for preparing a delicious meal," Rubric chuckled, eliciting laughter from the group.

"Thank you! I agree, it was quite delightful. I'll catch up with you all at dawn," he replied, settling comfortably just a few feet from the fire.

"Rest well, my friends. I'll see you at the first light," the leader said as he laid out his bedding next to Sirine, wrapping up his day.

Morning broke with a breathtaking blue sky. Birds sang cheerfully overhead, while small creatures darted through the lush, tall grass. Rolyn's horse, along with the others, trotted into the campsite, stirring the warriors from their slumber.

"We've slept longer than I intended," Rubric said with a wide yawn, rising to his feet and tossing his hair back. "I'm sure the freedom fighters are aware of our presence. Their scouts will be closing in on us as we descend the next mountainside. If we keep our weapons sheathed, they'll respect our request and lead us to their camp leader." He approached Sirine, who was gently running her fingers through her hair.

"Well, my lady, are you ready to welcome a new day?" He placed a soft kiss on her cheek, took her hand, and guided her toward her horse.

"Yes! I always look forward to the thrill of a new day and the mysteries it may hold," she replied, her smile radiant.

Rubric took a moment to survey the camp, noting that the warriors had extinguished the fire. The campsite was tidy, and all his companions were mounted and ready for the journey ahead.

"Time is critical. We must leave soon," Rolyn urged, steering the group toward the next steep, foliage-laden mountainside. His elf senses tingled, alerting him to subtle shifts in the wind—signs that they were being watched.

As they traversed the rugged terrain, the team faced several challenges. At one point, Zilar spotted a snapped twig with a distinct, unnatural break. They paused at the peak, captivated by the breathtaking view; a vibrant sea of golden flowers unfolded before them.

Sirine radiated joy as she took in the landscape, inhaling the rich, sweet scent that permeated the air.

"This place brings back memories of my first adventure beyond Pildar's fortress," she said, her smile brightening the moment.

Ari scanned the distant landscape, spotting another steep, forested range. "I truly hope we can steer clear of another treacherous woodland," she sighed.

"Let's get moving; we need to reach the Candora Forest, where the freedom warriors' stronghold lies," Rolyn declared, mounting his horse with determination.

"Lance, it's odd that we haven't encountered any scouts from the freedom fighters," Zilar remarked, riding closely beside him.

"I have a feeling they've been following us since we left camp this morning," Rubric replied, his eyes sweeping over the sturdy tree trunks ahead.

As a gentle northern breeze descended from the mountain, the riders made their way through the vibrant meadow adorned with blooming flowers.

Taking the lead, Rolyn began to ascend the next mountainside.

"You are trespassing on Kandora's land!" a deep voice thundered through the trees.

"Stop!" commanded the lead scout, his eyes scanning the surrounding trees. He dismounted, prompting Lance and Rolyn to follow suit.

"We come in peace," Rubric said firmly.

The riders stiffened as a chorus of snapping branches erupted around them, rising tension in the air.

In a flash, six scouts appeared from their concealed positions. A vibrant green banner danced from their horses' saddles, and each scout sported a matching green wristband on their right arm.

"Take us to your chief officer. We bear urgent news that concerns everyone in this realm," the commander insisted, locking eyes with the nearest scout, whose brown gaze met his.

The tall, blond scout frowned with worry, his blue eyes widening as he replied, "The only threat we face comes from Pildar. He believes that no man, woman, or child should know freedom."

"That is no longer true. Darkness has infiltrated our land. An army of sinister creatures will swarm us like a relentless horde of locusts, determined to eradicate every human, elf, and dwarf, either by death or by shadows. You must guide us to your leader before it's too late. I will reveal everything I know, but we must act swiftly," the leader pressed, urgency etched across his features.

"First, you must relinquish your weapons, and then I will escort you to our leaders," the chief scout ordered, standing resolutely with his sword lowered.

Rubric unsheathed his sword and handed it to the scout beside him. Lance gestured for the others to lower their arms. In the canopy above, white eagles perched in silent witness.

Lundar turned to Efura. "We must pursue them," he said as the warriors from Falcon Ridge mounted their steeds.

Rolyn, Rubric, and Lance closely followed the two scouts. The women rode alongside the men they cherished, their presence anchoring the group with quiet reassurance. Behind them, the rest of their companions formed a solemn procession.

At the rear, four rebels kept a vigilant watch, ensuring no enemy forces followed.

As they climbed another mountainside, a cluster of white clouds welcomed the horsemen, adding a touch of majesty to their journey.

18th Chapter

R ubric and his comrades advanced as the sun sank behind the Eastern Mountains. The team descended the third peak and discovered a creek flowing alongside the northern edge of the forest.

The banks were adorned with vibrant yellow and purple flowers, while smooth pebbles glimmered beneath the stream's surface. Across the water, the intruders caught sight of the flickering lights from numerous campfires at the base camp. Concealed within the eastern mountainside lay a vast chamber, shrouded by dense foliage.

As the riders delved deeper into the Kandora's fortress territory, the environment shifted around them. Five men crafting weapons worked nearby, just a few feet from the brook on their right, their hammers echoing against stone. To the west, a sprawling garden stretched fifty feet from the edge of the forest—a contrast to the battle-forged air.

The appearance of the outsiders sent a wave of fear through the Kandora women, who hurriedly gathered their children and retreated into their homes. In stark contrast, the liberation fighters surged toward the water's edge, unsheathing swords as they moved toward the creek. The head scout adeptly navigated the lush, chilly brook, while Rubric and his companions closely observed the scout's body language, a skill they had honed over time.

With a commanding tone, the head scout called out, "Bring the travelers." His raised arm signaled readiness, and others swiftly echoed his words. With his slender build and dark hair, the scout led a formation of twenty-five soldiers, their movement marked by discipline and urgency.

A refreshing breeze rustled the leaves as the riders crossed the river, their horses splashing through the cool water, grateful for relief from the day's heat.

Sirine slowed her mount, gazing into the glimmering green surface of the creek. The enchanting ripples created by her galloping horse left her mesmerized. Keeping a safe distance from the pounding hooves, she observed fish darting away, startled by movement, while a stubborn green-brown frog remained steadfast on a rock by the flower-laden bank.

The intruders sprinted across the fortress grounds, led by their vigilant scouts. Zilar, Rubric, Lance, and the elves dismounted from their steeds, taking a moment to admire the splendor of the vast chamber before stepping inside. Warm torchlight spilled from the entrance, casting flickering shadows on the stone walls. Outside, Ari and Sirine remained with the horses, their expressions a mix of curiosity and concern as they watched the group disappear into the hall.

As the four fighters from Falcon Ridge peered into the room, their eyes were drawn to a long table lined with stools against the western wall, where five councilmen stood ready to greet them with composed but expectant expressions.

"We have caught wind of your troubling tales regarding a malevolent horde of monsters. This threat is unfamiliar to us. Please, share your knowledge," urged a tall, clean-shaven man with long, flowing black hair cascading to his shoulders.

The team moved forward, their leader stepping up to address the council.

"Tomar has returned," he began solemnly. "His army of beasts grows stronger with each passing day. He has forged an alliance with a nefarious sorceress, giving rise to a legion of horrifying creatures. Such a vast army has never been seen before. They have taken refuge in Stragon Valley."

Rubric's voice gained weight as he stepped closer.

"I intend to gather a formidable force in the Valley of Tonepass. After our meeting, we will journey to the realms of the Dwarves and Elves. They must be alerted to the peril threatening their lands. We must unite in this battle. I implore you to send as many warriors as you can."

With a measured breath, Rubric stepped back, motioning for Rolyn to take his place.

The speaker, visibly shaken by the news, voiced his concerns. "How can we possibly hope to prevail against such overwhelming despair?"

"Our coalition will include the Eagle Dynasty, two zundars who can transform into dragons, and Easha, the Sorceress of Light. It is essential that we rally as many dwarves and elves as we can. If you wish to support our mission, we will convene in the Valley of Tonepass in fifteen days. We have a total of seventeen days to set traps along the tree line before the sinister army launches its vicious assault. Clearly, an ambush would be futile, as the dark sorcerers employ crows as their scouts, keeping them updated on any intruders. We will bide our time until the dark infantry enters the Valley of Tonepass, and then we will strike," Rolyn declared, stepping closer to Rubric as he observed the worried expressions of the councilors.

Then Lance moved forward.

"Lundar, the white eagle, overheard the malevolent sorcerer announce that their initial target will be Pildar's Stronghold. The guards will be alerted when they see the sky darken with Tomar's spies. The Potentate's army is a formidable force, boasting over five thousand warriors. They will obliterate many of the sorcerer's minions, but we will still contend with the remaining beasts. Tomar has grown even more powerful after absorbing his wife's magical essence. Only Easha has the strength to defeat him. We will draw the army's focus onto ourselves, allowing the sorceress to eliminate Tomar. Tomorrow morning, my allies and I will set off for the Kingdom of Dwarves, heading eastward over the Middrom Mountains. In fifteen days, the volunteers who have pledged their support must assemble in the Tonepass Valley."

Lance carefully observed the council members' reactions, each face tense with apprehension.

The speaker stood up, placing his hands firmly on the desk.

"At dawn, after we contemplate your words, we will announce our decision," he assured them. "A scout will guide you to your campsite for the night."

The meeting adjourned. Rubric and his companions exited the chamber, following the scout through stone corridors to a snug hut nestled beneath the fortress walls. Inside, a warm fire crackled invitingly.

Without a word, the scout pivoted and made his way back to the council.

"Do you believe they will lend us their support?" Sirine inquired, observing the creases of worry etched on Rubric's forehead.

"If they choose not to assist us, the encroaching darkness will consume them as well." He placed a gentle kiss on her cheek and enveloped her in his arms, conveying that the warriors would join their cause if they wished to survive.

"Rubric, regardless of the outcome, we will fight side by side," Sirine promised.

"Yes, my dear. We must brace ourselves for a fierce confrontation. With you commanding Suhzar and Ari leading Gular, our odds of triumphing in this war are significantly enhanced." He smiled softly, tenderly taking her hand in his, and guided her to the table where Rolyn and Lance were seated, just as three women approached.

The group turned their gaze eastward, captivated by the women as they drew near. One carried a basket filled with freshly baked bread, another held a steaming pot of meat, and the third brought a jug of wine for their guests. The delicious aromas of the sizzling dishes intensified as the ladies approached.

"I hope you're all ready to eat," exclaimed a petite blonde with striking blond hair.

Standing nearest to her, Lance accepted two loaves of warm bread and a pot of meat.

"Thank you so much. I genuinely appreciate your generosity," he replied as he made his way toward the fire pit with the food.

The kind woman turned to leave, a smile brightening her face as she glanced up.

"Rolyn, what do you think our chances are in this battle?" Ari asked, her voice laced with concern.

Rolyn looked into the fire, thoughtful. "The future holds many uncertainties, Ari. No one who has experienced this place can foresee what lies ahead. While some place their trust in destiny, others remain skeptical. It's akin to trying to withstand a fierce gale. My dear, I vow this: we will confront this darkness with every ounce of our strength." Ari's breath caught as his words sank in. The warmth of the fire flickered against her face, casting soft shadows over her worried expression. Rolyn reached out slowly, a quiet reassurance in his gaze.

With quiet conviction, the elf extended her hand toward her— not simply in comfort, but as a pledge born of loyalty, love, and the promise of shared courage. Ari accepted the gesture, her fingers closing gently around his, sealing a silent understanding between them.

Rubric stirred beside them, breaking the reverie, and suggested, "Let's take a moment to unwind and savor this time together. Once the council wraps up, we'll make our way to the Middrom Mountains, following the most straightforward route to the Dwarves' Kingdom. It should take us around five days. It would be wonderful if the liberation fighters could send reinforcements to Tonepass Valley."

Sirine, seated at his side, met his gaze with both warmth and worry. "Do you genuinely think they'll provide help?"

"Without a doubt, I believe many will come to our aid in Tonepass." He pressed a gentle kiss to her lips, assuring her that they would make the right decision. "Once we receive their response, we'll head east. Since I've never traveled this route before, we must proceed with caution. Rolyn, have you ever ventured into Ange's territory?"

Rolyn nodded slowly. "Yes, when I was younger. I don't recall much, and I'm certain it has changed since then."

A hush returned, wrapping the circle of warriors in a moment of fragile peace. The fire crackled softly, and above, the stars blinked into view one by one. As the night deepened, the Kandoran Freedom Fighters secured their supplies, and the visitors drifted toward slumber, drawn into dreams under the quiet watch of the moon.

At first light, just as the chill of morning began to lift, the group was awakened by the call of a voice.

"A meeting with our leader is essential. Follow me," the scout instructed, his cloak swirling behind him as he turned toward the stone corridors. Rubric and his companions followed, footfalls echoing as they entered the hall once more. The chamber was awash in pale sunlight, filtering through narrow windows cut into the fortress walls. Ten Kandoran leaders stood assembled, grim and alert.

"Let's not waste time; we have a lot to cover," spoke the man at the head of the table, his voice rough from long nights. "Eight hundred warriors have committed to our cause. They promise to gather at Tonepass Valley in just fifteen days. We need three hundred of them here to protect our families. We cannot leave the women and children behind."

Rubric stepped forward, resolute. "Your support means everything to us, and I truly value your choice," Rubric replied. "Now, we shall head towards the dwarfs' lands." With a solemn bow, the travelers turned and exited the chamber, the decision like a torch passed between allies.

Outside, a guard with striking mercury-red hair and a wild, bushy beard guided the newcomers back to their encampment beneath the waking sky.

Sirine gazed up at the brightening sky, where clouds sailed gently overhead. The morning air was crisp, filled with the scent of pine and dew. A quiet sense of readiness hummed beneath her skin.

Moments later, Rolyn emerged with a glint of triumph in his expression.

"Ari, Sirine, we have incredible news! The Kandorans have agreed to send troops," Rolyn announced, reassuring them that a larger force would significantly improve their odds against the dark powers.

The princess met the elf's eyes and replied, "I'm thankful they made the right decision. Do you believe the dwarves and elves will join us in this fight?"

Rolyn offered her a steady nod. "They will certainly send a substantial number of troops. But for now, we need to rest.

Tomorrow will be a long day," He placed a kiss on her lips, wrapping his arm around her waist as they settled in. He laid out the bedding for both of them on the ground beside the crackling fire.

As night fell, the inhabitants of the base camp drifted into slumber, enveloping the area in a profound silence. The sky turned into a dark canvas, with stars twinkling brightly, while the bonfires dimmed to glowing embers. As time passed, the soft chirping of crickets filled the air around the fortress.

19th Chapter

As Sirine awoke from her dreams, the sun began to rise over the Kinnick Mountains, casting a soft glow across the landscape. Around her, her companions remained bundled in peaceful slumber, their breathing steady, their weapons resting by their sides. She sat up slowly, stretching as her gaze drifted toward the treetops, hoping to catch a glimpse of the elusive white eagles. But the sky was silent.

Lundar and Efura were likely off on an early hunt, she thought, imagining them soaring above the valley or weaving through underbrush. Her gaze swept over the fortress, and a sense of comfort enveloped her, knowing that hundreds of soldiers and their families made this small refuge their home, easing the burden of their protection.

The stars she had been admiring just hours before were starting to fade as the dawn approached. She rubbed her neck absentmindedly, lost in contemplation.

Our adventure into the unknown awaits us. I miss Suhzar. Can he see the stars as clearly as I do? I know he carries the weight of guilt for not recognizing the threat sooner, but it's a burden he shouldn't bear alone. I wish he could let go of that guilt. Thankfully, our luck changed when the sorceress sent Lundar to scout the ominous skies. We will catch the enemy by surprise and defend our home with strength. There's no way darkness will conquer our sanctuary.

Sirine looked up just in time to see Rolyn and Ari stirring from their sleep, shifting beneath their blankets. She smiled at the sight before her attention was pulled eastward, where a woman was approaching along the path, pushing a wooden cart that glided effortlessly over the stones.

"Your breakfast has arrived! I hope you're feeling hungry on this lovely morning," the woman called warmly, her voice a melody against the quiet hum of daybreak.

"Rise and shine, my friends; the day awaits us!" the elf declared. He stood to assist the woman with the striking red hair as she began to distribute the meal for their eager companions.

Zilar got to his feet, savoring the delightful scent of freshly baked bread. "You truly exemplify grace. We are grateful for your generosity," he remarked sincerely. The woman beamed at him, then turned to head home, but paused to glance back at the cheerful group enjoying their breakfast.

One of the volunteers from Falcon Ridge exclaimed, "I've never tasted blueberry sauce before! It's absolutely scrumptious!" as he relished the lingering flavor on his lips and fingers.

"You're right," Rubric replied. "I found the sauce to be quite distinctive; it paired perfectly with the warm bread. Now that we've finished our meal, we should tidy up our camp before heading to the Kingdom of Dwarves." As he stretched and bent down to gather his bedding, he noticed a man approaching and called out to his friends, "A scout is making his way toward us."

The fighter reached the clearing and came to a silent halt, his gaze sweeping across the gathered travelers.

Rubric stepped forward and said, "It's fortunate you've arrived. We're about to set off, and it would be wonderful if you could guide us back across the stream."

The scout dipped his head respectfully. "It would be my pleasure. Meeting such courageous men has been an extraordinary experience for me. I will take you across the brook; just follow my lead. We shall reunite in the Valley of Tonepass in fifteen days."

The scout observed the Falcon Ridge Warriors until they disappeared from sight, then mounted his horse and joined the other scouts patrolling their territory.

He lingered for a moment, watching the Falcon Ridge warriors disappear into the forest's edge, their silhouettes framed by golden shafts of light. Then, with silent precision, he mounted his horse and rode off to rejoin the other scouts patrolling their designated area.

Rolyn and his team directed their attention eastward toward the Candora Forest. The air buzzed with anticipation as their journey continued on. Sirine glanced up and spotted a pair of stunning white eagles just a short distance away. It dawned on her that they had carefully mapped out their journey. "I feel much more secure with my friends scouting ahead," she remarked, warmth of her smile reflecting a deep confidence in those she journeyed with.

The Candora Forest extended to the east of Rolyn and his companions.

Behind the group, Lance noticed the sun dipping low in the sky behind them. Its golden rays bled across the horizon, painting the leaves with firelight. As the riders veered northeast, the late summer leaves danced in the gentle breeze. The sound of their horses' hooves crunching on the fragile foliage filled the atmosphere, and a sense of unease washed over them. The towering trees swayed as the cool wind whispered through their branches.

Ari observed Lundar and Efura gliding gracefully above. On the ground below, Rubric, Lance, and Rolyn rode in unison, forming a protective barrier. Zilar and the fifteen warriors from Falcon Ridge followed closely behind, their blades ready to respond to any potential ambush.

Sirine tilted her head to the right, examining the leaves in their myriad shades of green. *It's incredible how the leaves cling to the branches, even when the wind howls,* she mused. Surrounded by grand oak trees, she felt an extraordinary sense of liberation as the sunlight dappled through the canopy. Her face lit up, warmed by the stunning landscape. The former slave girl reflected on her time serving Pildar, the Ruler of Enwood, as she breathed in the rich scent of oak and gazed at the vast blue sky. Memories flooded back of the stories Suhzar had shared with her.

Mum and Pa, my heart aches with a profound longing for you. I can sense your protective presence guiding my journey. I have become the key that liberated Seledor from the darkness, and now I ride high upon a dragon's back. Is it merely our shared bloodline that has led me to this extraordinary fate? My life has evolved into a vibrant tapestry filled with mysterious adventures.

Up ahead, Sirine gazed at Rubric, her heart swelling with admiration as he took charge. The thought of marrying him and starting a family brought her immense joy, and a radiant smile spread across her face.

As they navigated the sixth curve of the mountain path, her eyes drifted to the left, where she spotted Ari, the Princess of Birchwood, sitting confidently in her saddle. Shifting her gaze westward, she observed the sun dipping behind the majestic Atron Mountains.

Rolyn raised a hand, bringing the group to a halt. He spoke firmly, yet with care. "We'll camp here for the night. It's not wise to approach Denmora Marsh after dark; I've heard unsettling tales about that area. At dawn, we'll circle around the marsh's perimeter." With resolve, he dismounted and walked over to Ari.

"I can dismount my horse without your help. I've been riding since I was a child." Ari said coolly, her pride undimmed.

Rolyn's expression softened. "My upbringing instilled in me a deep respect for women and the importance of offering support, so I sincerely apologize if I have offended you." With gentle hands, the elf helped her down, his sincerity evident as he placed a soft kiss on her cheek and wrapped her in a quiet embrace.

"Rolyn, as time goes on, we will explore each other's cultures and embrace them." She held his hand tightly, gazing into his eyes before turning back to their companions.

Zilar gave a nod toward the eastern grove. "I'll collect some wood and ignite a big bonfire to keep us warm," he said, striding off with purpose, his silhouette swallowed gradually by the tree line.

As the group waited, a gentle quiet settled over the clearing. Ari scanned the towering canopy, eyes darting hopefully among the branches in search of eagles—but the skies remained still. With a resigned sigh, she opened her pouch, revealing dried rabbit and berries. *They must be out hunting,* she thought, fingering the edges of the pouch with quiet disappointment.

"Who wants some meat or berries?" she called out, breaking the silence, her eyes glimmering with curiosity as she sampled a piece of the succulent fruit.

Moments later, the rustle of leaves and crunch of twigs signaled Zilar's return. His arms were full of dry branches, his steps slower now. He placed the gathered wood by a stone ring at the center of camp, knelt to strike flint, and coaxed the fire to life. The flames soon flickered and danced, casting golden light on weary faces.

Wiping sweat from his brow, Zilar settled against a nearby log. Exhaustion tugged at his limbs. "No, I'm too tired to eat," he murmured, his eyes half-lidded. He longed for sleep more than sustenance.

The elf beside the princess chimed in, "I'd appreciate a bit of meat before we settle in for the night."

The riders gathered around the campfire, chewing dried elk and sipping cool water from leather flasks. The warmth of the meal softened the weariness etched into their faces.

"Ari, I saw you glancing toward the woods. You must be looking for Efura and Lundar. They're likely out hunting and will return shortly." Just as the elf finished speaking, as if summoned by his words, a pair of eagles swept into view, their majestic wings slicing through the fading twilight. They landed silently in the trees above, feathers glowing faintly in the firelight. "They are truly magnificent," the elf whispered, planting a gentle kiss on her cheek.

Ari's eyes lingered on the eagles. "Yes, their presence brings me tranquility. Would you like some extra meat?"

"No, but I'll set up our bedding while you put the food away," he replied. Rising to his feet, the elf tossed aside the bedding and spread them out on the ground.

Ari nodded with gratitude as they prepared for the night, stating, "Rolyn, your kindness truly matters." The camp gradually fell into a peaceful hush, with most of the exhausted riders drifting off to sleep, leaving only Sirine awake. Her thoughts wandered to the marsh, where the wind howled menacingly around her.

Rolyn sensed a twinge of discomfort about the marsh, but it doesn't trouble me. My childhood had been tainted by cruelty and betrayal. The most haunting memory was of being trapped in a box, forced to listen to the terrifying demise of my family at the hands of Pildar's men. She often pondered that if her parents hadn't hidden her away, she might have been able to save them.

As waves of sorrow washed over her, she felt a constriction in her throat.

I will not linger on the painful moments of my past; I refuse to let them dictate my future. That will not define my fate. She vowed silently.

After bolstering her spirits, Sirine gazed up at the shimmering stars, wondering if Suhzar could see them as well. She remained lost in the constellations, their light a balm to her wounds. And when sleep finally came, it held her gently—as if the night itself embraced her.

• • •

As the first light of dawn broke over the East Kinnick Mountains, the shadows began to recede, painting the landscape in soft gold.

While the riders continued their slumber in the camp, Lance stirred and stood up. He surveyed the surroundings and declared, "It's time to wake up. Our days will be long if we hope to reach the Kingdom of Dwarfs in three days." He shook off his bedding and draped it over his saddle, tidying up his area.

"I agree," the chief warrior replied, turning to Sirine and planting a fervent kiss on her lips.

As Rubric walked beside Rolyn, he remarked, "You should take the lead since you're most familiar with this region."

Rolyn nodded slowly. "I don't recall ever taking this path during my childhood. This area was once adorned with magnificent rock canyons, but they have transformed dramatically. I'll do my utmost to lead us through. We'll navigate the wetlands in a single line," he instructed his companions as they journeyed eastward.

The undulating hills evoked cherished memories of Ari's homeland—the Kingdom of Birchwood. A flurry of thoughts swirled in her mind. *I hope my family received my message. I intend to visit them in the fall. I wish they wouldn't worry about me.* She cast a glance at the tall, golden-haired elf she held dear. *Will my parents accept my choice to marry the man I love?*

Shaking off her reverie, Ari turned to Sirine with renewed curiosity. "This is the first time I've seen a place like this. Have you noticed the black and brown weeds blanketing the ground, along with the diverse heights and hues of the grass? Look at the vibrant aquatic plants flourishing in the serene, deep pools. I try to take in the entire marsh, but it becomes overwhelming. We need to push deeper into this challenging terrain."

Rolyn swiftly turned, urgency tinging his voice as he warned his friends, "There are floating eyes in the water. Don't look at them!"

Despite the caution, the group found themselves irresistibly captivated by the enchanting eyes, marked with gray and black veins.

Ari commented, "It seems like the eyes are twitching. They just keep staring at us." She rubbed her arms, a shiver running down her spine.

Above them, the Eagles circled low, weaving through the winding trails of the wetland alongside their companions.

Sirine's complexion drained as she trembled, inhaling deeply to regain her composure.

Sensing the rising tension among his friends, Rolyn called out, "Look away! They can put you under their spell. Stay focused on what's ahead!"

Yet, Sirine's curiosity got the better of her when she spotted a three-inch eyeball that intrigued her. It leaped from the water and landed on her shoulder just as she turned her head.

Ari was caught off guard when Sirine's startled horse snorted and bolted, tossing the princess to the ground as the creature reared in fright.

In a flash, Lundar swooped down, his talon snatching the eye from Sirine's shoulder and with a triumphant screech, he soared high above the treetops.

Ari, noticing her restless horse circling around, took a moment to soothe it before remounting.

"Are you alright, Ari? I'm really sorry for bumping into you. I just want to get out of here," Sirine said, her voice laced with concern.

"I'm fine. It wasn't your fault. We need to move!" Ari replied firmly.

With urgency, the riders urged their horses forward, racing toward the marsh's exit. But a sudden cry from the eagles made them pause. Ahead, a colossal creature rested upon a jagged rock, motionless but unmistakably alive.

A deep rumble echoed through the air.

Before them loomed a terrifying creature, its single eye glaring down from the highest rock in the rugged landscape.

In that moment, they soon understood that this beast was the protector of the marsh.

With a thunderous roar, the colossal creature sprang from its rocky perch and charged toward the intruders.

Rubric shouted, "We need to move quickly before the monster blocks our escape!" As he rode alongside the women, Rolyn urged, "Keep pushing ahead. The beast is closing in on us." The team of riders fled the swamp, their hearts pounding. The elf knew that if they were cornered, the consequences would be dire.

As Sirine tilted her head, she saw the creature come to an abrupt halt. A chilling screech reverberated through the land, serving as a stark warning to the intruders.

Zilar paused, eyes wide and remarked, "The monster is warning us never to return." He shivered at the thought. Sirine looked up and called out, "Lundar, thank you for your help!" while waving at him.

She trembled uncontrollably, her gaze flickering to her shoulder, where the eye had once been.

The elf, catching his breath, cautioned that the terrain would only become more treacherous if they pressed on. Raising an eyebrow, he turned his attention to the lead warrior. "Rubric, is this path the safest option? I've never encountered floating eyes in the wetlands before."

After a moment of contemplation, Rubric declared, "Let's take a short break before we proceed." He dismounted from his horse and added, "Rolyn, we need to alert the others that we might be walking into a dangerous trap."

As the group halted, Rolyn interjected, "I must warn you about the threats that lie ahead. If we continue down this route, we could find ourselves in serious danger; many lives could be at risk." His expression was somber as he voiced his concerns. "It would be wise to turn back, even considering the distance we've traveled. Our future is fraught with peril." He wrapped his arm around Ari's waist, who listened intently.

Sirine asked, "What dangers are we facing?" A hint of concern flickered in her right eye as she grasped Rubric's hand tightly

"If there are hidden watchers lurking in the marshes, then we can be sure there are other unseen threats; I can't say for certain. Raise your hand if you wish to proceed."

With resolve, Tackar and the volunteers from Falcon Ridge stood up.

"We must move forward. Turning back is not an option," Tackar declared.

After a brief moment of silent agreement, Rolyn gently squeezed Ari's hand.

Rubric wrapped his arm around Sirine's waist. "Do not worry, my dear. The challenges we will face at Tonepass will be greater than anything we've encountered so far, but we will overcome our enemies," he comforted her as he assisted her onto her horse.

The group pressed on, with the elf leading despite his unease about what awaited them. As they journeyed eastward, the gathering darkness signaled their approach to the Arista Mountains, prompting them to stop for the night.

As the sun dipped below the horizon, Zilar let out a deep breath, feeling a wave of relief. "It has been a long day! My legs feel numb," he remarked, stretching his tired muscles.

Lance, echoing the sentiment, nodded with a weary smile. "I can't wait to close my eyes and leave this day behind." He settled into his bedroll, joined by the others as they all prepared for a well-deserved rest.

20th Chapter

By mid-morning, ominous dark clouds began to gather from the east, saturating the air with the foreboding scent of an impending storm. The wind howled fiercely, a wild herald of the tempest looming on the horizon. Trees bent and groaned under its force, their branches clawing at the sky like desperate hands.

Understanding the urgency of their predicament, Rubric realized they needed to seek shelter before the rain unleashed its wrath. They ventured into a shadowy valley, where towering rock formations loomed like ancient sentinels, casting jagged shadows across the ground. The terrain was treacherous—slick stone, uneven paths, and the eerie silence of a place long abandoned by light.

"Rubric, do you see these footprints?" Tackar asked, his voice tinged with anxiety as he crouched to examine the ground.

The team clustered around him, their eyes widening at the sight of the enormous impressions embedded in the soil. Each print was nearly ten feet long, the edges deep and sharp, as though the creature that made them carried the weight of a mountain.

"We're in deep trouble," Omond breathed, his voice quaking as he stared at the monstrous tracks. Just then, low, menacing grunts reverberated through the gorge like a warning from the underworld.

"Unsheathe your swords! I can feel a clash is about to happen," Rubric commanded, worry visible on his face.

Although Tackar and his Falcon Ridge warriors had never encountered real battles, their training had prepared them—albeit against foes far less formidable than what now stalked them. The air grew heavier, thick with dread, as if the storm itself were watching.

Tackar furrowed his brow in contemplation and suggested, "Maybe we should backtrack and look for a different path to the Valley of Tonepass."

"It's too late for that now," Rubric replied grimly, his grip on the sword hilt growing firmer. His eyes scanned the horizon, searching for movement in the shadows.

"I'm convinced the stalkers have blocked all the exits from the valley," Ari interjected. "There are massive boulders to the north. We could split up and navigate around them."

"That's a brilliant idea," Rolyn replied. "But I worry that the mutants will eventually find us. These rocks will provide some cover. Let's divide into four teams. Tackar and Lance, take half the men and conceal yourselves behind the first cluster of boulders."

"Omond, Zilar, and the others should seek refuge behind the second group of rocks. I'll stay here with the women and Rolyn. Get your swords ready. When they arrive, aim for their bodies from below." With that command, Rubric dashed towards the rocky formations to the west, while the three groups of warriors took their positions behind their makeshift defenses. The valley lay still, its silence broken only by the distant rumble of thunder and the whisper of wind through stone.

A flash of lightning illuminated the distant mountains, casting eerie silhouettes across the terrain. As the warriors waited, breath held and blades drawn, the first drops of rain began to fall—cold, deliberate, and heavy—causing the ground to shudder beneath their feet. Then came the sound—slow, deliberate footsteps echoing through the gorge. Not the hurried gait of a beast, but the confident stride of something that knew it was feared. The grunts grew louder, more guttural, accompanied by the scraping of claws against rock.

"Stay vigilant! The creatures are closing in quickly," Lance whispered, his voice barely audible over the rising wind. Moments later, two enormous beasts emerged from the mist. The first barreled in from the north, its hulking form crashing through the underbrush, while the second slithered from the southern valley, its eyes glowing faintly in the gloom.

Lance glanced at Tackar, urgency etched onto his face. "They're gigantic," he muttered, both of them staring at the hideous mutants with their distorted features and hairless heads. Towering even over trolls, they bore a grotesque resemblance to gilzdars. Their muscular arms and legs rippled with unnatural strength, and their breath steamed in the cold air like smoke from a forge.

At the same time, Rolyn and Rubric positioned themselves at the brink of the rocky outcrop, eyes scanning the shifting shadows. Out of nowhere, a colossal silhouette advanced toward the two piles of stones. Tackar and Omond shared a wordless cue, placing their fingers against their lips. The tiniest of the giants crept forward, its movements cautious but deliberate. Their commander motioned to the warriors, indicating that the time to act had come.

With unwavering resolve, the warriors surged from their hiding places, blades flashing as they plunged their swords into the foes lurking among the shadows and behind the massive stones. Steel met flesh with a sickening crunch.

Suddenly, from behind the foremost boulder, a terrifying creature sprang forth, its roar splitting the air. It seized three of Tackar's fighters in its massive claws and smashed them brutally against the jagged wall. In a single, monstrous motion, it then flung nine members of Omond's squad over the towering rock formation like rag dolls.

Omond roared, "Blind the monster; aim for its eyes!"

A warrior brandishing twin swords dashed forward, leaping onto the largest boulder near the beast, raising his blades high. With a fierce cry, he plunged his swords deep into the giant's eyes.

A chilling wail of agony reverberated through the canyon, shaking the very bones of the valley. The creature staggered, struggling to maintain its balance as the ground quaked beneath it. Blood poured from its eyes as it attempted to protect its face. It toppled backward, colliding with the giant that Rolyn and Rubric's teams were engaged in combat with. Dazed and disoriented, the beast crashed against the basin wall, and a colossal boulder, dislodged from above, smashed its skull, snapping its neck in a heartbeat. The giant collapsed, lifeless, its body crumpling like a felled tree.

Omond shouted, "Rubric, we're coming to assist in bringing down the beast!"

A bolt of lightning split the sky, illuminating the turmoil as it struck the wall of the Upper East Valley. The light drizzle escalated into a torrential downpour, inundating the valley below. Water coursed through the ravine, and small stones began to cascade from the cliffside, clattering like bones tossed by fate.

The monstrous beast loomed over the battlefield, its grotesque form towering above the chaos. With a sudden lurch, it lunged forward—its massive arms sweeping through the storm like scythes. Three warriors who had rushed to support Rubric were snatched mid-stride, caught in the creature's crushing grip. Their weapons fell from their hands as they struggled, suspended helplessly above the mud.

"Let my brothers go!" Tackar bellowed, charging at the creature and driving his sword deep into its right thigh.

With a bone-chilling roar, the beast seized Tackar by the head, shaking him violently until his head was wrenched from his body. Blood sprayed across the stones as the creature hurled the captured warriors to the ground, where jagged rocks rained down, embedding themselves in their flesh.

"Help! We're stuck! The mud is too thick!" the wounded fighters cried, struggling to rise as the ground clung to them like a curse.

Rolyn and Lance dashed to help the fallen men, but their attempts were in vain.

The giant turned its gaze toward them, eyes gleaming with malice. With a thunderous step, it crushed the helpless men beneath its enormous foot, their screams silenced in an instant.

With fierce determination, Rubric and Omond leapt from a nearby boulder. With precision and power, they drove their swords deep into the giant's skull, the steel biting through the bone. The beast staggered, then collapsed with a deafening crash.

Sirine and Ari shared a determined look, nodding in agreement before dashing forward to jump onto the beast's chest. Sirine struck at its throat with a swift, slicing blow, while Ari plunged her sword into its heart, twisting the blade with all her strength.

The creature convulsed violently, its massive limbs flailing. It flung the women aside with a final burst of rage, sending them crashing to the ground. Blood poured from its throat as it clutched the wound, its breath ragged and shallow.

"De t al!" the dying giant rasped, its voice a foreboding warning of death to all.

"Ari, Sirine, are you both alright?" The chief warrior, shocked by the sight before him, asked with heartfelt worry.

"We're fine, just a few cuts and bruises," they reassured him.

Rolyn and Rubric wrapped their partners in tight, protective hugs, their relief palpable in the midst of the carnage.

Omond's voice trembled with sorrow. "So many friends have perished in this fight." The warriors looked around, their hearts heavy. Mangled bodies lay strewn across the battlefield, limbs twisted unnaturally, eyes frozen in final terror. The sight churned their stomachs and hollowed their spirits.

With heavy hearts, they collected their fallen comrades from the drenched ground, gently placing them upon their steeds before pausing to mourn. Rain continued to fall, soft and relentless, as if the heavens mourned with them. The living bowed their heads in sorrow. Rolyn broke the stillness, his voice steady but thick with emotion.

"I pay tribute to your courage, dear friends. You are beloved, and your legacies will live on. Rest peacefully, my brothers."

As the rain cascaded from the gloomy heavens, it cleansed the traces of blood and grime, sanctifying the ground where heroes had fallen.

Rubric wrapped his arm around Sirine, offering her solace.

Ari leaned against Rolyn, tears streaming down her cheeks as she mourned the tragedy that had unfolded.

The group departed from the canyon, a place that had exacted such a heavy toll. Behind them lay the echoes of battle, soaked in sorrow.

Omond wiped away a tear and proclaimed, "I will bring our fighters back to Falcon Ridge."

The chief warrior nodded solemnly, "Will you join us in the Tonepass Mountains?"

"Yes, I'll rally more warriors to join our cause." He noted that his allies from the south would bolster their fight against the dark army, securing his swords at his waist.

Rubric clasped his hand and said, "I'll meet you in Tonepass."

With one final look at the battlefield, Omond turned westward toward Falcon Ridge, his steps heavy with grief, yet driven by duty.

As the rain eased, rays of sunlight pierced the gloomy sky, casting golden streaks across the drenched landscape.

Zilar broke the silence, his brow furrowed. "Do you think those massive mutants that attacked us were part of the dark army?"

Lance rubbed his arms, affirming, "I'm convinced those creatures broke free from the dark fortress."

Rubric's team pressed onward with sorrow thick in the atmosphere. Silence enveloped them as they navigated the rugged paths behind Rolyn, each step echoing with the weight of loss.

"We need to remain vigilant. I have no idea what threats await us," Rolyn cautioned before stepping into the woods, his hand resting on the hilt of his blade.

The day gradually dimmed as the sun slipped away, yielding to the encroaching night that enveloped the weary travelers.

"It's time to rest," Rubric declared, dismounting his horse and approaching Sirine. He kissed her gently and whispered, "You, my love, have truly become a formidable warrior with that sword."

Rolyn stood beside Ari, inhaling deeply before suggesting, "We should avoid lighting a fire. In this perilous place, silence is our greatest ally." He began to arrange his bedding near the princesses, his eyes scanning the dark woods.

Ari quietly unpacked their supplies, distributing them among the group. Though exhausted, the travelers found little solace in sleep, haunted by the horrors of the previous day.

As the final hours of the night wore thin, Rubric kept silent watch near the flickering remnants of their campfire, his eyes scanning the darkened terrain. When the first blush of dawn painted the mountain sky in warm golden light, he stood and stretched, weariness tugging at his limbs but purpose lighting his face.

The soft salmon-hued clouds drifted over the Eastern Mountains, their snow-capped peaks glowing in the morning sun.

Sirine rubbed her weary eyes and admired the view, inhaling the crisp morning air and savoring its purity before releasing it with a sigh.

Rubric, drawn by the sight of his beautiful companion bathed in morning light, felt a quiet joy stir within him. A smile spread across his face as he stepped closer, leaning in to kiss her softly. "Good morning, my dear," he whispered. Rising to his feet, he added, "We must get up and continue our journey, despite the restless night." With steady resolve, the seasoned fighter rallied the rest of the group.

Stirred by the shifting rhythm of morning preparations, Ari awoke with a groggy murmur, rubbing sleep from her eyes as dawn spilled across the rugged terrain. From her saddlebag, she retrieved a pouch of dried meat, the familiar scent grounding her. "Everyone requires some food to keep their strength up," she murmured as she opened the food pouch and shared its contents with the group. The gesture of sharing, though simple, reaffirmed the bond forming among the group—a bond forged not by blood, but by shared danger.

Rubric, ever the focused leader, took one last bite before swinging onto his horse. "Now that we've had our meal, we must press on," he directed, mounting his horse and leading the party up the mountainside. As the caravan began its ascent, the horses snorted and pawed at the ground, unease rippling through their muscles.

Rolyn, riding closer to the front, tilted his head, "I hear a low growl coming from ahead."

It was faint, but primal—like a warning carved into the wind itself.

The group halted; their senses heightened.

"The northwest territory isn't typically home to grizzly bears, even if that sounds like one," Lance noted, drawing his sword. "We can't risk a confrontation with bears right now."

Rubric nodded, pushing his mount forward, signaling the others to stay close. But the growl deepened, vibrating through the ravine.

"Bears aren't the source of that noise. They don't hunt in packs, and mountain lions are uncommon here. Whatever it is, it's approaching," Zilar cautioned, scanning the surroundings with keen eyes.

Rubric commanded, his sword shimmering in the dim light. "We need to form a defensive circle; it's our best chance against whatever is tracking us." He flexed his right arm, prepared for the challenge ahead.

From the shadows of the forest, emerged a horror no beast should match: grotesque rats, easily taller than a man, with tails like whips and fangs honed for carnage. Eight in all, slinking from shadow into half-light.

As one of the mutants lunged at her, Ari instinctively drew her sword. The creature dodged her strike, narrowly escaping, and charged forward. A wave of panic surged through her as she screamed and kicked at the beast.

Before it could strike again, an elf blade pierced its heart. The mysterious elf emerged like a whisper of death. The rat crumpled instantly, effectively eliminating the danger.

With their alpha slain, the remaining mutant rats realized their defeat was imminent and scurried back into the forest's shadows.

Rolyn was by Ari's side in moments, lifting her gently and guiding her to a fallen log. His hand on her waist lingered just enough to show care, not intrusion.

"Thank you for your assistance," she said, her voice filled with gratitude.

"Of course, my lady. I'll be back shortly." With that, Rolyn dashed off toward his horse. He swiftly searched through his saddlebag and retrieved a crystal-clear jar. Returning to her side, he applied a salve to her wound, its herbal scent mingling with pine and ash. "This will keep your cut clean," he assured her as their companions gathered around.

"Do you think you can ride? We can take the rest of the day to rest if you need it," Rubric inquired, noticing the severity of her injury along with the many cuts and bruises that marred her skin.

Ari exhaled through clenched teeth, her fingers pressing against her ribs to steady the throb. "Yes, we must press on. I've endured worse than this," she replied, voice strained but resolute.

Rolyn stepped beside her, offering his arm without a word. She grasped it, her knuckles whitening as he helped her mount the horse. Her saddle dug into her side, but she bit back the pain, determined not to burden the others further. Behind her, Sirine silently watched, her eyes scanning the treetops—as if expecting something to pounce.

With a curt nod, Rubric turned his steed and led the party into the narrow pass that marked the border of the dwarfs' territory. The terrain shifted subtly—rocks grew sharper, trees stockier, and faint markings etched into stones hinted that eyes watched from the hidden corners of the world.

"We'll set up camp for the night right here," Rolyn said as the group entered a sheltered clearing tucked between two jagged boulders. The sun was beginning its descent, casting long shadows that danced along the cliff face. "I'm sure the dwarf scouts have spotted us and will keep an eye on us until dawn."

He then assisted Ari down from the saddle with careful precision, mindful not to worsen her wounds. As she settled onto a nearby log, Lance struck flint against steel until flame licked the bundle of dry twigs, blooming into a sturdy campfire.

Yet despite the promise of comfort, the group was subdued. The day's ambush had drained more than just their stamina—it had left cracks in their resolve. The mutant rats, the elf's sudden appearance, the unnatural growl from deep within the mountains—all lingered like shadows behind their eyes. Hunger was present, yet no one reached for food. The silence was a shared language now, a lull born from exhaustion and growing unease.

They'd crossed into dwarfs' territory, but no one spoke of alliances or diplomacy. Not tonight. One by one, the travelers withdrew into their bedrolls, fading into the flickering half-light.

21st Chapter

❖

Before the first light of dawn fully emerged, the intruders were met with a sound they recognized all too well.

"You are trespassing on dwarf territory. Depart at once," a powerful voice echoed through the stillness—gravelly, unmistakable, and filled with authority.

Lance blinked against the dim glow of the dying campfire and looked up to see Arrow standing over him, flame-red beard braided tightly, an ornate axe gleaming in his grasp.

"It's been a while, Arrow," Lance replied, rising to his feet and extending a hand toward the dwarf.

Arrow lowered his weapon and clasped the warrior's hand firmly. "Warriors! I didn't expect to find you here," he said, glancing at the others. "What brings you to this part of the world? The last time you visited, it was with grim tidings. I hope your news is brighter today."

"Regrettably, we come with troubling news once more, my friend. Darkness has returned to our lands, and it's worse than before." Rubric interjected as he stepped beside Lance, "We need to speak with your council."

"I don't need permission to take you to our stronghold. You warriors are always welcome. Follow me," Arrow replied.

The weary team gathered their belongings, loaded them onto their horses, and mounted up. Ari gritted her teeth as she climbed into her saddle, pain still clinging to her ribs, while Sirine whispered quiet reassurances from behind. They trailed behind the red-haired dwarf along a tree-lined path. Behind them, ten dwarfs' scouts emerged like mist from the underbrush, their armor glinting beneath the early light as they fell into silent formation. As the sun began to rise behind Kinnick Mountain, its golden hue spilled across a familiar meadow, stretching before them in a burst of life.

Ari's eyes widened, momentarily forgetting the pain, "This place is stunning!" she said with a breathless smile, her voice softened by awe. The scent of soil and blossom surrounded her, the crisp mountain air filling her lungs. She knew this vision of beauty would remain etched in memory—an oasis before the storm. The group pressed onward, their horses steady beneath them as the path narrowed. Arrow led the way until they reached the base of South Mountain.

"Follow me, and I'll guide you along the hidden mountain path," Arrow announced, leading the group southward into the rocky corridor.

The party maneuvered into a single-file line, shadows dancing along the rocky corridor walls. Ari glanced at the damp stone beside her, recalling past journeys through this very passage. Suddenly, a shower of pebbles cascaded from above, bouncing across the uneven ground.

"Ouch!" the princess whispered softly as a small rock hit her shoulder. But when she finally spotted the light ahead, a wave of relief washed over her like a gentle tide.

The Falcon Ridge warriors stepped out from the mountain passage into the expansive, well-known terrain. By the time they arrived at the dwarfs' territory, the sun had risen above the eastern treetops, bathing the fortress grounds in a warm light, alive with the glow of campfires. Dwarf women, no taller than seventeen inches, were busy preparing breakfast. Their swift movements and cheerful chatter brought a sense of peace.

"You can set up camp here as you have in the past. I'll return shortly," Arrow informed Rubric. "I need to notify the council speaker that a meeting is necessary."

From afar, Spring spotted her friends gathered near the edge of the bustling fortress and eagerly pushed her cart filled with delectable food toward them. The warm aroma of oats and honey drifted ahead of her like a friendly breeze.

"It's so great to see all of you again! I take it you're hungry?" she called out cheerfully.

Zilar, still seated on the grass, rose with a welcoming smile and stepped forward to help the proud dwarf arrange the steaming oats, honey, and blueberries across the soft patch of green. "Thank you for your kindness, Spring," he said, nodding in appreciation. After a final grin, Spring turned and vanished into the swirl of fortress activity.

As the group began to eat, Lance stretched his arms overhead, casting a casual glance down the path. He nodded toward an approaching figure. "Arrow is coming this way."

Their conversation fell to a hush as the dwarf named Arrow neared, his gait purposeful and firm. Without preamble, he gestured for Rubric and his companions to follow. "Let's go." The group fell into step behind him as he led them fifty paces toward the grand council chamber. Four statues of dwarves flanked the imposing entrance; their features chiseled with reverence—the likenesses of ancient dwarfs' heroes guarding the threshold. Arrow gestured for the visitors to enter as the guards in dark uniforms swung the doors wide open. Inside, nine dwarves clad in green robes were seated upon a polished bench carved from mountain oak. The chamber was quiet, save for the faint rustling of the untouched green-and-white drapes that hung like sentries at either side.

Rubric and his friends bowed in respect.

"We have come to alert you about a new dark army of beasts, one that is more powerful than any we have encountered before," Rubric began, his voice steady. "In the Stragon Valley, this army is gaining strength. To succeed in this battle, we must join forces."

His words hung in the air like a challenge, met only by the soft rustling of the council's robes and the hushed exchange of whispers among the dwarves seated on the bench. Their faces remained stoic, unreadable beneath the flickering light that filtered through the towering windows. After a brief pause, the dwarf at the center stood up.

"It's late. You will spend the night in the fortress. We'll continue our discussion at dawn," he declared. Rubric furrowed his brow, instinctively turning toward the nearest window, where sunlight still poured across the chamber's stone floor. Puzzled, his companions exchanged quiet glances—but none dared question the council's word. Without another word, the council members rose in silence and filed out, their expressions unreadable as they passed by the gently swaying curtains.

The group looked at one another, puzzled by the early dismissal.

Arrow approached and gestured calmly. "You will be our guests," he said, leading them back toward the courtyard. Without another word, he then turned and made his way back to the meeting room.

As they settled once more by their camp, Zilar leaned closer to Rubric, his tone quiet and uncertain. "Do you think the dwarves will ally with us in Tonepass, Rubric?"

Rubric watched the entrance of the council chamber for a long moment. "I can't say for sure. If darkness takes hold, they will undoubtedly fall; I have no doubt about that," he replied.

As time went by, the guests took advantage of the unexpected reprieve—savoring food, drink, and moments of ease under the sun-dappled courtyard.

"We plan to head to the Kingdom of Elves soon," Rolyn said, tossing a glance at the southern horizon. "But we're still unsure of the route."

Lance absentmindedly fiddled with a stick in front of him and suggested, "Perhaps the dwarves could create a map for us. They must know the way."

"You're right, I am sure they are familiar with the route," Rolyn agreed, his gaze sweeping over the fortress grounds.

As the afternoon waned, bonfires began to crackle to life throughout the courtyard. Their glow bathed the stone walls in amber light, while the aroma of sizzling meat and simmering stews filled the air. Families gathered—laughter echoing among the carved columns and garden terraces. Wisps of smoke curled into the twilight sky, mingling with the scent of roasted quail, fresh cornbread, and wild vegetable stew.

Ari stood among the crowd, chuckling as she placed a hand on her rumbling stomach. "This feels so familiar to me," she murmured, her voice soft with nostalgia. Her eyes swept over the courtyard, where bonfires crackled and laughter spilled into the twilight air like music.

The evening feast kicked off with a jug of ale. Dwarf women arranged long tables just a few inches apart in the center of the courtyard, laden with hearty food and steaming drink. Carpenters and blacksmiths hurried to finish their day's work, washing off dust and sweat before joining the celebration. Children darted forward, laughter rising as they scrambled toward the feast.

"Come join us for a meal!" Arrow shouted, lifting a jug of ale and waving toward Rubric and his companions.

Music rose into the air, stringed instruments and drums blending with the clinking of mugs and warm voices. The fortress pulsed with life.

Rubric and his friends shared a laugh as they watched the vibrant festivities unfold. The gloom of war lifted—if only for an evening.

Rolyn turned to Ari with a playful grin, "Will you dance with me?" he asked, extending his hand.

"What a delightful invitation!" she exclaimed, eagerly taking his hand. "I would love to dance with you. Let's keep moving until the music fades into the night."

As the moon drifted westward above the mountains, casting a silvery light over the courtyard, Zilar quietly reminded them, "We should return to camp now. Tomorrow, we embark on the challenging journey to the Kingdom of Elves after our meeting."

"I agree," Rubric replied with a nod as he and the others wrapped up their night and made their way back to camp.

• • •

Dawn broke gently, bringing a warm late summer breeze. Sunlight spilled over the peaks of the Kinnick Mountains, stirring the fortress to life.

Sirine stood quietly beside Zilar, both gazing up into the brightening sky. Two eagles soared gracefully above, their wings stretched wide as they circled downward. Curiosity sparked within her—what could have brought them here? A flicker of worry passed through her thoughts as she hoped for their safety, watching them land with effortless poise on a delicate branch nearby.

Lundar's voice rang out, clear and urgent, "Sirine, we must depart at once. Efura's Pa has called for us. Our presence is urgently needed. I'm certain they've formulated a plan to confront the dark forces."

Without hesitation, Sirine nodded. "I'll inform the others of your departure."

Efura added with calm resolve, saying, "We'll reconvene in Tonepass Valley." With that, the two eagles ascended once more, wings slicing through the sky until they vanished beyond the treetops. As the sky cleared in their wake, movement stirred on the nearby path. Zilar's eyes lit up, and he raised his arms in delight. "Look! It's Spring, and she's approaching us with her cart!"

"Good morning! I trust you had a peaceful night," Spring greeted them with a radiant smile. "I've brought honey oats and fresh bread for everyone."

"Yes," Lance replied, beaming. "I slept like a baby." He stretched and stood, the chill of dawn fading from his bones as he moved to help lay out the food by the fire.

The group gathered for breakfast, enjoying the simple warmth of shared food and calm conversation. Once the meal was finished, they packed up their camp and prepared for what lay ahead.

Their chatter faded as they noticed a dwarf approaching, prompting Rolyn to remark, "Rubric, Arrow is rushing toward us."

Rubric nodded. "Let's go; the council is about to commence."

The warriors followed Arrow through the stone corridors into the meeting room, where the dwarfs awaited them. The one in the center urged, "Please, state your request again."

Rubric stepped forward with assurance.

"The malevolent sorcerer Tomar has somehow managed to survive. He has amassed a fearsome army of monstrous creatures, bolstered by a dark sorceress. The black crows act as their spies, keeping a vigilant watch over everything. Attempting a surprise attack would be futile. Our only hope lies in luring them to us," Rubric articulated before stepping back into formation.

Lance advanced with determination, taking two confident steps forward.

"The Valley of Tonepass will be our battlefield. We'll lay out a series of lethal traps to ensure that many of the beasts perish as they charge in. Eight hundred Kandora warriors are on their way to Tonepass Valley to join our ranks and are expected to arrive in eleven days. We believe the dark army will strike the Stronghold of Enwood, ideally taking out a significant number of their creatures. However, if that doesn't happen, we must be ready. Please send as many fighters as you can, as we requested. They need to reach Tonepass within the eleven-day timeframe. After the council meeting, we will proceed to the Kingdom of Elves to recruit more allies," Lance communicated to the gathering before stepping back to rejoin his fellow warriors.

The chief dwarf rose, cleared his throat, and placed his hands firmly on the bench.

"We had an extensive discussion last night and determined that our only course of action is to fight alongside you. You will have the backing of eight hundred warriors for this battle. To protect our families, the rest must stay behind." The dwarf representative declared, "Our fighters will arrive at Tonepass as you requested." Without further ceremony, the attendees stood and exited the chamber through the curtain-lined archways.

Once outside the chamber, Rubric said, "Arrow, it's time for us to depart. Can you guide us through the hidden passage?"

"Certainly, my friend, it would be a delight."

Arrow led them back to their accommodations, where they found that Spring had arranged provisions for their journey. The riders began to load their belongings onto their horses.

Lance and Zilar followed as Arrow guided them toward the concealed tunnel. Rubric and Rolyn walked alongside the women, quiet but watchful, with three dwarf guards trailing in formation like moss-covered statues come to life.

As they approached the exit, a hush fell over the group, the weight of departure settling gently in the air. Lance turned to his companion and said, "I'll catch you in Tonepass." Arrow responded with a strong handshake before vanishing back into the tunnel, leaving no trace of its existence.

Sirine paused, casting one last glance over her shoulder, but the tunnel had completely disappeared. She rubbed her aching right shoulder, the strain of travel settling into her bones as the warriors resumed their march.

A soft morning breeze danced behind them, trailing through the lush grass like a farewell. Its gentle whispers faded as the land shifted—green giving way to stone, the wild beauty of the valley yielding to a wide, rocky expanse that beckoned them forward into uncertainty.

With a heavy sigh, Sirine voiced her yearning, "I miss the soft whisper of summer leaves in the breeze." Her expression darkened as she looked toward the barren hills. "I sense danger lurking in the desolate, rocky mountains ahead." None of the others spoke, yet their silence told her they felt it too.

By dusk, the sun slipped behind the jagged silhouette of the Atron Mountains.

"We're about to enter a canyon I've never ventured into before," Rolyn announced as he dismounted and made his way to Ari's side. "Let's set up camp here and wait for dawn to explore the gorge."

He took her hand and pressed a kiss to it, his gaze lingering. "After a long day of riding, how are you holding up?"

"I'm feeling a bit achy, but I'm healing quickly thanks to the rest I had in the dwarves' stronghold," she admitted.

"I'm really looking forward to some sleep," Lance groaned as he slid off his horse, already unrolling his bedding and stifling a yawn.

Rolyn nodded in agreement as he settled beside Ari. "If we skip dinner tonight, we'll need to eat before we head out tomorrow," he reminded his companions, who all acknowledged his point with nods, the weariness of the day settling in their bones.

Above them, the moon cast a soft, silvery glow over the clearing where the warriors had gathered for a night of much-needed rest. The gentle rustle of leaves and distant hoots of nocturnal creatures provided a lullaby of sorts, easing them into sleep.

22nd Chapter

A s the first light of dawn crept over the horizon, the Falcon Ridge fighter halted at the brink of a narrow ravine. The terrain ahead was jagged and uncertain.

Rolyn dismounted his horse, his boots crunching softly against the gravel. "I'm uncertain about the dangers that may lurk in this gorge," he said, scanning the shadowed path ahead. "I can't evaluate any threats. We should lead the horses on foot." He gently stroked his horse's neck before taking hold of the reins.

The others followed suit, carefully guiding their steeds along the winding path flanked by steep cliffs. The sun had already climbed past midmorning, but drifting clouds began to dim its light, casting a muted haze over the canyon.

Sirine shivered as a tingling sensation crept up the nape of her neck. "This route to the Kingdom of Elves feels perilous," she murmured, her voice low. "But I know it's the quickest way, and we're running out of time."

Rolyn shouted, his eyes locked on the winding trail ahead. "We've made it halfway through the rocky terrain; let's pause for a moment to regain our strength before pushing on." He stopped, eyes narrowing on the winding trail. A faint frown creased his brow. "Do you notice that fog creeping toward us? It seems to be drawing nearer," his gaze swept the canyon walls, searching for movement. "Could it be that the canyon is swarming with insects?" He hesitated, stroking his chin thoughtfully. "Let's gather close; our horses are becoming restless, sensing something is off. Why do I keep hearing the sound of small stones tumbling around us? The path is getting tighter, and it's filling me with unease. I can sense danger approaching. We need to pick up the pace," he urged his companions.

"I share Rolyn's concern," Rubric said, his expression tightening. He glanced toward the fog and tightened his grip on the reins. "We must hurry."

As they pressed forward, a strange movement caught their eyes—far ahead, a cluster of shapes hovered in the haze, no bigger than insects at first glance. The team urged their horses to bunch closer together.

A sudden shriek cut through the canyon. "Look! They're stone creatures soaring through the air!" Ari cried, just as one swooped down and landed boldly on her shoulder.

"Ouch! It just bit me!" Zilar exclaimed, twisting his arm as he tried to shake it off.

"Quick! The mutants are trying to cut us off. They must thrive on flesh!" Rolyn warned, his voice carrying over the pounding of hooves. "Hop on your horses; we have to sprint for the exit. If they catch us, we'll end up as their next meal."

The warning came too late—the creatures were already all around them. Small, white rock mutants swarmed the air like shards of living stone, snapping at man and beast alike. Each time the attackers' bit, the horses reared back, snorting in alarm.

"It's difficult to breathe and see through all this dust," Zilar cried, yanking his cloak over his mouth and nose.

The warriors battled fiercely, blades flashing and hooves pounding, until they finally broke free from the ravine's grip. Dust settled behind them like a fading storm. "I've never witnessed bloodsuckers flying with such ferocity," Rolyn said, his breathing heavy. "We must locate a cluster of Mint Walloon flowers."

"Why are those flowers so crucial, Rolyn?" Ari asked, her voice tinged with doubt.

"The petals of this flower aid in drawing out the toxins from bites. Elves have utilized this bloom for as long as I can recall," Rolyn explained, trotting beside Rubric. "Be on the lookout for the Golden Koos soaring above. These birds have a special affinity for these plants." He continued, "When we reach the peak of the mountain, we should catch sight of them gracefully gliding over the blossoms."

Zilar frowned, still rubbing at the red welts on his arms. "How will I recognize the birds when I come across them?"

"The birds' shimmer with a celestial glow," Rolyn replied, scratching at the bothersome lumps on his arms. "Their wingtips and crowns twinkle in radiant gold, and their forms carry a softer shade of that same light."

As they pressed on, the rocky path gradually softened beneath their mounts' hooves. The group navigated a lush terrain adorned with towering plants, a welcome contrast to the harsh rocks they had recently crossed. Upon reaching the summit, the warriors reined in their horses, eyes scanning the heavens for the elusive birds.

"Look! The sky sparkles like diamonds in the west!" Zilar shouted, his excitement contagious as he pointed toward the birds darting about.

"Yes, young one. You've found the Golden Koos and the flowers we need to heal our wounds," came Rolyn's reply. Without delay, the riders made their way down the mountainside, winding through narrow slopes until they reached a meadow awash in vibrant blooms.

"They're incredible! They look like tiny sparks of light," Ari shouted, captivated by the sight of the birds playing in the meadow.

At that moment, a particularly bold Koo fluttered down and perched lightly on Sirine's shoulder as they entered a small valley filled with purple and orange flowers. She felt a wave of joy as the charming little bird brushed its soft feathers against her cheek.

The warriors dismounted swiftly, moving among the blooms with a mix of urgency and awe. They knelt to gather the aromatic petals scattered across the meadow, the scent sweet and calming in the warm air.

"This flower is truly enchanting, Rolyn!" Zilar exclaimed, his eyes wide with wonder as he watched the large bump on his arm disappear. He continued to caress the flower against his face and neck, his joy evident.

"I believe we should collect some of these blooms," Rolyn suggested, gently placing the vivid flowers into his saddlebag. "They could prove useful later on."

"That's a brilliant idea," Rubric agreed, "but we also need to explore their other qualities." The warriors nodded in unison, observing their bumps fade away. "Perhaps their potency will increase as they dry."

Rolyn turned to his comrades and declared, "By nightfall, we will arrive at the Kingdom of Elves. The elf scouts will undoubtedly sense our presence after dark." With that, Rubric, along with the elf, led them through the rugged mountain paths until they finally reached their destination.

As the sun dipped behind the Atron Mountains, the riders halted for the night after descending the sixth peak. Fatigue enveloped them like a heavy shroud, leaving them too drained to eat. They chose to forgo the fire and ended the day in silent reflection beneath the cooling sky.

At dawn, their rest was broken. The warriors awoke to find themselves surrounded.

A commanding voice shattered the morning calm, proclaiming, "You have intruded upon the Kingdom of the High Sun Elves and must leave at once."

When Rubric opened his blue eyes, he was met with the sight of arrows pointed at them by the elves. Nearby, Lance and the lead warrior stood with their hands raised in surrender.

"We have come to warn you of a rising, malevolent army. We seek a meeting with your High Council," Rolyn said, standing to join his companions.

"Lagar, we must call a council with Kendar," Rubric urged, his tone urgent and his face etched with concern.

"As I seek the chief's approval and gather the council members, darkness will have descended," Lagar replied. "You will be staying at my home during your visit, and a scout will guide you there. Please make yourselves at home," his eyes drifted briefly toward the north before he turned to give orders.

"Come with me. I'll show you where you will spend the night," said a scout with striking blue-tinted hair. Just twenty feet to the south, across the fortress, the travelers noticed a robust wooden building. "This will serve as your home until the meeting is arranged. Lagar has an abundance of food and ale to keep you satisfied while you wait." With that, the elf turned and departed.

The warriors passed through an east-facing archway and entered the expansive stone structure. The west wall was adorned with stained glass windows, showcasing a vibrant rainbow arching over a herd of antelopes grazing on lush grass.

Rubric noticed a small seal at the bottom of the stained glass, marking it as Lagar's family crest. The room was filled with intricately carved redwood furniture, including eight high-backed chairs surrounding a large central table. An iron wood-burning stove stood in the kitchen, while three neatly made beds lined the southern wall. The north wall featured elaborately carved redwood cabinets, and the floor was covered with soft bearskin rugs.

As Rubric and his companions absorbed the details of their new surroundings, time seemed to slip away. The light dimmed, and the sun dipped lower toward the West Mountains, casting the room in a warm, fading glow.

Outside, Zilar and his companion stepped into the open air, spotting the same scout they met earlier, making his way from the north.

"The time for the council had come. Let me escort you to the chamber," the elf declared to the guests.

The team trailed behind the scout until he stopped in front of a lavish chamber entrance.

The warriors climbed the radiant white stone steps alongside the elf, reaching a grand entrance flanked by six sentinels on each side. As the double doors, adorned with golden embellishments, swung wide, they were welcomed into a splendid hall filled with stunning sculptures of the Great Elves. The elaborate carvings on the ceiling and walls were unfamiliar to them, prompting a respectful bow as they entered, embodying the essence of true warriors.

"Welcome! It's a pleasure to see you again, though I wish the news you bring were not so dire," Chief Kendar greeted, recognizing the team from the dwarfs' council.

Rubric stepped forward, taking a moment to collect his thoughts. "Indeed, the forces of darkness have returned to our homeland. I must relay what I shared with the dwarves and the Kandoran rebels."

He drew a steady breath before speaking. "Tomar, the malevolent sorcerer, has resurfaced, and his power has surged to alarming levels. It is rumored that he has absorbed his wife's abilities, making him nearly invincible. Together with a dark sorceress, he has gathered a formidable army of fearsome creatures, each enhanced in intelligence, strength, and savagery. They are currently stationed in Stragon Valley, growing stronger with each passing day. To have any hope of combating this evil, we must unite our warriors. The dwarves and freedom fighters are en route to

Tonepass Valley to strengthen our defenses against this deadly horde." He gathered his thoughts, then went on.

"Easha, the powerful white sorceress, accompanied by two dragon-shifting zundars and the eagle colony, will lend their strength in this battle. A surprise assault would be futile, as they have crow spies keeping a close watch on our every move. We must remain patient until the dark forces draw near. Once they enter the valley, we will strike back. Rumors suggest that their first target will be the Enwood Stronghold. The Rulers' scouts will undoubtedly notify the fortress when the mutant army approaches." Rubric's voice softened as he reached for the water at his side, taking a sip before continuing.

"The Enwood army boasts over five thousand warriors. Even if Pildar's forces manage to eliminate a considerable number of the beasts, we will still have to confront Tomar and his sorceress. Easha, the Sorceress, is our greatest hope against the malevolent sorcerer. We will create a diversion, then take out his sorceress and the remaining troops. Rolyn will provide you with the specifics of our strategy," Rubric announced as he stepped back to rejoin the group.

The room grew still as Rolyn moved to the center. Every eye was fixed on him, the crackle of the council hall's torches the only sound.

"We have explored various strategies," Rolyn began, his voice steady, "and concluded that our most effective defense lies in setting lethal traps along the tree line of the Valley of Tonepass. This approach will eliminate many creatures before the battle even begins. I implore you to stand with us in this critical fight against the forces of darkness. If you agree to send warriors, they must arrive in Tonepass within seven days. We will have fourteen days to prepare and fortify our defenses against the dark army. Tomar's primary goal is to eliminate the powerful white Sorceress. He believes that once she is defeated, he will face no further opposition in claiming Seledor," Rolyn stated, watching Kendar's response. Slowly, the chief rose, adjusting his robe with measured dignity.

"The council and I have decided to face the encroaching darkness with unwavering resolve," Kendar declared. "We will dispatch two thousand warriors to stand by your side in battle. They will convene on the appointed day," he assured, then, without further ceremony, he turned and disappeared behind the shimmering golden curtains.

The tension in the room eased. Lagar stepped forward with a warm smile. "Let's take a break and enjoy a meal," he said, gesturing for them to follow.

The offer was welcome after the long discussions. "Thanks, Lagar; resting in a hut sounds wonderful," Rolyn replied, appreciating the offer.

"I've stashed cots beneath each bed for you, Rolyn," Lagar mentioned as they made their way through the corridors.

Grateful for the gesture, Rolyn responded, "You and the women can take the beds; the rest of us will make do with the cots."

They followed Lagar into a spacious dining hall, where long redwood tables gleamed under the soft light of hanging crystal lanterns. Platters of roasted vegetables, fresh bread, and steaming venison stew awaited them, alongside jugs of sweet, spiced ale. The warriors ate heartily, speaking little at first, but the warmth of the food and the mellow drink slowly loosened their tongues. Lagar shared tales of the High Sun Elves' victories and festivals, and for a short time, the worries of the coming war seemed far away.

When the meal was done and the tables cleared, Lagar led them through the quiet corridors to their quarters. Lance and Rolyn quickly retrieved the cots and set them up. Sirine's bed was conveniently placed right next to Rubric's cot, while the elf adjusted his cot next to Ari's. The soft glow from a nearby lantern bathed the room in gold as they prepared to wind down for the night.

Outside, the fortress was silent, save for the distant whisper of wind in the trees.

By the time dawn approached, that whisper had turned into a restless murmur. Ominous storm clouds loomed on the horizon, casting a grey pall over the elves' stronghold.

"If we want to reach our destination in three days, we need to start packing now. I hope we can miss the storm," the lead warrior stated, tightening the straps on his pack and securing his bedding to his horse. "If not, we'll seek shelter along the way."

Rolyn turned to their host, "Lagar, it would be amazing if you could guide us through the passage."

"Not only will I lead you through the tunnel, but it would also be an honor to travel with you again," Lagar replied warmly.

With their gear packed and weapons checked, the seven warriors mounted their horses. The fortress gates opened with a low groan, and the group rode northward toward the Valley of Tonepass. Behind them, the towers of the elf's kingdom faded into the mist, while ahead, the storm's shadow stretched across the land.

23rd Chapter

Far to the west, Pildar's Bastion loomed majestically atop a hill in the bustling Kingdom of Enwood, just beyond the Seabray River. The southern section of the fortress had been recently dismantled to facilitate a significant expansion for his ever-growing army.

Robust stone walls encircled the stronghold, their height and thickness rendering it nearly impregnable. Beyond them, the outer defenses were constructed from long timber beams, firmly secured with heavy chain pulleys.

To bolster security, guards would raise the wooden slats against the palace walls each night, locking the fortress into a state of fortified slumber. When the wide, flat timber panels were lowered, the Ruler felt assured that they would obliterate any threat bold enough to approach.

Surrounding the fortress was a treacherous moat filled with tainted, stagnant water. Anyone foolish enough to attempt a crossing would meet a grim fate, ensnared by deadly traps lurking just beneath the surface. Each corner of the stone edifice was crowned with towering spires, where guards clad in black vigilantly scanned for any signs of intruders. A long, sturdy timber drawbridge spanned the moat, ensuring that no one could enter or exit without permission.

"Guard, summon Marco at once!" Pildar commanded, rising from his luxurious red and white velvet royal seat and striding purposefully across the grand chamber. His face flushed with fury, prompting the head warrior to leap into action at the Ruler's behest.

"I must act quickly," the guard muttered under his breath, "or I'll face the Ruler's ire."

Hastily making his way through the entrance, Marco entered the Potentate's chamber moments later. "Yes, my Ruler, you called for me," he sighed, kneeling briefly before standing again.

"How many soldiers are currently under my command?" Pildar glared at the lead warrior, whose short arms and wiry, mercury-red hair shimmered in the light.

"We currently have five thousand troops and are in the process of expanding, my lord," Marco replied carefully.

Pildar's left foot tapped impatiently. His arms were crossed, and his brow was furrowed—clear signs the Ruler's frustration was escalating.

"Am I not the most powerful Ruler in Seledor because of the might of my army? Isn't that true?"

"Yes, my lord, that is true. I know of no army as formidable as yours," Marco replied, trying to gauge Pildar's mood.

"Then why do the liberation militants continue to operate freely? I will not tolerate this! I demand that the rebels be either eliminated or conscripted into my ranks!" Pildar roared. He hurled a chair across the room, the crash echoing off the stone walls. "Take eight hundred fighters to carry out my orders!"

"Forgive me, my lord, but the rebels are always on the move." Marco's complexion paled as he spoke, his throat dry with fear.

"Are you implying that you are foolish? Only a fool would fail to track the rebels!" Pildar shouted, slamming his fist on the table, causing his ale mug to rattle.

"I swear to you, my lord, I will either eliminate or capture the traitors as you command. We will set out at dawn." Marco took a step back from Pildar, beads of sweat glistening on his forehead.

"Why not leave at once?" the unyielding sovereign bellowed. "I demand you obey my orders without delay!" With that, he hurled the mug at the knight. The stein shattered against the wall as Marco deftly dodged the flying object.

"I agree; we will depart once our Keepers of the Armor have readied our horses for battle." Marco exited the chamber, his boots echoing on the stronghold's stone floor, flecked with gold, as he navigated through the chilly corridors, turning left and then right.

On the southern wall, hung an impressive charcoal portrait of Pildar, embellished with gold accents. The hallways sparkled with gold, silver, and precious stones.

Oil lanterns illuminated the corridor, spaced ten feet apart and perched on golden stone ledges.

Guards clad in blue uniforms stood vigilant at every corner, watching silently as Marco strode past. Marco stepped outside and crossed the courtyard towards the living quarters. The determined fighter entered the room with intent. The sharp sound of Marco's sword clanging against a metal barrel signaled to the others that a meeting was about to begin.

The men hurried to the meeting room. Marco stood confidently before them, hands resting on the podium, and declared, "We will pursue the rebels as commanded by Pildar. They will meet their end unless they join the royal army. Keepers, prepare the horses and gather the armor." At this command, a young boy dashed into the next room to alert the others. The sound of hurried footsteps and the clatter of armor soon filled the air as the Keepers moved to obey.

As the sun reached its zenith, the Sovereign's army mounted their warhorses, and the call to action resonated as Marco thrust his arm forward. "We ride!" he shouted, and the riders fell into formation, maintaining a respectful twenty-foot distance behind him as they crossed the vast drawbridge in pairs.

With urgency, the soldiers sped eastward towards the Seabray River, where a large barge awaited them at the water's edge. The fighter recognized it as their vessel, ready to ferry them across the flowing waters. They quickly arrived at the riverbank and halted.

"Dismount!" Marco commanded, and the men swiftly dismounted, leading their horses onto the swaying deck of the ship, which rocked with the current.

"Board the ship immediately! What's causing the delay? Are you scared of the water?" The commander's voice boomed across the deck as he ran his fingers through his hair in frustration. The soldiers carefully led their hesitant horses onto the vessel, but progress was slow. After a grueling three hours, two hundred soldiers and their steeds were finally on board. Marco took a deep breath, his complexion paling as sweat trickled down his forehead. He wiped his clammy palm across his shirt.

"Tollack, Rodder, help me get on the ship. My vision is blurring. Hurry!" he yelled, panic creeping into his voice. "We don't have all day," he added, gripped by the fear of the rushing river.

"Captain, you will disembark at Dragon Cove," he was reminded once they were aboard. Marco replied with authority, "Take the quickest route."

"Excuse me, Marco," Bors, the second-in-command, interjected cautiously. "I mean no disrespect, but we should dock well before reaching Dragon Cove. If we don't, our journey will take twice as long. The Candora Mountains lie to the north, not the south."

"I know these mountains like the back of my hand. Do not question my judgment. I am your Master. Disobey me again, and you will face the consequences. Get out of my sight!" he bellowed, his forehead veins throbbing with intensity.

The barge rocked violently on the turbulent waters, sending waves of dread through Marco. The river's menacing currents filled his mind, draining the color from his face as panic set in. Sweat formed on his freckled skin, and his breathing quickened, signaling the onset of another anxiety attack. The warriors around him noticed his distress but chose to remain silent, wary of the potential fallout from any show of concern.

After what seemed like an age, the ship finally docked at Dragon Cove. Following Marco, two hundred men and their horses disembarked, completing the journey with a total of eight hundred warriors across four trips.

The Master's voice rang out, "Mount up!" The knights swiftly climbed onto their horses and rode a short distance from the riverbank, where their leader brought them to a halt.

As the sun dipped behind the West Atron Mountains, Marco reined in his horse and dismounted. He climbed onto a large boulder and raised his arms in triumph, the evening breeze playfully ruffling his hair.

Curious soldiers gathered around, expecting orders and eager to hear his plan.

Taking a deep breath, Marco declared coldly, "You will set up camp tonight without food or warmth. This is your punishment for delaying our departure from the ship."

He stepped down from the boulder, led his horse away from the group, and began building a small fire. From his saddlebag, he retrieved his provisions and settled onto a log beside the flames, enjoying the meal he had brought while facing his men.

With a low chuckle, Marco teased, "I hope you enjoy your night." The sight of his men shivering in the darkness, cold and hungry, amused him as he nestled comfortably in his warm blankets, his stomach satisfied.

Not far away, Bors, the second-in-command, approached his loyal companions, a puzzled expression on his face.

"Where are Marco's guards?" he asked, tossing his bedding onto the ground as a tall, slender soldier with brown hair glanced at him, clearly bewildered.

"He stubbornly refuses to share his rations with anyone, not even his fellow allies. He's a spiteful, malevolent man," Bors asserted, then crouched down to whisper, "If we want to succeed in this mission, we must eliminate Marco, or he'll lead us to our doom."

A worried soldier with thin, dirty-blonde hair stood to Bors' left and interjected, "This mission poses significant risks. Most of the men are loyal to the commander. We must act quickly to prevent any doubts about what transpired."

"Exactly, that's right. We need a foolproof strategy," Bors concurred.

Edgar, a stocky figure with jet-black hair and deep brown eyes, leaned in and whispered, "I spotted a toxic plant when I disembarked from the barge." His right eye twitched with unease.

"That's a smart idea," Bors said, eyes narrowing in thought. "You can slip out tonight after everyone has gone to sleep to gather the plant. Just be careful not to poison yourself. I'll crush it and prepare the juice for Marco. Does anyone have a small, sharp tool? I'll make two punctures in Marco's leg. Everyone will think he was bitten by a venomous snake or spider."

"I saw a thorn bush just behind the trees where we're standing," another warrior chimed in, pointing into the shadows. "I'm sure it will do the trick."

"Edgar, we'll pretend to be asleep, and I'll nudge you when it's time to set our plan in motion. The moonlight will be bright enough for you to locate the plant," Bors instructed as he laid out his bedding on the ground, keeping his movements casual.

"I hear something in the trees behind us," Bors said, standing up and moving closer to the nearest trees. As he peered through the underbrush, he spotted a thorn bush. He carefully plucked a sharp thorn from its branch and tucked it into his pocket. When he returned to the camp, his companions were lying still, feigning sleep beneath the pale light of the moon.

• • •

Edgar stirred, rising to his feet as the half-moon cast a cold sheen over the slumbering warriors. He surveyed the surroundings, straining to catch any hint of movement. Satisfied that everyone was still asleep, the knight stealthily made his way into the trees, heading towards the Seabray River. The biting cold wind stung his skin, and adrenaline surged through him. Each rustle of the leaves heightened his anxiety, causing his hands to shake and his throat to feel parched. He halted, listening intently, his mind racing with thoughts.

The moonlight will guide me to the river. I'll trace the horses' tracks until I reach the water's edge, he thought.

When the pale gleam of the Seabray came into view, he also spotted the hazardous plant they sought. He crouched down, contemplating his next move. *I need to gather some leaves to shield my hands.*

After a swift scan of the area, he spotted a leafy bush just three feet away and quickly collected twenty leaves, urgency swirling in his thoughts.

These should be enough to protect me from the poison, he thought, glancing up. *I hadn't noticed the moonlight shimmering on the river's surface until now.*

After a brief moment of taking in the water's beauty, he placed the leaves on a small hedge and approached the riverbank, plunging his hands into the icy water. The cold bit into his skin, but he forced himself to continue, coating his fingers with a thick layer of mud.

Perched on a log, he reminded himself, *I'll uproot the plant once the mud has dried.*

Five minutes passed, and he shook off the excess dirt.

The mud had hardened.

With care, he grasped the toxic bush by its roots, lifted it from the ground, and set it atop the shrub before standing up to retrieve his makeshift gloves.

I need to hurry back to camp before anyone notices, he told himself, scanning the trees before heading back.

Meanwhile, the second-in-command remained alert, eyes fixed on the forest's edge, eagerly awaiting Edgar's return.

A dark silhouette slipped behind a tree, bathed in moonlight. Bors rose and made his way to his waiting companion. He gathered the plant, set it on a rock, and crushed the leaves with a smaller stone until their liquid oozed out. Using a twig, he carefully extracted the toxic essence from a leaf, burying the leftover poison deep in the soil to erase any trace of its source.

With the poison secured, Bors crept to Marco's side while he was still in slumber. Kneeling beside him, he pressed his thumb against Marco's chin, pried his mouth open, and let the deadly liquid flow inside. He waited, listening to the steady rhythm of Marco's breathing, and after a few tense moments, ensured that no sign of the substance remained. The two men lingered until the moon hung low over the Western Mountains. Then, with precise, practiced movements, Bors retrieved the thorn from his pocket, lifted Marco's pant leg, and made two quick punctures on his left ankle—just deep enough to mimic the bite of a venomous creature. They slipped to their bedrolls, blending once more into the circle of sleeping warriors.

24th Chapter

The biting wind carried whispers as it danced through the branches of the trees. The sun began to rise over the Kinnick Mountains, painting the dawn in soft shades of pink. The soldiers of Pildar stirred from their slumber, feeling the chill and hunger gnawing at their insides.

Tundar, the third-in-command, rose and remarked, "Marco is still asleep," he said, frowning. "This isn't like him. His fire still flickers, yet he lies motionless. We should rouse him; he may be unwell." He rubbed his arms for warmth as he and ten comrades approached Marco's resting place.

One of the warriors spoke up, "Commander, forgive my bluntness, but it's time for you to wake up."

Marco remained unresponsive. Tundar grasped his stiff arm, searching for any sign of life, but found none.

"I fear Marco is dead!" a tall, blond guard exclaimed; his voice laced with escalating anxiety. The fighters instinctively encircled their leader protectively as Tundar declared, "This can't be right. He must still be alive." He crouched beside Marco, eyes scanning the still form. The fire crackled nearby, casting flickering shadows across the warrior's face. At that moment, another loyal guard with shoulder-length black hair reached out to touch the Master Warrior, only to be met with the unsettling chill of his skin. "This is strange; he was perfectly healthy when he went to sleep."

Tundar pressed his fingers against Marco's neck, hoping for a pulse. Nothing. "You're right; Marco is gone, but how did this happen?" He leaned in closer, desperately seeking any signs that might explain the tragedy. As he examined the body, he lifted Marco's left leg and spotted two tiny puncture wounds near the ankle. "A snake must have bitten him," he concluded grimly. "The fire likely attracted it. What should we do now?" Confusion clouded his mind, mirroring the uncertainty felt by his comrades. The realization settled over the group like a shroud. No one spoke. The wind rustled through the trees, as if nature itself mourned the loss.

Edgar stepped forward, his tone steady but solemn. "Bors, the second-in-command, is now our Commander. He will lead us into battle."

News quickly spread through the ranks that Bors had assumed command and that Marco had perished. The camp, once filled with quiet camaraderie, now buzzed with tension and grief.

Bors stepped forward from the edge of the clearing, his armor dusted with frost, his face grim. He looked down at Marco's body for a long moment before speaking.

"We will give Marco a dignified burial. Gather wood and stack it high around him. Then we will follow Pildar's orders," Bors declared with authority.

"No! I will take my friend back to the fortress for a proper burial," Derdar, one of Marco's devoted guards, protested, crossing his arms defiantly.

"That's not an option. Marco has no family at the stronghold. Pildar will be furious if we return with him, and we will face the consequences. I am in charge now. Collect the wood as I instructed!" Bors shouted, his expression firm.

Reluctantly, the warriors obeyed. They gathered firewood from the surrounding brush, stacking it high around Marco's body. The flames soon roared to life, consuming their fallen commander in a blaze of orange and ash. Smoke curled into the sky, carrying the scent of burning pine and loss.

"It's time to saddle up," Bors commanded, mounting his stallion and steering his men northward toward the Candora Mountains. "We have a lengthy journey ahead," he added, wiping the sweat from his forehead.

• • •

As the caravan moved forward, whispers rippled through the ranks. The news of Marco's death had unsettled the riders, creating a quiet divide between his loyal followers and the rest.

"Tundar," Edgar said, riding alongside him, "why can't you accept that a venomous bite led to Marco's death? He chose to sit alone by the fire, and that was his own doing. I bet he had food scraps all over him."

Tundar's jaw tightened. "I refuse to accept your version of events." He spat into the dirt, then wiped his mouth with the back of his hand. "I believe one of his own men took him out."

Edgar's eyes narrowed. "Let's not forget, Marco was a merciless killer who reveled in the slaughter of innocent villagers. At the very least, we should stop this rumor. We can't afford a rebellion among the riders."

"No, he was my friend." Tundar's face flushed with anger.

"If he was truly your friend, you would have shared a camp with him. But he was cruel and selfish, only looking out for himself. He got what he deserved," Edgar retorted sharply.

"That's a lie," Tundar shot back, and in a flash of rage, kicked Edgar's horse, making it stumble.

"My horse nearly went down!" Edgar roared. "He could have been injured!"

Furious, Edgar yanked Tundar off his mount. The two men tumbled into the dust, fists clenched, eyes blazing. Around them, the other riders slowed, watching the confrontation unfold. Edgar stormed off, brushing dirt from his tunic as he raced toward Bors, who rode ahead at the front of the column.

"My friend, Tundar and Marco's supporters will soon rise up," Edgar muttered, his voice low and troubled. "They won't stop spreading the rumor that he was murdered."

Bors didn't flinch. "Don't worry, my friend; by morning, I'll find a way to quiet the story about Marco." He turned in the saddle, scanning the horizon. The sun dipped low, casting long shadows across the rocky terrain. "Night is approaching," he said. Then, raising his voice, he called out to the riders, "We'll stop for the night once we reach the baseline!" The senior commander placed a hand on his thigh, tilted his head back, and shook the dust from his hair before urging his horse forward.

When they arrived at a vast open stretch of land, Bors reined in his stallion and called out to his men, "Night is almost upon us. We'll set up camp here for the night."

The warriors dismounted from their horses, their boots crunching against dry ground as they spread out to establish their camps. Edgar joined Bors as they surveyed the scene, taking in the sight of more than fifty campsites. As the day drew to a close, the fighters gathered around the fires, relishing a hearty meal of venison. The scent of roasted meat mingled with the smoke, drifting across the camp like a balm against the weariness of the journey.

But Bors found no comfort in the food or fire. Throughout the night, he wrestled with his thoughts.

I need to come up with a plan to dispel any growing suspicions. The thought of the soldiers rebelling over Marco's death fills me with dread. My strategy is to divide the troops into two groups. I can isolate the troublemakers and keep control. I believe this will be effective; I am confident of it.

As dawn broke, a brisk wind swept through the camp, stirring the embers and sending wisps of smoke spiraling into the clear midsummer sky. The warriors stirred from sleep, their cloaks drawn tight against the chill.

After a quick morning meal, Bors climbed onto a high rock overlooking the camp. He struck his metal water jug with his sword, the clang echoing across the clearing. Loose sand shifted beneath his boots as his brown hair danced in the breeze.

"I have decided: we need to divide into two teams. This is the quickest way to track down the rebels," he announced, observing the soldiers' responses. "One group will move west, while the other will head north. Tundar, you will be in charge of the western team." His tone was resolute, and his expression reflected his determination. "I will lead the remaining troops going north."

Tundar responded, "I haven't explored the western territory before, and I'm not familiar with the landscape we might face." He considered Bors's decision to split their forces.

Bors continued, "When you encounter a rock formation, turn right and follow the well-worn dirt path. That will lead you back to us. We'll regroup in the Candora Mountains in three days."

The second leader agreed with a nod, saying, "That appears to be quite simple."

"Prepare to set off!" the chief ordered, gesturing for the two teams to depart in different directions.

As the northern group advanced through a narrow gorge, Edgar rode alongside Bors, his voice low and cautious. "Should they follow your suggestion and veer to the right, they could stumble upon a hidden cliff that would plunge them onto the sharp rocks beneath."

Bors didn't look back. "Exactly; they must stay alert to avoid danger."

• • •

Three days went by without a trace of Tundar and his troops.

Bors came to a stop and faced his warriors. "We have just one day left before we reach the Candora Mountains. Get ready for a fierce battle. It would be beneficial if Tundar and his men could rendezvous with us there." At that moment, he noticed a glimmer of light from a figure three trees away to the east, partially obscured by foliage. He waved his arm in a wide arc.

The warriors instantly understood. They fanned out, surrounding the mysterious figure with practiced precision. The trees creaked as the wind whistled through the forest, and dry leaves twirled above the forest floor, adding a sense of electric tension to the moment.

A voice rang out, firm and commanding. "There's no escape, so you must surrender. We mean you no harm." With his sword drawn, a formidable warrior inquired, "What brings you here alone?" The tall stranger, standing at six feet with a powerful build, came to a stop. His light-brown hair, pulled back, shimmered in the sunlight as he stood with confidence, two swords gripped tightly at his sides. "Seledor is on the brink of an assault from an army tainted by dark magic. They will annihilate anyone who opposes them. I've come to carve a path for the brave souls ready to confront these beasts."

Bors, disturbed by the revelation, responded, "We've received no word about this impending conflict."

"In eighteen days, they will launch their attack, starting with the stronghold of Pildar. You need to go back and alert the fortress. Get them ready for the impending battle," the stranger urged, identifying them as soldiers of Pildar by their distinctive armor.

Riding next to the stranger, Bors declared, "You are our prisoner now and will come with us to notify the ruler about this looming threat."

The stranger's gaze hardened. "I refuse to yield. You can either take my life or allow me to walk free, but I will not bow down. I will resist until my final breath, and you, along with many others, will face your demise alongside me. I urge you to journey to Stragon Valley to uncover the truth for yourselves. However, be forewarned: before you reach the fortress of the sinister forces, you and your men will endure a merciless slaughter." The stranger continued, "You are invited to join our battle against the dark army." Then, with a quick flick of his wrist, he spun his twin swords in a blur of motion, severing two thick branches from a nearby tree with effortless precision.

Bors inhaled deeply, gathering his resolve before addressing his enthusiastic soldiers whose eyes were wide with uncertainty and awe.

"Pildar will be displeased with our return if we arrive without the other soldiers. If you are prepared to face the forces of darkness, lift your swords high. Those who wish to withdraw may return to the fortress and report our situation to the Ruler and the townspeople," Bors announced.

A moment of silence passed—fifty valiant fighters advanced, swords held aloft, ready to confront the encroaching shadows. Meanwhile, the remaining soldiers turned back, making their way toward the safety of Enwood Stronghold.

"I am Bors, the leader of this group. We will unite with you to confront the dark army," he declared.

"My companions refer to me as Omond. The trek to the Valley of Tonepass is lengthy and filled with peril. This valley will serve as our battlefield," the stranger replied, sheathing his blades.

"Omond, can you lead us to the Tonepass Mountains? I am not well-acquainted with this territory. If we are to aid in the battle against the dark forces, we must remain on the right path," Bors asked.

Omond gave a single nod. "I will guide you."

The men shed their armor, letting it clatter to the ground below like falling shields. They mounted their horses, lighter and faster now, ready for the journey ahead.

At the front rode Omond, twin swords strapped across his back, astride a black stallion. Behind him, fifty warriors followed, their eyes fixed on the horizon as they rode north—toward the Valley of Tonepass, and the battle that would decide their fate.

25th Chapter

A s the final stars faded from the sky, dawn began to stir. The sky unfolded in a stunning panorama, painted with hues of deep blue and soft gold. The sun began to rise over the Kinnick Mountains, casting a gentle warmth across the rugged terrain and illuminating the early morning mist that clung to the trees.

Omond stirred first. Rising from his bedroll, he scanned the campsite, observing that his companions were still deep in slumber, and called out, "It's time to rise. The days are passing quickly, and we have a long journey ahead." The call roused the camp. Groggy murmurs followed as men sat up, blinking against the light. Omond scattered dirt over the fading embers with his right foot—a silent signal that rippled through the other camps.

Without pausing for breakfast, the group mounted their horses and started their descent down the rugged mountainside. An air of tension lingered as the riders maneuvered through the rocky trails and dense underbrush. The sun enveloped the horsemen in warmth at the base of the East Mountains. They traversed a meadow alive with vibrant yellow flowers set against a backdrop of rich greenery. As they continued northward, the sweet fragrances of oak and wildflowers diminished, giving way to the ascent of a new, unfamiliar mountain range.

Sensing the shift, Omond slowed his stallion and raised a hand. "The expansive branches of the trees conceal numerous threats. We must remain vigilant about our surroundings. Let's reduce our speed; this will help us steer clear of any unexpected dangers."

The riders nodded, adjusting their formation. The sound of hooves softened as they moved more deliberately, eyes scanning the dense foliage above and around them. Time stretched thin as the afternoon wore on. As the afternoon sun began its descent, tiny specks of dust danced in the air, caught in the waning light. The leaves whispered, and the branches swayed softly. The group's unease intensified, urging them to carefully survey their environment.

Edgar, riding near the front, nervously rubbed his jaw as Omond brought the column to a halt.

"We will proceed into Cadrem Forest in a single line," he instructed. "This forest may conceal hidden dangers. Be cautious of gopher holes; they could cause your horse to stumble and fall." With a sweeping motion, the leader signaled for them to move into the smallest forest in the realm of Seledor.

As they made their way through the towering trees, shadows danced on the ground, cast by sunlight filtering through the leaves.

The sound of hooves on soft ground replaced the clatter of stone. The forest was quiet—too quiet. No birdsong. No rustling of small creatures. Just the creak of saddles and the occasional snort from a wary horse. A tall man with vibrant red hair glanced between the trunks and commented, "It's strange that we haven't seen any wildlife."

His words lingered in the silence. Moments later, the group stepped out from the shadows of the great trees into a desolate meadow. The grass was brittle, the soil cracked—devoid of flowers and untouched by life. A stillness hung over the land like a warning. Omond scanned the terrain ahead and said, "We are approaching the Valley of Tonepass. If we shift our course to the north, we can avoid the Kinnick Mountains to our east. In just two days, we will reach the Tonepass Mountains. Remain alert for any foes that may appear."

Suddenly, the horses lifted their heads, ears twitching, nostrils flaring. A sharp chorus of neighs broke the silence.

"Draw your swords!" the leader commanded, adding, "The horses can sense a threat that we cannot see."

A cloud of dust billowed in the western sky, indicating that creatures were lurking in the basin. The riders turned toward it, eyes narrowing as the haze thickened. Then they saw them. Dark shapes surged forward—swift, unnatural, relentless. The gilzdars.

Omond shouted, urging his horse forward, "We must flee; we stand no chance in this battle!"

With urgency, the riders turned their steeds and raced across the barren meadow, hooves pounding against dry ground. Dust rose in thick clouds behind them as the ground trembled beneath their flight.

"Death!" the gilzdars shouted, brandishing their weapons high in the air.

Bors glanced back. The grotesque mutants surged forward, their glossy black scales glinting in the sunlight. Their heads were reptilian and cruel, their eyes burning with bloodlust.

"Launch the catapult! Annihilate the humans!" ordered the largest of the beasts.

A thunderous crack split the air. The monsters unleashed a ferocious barrage. Massive boulders fell from the sky, crashing down on the retreating soldiers. The ground shook with each impact. Screams echoed across the valley as men and horses were struck, thrown, or crushed beneath the falling stone. Those who managed to escape were left with bruises from the debris. Injured horses and men crumpled to the ground, while the unscathed scrambled onto the nearest mount, desperate to escape the chaos.

Some of the wounded, unable to flee, made a grim choice—choosing death over the torment of being devoured by the advancing gilzdars. The unyielding downpour of stones persisted, sending plumes of dust and rubble into the air, obscuring the battlefield in a choking haze. The booming impacts of the rocks striking the ground echoed the danger presented by the creatures. A dense cluster of trees appeared ahead, concealing a narrow stream that shimmered in the fading light. The riders plunged into the thicket, the sound of hooves muffled by soft soil and fallen leaves. The crisp water of the stream offered a moment of solace. Horses drank eagerly, their sides heaving. Men knelt, splashing their faces, letting the coolness soothe their bruises and burns.

The catapults had fallen silent. Edgar paused to let his horse drink, the animal snorting gently. "I can no longer hear the gilzdars' war cries, but it's a tragedy that we've lost twenty-three of our brothers," the commander lamented. The group listened as the once-mighty roars faded into the gentle afternoon breeze.

"Why have the gilzdars stopped their assault?" Edgar inquired, turning to Bors for insight.

A blonde rider speculated, "Could it be that they fear venturing into unknown territory?"

Omond scanned the area thoughtfully before responding, "The mutants show no concern for their surroundings, no matter where they are. There must be something here that terrifies them. We must move forward with caution."

Once the animals were refreshed, they pressed on, traversing two small hills until they reached an expansive, verdant landscape.

As they paused to take in the view, the leader declared, "It's time we take a break; the view is unobstructed." Bors gazed upward, watching a flock of mallard ducks glide effortlessly northward against the backdrop of a clear sky. The moment felt almost serene—until something caught his eye. His attention was soon drawn to an unusual creature sitting on a distant ridge to the north. Curiosity piqued, he called out to his companions, "There's a gigantic beast observing us from the cliff! Its head resembles that of a buffalo, but it's three times larger than an average bear." He wiped the sweat from his brow, his hands trembling as he pushed his hair back. "Could these creatures pose a danger to the gilzdars? If that's true, we're in deep trouble."

Omond's eyes widened, and he quickly mounted his horse, exclaiming, "That creature looks like a hybrid. I'm certain they inhabit this area, and since I've never seen this specific beast before, we need to leave their territory immediately." He spurred his horse into a gallop, heading toward the forest.

His companions swiftly followed, their hearts racing as a strange growl echoed ominously through the valley.

Bors turned in the saddle, eyes scanning the horizon. "We're surrounded by monsters!" he shouted.

The group came to a sudden halt. Swords were drawn in unison, the metallic hiss slicing through the tense air. Horses shifted nervously beneath their riders, hooves pawing at the ground, nostrils flaring.

From all sides, mutants emerged—massive beings that exhibited features of both buffalo and grizzly bears, encircling the intruders with menacing intent. Their eyes glowed faintly, and their breath steamed in the cool valley air. Muscles rippled beneath thick hides as they encircled the intruders, growling and snarling.

Omond's voice trembled as he urged, "Our only chance is to break through their ranks. If we stay here, we won't survive. Once you get past them, turn left, and we'll regroup."

Without hesitation, four squads of seven fighters formed up behind the dual-wielding warrior and Lucan, the third in command. The warriors tightened their grips, eyes locked on the wall of beasts ahead.

"Charge!" the leaders shouted as they spurred their horses forward, crashing into the half-breeds. The collision sent the smaller creatures tumbling as they broke through the attackers' lines.

With a swift strike, Omond slit the throat of the closest mutant. Blood sprayed across the grass as the beast collapsed. Behind him, the others surged forward, crashing into the hideous creatures with fury and desperation. Twenty men breached the defenses of the beasts, carving a path through the chaos.

But the victory was short-lived. The mutants regrouped quickly, their massive forms closing in around the fighters. Roars echoed through the valley as claws tore through armor and bone.

When Lucan and Omond finally came to a stop, breath heaving, they turned to see the horror behind them. Ten men were ensnared; it was too late for them. The mutants had overpowered them and were now feasting on their fallen allies. The sounds of tearing flesh and agonized screams filled the air, a grotesque symphony of death.

The surviving riders retreated from the domain of the beasts, mourning the loss of more of their comrades. Once they felt secure, the remaining members dismounted and gathered in a somber circle, their heads bowed in sorrow.

Tears welled in Edgar's eyes, his expression a mix of grief and despair. "It's truly devastating to bid farewell to our friends. They are heading to a better place, and one day, we will join them there." He lowered his gaze in tribute to the fallen, whispering, "We will always hold dear the memories of those we have lost." No one spoke. The silence was sacred.

Eventually, Omond shattered the heavy silence, guiding them up the mountainside. "By tomorrow evening, we should reach Tonepass Valley. Our safety will be guaranteed once we reach the summit of the second mountain, where we will set up camp for the night."

As the group continued onward, the men ascended the steep path, shrouded in dense foliage. The trail was narrow and winding, the air thick with the scent of moss and pine. Given the recent events, they were anxious about what further calamities might lie ahead.

Lucan rode beside Omond, his eyes scanning the terrain. Bors and Edgar trailed behind, their silence a reflection of the weight they carried. By the time they settled down for the night, the sun had vanished behind the Atron Mountains.

"This area is secure. I know it well," Omond declared as he dismounted. "We can start a fire to keep warm."

"I think it's time for a hunt," Edgar suggested, glancing toward the eastern woods.

"I'll join you," replied Jargar, the lean warrior with tousled dark blonde hair. The two men grabbed their weapons and ventured into the trees, disappearing into the growing dusk.

The remaining riders dismounted and began to kindle a fire. As the refreshing evening breeze flowed around them, they huddled close, captivated by the dancing flames and the wisps of smoke rising into the starlit sky. The crackling fire offered warmth, but more than that—it offered comfort.

Lucan picked up two forked branches and began pounding them on opposite sides of the roaring flames. He bent down to retrieve another stick, sharpened one end, and set it aside. Then, he rejoined the group, saying, "We can put the meat on the spit to roast once the hunters return."

A heavy silence fell over them. Though the fire flickered and the wind whispered through the trees, their thoughts remained with the fallen. Each man sat quietly, grieving the comrades lost to the valley's horrors.

As the exhausted group gathered around the flickering campfire, the eerie hoots of owls resonated from the dark woods to the north. The sound was haunting, yet strangely grounding. Omond inhaled deeply, breaking the silence with a hopeful tone. "I can't wait for the hunters to come back so we can enjoy a feast and leave this dreadful day behind us." He rubbed his hands together to generate warmth, massaged his chilled arms, and carefully placed his swords beside him—just as the hunters stepped out from the shadows.

Jargar and Edgar returned to the camp, their faces lit by firelight, proudly bearing a small boar. They presented it to Lucan, who nodded in approval and immediately set to work. With skilled hands, he cleaned the animal before skewering it over the sizzling fire. Before long, the air was infused with a mouthwatering scent as the juices from the roasting meat dripped into the flames, igniting a shower of sparks that danced upward into the night. "If you're feeling hungry, come and join us," Lucan called out, his voice filled with warmth and hospitality. The exhausted men gathered around the inviting glow of the fire, silently grateful for their survival amidst the day's horrors.

As they savored their meal, Omond's expression turned serious. "Today has been bleak, and many of us might not make it back from the battle against the darkness. I won't judge anyone who decides to stay behind rather than march to Tonepass." He cut another piece of meat, his face reflecting the weight of his words. "We've witnessed far too many lives lost; keep in mind that if the forces of darkness prevail, all that is good in this land will vanish. You have until dawn to decide, but for now, let's seek some rest. Tomorrow, we must move quickly; reaching Tonepass on time is essential."

The fire crackled as his words settled over the group. Gradually, the camp embraced a serene stillness. The men lay down beneath the stars, cloaks pulled tight, weapons within reach. The fire burned low, its glow casting soft shadows across their faces. It was the only sound in the quiet night—their silent companion as they drifted into uneasy sleep.

26th Chapter

The first rays of dawn broke through the horizon, painting the sky in soft hues of blue and bathing the Falcon Ridge warriors' camp in a warm, comforting glow. The grass shimmered with dew, sparkling like a multitude of tiny gems as the sun began to rise.

Sirine stirred from her dreams, stretching her arms wide and drinking in the breathtaking panorama above. Three delicate white clouds drifted lazily, touched by a hint of purple as the sun ascended. Breathing in the fresh scent of the grass, a smile spread across her face. The gentle rustling of leaves in the wind reached her ears, grounding her in the serenity of the moment. To her right stood her dear companion, Rubric, his expression clouded with concern over the looming battle against the darkness.

Lance stirred from his slumber, his joyful voice echoing as he greeted Sirine with a bright, "Good morning!" He wasted no time in starting a fire, and before long, the rest of the group began to awaken, lured by the fire's cozy glow.

Rubric moved closer, planting a soft kiss on Sirine's lips. "Good morning, my love. Did you rest well?" He enveloped her in his strong arms, placing a gentle kiss on her cheek.

She leaned into him, her voice low. "Not quite; I tossed and turned throughout the night. The thoughts of the impending battle against evil kept me awake," she admitted, suppressing a yawn with her hand.

"I can sense your uneasiness," he said, his tone steady and reassuring. "Rest assured, we will do everything possible to protect our homeland. We will not be harmed. At this moment, three brave groups of fighters are making their way to Tonepass Valley to join us in this fight. We will overcome the dark forces."

Sirine looked into his eyes, drawing strength from his conviction. "You're right. I trust your words. The shadows will never conquer Seledor as long as we stand united," she responded, planting a gentle kiss on his lips. Her gaze then drifted to the right, where she saw Rolyn tenderly holding Princess Ari. A smile blossomed on her face, knowing that love had also taken root between them, even amid the looming storm.

"We must gather our horses and press on," the commander directed his men.

Rubric and Rolyn fell in step behind Sirine and Ari as the group made their way to the horses. Once mounted, they set off again, heading northward toward Tonepass Valley.

Zilar rode alongside Rolyn and inquired, "When do you think we'll reach the Valley of Tonepass?" His voice carried the weight of fatigue from their arduous journey.

Rolyn glanced at him, then back at the winding trail. "We should arrive at the sorceress's cottage by late tonight or at dawn tomorrow. However, today will be long, so we need to pick up the pace," Rolyn responded, resting his hand on his thigh. "After that, we'll formulate a robust defense strategy to safeguard our homes." His eyes remained fixed on the winding trail ahead.

As they continued, they traversed a mountainous region where ancient oak trees towered above. Their thick trunks and sprawling branches dipped low, casting shadows across the trail. The sky darkened as clouds began to gather, heavy and brooding.

Lagar glanced up at the sky, weaving through the branches, and declared, "Don't worry, it won't rain." He noticed a gray cloud drifting by while rubbing his right eye. "Stay vigilant for any signs of danger. Trouble can hide in the shadows."

Descending from the highlands, the group entered a rugged landscape dotted with jagged rock formations. As dusk settled in, the fatigued adventurers finally established their campsite for the night. A comforting fire eased their sore muscles and joints as they came together to enjoy some dried venison.

Lagar leaned back, patting his stomach with satisfaction. "The food and drink have truly filled my stomach. Today's trek was long and challenging. I can hardly wait to rest. Morning will come before we're ready for it." He shifted his bedroll a few feet from the dancing flames, letting the warmth fade into the cool night air.

One by one, the others followed suit, settling into their places as a serene stillness descended over the campsite.

As dawn broke over the East Kinnick Mountains, a brisk wind whistled through the trees, rustling leaves and stirring the sleeping camp. The group awoke later than usual, their bodies heavy with fatigue.

Zilar stood tall, shaking out his hands before stretching his limbs with a groan. Nearby, Rubric helped Sirine to her feet, brushing off their bedding. "A new day has arrived. We need to get moving if we want to reach Tonepass by nightfall," he urged his companions.

The riders moved slowly, their muscles stiff from the previous day's climb. Rolyn unwrapped the remnants of last night's meal, offering them to the group. "It's time for a snack to keep our energy up," he said, grimacing as he turned his stiff neck.

Lance moved closer to the food, nodding in agreement. "Yes. Who knows when we'll get another chance to eat?"

By the dancing flames of the campfire, the travelers indulged in honey bread, their hearts buoyed by the prospect of nearing Tonepass. Once the campsite was tidied and gear secured, they mounted their horses and resumed their journey. Upon reaching the peak of the mountain, they dismounted and gazed at the stunning expanse of the Valley of Tonepass that lay before them. The sight of Easha's quaint cottage filled them with eager anticipation.

The sun's gentle warmth kissed their faces as they gazed out over a lively meadow, where purple and yellow flowers swayed in the breeze, shimmering like brushstrokes on a living canvas. From the cottage chimney, tendrils of white smoke curled into the air, carrying a delightful aroma that danced with the wind.

As they made their way along the twisting mountain trail, the riders moved with caution, acutely aware that one wrong step could spell trouble. They took a moment to pause. Before riding into the Valley

Zilar slid off his mount, stretching his back with a sigh. "I can't shake the thought of whether the white sorceress is still in slumber. I wish our visit could be under more joyful circumstances."

Rolyn nodded in agreement, his gaze fixed on the cottage below. "I have no doubt she's awake, eagerly anticipating our arrival."

A soft, familiar voice chimed in, settling gently on Sirine's shoulder. "It's been far too long since we last met. Sirine, you've been truly missed," the zundar chimed in.

She turned, her smile radiant. "Suhzar," she replied warmly. "You've been missed as well."

The warriors leaned in, recognizing the voice of the hidden zundar. As they approached Easha's cottage, Suhzar began to speak, his tone tinged with sorrow.

"My friends, it is truly disheartening that our gathering is marred by such grim tidings. I had hoped we had banished evil from this land, but it seems that was merely a fleeting illusion. The challenges that lie ahead will surely be perilous. Sirine, as the warriors strengthen their defenses, we must hone our aerial abilities to brace ourselves for the relentless shadows threatening to consume Seledor."

Taking a moment to inhale deeply, Suhzar absentmindedly scratched his nose with his wing. "Once this battle is over, Sirine, you and the others should find sanctuary in the Middrom Mountains, close to the Zundars' cave. As the current protector of Seledor and a dragon rider, it is our responsibility to defend our homeland. The horrors I encountered in Stragon Valley left me breathless; the return of darkness was astonishing, its might far exceeding my expectations," the zundar lamented, a trace of sorrow in his tone.

"I can't help but ponder if there was a way to prevent the darkness from gaining such power. This is a weight I bear, but together, we will stand against the encroaching shadows that threaten the land," he proclaimed as they neared Easha's cottage. Upon reaching the porch, the sorceress opened the door, her flowing white robe trailing gracefully behind her like mist, and her hair cascading beautifully over her shoulders in soft waves.

Rubric welcomed Easha with a friendly smile, saying, "We've journeyed far to assist you in dispelling the darkness." He stood confidently, feet firmly planted, with Sirine by his side.

Easha's eyes softened. "I am truly grateful for your companionship. Please, come inside; I've prepared a feast for you all. There's more than enough for everyone," she said, leading them to a table laden with steaming bowls of oats.

The delicious scent of the warm dish wafted through the air, awakening the warriors' appetites. As they settled in and began to eat, a peaceful silence filled the room, broken only by the soft clinking of spoons and the occasional satisfied sigh. Eventually, Lagar rose and commented, "The meal you've made is fantastic. Your kindness is deeply appreciated."

Sirine chimed in, "Thank you, Easha. I absolutely adore the honey oats. The blend of sweet berries and creamy oats always leaves me feeling fulfilled and invigorated. Will you share your secret with me one day?"

Easha chuckled, her smile warm. "Yes! Once our mission is accomplished, I'll share my recipe with you. It's quite straightforward, though I do add a special ingredient my pa taught me, passed down through our family."

Rubric rose from his chair, gently placing a comforting hand on Sirine's shoulder before turning to Easha. "Do you remember the first time we realized that magic surrounded us?" he asked, a nostalgic chuckle escaping his lips as his eyes sparkled with joy. "I can still picture the looks on our friends' faces."

Easha's eyes lit up with fond memories as she replied, "Yes, that was such an enchanting moment, one I will always hold dear."

Rubric nodded, his expression a mix of gravity and warmth. "Those were remarkable times that forged our bond for eternity."

"I can recall it vividly. We were incredibly lucky that day," Sirine chimed in, her voice soft with reflection. "It was a pivotal moment that transformed everything for us."

"Without a doubt, it was a day to cherish," Zilar remarked, as he topped off his bowl with more oatmeal and reached for a slice of bread drizzled with honey. "I've learned that anything is achievable," he said, flashing a grin that lit up his face.

Easha beamed, a wave of nostalgia washing over her as she took in the familiar faces around her. The simple act of sharing a meal stirred a cascade of joyful memories—of battles fought, victories won, and quiet moments like this that reminded them of what they were fighting for.

Around the table, laughter bubbled up, mingling with the hum of lively conversation. The room glowed with warmth—not just from the fire, but from the deep camaraderie that bound them together. Each bite of food, each shared story, was a thread in the tapestry of their unity—a quiet but powerful reminder that they were not alone.

27th Chapter

The northern wind howled fiercely through the trees, its branches scraping against the cottage window like restless fingers.

"Just a moment," Easha replied, pointing her index finger at the window and drawing the curtains closed. "Now that my home is concealed from unwanted eyes, we can strategize. How many warriors will stand with us in this battle?"

Rubric straightened, taking a sip of water before answering. "We have the backing of two thousand elves, eight hundred dwarves, and another eight hundred freedom fighters. They will arrive in two days, giving us fourteen days to strengthen our defenses along the tree line. By the time the dark army attacks, we will be prepared."

Easha listened closely, cradling her tea as she absorbed the warrior's strategy.

"Rubric, you know Tomar is planning an initial strike on the Stronghold of Enwood," she said, tilting her head to meet his eyes.

"Indeed, Pildar commands a formidable force. Assaulting the fortress will be a significant challenge. The dark army will encounter fierce resistance. While I doubt their warriors can wipe out the entire horde, many of the mutants will surely fall. Defeating those colossal creatures would be a major triumph." He paused for another sip before continuing. "We'll set various traps along the forest's edge. With the dragons' help, we can take down Mirra; however, you alone have the power to defeat Tomar. If the sorcerer is vanquished, the creatures will scatter, and the spell may be broken—if fortune favors us." Rubric noticed Sirine's unease as she looked down, shifting her right foot. Rising from his chair, he took her hand, squeezed it gently, and pressed a kiss to her cheek.

The cottage was shrouded in contemplative quiet as the warriors stood and began gathering their things. Sirine moved to clear the table, her hands steady but her thoughts elsewhere. "We'll help you tidy up before we head out to join the others," she offered, glancing toward Easha.

"No, thank you. I can manage," Easha replied, her palm moving across the table's surface. A brief flash of white light flickered and vanished, leaving it spotless. "I've been studying diligently since we last met. You're both welcome to stay with me if you'd like," the sorceress offered as they paused at the threshold.

Sirine looked at Rubric, gripping his hand firmly. "No, thank you; we should stick together."

Rubric nodded, his gaze lingering on Easha for a moment. Then he turned and called out to the others, "It's time for us to set up camp," and then he stepped outside.

A gust of wind swept through the doorway as the group exited, rustling cloaks and stirring the embers in the hearth. Lagar lingered, the last to leave. He turned to Easha, captivated by the depth of her striking blue eyes, and bowed slightly. "Thank you for the wonderful meal. It's a pleasure to be in your company again."

"Thank you, Lagar, but there's no need for that," she replied, her smile bright as their eyes met for a brief moment.

"I hold you in high regard, sorceress; you deserve my respect. Without you, we would be lost in darkness. Do you have a preferred spot for our camp?"

"Lagar, I appreciate your company, too. You can set up camp near the cottage. I'll speak with the leaders when the other fighters arrive."

"You possess great wisdom, my lady. Until the siege begins, we shall convene in council each morning. Communication is essential to our success." He took Easha's hand and pressed a gentle kiss to it.

Her heart swelled with joy as she whispered, "I've never known such kindness," she whispered, watching him leave before closing the door behind him.

Outside, the group began to settle in. Rolyn led the warriors to the right side of the hut, halting approximately twenty-five feet from the cottage.

Lance spread out his bedding on the ground and took a moment to survey the area. Suhzar perched on Sirine's shoulder, assisting the others in setting up the campsite. Rubric nudged a small stone aside before laying down his bedding on the grass. "In two days, we'll have thirty-six hundred fighters arriving. This expansive valley can easily accommodate them. Our primary concern will be securing enough food. We need to construct a large corral to hold a herd of deer or elk. Suhzar, please speak with Gular and inform him that we require his assistance. You two can catch some deer and elk on your way back. Additionally, find out where the fighters are coming from; knowing their arrival time would be advantageous."

"It would be a privilege. Reuniting with my rider is essential," the zundar responded, soaring into the meadow. The fighters observed as a dazzling flash of light blue brightened the valley when Suhzar transformed into a stunning blue-and-white dragon. The dragon touched down, the rider climbed aboard, and together they soared into the sky, disappearing from view.

Sirine exclaimed, "It's incredible to be airborne once more." Her face radiated joy as she admired the trees beneath them.

Meanwhile, Rolyn continued his conversation with the others and informed, "Rubric, I've spotted a waterfall to the north. That will be our water supply." Lance nodded, surveying the vibrant green valley. "Each camp will require several latrines," he remarked, emphasizing the need to protect its beauty as much as possible.

• • •

A refreshing breeze swept over the defenders as noon approached, stirring cloaks and lifting strands of hair. The valley buzzed with quiet determination as each warrior immersed themselves in their tasks, preparing for the days ahead.

As dusk began to cast its enchanting glow across the treetops, Sirine and the dragon landed gracefully behind the cottage. The dragon's wings shimmered in the fading light as he touched down. Sirine elegantly dismounted and made her way back to the camp, while Suhzar soared back into the sky.

"Sirine, did you see any of the fighters heading our way?" Lance asked, his curiosity evident in his raised eyebrows.

"Yes, the elves are expected to arrive by nightfall. The freedom fighters from the west will join us at dawn, but the dwarves are moving at a slower pace and will likely need an extra day."

She replied, brushing a leaf from her shoulder. "Additionally, we have spotted a small, unidentified group of men approaching our vicinity. Suhzar is heading back to consult with Gular and has asked me to let you know that the meat you requested will be delivered tomorrow."

Rubric stepped forward, wrapping his arms gently around Sirine's waist. They stood together, watching the horizon as Lance and Zilar approached, their faces lit by the soft amber glow of the setting sun.

. . .

As the sun dipped below the peaks of the West Atron Mountains, the elves made their majestic arrival. Their banners fluttered in the breeze, and the rhythmic beat of hooves echoed across the valley floor. Rolyn, Lagar, and Rubric rode forth to welcome them, their expressions bright with anticipation.

"Greetings! It's wonderful to see you," Rolyn declared with excitement.

Under Lagar's direction, the two thousand elves began to establish their camp in the valley's western region. Their movements were swift and graceful, each tent rising with practiced ease, each fire lit with quiet precision.

As the sun continued to lower in the sky, Easha stepped out of her front door. Her flowing white robe swirled gracefully with her movements, and her conical white hat framed her long, jet-black hair, which shimmered in the light. The sorceress paused at the threshold and took in the scene of the valley, where the two thousand fighters were settling into their designated area in the west.

The elves' bonfire crackled merrily, sending lively sparks of yellow and orange dancing into the night, casting a cozy glow across the twilight sky. She could catch snippets of conversation swirling around her, quiet discussions of tactics, whispered plans to confront the looming threat. The elves moved with purpose, their eyes sharp, their spirits steady as they readied themselves for the night ahead. Easha stood silently, absorbing the moment. The valley, once quiet and untouched, now pulsed with life and resolve. The gathering had begun.

• • •

As nightfall blanketed the land in velvet darkness, the defenders braced themselves for the expected arrival of reinforcements. The valley, once bustling with motion, now quieted under the watchful gaze of the stars.

Rubric stretched and yawned, grasping Sirine's hand. "It's time we end our day," he announced to the group.

Zilar nodded in affirmation, "I'm prepared, my friend. The kilns, corrals, and latrines are complete. I'm feeling rather exhausted and could use a bit of rest," he remarked, falling in line with the others as they headed toward their sleeping quarters.

As the warriors settled into their beds, the valley slumbered beneath a velvet sky, where constellations traced ancient stories above the sleeping warriors.

When dawn arrived, casting golden hues across the horizon, the fighters continued to enjoy a deep, peaceful sleep, their bodies recovering from the day's labors. But the quiet was soon stirred.

Rolyn, Rubric, and Lance were awakened by urgent whispers and hurried footsteps. News had arrived—the freedom fighters had come. Without delay, the trio mounted their horses and rode into the valley, hooves thudding softly against the dew-kissed ground.

"I'm Rubric," he said, extending a hand as they approached the newcomers.

"I'm Author, the leader of this group. We came to unite to protect our homes," came the reply, firm and resolute.

Rubric nodded with gratitude. "Thank you for joining our mission. You can set up your camp in the southwest corner of the valley. Once you're settled in, feel free to visit with the others. Have a great morning, and I'll talk with you later." With that, the three made their way back to their campsite.

• • •

By noon, Gular and Suhzar returned to the camp, each hauling ten elk, which they carefully placed in the corral. The scent of fresh game mingled with the crisp mountain air, drawing curious glances from nearby warriors.

Overhead, majestic dragons soared through the sky, their wings slicing the air with effortless grace. The newcomers gazed in wonder as majestic dragons elegantly descended behind the cottage, their scales shimmering like polished gemstones in the sunlight.

The zundars—shape-shifting companions of their riders— swiftly morphed and soared toward their chosen partners, eager to reunite.

"Ari, it's such a delight to be with you again. I've really missed your presence," Gular said, settling on the princess's shoulder and gently nuzzling her golden locks, expressing his affection.

"I've missed you as well," Ari replied warmly. "I'm doing well. How is your family?"

"Mobee is flourishing. The little ones are growing up so quickly! Their endless energy makes me feel so old," he laughed.

"I can certainly understand that," she responded, reflecting on her own youthful experiences. "Did Suhzar mention that there's a council meeting planned for tomorrow at dusk, right after the dwarves arrive? The first and second in command from every group will be attending. We are free the rest of the day until then."

Gular's wings twitched with anticipation. "Ari, we should practice our maneuvers. Together, we make a formidable team."

"You're right. Gular, I've been eagerly anticipating flying again." She nodded enthusiastically, her face lighting up with excitement.

"Do you want to inform Rolyn that you're joining me?" His eyes glimmered like precious emeralds.

"No, he's busy with the fighters. He'll see us when we take off."

With a graceful leap, Gular lifted from her shoulder, morphing into his dragon form midair. He landed with a soft thud, kneeling before her.

Ari climbed onto his sleek back, giving him a gentle pat. With a powerful thrust of his wings, they soared into the bright blue sky, gliding over the camps scattered throughout Tonepass Valley.

Rolyn looked up and waved as they passed overhead. The sight of his love radiant and free in the sky filled the elf with a quiet warmth that lingered in his chest.

Nearby, Sirine leaned close to Rubric and kissed his cheek. "Did you notice how the dragon vanishes into the blue sky? Will that help us in the battle?"

Rubric considered the question, his gaze still fixed on the horizon. "It could, but I'm uncertain if the sorcerers with their magical abilities can spot them."

"I wish they were blinded to their presence," Sirine murmured, as they strolled toward Rolyn.

As time went on, the airborne warriors performed breathtaking dragon spins, thrilling nose dives, playful sideways loops, and smooth touch-and-go maneuvers that left trails of wind and wonder in their wake. The valley below watched in awe, inspired by the display of unity and power.

When dusk began to settle, Gular's voice echoed through the wind, "It's time to return to camp."

"I agree," Ari responded, tucking her hair into her shirt after securing it back.

With a graceful turn, the dragon angled northward, wings slicing through the cooling air. From their elevated vantage, they spotted the encampment below and saw fighters scattered across the terrain like pieces of a living mosaic.

In mere moments, the aerial warriors reached the heart of Tonepass Valley. The sight of so many defenders, each one preparing for the trials ahead, stirred a wave of quiet assurance in both dragon and rider. Together, they felt the strength of unity and the promise of triumph against the looming darkness.

Once they landed, Ari took a moment to wait for Gular before heading towards Rolyn and Rubric, who were eagerly anticipating her arrival.

"Ari, how did your day go?" the elf inquired, planting a soft kiss on her forehead.

"It was fantastic! We delved into various strategies that I think will significantly benefit our mission," Ari responded, her grin widening.

As the stars began to shimmer in the night sky, Rubric clasped Sirine's hand while they made their way back to camp after a fruitful day. In just a few hours, the once-bustling Tonepass Valley settled into a profound calm. Fires dimmed, voices softened, and the land settled into a hush—holding its breath beneath the stars for what the coming days would bring.

28th Chapter

The morning sun bathed the landscape in a soft, inviting warmth—a delightful surprise for this season.

The Sorceress of Light stepped onto her porch, cradling a delicate white cup filled with fragrant rosemary tea, her gaze sweeping over the valley. Just as she raised the cup to her lips, her eyes caught sight of countless fighters assembled below, their armor glinting in the golden light, readying themselves for the impending battle.

"What a remarkable gathering of combatants prepared to stand against evil," she mused, resting her hand against the cup. A flicker of doubt crossed her mind as she pondered whether she truly had the strength to confront her fate and vanquish Tomar. Just then, the sharp sound of snapping branches broke the silence, prompting her to inhale deeply, her senses alert.

"What causes that noise?" she asked aloud, turning her head to the right.

To her astonishment, eight hundred dwarves emerged from the surrounding trees, their small but sturdy figures marching with unwavering determination into the valley.

Nearby, Zilar and Lance, who had been walking together, perked up at the sound of the approaching company. Without hesitation, they swiftly mounted their horses and rode southward to intercept the newcomers.

"Arrow, it's a pleasure to see you and your troops," Zilar called out warmly. "We are genuinely grateful for your assistance. Let me lead you to your campsite."

Lance gestured toward the northeastern part of the valley. "Feel free to set up camp here. Afterwards, you can visit with the others."

"Your kindness is greatly appreciated," Arrow replied gratefully. "We'll come by once we're settled." He then dismounted, followed closely by his eager companions, their faces lit with anticipation and their spirits buoyed by camaraderie as they began preparing their camp.

• • •

With the first rays of dawn breaking over the horizon, a gentle breeze danced through the verdant trees and swept into the valley, where the men gathered in clusters, animatedly exchanging ideas with their fellow fighters.

Around a flickering campfire, Rubric and the dragon rider's companions formed a loose circle, the flames casting a warm, golden glow on their faces.

Sirine's gaze drifted toward the cottage, where the Sorceress of Light leaned against the cottage wall, her expression thoughtful.

"Easha has awakened," Sirine said softly, turning to Rubric. "I want to take this opportunity to spend some time with her." She placed a soft kiss on his cheek before rising to her feet. As she approached the cottage, the dragon rider noticed a flurry of tiny, luminous creatures flitting about in the morning air.

"My friends have chosen to remain here until the conflict subsides. They find solace in this sanctuary," the sorceress said, without being asked.

As she gazed across the meadow, Sirine observed the horses galloping freely through the verdant valley, their hooves disturbing the delicate homes of the small creatures that lived there.

"Sirine, there's no reason to worry," Easha reassured her, acknowledging her concern for the animals and added, "This place will mend itself. In the meantime, my little friends will adapt and find their place near me."

Sirine's cheeks flushed with a warm hue as she responded, "I had no idea you could perceive my emotions."

"My dear friend, your feelings are quite clear. You radiate with a sincere heart and an energetic soul," she remarked. "I sense that you haven't completely accepted your true journey."

Just then, Rubric stepped into view, his hair tousled by the breeze. With purposeful strides, he approached and placed his right foot on a nearby rock, striking a confident pose.

"Easha, should we convene the council at your place?" he asked, his voice firm but respectful.

"Rubric, that's a brilliant suggestion! It would be the safest place to meet in case Tomar dispatches his spies," she agreed, gently tucking a stray lock of hair behind her ear.

"Perfect! I'll set off right away to inform the camp leaders about our meeting," he replied, planting a gentle kiss on Sirine's cheek before he left.

The two women watched Rubric as he exchanged words with Lance and Lagar, then quietly turned and entered the cottage together, the morning light casting soft shadows behind them.

Meanwhile, Rubric quickened his pace, urgency guiding his steps.

"Lance, it's time to let the leaders know that a council will convene at dusk tonight. I'll head to the campground on the right side of the valley. It would be great if you could take care of the left side," Rubric added quickly. "We'll get this done in no time."

Lance nodded. "We'll ride together a bit, then split when the path divides."

Rubric gestured to Lagar. "Come with us. We'll need more eyes on the road."

The three riders mounted their horses and galloped toward the nearest camps, their cloaks billowing behind them.

As they neared the elves' domain, snippets of dialogue drifted through the air. Startled, Rubric and Lagar instinctively unsheathed their swords when a figure emerged from the trees.

"Omond!" Lance exclaimed, recognizing the elf immediately. He dismounted and approached with a wide smile. "It's wonderful to see you again! It feels like it's been forever since we last spoke. I thought you would have found us after you left, and I've been eager to hear about your journeys." He gestured toward Rubric, who waited nearby. "I need to join Rubric to inform the other camp leaders about the meeting schedule. Please feel free to set up your camp wherever you wish. I'm really curious to hear what held you up when we meet again." With a warm smile, Lance knelt to clasp his old friend's hand, the bond between them evident in the quiet gesture.

The riders pressed on, their horses kicking up dust as the path forked ahead. Here, Lance turned toward the western slope, while Rubric urged his steed eastward. The two warriors set off on a mission to visit each encampment, sharing the news of the upcoming gathering at the sorceress's cottage.

As Rubric arrived at the dwarves' campsite, Arrow stepped forward with a concerned expression. "Have you noticed how the sky in the northeast over Stragon Valley has been getting darker?"

Rubric nodded, his gaze following the direction of Arrow's outstretched hand. "Indeed, I've sensed a wave of negative energy. Although the morning feels warm, there's an unsettling chill in the air. The darkness is intensifying."

The dwarves exchanged uneasy glances. Rubric and the warriors who had once stood against the formidable dark forces recognized the signs. The shifting weather was no accident—it was a warning.

· · ·

In Tonepass Valley, the fighters convened in small clusters, their voices low and urgent as they strategized various methods to set deadly traps. The air buzzed with anticipation, the tang of iron and pine mingling in the breeze.

Meanwhile, inside the sorceress' cottage, Sirine and Suhzar lounged near the hearth, the flickering fire casting soft shadows across the room.

Easha rose from her seat and crossed to the door, opening it just as Ari raised her hand to knock.

She smiled warmly. "Welcome," she greeted, stepping aside to let her in. Gular, who had been perched on Ari's shoulder, became visible as she entered. The five of them gathered around the kitchen table, the wood worn smooth by years of use. The sorceress stretched her arms overhead and sighed. "I've never crafted a battle plan outside the Sorcerer's Secret Chamber."

Ari reached out and gently brushed her cheek, her touch tender. "Do you think that will impact our chances of winning this battle?"

She replied, tucking her right hand into her pocket, "I believe we need to formulate a plan right here. I am truly amazed by the sheer number of fighters who have come to this land to fight for justice. This only strengthens my belief that victory is within our grasp."

• • •

Efura and Lundar glided gracefully above the valley, their white feathers gleaming in the fading light. From above, their keen eyes scanned the landscape beneath them as they spotted a large gathering of combatants, a formidable testament to their strength and determination. Their journey led them to the sorceress's cottage, where they landed gently at the entrance.

A series of three firm knocks resonated in the air. Sirine, anticipating Lundar's arrival, opened the door swiftly. Her eyes widened with delight at the sight of the two majestic eagles waiting patiently

With a welcoming gesture, she stepped aside and invited, "Please, come in." The eagles strolled through the doorway in a captivating display.

Ari was there to greet them. "It's wonderful to see you both." She guided Lundar and Efura to the table, where conversations flowed freely. The room buzzed with energy as plans and hopes mingled. "We were just admiring the impressive number of supporters gathered to face the impending darkness," she noted.

As the sun dipped below the horizon, Easha moved to the door. "We should step outside to welcome the arriving fighters," she said. Outside, eight leaders approached—two from each of the four factions, flanked by Rubric and his allies.

The riders dismounted, tying their horses to a sturdy branch of a nearby tree.

"Welcome!" The sorceress invited the men into a spacious room, announcing, "There's ample room in the den for everyone." At the heart of the chamber stood a long table surrounded by sixteen chairs.

Rubric and Sirine took their places next to each other, closely followed by Rolyn and Ari. Suhzar settled near Efura and Lundar, ready to contribute.

In the center of the table, two zundars hovered with their wings softly fluttering, releasing a shimmering cloud of magical dust that filled the room, enabling everyone to absorb their silent message.

Suhzar leaned forward, his voice calm but resolute. "I understand your surprise, and I'd like to share my perspective. It's crucial to remain receptive to fresh ideas. Our dragon riders, Ari and Sirine, are keen to enhance their archery abilities. While our riders are skilled at taking down enemies with arrows, Gular and I can also launch boulders at them." Suhzar pointed out, "Attacking from above is an effective tactic for eliminating multiple beasts." The council murmured in agreement, heads nodding thoughtfully.

"That's an exceptionally wise suggestion. The riders should commence their training at dawn. Do you have any recommendations for the best equipment to ensure our safety?" one of the faction's leaders inquired, observing the reactions around the table.

Gular and Suhzar exchanged a glance and stepped aside to let the eagles participate in their discussion. "Pardon me, Rubric," Lundar began, his voice firm but respectful. "But we need to formulate a strategy to deal with Tomar's spies."

He turned to the gathered leaders. "I had an extensive conversation with the Eagle Council. They are worried that the Eagle Dynasty could face extinction if darkness prevails. The Eagles have agreed to eliminate the spies. Four days before the evil reaches Tonepass, they will dispatch birds to keep an eye on you. Our strategy is designed to prevent the crows from warning them about your concealed traps." He paused, letting the weight of his words settle. "We will ambush the crows once they have crossed back the Seabray River. We expect that the encounter with Pildar's men will wear out the sorcerers. We'll take out the birds as soon as they settle in for the night." Lundar reassured them, "We will transport them to the Eagles' Nest."

"I am grateful. You have pinpointed a crucial solution. Our defense strategy would have crumbled without your prompt help." The commander acknowledged this with a nod.

Lance stood up, leaning over the table as he scanned the room and inquired, "What kinds of deadly devices can we assemble quickly?"

A tall, brown-haired freedom fighter suggested, "We can dig trenches along the northern tree line and conceal sharp spikes among the foliage. Many will fall victim to the traps as they pass through."

Lagar, lost in thought, stroked his chin before speaking, "We can string twine two inches off the ground. When triggered, it will cause spiked tree trunks to topple, eliminating anyone in their way."

Omond noticed the sorceress nearby and asked, "Could you create a sticky substance? If so, we could set up a mire trap by spreading the thick liquid among the trees, blocking the monsters from entering the valley."

"Of course, Omond, that's a brilliant idea. I'll have it ready for you by dawn. The ingredients need to be kept at the right temperature to ensure their effectiveness. After that, I'll devise a plan to confront Tomar," she replied, her brow creased as she rubbed her arm. "It will be a formidable challenge."

Arrow added, "We can create explosives using corn flour, allowing us to hit the attackers from a distance. The dragon riders can drop them from above, and we can set up spring-loaded traps between two trees." He also proposed constructing barriers with wooden supports to hinder the intruders' advance.

"You possess an incredible wealth of creative ideas," Rubric said, addressing the group. "The variety of traps we can deploy greatly enhances our likelihood of success. Now, it's up to each team to decide which traps to implement."

Lagar chimed in, "We have a sizable team dedicated to crafting the spiked tree trunks. Once we complete that, we'll lend our support to the others."

Rolyn squeezed Ari's hand and proclaimed, "I will instruct the dragon riders on how to effectively use the bow and arrow."

Omond announced, "We will distribute the thick substance created by the sorceress."

Arrow rubbed his chin in contemplation and remarked, "We'll handle the explosives, as we have the necessary expertise."

"Lagar," someone added, "we can place the razor-sharp spikes in the trenches and cover them with foliage."

The bluish-blond-haired elf nodded in agreement, saying, "We truly appreciate your assistance."

Rubric chimed in, offering, "Lance and my team are ready to back the rebels."

With the plan in place, Rubric helped Sirine to her feet and declared, "We'll bolster our defenses at dawn."

As the final words settled over the room, a quiet understanding passed among the fighters. One by one, they rose and began to file out of the cottage, their movements purposeful and silent. Outside, the night had fully descended, wrapping the valley in a cloak of shadow. Gular and Suhzar stood and joined their riders while the eagles took flight, their silhouettes vanishing into the dark sky as they sought shelter among the cliffs.

Soon, fires began to flicker throughout the valley, casting a warm light. The commanders mounted their horses and rode back to their camp, traversing the open meadow. Gathered around a roaring bonfire, the fighters engaged in serious discussions about the weapons they needed to forge and the traps they would set. Each voice carried the weight of purpose; each plan a thread in the tapestry of resistance.

As the protectors nestled down for the night, the moon climbed higher, casting a silver glow across the valley. Its brilliance eclipsed the stars, a silent guardian watching over those who had vowed to stand against the coming darkness.

29th Chapter

A brilliant sunrise bathed the clear sky in golden light, yet a sinister shadow loomed over the Valley of Stragon, obscuring the sun's gentle warmth with an ominous veil.

The sorcerer was the first to awaken, stretching his arms toward the heavens as he inhaled deeply, his gaze fixed on Mirra, who lay in serene slumber.

Tomar soon emerged from the bedchamber, his steps purposeful as he made his way to the site of the assault weapon. He gripped the base of the carrier, his hands wrapping around the beam as he shook it with vigor. "These carriers are remarkable," he muttered, inspecting the structure. "They will perfectly support my arsenal." With a quick flick of his finger, he cleared the stones that hindered the raft's wheels, watching them roll freely across the ground.

By the time Mirra stirred, she discovered that Tomar had already departed. She quickly dressed and made her way out of the palace.

The wind whipped through her hair, swirling dead leaves around her and momentarily obscuring her vision. She brushed her hair aside and pressed on. As she walked, the crunch of dry leaves underfoot harmonized with Tomar's distant commands.

"Pay close attention to my orders. Disobey, and you will face a slow, agonizing fate. Two of you will pull each cart with these chains," he directed, lifting the long chain that glinted in the morning light. "Four of you will push the cart," he added, motioning toward the creatures gathering around him. He moved with calculated precision, organizing the creatures into formation. After a meticulous inspection, he ensured everything was secure, his eyes scanning for flaws with ruthless precision.

Mirra flinched as Tomar's voice echoed just behind her, snapping her attention to the scene unfolding. She peered cautiously from her hiding place and gasped. The mutant rodents had been unleashed. Half of them were arranged in six rows of five, strategically placed in front of the weaponry, while the others formed ten rows of fifteen behind the rafts, their grotesque bodies twitching with anticipation. The trolls, massive and menacing, lumbered forward, prompting Mirra to duck behind a wooden wheel for cover.

"My dear, the time has come to initiate the assault," Tomar shouted, his voice slicing through the air. "Only take what is needed."

Mirra's breath caught in her throat. "I must remain concealed. If he spots me, he'll assume I'm spying on him."

Suddenly, a deafening crack shattered the tension—a tree had crashed down in the northern forest. The sorcerers recoiled, startled by the sound. Tomar pivoted sharply toward the woods, his voice booming with authority, "I know you felled that tree to provoke me!" His eyes blazed with fury as he scanned the tree line. "Do not test my patience, or I will reduce your homes to ashes."

Seizing the moment, Mirra slipped quietly back into the palace, her footsteps light and swift. The sorcerers' attention had shifted to the beavers now gathering near the fallen tree.

Moments later, she reemerged from the entrance, her expression calm and resolute. "I have everything I require," she declared, stepping forward to join Tomar.

Without hesitation, he reached for her. "Up you go," he said, hoisting her onto the first raft with ease, his hands gripping her waist securely.

As she turned to survey the horizon, her eyes caught sight of eight rafts in the distance, each one heavily laden with weapons. At the rear of the final raft sat a formidable catapult, flanked by four massive creatures at the back and two at the front—silent sentinels of destruction.

Derail landed beside her.

"You're safe here in the carrier," he assured her, lifting his gaze to meet hers.

"Where will you be?" she asked, her expression clouded with concern.

"I'll lead the army out of the valley until we reach the Seabray River."

"Does that mean it's safer for you? I want to be with you as we move forward." She narrowed her eyes at him, hands planted firmly on her hips.

The sorcerer hesitated, then spoke with quiet conviction. "I'm afraid it's too perilous. I must prioritize your safety so I can focus on our journey. You can join me after we've crossed the mountains, but for now, you need to stay here."

"No!" she shouted, stepping out of the war wagon and striding to the front. "We are strongest when we stand united," she declared, leaving Derail behind on the carrier.

He regarded her with a serious expression and cautioned, "You must remain alert for any carriers that might break loose. Do you understand?"

"Yes." The sorceress took his hand, her eyes sparkling with excitement.

Tomar climbed onto the first carrier, confronted the creatures, and declared, "The journey ahead is fraught with danger. Be careful as you maneuver the crafts. We can rest once we reach the peak!" With that, the sorcerer leapt from the carrier and began his ascent along the mountain trail. The sky was darkened by a swarm of crows circling ominously.

The wooden wheels of the rafts groaned under the weight of the timber weapons, creaking with every turn as the envoy climbed the rugged incline. Out of nowhere, the wheels of the final carrier slipped midway up the incline, veering off the edge and sending two beasts tumbling down the mountainside.

Mirra gasped. "Tomar, what just happened?" Her voice trembled with confusion. "I'm concerned we might have lost some of our creatures. Halting now would be far too risky. We can take a break once we find a flat spot. It's essential that we remain focused on the path ahead."

Tomar gave a curt nod, his jaw clenched. The army pressed on, struggling beneath the burden of the carriers. The ascent was grueling, but at last, the dark forces reached level ground just as the first rays of sunlight broke over the eastern horizon.

"Halt!" Tomar commanded, raising his hand. "The mountains are behind us now." He carefully lifted Mirra onto the first craft and turned to address the troops. "We can ride until we reach the river." He declared, standing tall on the first raft. "Keep moving."

Then, in a rare moment of tenderness, he leaned in and kissed Mirra softly on the cheek.

The convoy continued its march until it reached the banks of the Seabray River, where it finally came to a halt. A foreboding aura seemed to dim the sunlight around them, casting long shadows across the shore.

"I command you to lower the carriers into the water with care. Crows do not cross the river," he instructed, standing beside the sorceress on the leading vessel.

Mirra turned to Derail, her brow furrowed. "Derail, did you see what happened when the craft went over the cliff?"

"I hurried back to the carrier as soon as I heard the crash. I witnessed four giants and ten rats tumble off the edge as the carrier plummeted. Fortunately, the other mutants managed to pull it back onto the path, but we suffered the loss of fourteen fighters," he recounted.

With solemn precision, the trolgilzs, trolls, and rat warriors meticulously eased the enormous rafts into the flowing river. With the sun now standing at its highest point in the sky, the vessels set off on their voyage southward, heading toward their goal.

• • •

As noon drew near, a watchman atop the tower noticed a rising cloud of dark dust. The watcher recognized the urgency as five scouts raced toward the stronghold. The warning horn blared, signaling everyone about the approaching riders.

"Lower the drawbridge and open the gates!" the watchman commanded the gatekeeper. The heavy chains groaned as they worked to lower the bridge. With a thunderous creek, the enormous wooden and steel doors swung open, allowing the scouts to thunder into the fortress courtyard.

"Be mindful of the horses," the lead scout instructed as he dismounted, sweat glistening on his forehead. He rushed into the building and sprinted down the corridor, his boots pounding against the floor.

He burst into the Ruler's chamber, breath ragged. "Pildar, my lord, I bring dire news. A vast horde of creatures is advancing toward us, armed with a formidable array of weapons. Their rafts are currently drifting down the river. On the foremost weapon platform, two figures cloaked in black loomed ominously. The sky above them darkens, mirroring their malevolent presence. They are wicked sorcerers orchestrating a siege against our realm, commanding an overwhelming force." The scout warned the Potentate of the imminent danger facing the stronghold.

Pildar, seated upon his gilded throne, did not flinch. "I have no interest in your fears. My fortress is unassailable." He clapped his hands sharply and waved the scout away, dismissing him.

Dismissed but undeterred, the scout rushed back to the warriors' chamber, darting across the courtyard and urgently ringing the meeting bell.

"I bring an urgent message!" he cried to the gathering warriors. "A siege is imminent. A colossal and sinister army of dangerous mutants is marching toward us, and if they maintain their current pace, they will arrive in just two days. Their only goal is to seize Seledor and shroud it in darkness." He paced anxiously, his voice rising in intensity. "We must devise a plan to safeguard our homes. We need to face this threat with determination, but we must act with stealth. Pildar is convinced his walls cannot be breached." His voice quivered, and beads of sweat glistened on his brow. The defenders exchanged tense glances, then quickly set to work, crafting and implementing a strategy they hoped would remain hidden from the Ruler's prideful gaze.

Cauldrons brimming with scalding water were strategically placed beneath the tower openings. Enormous catapults, loaded with boulders, stood poised at both ends of the fortress walls. The upper entrance walls were rigged with explosives, ready to be detonated at a moment's notice. Stacks of bows and arrows leaned against the narrow slits of the towers, ready for swift deployment.

Along the battlements, the warriors crafted large metal funnels filled with sand, set to unleash a blinding torrent on any foes daring to climb the stone walls.

The soldiers meticulously examined the heavy wooden and steel planks securely fastened to the palace's exterior, ensuring that the release mechanisms operated perfectly. "I'm grateful that Pildar had the foresight to install those enormous flat timbers around the outer walls. When we release them, they will crash down with incredible force, obliterating everything in their path."

As dusk enveloped the land, a horn blared, signaling an imminent threat. Pildar, standing on his balcony, peered into the distance. His eyes widened in horror as he spotted the colossal beasts marching toward his fortress. A bead of sweat trickled down his forehead. He stumbled backward, his breath shallow, heart pounding against his ribs.

"Guards!" he cried out, clutching his chest. But it was too late. Pildar, overwhelmed by despair, dropped to his knees, letting out a gut-wrenching scream before collapsing face-first onto the cold stone floor—lifeless.

The courtyard erupted into motion.

The chief scout stepped forward, his voice cutting through the rising panic. "You must wait for my signal before we engage! As the creatures near the moat, release the heavy beams and reset them. They will crash down on the invaders, ensuring the annihilation of anyone who dares to approach."

"Archers, get ready to fire on my signal!" the chief defender bellowed, his gaze fixed on the advancing horde of rats. "Hold....hold..."

"Fire!" he ordered, his voice echoing through the air. Arrows soared over the palace ramparts in a deadly arc, aimed directly at the enemy ranks.

But the malevolent sorcerer raised his left wrist with a flick, and the air shimmered. The arrows veered off course, twisting unnaturally away from his troops and falling harmless on the floor. At the same moment, the palace's wall openings groaned open, releasing massive cauldrons brimming with scalding water and oil.

Mirra lifted her arms to her chest, bent her elbows, and opened her palms. Her magic surged, rekindling the churning liquid with a searing glow.

The soldiers cried out in pain as the scorching oil consumed them. Flesh blistered, armor melted, and the defenders of the fortress stood paralyzed with terror, witnessing a level of savagery they had never seen before.

"To the courtyard!" the commander bellowed. "It's time to unleash the catapults!"

The chief scout sprang into action, activating the catapult and proclaiming, "The invaders will never cross the perilous moat or breach the mighty palace walls."

With a thunderous roar, enormous boulders were hurled at Tomar's forces. Yet, with a simple wave of his hand, the sorcerer diverted the stones into the wide meadow.

"Release the fireballs," commanded the sorcerer.

Flames surged over the battlements, cascading into the courtyard like a fiery tide. Fighters screamed as they were consumed, their escape routes swallowed by infernos.

In the west tower of the Bastion, women and children huddled together in terror. The sorcerer turned their wrath toward them, summoning fireballs and hurling them against the stone walls, causing a powerful explosion that obliterated the left side of the tower in a cloud of smoke and rubble.

Outside, enormous boulders crashed down with devastating force, crushing two trolgilzs and twenty rats. The drawbridge groaned, then gave way—resulting in the demise of even more beasts plummeting to their deaths.

A short defender with blonde hair yelled, "Lower the planks!"

The enormous wooden beams crashed down, obliterating two of the colossal creatures that dared approach.

From atop a towering structure, a lone protector observed as a throng of men surged toward the fortress, swords unsheathed and poised for battle. He witnessed them cut down considerable numbers of rat soldiers.

Derail screeched, "Humans are attacking from our rear."

Spinning around, the sorceress spotted the advancing men— those who had vanquished the mutant rat warriors.

Mirra unleashed a shrill cry, "Advance, eliminate them!" The trolls roared in response, whirling around and charging at the riders.

The brave warriors quickly grasped their dire situation as they witnessed the monstrous horde advancing. The fighters leaped onto the shoulders of the towering giants, seizing their chance. With swift precision, Pildar's men drew their gleaming blades, slashing throats and toppling beasts with deadly intent. But the tide turned. Other giants roared in fury, snatching the horsemen mid-strike and hurling them to the ground with bone-shattering force. The clash of steel gave way to the sickening crunch of broken bodies.

Then came the trolgilzs. Three of the towering mutants emerged from the smoke, their grotesque forms silhouetted against the fire lit sky. The men, bloodied and breathless, spotted them and cried out, "Retreat!" However, it was too late; the mutants charged at the downed riders, shattering their skulls and drenching the ground with the blood of the valiant. And then—silence. Not a single defender remained upright.

30th Chapter

For the thousand surviving men, the journey was arduous, each step steeped in exhaustion and despair. Hope had long since faded, replaced by a grim determination to press on.

As they trudged forward, the captives noted how the trees, meadows, and forests had darkened, shrouded in a heavy gloom that smothered the sun's warmth and cast an eerie pall over the land.

"We will head north to the Atron Mountains and then cross the river," Tomar declared. "My aim is to descend from the North Mountains into the Valley of Tonepass." Standing tall on the first raft, he inhaled deeply, bracing himself for the trials ahead.

As dusk settled, the army reached the riverbank. The weary men pushed the rafts into the churning water, struggling against the fierce current as they tried to cross.

"Dock at the clearing by those trees to the right!" Tomar commanded, pointing toward the shadowed grove.

After three hours of relentless effort, the vessels were finally pulled ashore. The men collapsed onto the muddy banks, their limbs trembling with fatigue.

"We've had a long and fruitful day. Now it's time to rest. Trolgilzs, you will guard the camp. Keep a close watch on the humans; if they try to escape, eliminate them. Crows, stay away from the camp tonight," he added with a scowl. "Your noise disturbs my sleep."

The malevolent sorcerers took their place on the initial raft, closing their eyes in silent meditation.

Thirty trees distant, the crows gathered, preparing to roost for the night. Unbeknownst to them, danger lurked nearby.

Among the dense foliage, the eagles lay concealed, their forms bathed in the soft glow of the half-moon. Silent and poised, they waited for the signal.

With a piercing squawk, Lundar alerted his fellow warriors that the moment to strike had arrived. He descended swiftly from the southern skies, while Efura made her way from the north. The shrill calls of the two white eagles sent the crows into a panic, causing them to disperse wildly. In a stunning spectacle, hundreds of eagles dove down, captured their targets, and disappeared into the night without a trace.

The following morning, Tomar and Mirra awoke with the dawn, only to discover the skies devoid of birds. "Those silly creatures must have lost their way during the night. I'm confident they'll find us soon," he said, scanning the horizon from their raft. "However, we can't wait for them to return. They'll need to catch up," he added with a firm tone.

"It's time for us to head to our next destination," the sorcerer declared, guiding his troops southward toward the formidable Tonepass Mountains. The creatures followed closely behind the men of Enwood, who marched alongside the ominous army. The foul odor emanating from the dark forces unsettled the soldiers. For three exhausting days, Tomar's army continued its march, drawing nearer to the Valley of Tonepass.

"I can hardly believe the crows haven't caught up to us yet," he whispered, casting a wary glance at the sky. "I always thought they were smart birds," he mused, a hint of concern creeping into his tone.

•••

As the light dimmed in Tonepass, seventeen days had passed without anyone realizing. The lethal traps lay in wait, carefully arranged for the right moment to strike. Easha had crafted two strategies to eradicate the wicked sorcerer for good, prepared to select the most effective one as the situation unfolded. In the meantime, the warriors participated in tournaments to sharpen their fighting abilities, while the dragon riders evolved into adept archers, refining their skills with each passing day.

After enduring eighteen challenging days, the daylight started to wane, and the warriors felt the foreboding presence of the dark army approaching.

"When the shadowy forces arrive, we'll take refuge behind the sorceress's cottage," Rubric announced, stroking his chin and pulling his hair back with determination. "This will trick Tomar into thinking he has caught Easha off guard," he explained to his comrades.

"How are we going to fit behind the hut?" Zilar asked, a frown forming as he thoughtfully rubbed the back of his neck.

"We'll position ourselves just two feet from the back corners of the cottage. I'm confident our lines will stretch into the forest. The screams will herald the arrival of the dark forces. When we charge out to confront them, it will completely catch them off guard," Rubric insisted, swatting away a pesky fly.

"We need to tidy up our camps before we move," Rolyn advised his closest allies, encouraging them to spread the word about their plan.

Lance nodded in agreement, understanding that their ambush would be at risk if the sinister army became aware of their presence.

The protectors had painstakingly devised their defensive strategy. They dismantled their camps with precision, leaving no trace of their presence. The horses were hidden away in a secluded part of the forest, and the atmosphere was charged with tension. The defenders were acutely aware that the dark army was advancing toward the Valley of Tonepass.

"It's time for us to move," Rubric directed the leaders of each faction, his voice steady as the final preparations began.

Seven lines of fighters stealthily made their way behind the white and brown cottage, their movements deliberate and disciplined. Above them, dragons and their riders glided through the southern sky, their silhouettes barely visible against the fading light—silent, watchful, undetected.

Easha emerged from the cottage and headed toward the back. As she noticed the men in her garden, she felt a surge of gratitude seeing them tread carefully to avoid crushing her delicate plants. The fighters were dispersed among the trees, blending into the shadows. She made her way to Rubric, who was waiting for her.

"I hope everything unfolds as planned," she said softly, running her hand over the fabric of her robe in search of reassurance.

"Do not worry, sorceress. I believe in our victory. You must remain behind the cottage when the battle commences. I worry that Tomar will aim fireballs at your home, thinking you are inside," Rubric said, picking up on her anxiety.

"Indeed, you are correct. My animal companions will find safety behind the fighters." Easha agreed.

"That's good to hear; I'll make sure the men are cautious of the little animals," he promised, walking alongside Rolyn.

Easha watched as the creatures hurried away from the cottage, seeking refuge in the welcoming arms of the forest.

• • •

The atmosphere was thick with apprehension, amplifying the group's anxiety. Every rustle of leaves and distant howl seemed to echo louder than it should.

"Rolyn, let's alternate watching the perimeter while the others catch some rest," Rubric proposed, stepping up to be the first line of defense.

"I'll join you. There's no reason for one person to shoulder the responsibility of safeguarding our home when we are a team."

"I'm grateful to have you by my side, my friend." Rubric nodded in agreement, and the two settled onto the front porch, sheltered beneath the robust wooden beams, eyes scanning the horizon.

The dark forces lay in wait throughout the night, cloaked in silence.

"The sky is growing increasingly foreboding," Rolyn warned, signaling that malevolence was ready to strike Tonepass. Within half an hour, the traps were triggered, and the defenders were met with agonizing cries as sharp spikes pierced the flesh of the unsuspecting mutants.

The defenders knew then: the battle had begun. The sinister forces had arrived.

• • •

Tomar, Mirra, and Derail stood on the first platform when the realization of an ambush struck them like a sudden thunderclap.

"If only the crows hadn't lost their way, they might have warned us about these traps. Raven, take cover in that tree," the sorcerer commanded firmly. "Stay there, no matter what unfolds." He scanned the valley, searching for any signs of looming peril. The valley stretched before them, deceptively calm. But the silence was wrong. Too still.

From both sides of the cottage, enemy fighters emerged, pausing momentarily. Their swords glinted ominously in the dimming light.

"How foolish you are to believe you can defeat a sorcerer of my caliber!" Tomar bellowed, standing firmly next to the sorceress on the foremost raft. The morning breeze tousled his raven-black hair, accentuating his defiant posture.

Mirra quickly glanced to her right, reassured to see Derail safely hidden within the thick underbrush. Sunlight streamed through the foliage, forming a protective barrier against the ominous forces advancing from the east.

As the defenders of Tonepass advanced, they remained alert, their eyes fixed on the encroaching dark army.

"We will stand firm until they are right upon us," Rubric asserted, his grip steady on the hilt of his sword. "I will not jeopardize our traps by engaging them prematurely."

The elf archers prepared their bows, eager for the enemy's approach, while the dragon warriors lurked in the shadows, ready to strike.

"I can sense the fear we instill in the hearts of the humans," he sneered, pointing forward. "They will not dare confront us. Their terror is unmistakable." The mutant rodents, mounted on enormous rat-like creatures, surged ahead, only to vanish into the expansive trench.

Soon, the air was thick with the sounds of despair as the enormous wooden spikes impaled their bodies. The cries gradually faded into an unsettling hush, leaving only a piercing wail reverberating through the valley. The sorcerer understood that his front-line soldiers had succumbed to the deadly traps.

"Stop! Bring the cart back!" Tomar bellowed, his face flushed with rage as he realized he had lost even more of his army.

The sorceress looked down, alarmed to see they were perilously close to the edge of a spear trench.

"Pull us back immediately!" Tomar shouted, urgency tinging his voice.

The creatures strained to pull the heavy timber cart, muscles taut as they dragged it away from the trench's edge.

"I need twenty rats at the front!" he commanded, and the creatures sprang into action, driven solely by his orders.

"Disperse and locate a path around the ditch," he added, his arms crossed in a stance that dared the valley to defy him.

"Why didn't Tomar assign us to look for any dangers?" one of the captives murmured. "What are his real motives?"

Meanwhile, Tomar and Mirra kept their eyes fixed on the rodents sitting atop the cart, eagerly awaiting their return.

At last, the lead rat chirped, "Master, we've discovered a secure crossing."

With his foot hovering over the edge of the raft, he commanded, "Lead us to safety."

With the path revealed, the ominous army resumed its advance. Trolls grunted as they pushed the rolling carts deeper into the valley, the ground trembling beneath their weight.

31st Chapter

The sky turned ominously dark, signaling the approach of a malevolent force creeping into the valley. As Tomar moved through the trees, their leaves hung low in sorrow. Flowers drooped, and the grass adopted a gloomy tint. The white army was shrouded in an unsettling quiet, interrupted only by the growls of lurking beasts and the groans of war machines; even the birds had fallen silent, abandoning their joyful melodies.

Hidden within the underbrush, the archers crouched in readiness, forming the frontline defense. The elves readied their arrows, their bows taut and primed for the impending conflict.

"Fire!" Lagar commanded, his voice slicing through the stillness. He released his grip, and a storm of deadly arrows shot toward the enemy. With a quick flick of his left hand, Tomar altered their trajectory to the east. His gaze swept the valley, searching—probing—for the Sorceress of Light.

But she remained hidden, cloaked in brilliance and shadow, slipping past his reach with practiced ease.

I can't find her. My ultimate victory depends on defeating the white sorceress, he thought with a sinister laugh.

● ● ●

Zilar's expression darkened with worry.

"Why aren't they using their catapults, Rubric?"

Rubric narrowed his eyes at the distant attackers and replied, "I believe Tomar designed those weapons just to instill fear in us."

Beyond the tree line, the Tonepass Army braced for the impending clash. Towering trolls, fierce gilzdars, hulking trolgilzs, and grotesque mutant rats formed a wall of muscle and menace. Just past the forest's edge, hidden traps lay in wait—an essential second line of defense.

Moments later, the air resonated with desperate screams as the traps activated. Spikes, snares, and pits claimed their victims in brutal succession. The defenders, watching from their positions, recognized the shift: the upper hand was now theirs.

The elves fashioned a sturdy ladder, enabling their allies to climb and leap onto the backs of the half-breeds. With swift and accurate strikes, their swords found the monsters' skulls, swiftly ending their reign of terror.

"I can spot the third line of defense for the Tonepass fighters," one elf noted, scanning the distant landscape with practiced eyes.

Above the chaos, the dragons and their riders moved unseen, the storm clouds cloaking their forms in shifting shadow. As they glided over the battlefield, Ari and Sirine unleashed a barrage of arrows and explosives, raining destruction upon the advancing foes. Explosions lit the valley in bursts of fire and smoke. For a fleeting moment, the riders thought they had struck a decisive blow—until the dark army pressed on through the fire, their ranks unbroken.

Deep within the valley, mutated rats clawed and tore at soldiers in close combat; the sickening sound of metal tearing through flesh echoed across the battlefield, a grim symphony of chaos.

Meanwhile, Easha crouched in silence, hidden beneath a veil of enchantment, while Tomar prowled the area like a predator. The sorcerer's fireballs illuminated the ground close to the cottage, creating flickering shadows that danced in the dim light of evil.

Above the fray, Suhzar soared once more, wings straining against the smoke-choked sky. Determined to draw Tomar's attention, the dragon roared defiantly.

Tomar's eyes narrowed—he calculated the beast's altitude and velocity, then hurled another fireball. It struck Suhzar's wing with a deafening crack, sending the dragon into a spiraling descent.

Sirine was thrown from the saddle, her scream lost in the roar of battle. But Suhzar's talon snatched her mid-fall. She clung to him, heart pounding, knowing that staying in his grip during the descent would mean certain death.

"No!" Rubric yelled, his voice raw with panic as he watched them plummet. His heart ached with the helplessness of being unable to save her.

With determination, Sirine sprang into action, grasping his tail and climbing until she reached his back.

"Get ready to jump as we approach the ground; I can't control my landing," Suhzar growled.

As they vanished behind the towering peaks of the Tonepass Mountains, Rubric's eyes remained fixed on them, unwilling to look away.

Suhzar is in pain, Gular, Ari thought. *It fills me with sorrow. I wish we could help, but our battle must take precedence.* Ari trembled, her fist clenched tightly. "I see four elves heading toward the dark sorceress," she observed. "Suhzar's fall has caught her attention."

Mirra disembarked from the raft behind Tomar, her eyes scanning the heavens.

"Stay strong, Ari," Gular urged, his voice steady despite the chaos. "We'll divert their attention to us." With a great surge of wings, Gular carried Ari upward. The blasts erupted around the malevolent army, scattering soldiers and forcing Tomar to recoil in bewilderment. As he searched the skies for the source of devastation, another blue-and-white dragon emerged, cutting through the clouds with a piercing roar.

"There were two dragons," Tomar spat, stunned. "Get the weapons ready! Bring down the dragon just like you did the last one!" He raised his left arm high, signaling the barrage.

Derail watched as the elves approached Mirra. He let out a sharp cry of warning—a raw, aching sound that echoed across the battlefield. His obsidian feathers bristled with dread as he watched the elves close in on Mirra. He flapped his wings against the invisible bindings of Tomar's spell, desperate to intervene, but the magic held firm. Powerless, he could only bear witness. Mirra remained unaware of the chaos surrounding her.

The elves approached Mirra with silent precision, and in a swift, merciless act, Lagar slit her throat before decapitating her. The act was brutal, final.

Derail let out a mournful caw, his voice cracking with grief. He bowed his head, his beak trembling as he tucked it beneath his wing. The world blurred around him, the chaos of war reduced to a single, unbearable truth: she was gone.

He remembered the way she used to feed him bits of dried fruit, how she whispered secrets to him when no one else was listening. She had trusted him—not just as a messenger, but as a companion. And now, her voice was silenced.

The raven's talons clenched the bark of the tree, his instincts screaming to take flight, to circle her fallen form, to scream until the skies wept. But Tomar's command still bound him, and duty warred with sorrow in his hollow bones. Above him, the clouds churned. Below, the battle raged. But in Derail's heart, a storm of mourning had already begun. The battle was far from over.

• • •

Suhzar's wings trembled as he fought to stay aloft, each beat slower than the last. The wind tore at his scales, and pain lanced through his fractured wing. Below, the ground spun in dizzying spirals. He was falling. Easha, hidden behind the cottage, caught sight of the injured dragon. She realized her allies would soon touch down near the Secret Sorcerer's Chamber. The brim of her hat shimmered with golden light. With a whispered incantation, she vanished from her hiding place and reappeared in the valley, her boots sinking into the soft moss. She raised her arms to the sky, the sunlight catching the golden embellishments of her sorceress hat like fire. Just as she observed the dragon plummeting, she summoned a radiant beam of light that wrapped around him like a silken tether. The warriors drifted downward, cradled by her magic, until they touched the ground with barely a sound.

"Suhzar, are you both alright?" she asked, her voice gentle but urgent.

"I'm fine, though I do have a few fractures in my wing," the dragon replied as he transformed into a zundar.

Easha guided the two warriors into the main chamber, her hands already glowing with healing energy. She examined the injury with practiced care. "Fortunately, the bones haven't pierced the skin," she murmured, wrapping the wing with soft, enchanted cloth. "I'll wrap your wing to aid in its recovery."

Sirine exhaled, her adrenaline still surging. "I've never experienced such an adrenaline rush," she said, her voice trembling with awe. "Suhzar, if it weren't for your quick thinking and maneuvers to slow us down, we would have crashed before Easha could reach us."

As Easha tended to Suhzar's injury, Sirine gently shifted the dragon's attention, keeping her calm. Once the sorceress finished wrapping the fractured wing, Sirine carefully lifted the zundar and perched him on her shoulder, her touch reverent and steady.

Suhzar's eyes gleamed with renewed resolve. "We are ready to return to the battlefield."

Sirine met his gaze and nodded. "Back to the battle," she echoed. They descended quietly behind her cottage, slipping into the shadows, concealed from any watchful eyes.

• • •

When Tomar saw Mirra fall, the world seemed to fracture around him. Time slowed. The battlefield noise dulled to a distant hum. Her lifeless body lay crumpled in the dirt, and for a moment, he forgot the war, the power, the vengeance—everything but her. A strangled sound escaped his throat, half-roar, half-sob. Rage surged through him, raw and volcanic, burning hotter than any fire he could conjure. His hands trembled, not from weakness, but from the unbearable weight of loss. He raised both arms and unleashed a torrent of flame toward the combatants, his magic fueled by grief. The blaze tore through the air, forcing defenders to raise their shields in desperate defense. The inferno was not strategic—it was personal. Above, Derail flapped his wings, trying to intervene. The raven's cry was mournful, echoing Tomar's anguish. Tomar signaled sharply, and Derail dipped his head, bound by loyalty and sorrow.

The Tonepass army appeared to be on the verge of defeat, with numerous soldiers already down. Yet, despite their exhaustion, the men held their positions with resolute determination.

In an instant, the dragon spirit emerged. As the apparition swept through the remaining trolls, it compelled the monstrous foes to kneel. The giants toppled as the Enwood captives launched their relentless attack.

Tomar's rage erupted like a volcano as he bellowed at the tumultuous sky, realizing that Pildar's men had betrayed him. The ground shook beneath him, cracked by the flashes of lightning, while ominous thunder rolled overhead. In a fit of fury, the dark sorcerer unleashed his vengeance on the traitors, effortlessly lifting them into the air. With a swift flick of his wrist, he sent them crashing into the towering trees of the forest, snuffing out their lives in an instant. But even their deaths gave him no satisfaction. Vengeance was too small a price. Tomar understood that to secure victory, he needed to eliminate Easha and capture the dragon ghost.

"It's time to face the specter," he murmured, his gaze sweeping the area until it settled on a small, hollow log. He pointed at it, reciting an incantation. It began to levitate, and with a flick of his left hand, he transformed it into a lidded urn. A swirling vortex appeared as he traced glowing circles above the vessel with his hand. "When the apparition approaches this storm, it will be trapped within this prison forever." However, as he scanned the skies, he found nothing. "Where has the ghost gone?" he growled. "It must have sensed my dark energy and fled. I cannot afford to waste time—my beasts are falling."

The wind howled louder, as if mocking him. He secured the raft at the heart of the first platform, his eyes burning with grief and fury. The storm was rising—and so was he.

• • •

Easha, concealed behind the cottage, held her breath shallow and steady as she watched Tomar become mesmerized by the turmoil unfolding around him. The wind howled, tugging at the edges of her cloak. She leaned closer to Sirine and Suhzar, murmuring, "Remain out of sight until I can seize Tomar." Together, the trio observed the battle from a distance.

The raft the sorcerer stood on swayed dangerously under the fierce winds, yet he stood unyielding, arms outstretched, feeding on the storm itself. His power was monstrous, the air around him warping and trembling with his wrath. Easha raised her hand, a lance of radiant light piercing the darkness. It caught the urn and tore it from his grasp.

Tomar's eyes widened, then narrowed. With a snarl, he hurled a torrent of shadow against her beam. The clash ripped the air apart, light and darkness colliding in thunderous waves. For a moment, it seemed his will might overwhelm hers.

But Easha did not yield. Planting her feet, she shouted a single word that rang like a blade across the sky:

"AMUCLO!"

A shimmering cloth of magic burst into being, spinning through the air and wrapping itself around the urn. Tomar bellowed in fury as the vortex turned against him. Shadows writhed from his body, clawing to escape, but the cloth constricted, sealing the vessel shut with a deafening crack of thunder.

The sorcerer's scream split the heavens as the storm began to collapse in on itself. His beasts shrieked in terror. The twisted rats dropped to the ground, reverting to their natural forms and scattering into the forest. The rest of his warped creations fell writhing, their confusion heavy in the air.

At last, silence fell. The storm was broken.

And yet, even bound, Tomar's presence lingered—his hatred coiled within the urn like a living flame. Easha tightened the magical cloth, ensuring the vessel was sealed. The dark energy pulsed faintly beneath her fingers, but the spell held.

The mutated rats scurried back into the forest's shadows. The other creatures lay defeated, their bewilderment hanging heavy in the air.

• • •

Easha rushed into the cottage, clutching Tomar's prison firmly. The dark energy radiating from the urn pulsed against her skin, nearly unbearable in its intensity.

I need to steady myself and focus on keeping Tomar contained, she thought, her throat dry, and her body quaking. Her breath came in rapid bursts, and her heart pounded as tension surged through her limbs. A tingling sensation flickered at her fingertips as she crossed the room. She paused at the threshold of the chamber that had once held the Sormara. Taking a deep breath, she stepped inside and whispered, "I can do this." Upon opening the crypt, she was met with the glimmering, enchanted white satin cloths that still shimmered with magic.

"I must dust the satins with more white powder. This will stop Tomar from reaching out to other dark sorcerers."

She turned and sprinted to the pantry, her eyes scanning the shelves in desperation until they landed on a jar filled with shimmering white powder. She quickly grabbed it and rushed back to the tomb, her focus unwavering as she bit her lower lip in determination.

The image of Sormara lying in the coffin felt like a haunting echo of the past. "I wish I had been able to defeat Tomar. He has returned as a spirit once more. How can I ensure he is permanently banished?"

After lifting the urn with care, Easha gently placed it inside the crypt. Taking the ancient stone, she sealed the tomb shut, her magic weaving through the cracks like molten silver. Two layers of satin she laid across it—one forwarding, one for concealment—then scattered tainted white stones along the seam. "For added protection, I'll place these three gold bars on top." With a flick of her wrist, the dark stones transformed into a brilliant white, and the gold bars settled firmly in place, locking the enchantment.

Easha stood tall, her voice cold and resolute. "Tomar, your time in eternal confinement has come." With a swift motion of her wrist, the prison disappeared, only to reappear on the pristine mantle above the fireplace. It glowed faintly like a star contained in stone. Slowly, Easha walked over to the north wall and carefully took down a portrait of her parents, cradling it tenderly. For a long moment, she simply held it, eyes glistening. Then she carried it to the hearth, where the urn now rested. "Mum and Pa, please keep watch over this for me."

Her lips brushed the portrait in a soft kiss before she set it gently in its new place beside the prison of Tomar.

• • •

Rubric mounted his horse and called out to his men, "I need to find Sirine." At that moment, he caught sight of the sorceress, along with Sirine and Suhzar, stepping out from behind the cottage.

Relief surged through him. He spurred forward, leapt from his saddle, and pulled her into a fierce embrace. "I was so worried about you!" he said, voice thick with emotion. "I feared you might be injured or worse. The thought of it made my heart ache. How did you get here?"

Sirine clung to him, her eyes glistening. "As Suhzar and I plummeted from the sky, he urged me to leap off his back before we reached the ground, or I would have no chance to survive. It was dire. At that moment, we saw Easha. She watched us fall and realized we were nearing the hidden chamber. She teleported herself just in time to catch us and halt our descent."

Rubric took her hands in his, searching her eyes as though to convince himself she was truly there. His chest heaved, his voice breaking. "I realize this may not be the perfect moment—gods know the field still reeks of smoke and sorrow—but I can't let this opportunity slip away. Today showed me how fragile life is. I almost lost you, and I will not wait for another dawn to tell you what my heart has long known."

He dropped to one knee, still holding her trembling hands. "Sirine, will you be my bride?"

For a heartbeat, silence hung between them, broken only by the wind stirring the ruined field. Then Sirine leapt into his embrace, joy shining through her tears. "Yes, my love. Yes!"

Their reunion brought a spark of hope, yet around them the valley lay in silence, thick with the weight of loss. Seven hundred elves, along with dwarves and men beyond counting, would not rise again.

The survivors gathered in mourning. Elves moved with reverent care, lifting their fallen onto horses—seven hundred noble warriors draped across saddles in a grim, silent procession. The air was thick with grief, yet laced with honor.

Lagar's voice rose above the hush, strained but unyielding. "We will bring our fallen heroes back to their families."

He stepped closer to where Easha stood, her heart suddenly heavy with emotion as Lagar wrapped his arms around her. The warmth of his embrace sent a shiver through her, and as he gently tilted her chin upward, their eyes locked in a moment that felt both fleeting and eternal. With a soft kiss on her cheek, he whispered words that resonated deeply within her, "Thank you. Without you, my lady, the shadow would have triumphed. I promise—we will meet again."

After this tender exchange, he retreated to join his comrades, who awaited him with solemn expressions.

The elves mounted their majestic steeds, their heads bowed in a silent tribute to the bond they shared and the journey that lay ahead. They prayed in low voices that the souls of their kin would pass swiftly into the Spirit World of Nobles.

"Farewell, my friends; I hope our paths cross again one day," Lagar whispered as he took hold of the reins.

The column of thirteen hundred elves wound its way toward the Kinnick Mountains, a river of grief flowing out of the valley. The others stood in silence, watching until the last flicker of armor was lost to distance.

The air grew dense with an oppressive weight, saturated with the bitter scent of profound sorrow. Each inhalation felt laborious, as the lingering odor of death clung to the atmosphere.

With heavy hearts, the dwarves and freedom fighters turned to their own dead. Together, they gathered the fallen, their hands shaking as strands of hair fell across faces bowed in grief.

Arrow's voice trembled as he spoke gently, "We honor the bravery of our friends. A piece of us has been taken with you. We will always hold dear the sacrifices you made for our cause. We recognize your journey to join your ancestors. You will be profoundly missed." Tears brimmed in his eyes as his words fell into the silence.

Then the survivors set about their grim task. The carcasses of the dark creatures were dragged to the ravine, hurled into the abyss, and ignited. Blue-black flames leapt high, twisting like shadows in their death throes.

When the fire dimmed, the silence returned. Ari clutched Rolyn's hand tightly. "I hope we never have to face those dark forces again, Rolyn."

"Indeed, my love, I yearn for peace as well, but we both know that the dark forces will eventually resurface," he replied, softly kissing her cheek.

In that fierce clash between light and darkness, two thousand courageous warriors and countless Enwood fighters had perished.

32nd Chapter

The epic clash between good and evil resulted in the loss of countless brave souls. As the first light of dawn filtered through the trees on that chilly morning, their branches began to sway gently, as if mourning in silence. To the north of Easha's home, a raven perched upon a withered branch. Derail's black feathers caught the morning light, but his eyes—dark, glistening with tears—betrayed the sorrow within. The weight of heartache pressed on him, heavy as stone, and the brightness of the day only deepened his misery.

Derail was filled with grief at the sight of Tomar trapped inside the urn he had created. His dear friend, Mirra, was lost to him forever. The weight of his family's misfortunes bore down on his soul.

"My heart is in pain," he whispered, his troubled eyes glistening as he sighed and lowered his head.

Consumed by grief, he stared at the ground in silence. In a fleeting moment of despair, the raven shifted his gaze toward the north.

"What am I supposed to do now? Here I am, alone once more."

The raven trembled, his eyes growing wide as he tucked his head under his left wing.

"Tomar has granted me the gift of eternal life! Even though he is confined, his spirit remains strong. I will search for the hidden essence of the sorcerer. I must liberate him from his bonds once again."

The raven shook himself, wings spreading wide, his sorrow twisting into resolve. "I cannot stay in this miserable green valley; it makes me feel unwell. I will return to Stragon Valley, where I can find peace and formulate a plan to rescue my dark master."

With a renewed sense of purpose, the raven's keen eyes glimmered as he embraced his new quest to free his master. He took to the skies heading north, but not before Easha spotted him from her kitchen window. As she completed her chores, she commented, "It's rare to see a raven around here. It must be one of Tomar's spies." With a nonchalant shrug, she yawned and headed to her bedroom, never imagining the peril that still winged its way toward the horizon.

• • •

In the aftermath of the intense clash between light and darkness, Tonepass Valley started to step out from the shadows, its terrain gradually mending from the wounds of battle. The previously barren fields, scarred by the traces of conflict, began to flourish once more as colorful wildflowers broke through the ground, their hues symbolizing resilience. The atmosphere, once heavy with anxiety and sorrow, slowly changed, now filled with the delightful aroma of fresh soil and the whisper of leaves as the trees regained their vitality. Streams that had flowed murky from the chaos now glimmered in the sunlight, their waters clear and inviting, mirroring the renewed hope that began to seep into the valley.

• • •

Easha stirred from her slumber as the soft light of dawn began to seep through the curtains, casting a warm glow across her room. With a contented sigh, she reached her arms skyward, feeling the gentle stretch awaken her muscles, before swinging her legs over the edge of the bed. "Time to get up," she murmured to herself, though her heart felt reluctant to leave the warmth of dreams.

After a brief moment of wiggling her toes to shake off the remnants of sleep, she slipped her feet into her cozy white-and-tan slippers. With a sense of quiet anticipation, she padded softly down the hallway toward the kitchen. "Which tea will I enjoy today?" she mused, envisioning the fragrant aromas and soothing warmth that would soon fill her cup.

She filled the teapot with water and placed it on the cast-iron stove. Closing her eyes, she reached into a wicker basket overflowing with aromatic dried tea pouches, choosing one to add to the pot.

Moments later, the teapot emitted a joyful whistle. Easha reached for a delicate white cup from the lower shelf near the window, the air around her now infused with the sweet aroma of wild berries as steam spiraled upward. Yet as she worked, her thoughts strayed. How often had she stood in this very kitchen and felt the silence press in around her? She told herself she had chosen solitude, that it was easier not to hope—but hope was stubborn. In quiet moments, she found herself remembering those who had fought beside her. Remembering him.

She recalled the way his eyes had sought hers in the chaos of battle, the way his voice steadied when others faltered. A thousand memories pressed against her heart—his hand brushing hers in the hidden chamber, laughter shared beneath starlight, the quiet strength of his presence. She had buried those thoughts, certain they would never again belong to her.

Pouring herself a hot cup, she stepped out of the cottage into the brisk morning air. The coolness revitalized her, and a smile spread across her face as she gazed at the small white clouds drifting lazily overhead. "The clouds are breathtaking, and their shapes enchant me," she reflected. Yet beneath her words, her heart whispered something else: *How I wish I did not have to face this dawn alone.*

Shifting her gaze to the south, she admired the vibrant colors of the foliage. The sorceress inhaled deeply, savoring the rich scent of oak and blossoms, and declared, "I can feel the mighty oak trees standing sentinel over my home." Narrowing her eyes slightly, she murmured, "Someone is emerging from the forest. I can't quite see who it is." Easha concentrated intently, trying to identify the figure appearing from the southern tree line. She bit her cherry-red bottom lip, her brow furrowing in focus as the morning breeze playfully swept her hair aside.

For a heartbeat, time seemed to hold its breath. Her eyes lifted, locking with his across the distance. Recognition flared—swift, undeniable. The tall elf, standing at an impressive five feet eleven inches, darted forward with a sense of urgency, his lithe form gliding effortlessly over the forest floor. The air crackled with anticipation, and the elf's sharp, brown eyes were fixed intently on her, conveying a mix of determination and concern. Each step he took was purposeful, the soft crunch of twigs underfoot barely audible amidst the rustling leaves.

As he drew near, Easha instinctively smoothed the fabric of her robe, a gesture that felt both familiar and comforting. In that moment, a torrent of memories flooded her mind, each one a vivid snapshot of their shared journey through trials and tribulations. She recalled the countless nights spent strategizing under the stars, their laughter mingling with the whispers of the wind, and the fierce determination that had forged an unbreakable bond between them. Together, they had faced the shadows that threatened to engulf their world, their hearts intertwined in a dance of courage and resilience. Each challenge they overcame only deepened their connection, a testament to the strength they found in one another amidst the chaos.

At that moment, Lagar found himself standing before the sorceress on the porch.

"Good morning! I trust all is well?" Her eyes shimmered like the morning sun. "Did Rubric and his friends make it safely to the Middrom Mountains?"

He joined her on the porch, his expression easing.

"Everyone is in high spirits and gearing up for a grand wedding. It's set to take place in thirty moons. I've come to extend an invitation to their splendid celebration. Suhzar expressed interest in coming here, but I need to discuss something with you first."

"It's wonderful to have you here. Please, step inside. Would you like a cup of tea?" She lifted her cup with a warm smile.

"Absolutely, a cup of tea sounds wonderful," Lagar replied, holding the door open for her.

Easha's eyes lit up as she glanced back at him. She stepped into the room, and the elf followed her to a table positioned in the heart of the main area. Then, she quickly made her way to the kitchen.

Moments later, the whistle of a kettle filled the air, followed by the soft clinking of porcelain.

She returned, balancing two immaculate white cups. Steam curled upward in delicate spirals, drifting like mist across the room.

"I've prepared a unique tea blend just for you," she said, setting a cup before him. "I hope it pleases you. So, what brings you here today?"

Lagar rose from his seat and motioned her to take a place next to him. When she did, he searched her eyes, gathering his thoughts.

"I'm deeply intrigued by the art of potion-making," he admitted. "Knowing you are both a sorceress and a mage, I believe that mastering this skill could be crucial in future battles. The loss of so many lives weighs heavily on my heart. If I had been able to brew a healing potion, maybe I could have saved many of them."

Easha leaned her shoulder against his. The warmth they felt in their hearts served as a reminder of the past. The sorceress spoke softly, "You shouldn't blame yourself. We fought valiantly against the overwhelming dark army. It's important for us to focus on the future, one that I believe will be bright.

Her eyes softened as she added, "I haven't eaten yet, and I can imagine you must be quite hungry after such a long journey. Would you care for a bite to eat?"

Lagar smiled faintly, the weight in his chest easing. "Absolutely, a little something to eat would be wonderful."

"Make yourself comfortable," Easha rose up, straightening her robe before she made her way to the kitchen.

Lagar's eyes lingered on her graceful departure, a quiet warmth sparking in his chest.

Easha came back from the kitchen, carefully balancing a tray laden with honey oaks, wild fruits, and freshly squeezed apple juice. As she gently placed the food on the table, her gaze fell on the tome resting nearby. Her steps faltered; her face shifted to one of astonishment.

"Where did you come across this book on potions?" Her blue eyes glimmered with curiosity, and her sun-kissed face lit up with a radiant smile.

Lagar reached for it, fingers brushing the worn cover. "I was left at the gates of Kendar with this book in hand by my family, whom I have never known. My pa was an elf, though his features are merely a haze in my memory. I suspect my mum was a mage, as suggested by the contents of this tome. Long ago, a hundred warriors, including my parents, embarked on a quest, but they never returned. The power within me is unmistakable. I realize that my destiny does not align with the elves. Kendar urged me to seek my own path in the world. You are the only person I know who truly grasps the art of remedies." His voice was steady, but his eyes betrayed the vulnerability beneath. Lagar moved closer to her, extending the book with one hand while the other rested at his side.

She gently stroked the cover of the book with her right hand. "I can hardly believe there's a book dedicated to potions! What an incredible discovery!" She breathed the words as though afraid to break the moment. Then her lips curved into a smile, radiant and eager.

"I'm so excited, but my knowledge is limited. We need to delve deeper into potion-making. To truly master this craft, we must commit ourselves to our studies. After breakfast, let's explore the book together." Her eyes sparkled with excitement.

Their gazes lingered on one another, an unspoken understanding passing between them. Then, in companionable silence, they shared a simple meal of oats and berries. When Easha finished the berries, and she wiped her hands clean, Lagar rose and offered her his hand.

She accepted, rising gracefully, only for him to lean closer. Gently, he pressed a kiss to her cheek. His voice was low but sure. "Easha, we've stood together in battle for so long, and I've kept my feelings buried deep. I've longed to tell you that I've fallen for you since that day in the hidden chamber when our hands brushed. I've never felt this way about anyone else, but it was not the time to tell you. Easha, you are my destiny."

Her lips parted, a soft breath escaping her as her eyes glistened. For a moment, she simply looked at him, her heart racing as though it had been waiting for these words all along. "Lagar, I felt the same way. I had imagined a life alone after we parted from the last battle."

"Sorceress, I have never forgotten you. You were always on my mind. Kendar knew, here with you was where I belonged."

His hand rested gently on her shoulder, grounding her. His eyes, so earnest, held hers as though they could bridge every lost year and added, "It's astonishing to think that a book of potions has reunited us."

She smiled, radiant and unguarded. "I am thankful for that. I have an extra room where you can stay."

"Your generosity means so much to me, and I gratefully accept," he replied, taking her hand gently in his.

Easha's joy was palpable, her cheeks tinged with color as she confessed, "Lagar, I never anticipated encountering such generosity. I had resigned myself to a life of solitude, convinced that companionship was beyond my reach. I am truly thankful to have been proven wrong," she said, her smile illuminating her face. With a sparkle in her eyes, she continued, "After I tend to my garden and show you your room, then we can embark on our studies together."

She gestured for him to follow. "Let me take you to your room. Once you're settled, you're welcome to explore at your leisure."

Lagar trailed behind her into a concealed chamber.

As she opened the door, a warm aroma of rich oak filled the air. A magnificent oak bed with four robust posts rested against the west wall, its mattress dressed in a soft cream coverlet. Next to the bed, a nightstand held a white basin and pitcher, while a tall, wooden-framed mirror towered over the bureau.

The elf was drawn to the beautiful chandelier that elegantly adorned the center of the room. Lagar set down his belongings, though his thoughts were not on the room but on the woman who had welcomed him so openly. He soon returned to her side, his steps quick with quiet eagerness.

Together they stepped into the garden. Blossoms swayed in the morning breeze, the colors vibrant against the scars of war. Easha's heart lifted at the sight, and Lagar's gaze lingered on her, enchanted by the way her joy seemed to breathe life back into the land.

Easha stood beside the elf at the edge of her expansive garden.

"The war has really affected the plants," she said softly, brushing her fingertips along a wilted leaf. "However, I have faith that with time, rain, and sunlight, they will recover."

Jasper, her raccoon companion, scampered up eagerly. She laughed, lifting him to her shoulder, her hair falling across her cheek in a playful cascade.

"How are you on this beautiful morning, my dear friend?" she murmured, stroking his back.

Lagar watched, his heart tightening with affection for her. There was something in the way she moved—strength and gentleness intertwined—that made him certain she was unlike anyone he had ever known. "Lagar, this is Jasper, my friend. He's a miniature raccoon," she said, turning to him with a smile that nearly stole his breath.

Lagar inclined his head respectfully. "It's a pleasure to meet you, Jasper." He extended his hand, and the tiny creature leaned into his touch.

Easha strolled to the northern edge of the colorful garden, where she paused and settled down among the blossoms. Jasper leaped off her shoulder and scampered toward a ripe beet he planned to take home.

"My dear friend, I'm beginning to think you have a genuine love for those delicious beets. Next year, I plan to grow even more beets and maybe even an apricot tree. I'm certain you'll adore the sweetness of an apricot," she teased, as she pulled the vibrant purple beet from the soil.

Jasper nuzzled her hand, expressing his gratitude for her generosity. With the beet firmly in his mouth, the little raccoon hurried off, excited to savor his breakfast at home.

"I find that utterly delightful. I've never encountered a raccoon so trusting before. He must feel the warmth you exude," the elf remarked, his admiration evident.

Easha glanced at him, her smile touched with fondness. "I rescued Jasper from a hawk that had snatched his mum when he was merely a week old. Since that time, he has created his own family. Years ago, Jasper introduced me to them. They must be all grown up now, probably with families of their own."

For a moment, her voice trailed, and silence stretched between them. Then she rose, dusting her robe, and moved closer. The fabric shifted elegantly with her steps, catching Lagar's eye. "Lagar, are you prepared to embark on our journey into the future?"

His reply came with quiet conviction. "Yes, my lady, I am excited to delve into the craft of potion-making."

As they strolled side by side toward the cottage, they took a moment to appreciate the songbirds dancing around them.

"They appear to sing in perfect harmony with the nearby creatures," she observed.

"You're absolutely right; I hadn't noticed that before," he replied, marveling at how he hadn't noticed until she pointed it out.

At the threshold, he held the door open for her. Together, they entered and approached the table where the ancient tome rested. When she turned to him, their eyes caught—brief but intense. A smile passed between them, unspoken words shimmering like sunlight through leaves.

33rd Chapter

A wave of happiness washed over her, banishing the solitude that had once weighed her down.

They exchanged cheerful smiles and nodded enthusiastically as they began to explore the pages of the potion book.

"Easha," Lagar said softly, "I long to kiss you. This feeling has been with me since our first encounter."

"You have my consent," she replied, her voice barely above a whisper. "I've never shared a kiss with anyone before."

Lagar softly raised her chin, his gaze fixed on her captivating blue eyes, and placed a gentle kiss on her lips. As their eyes met again, she responded, deepening the kiss, their connection blooming like magic between them.

The elf leaned in closer, his voice a warm murmur, "You fill my heart with warmth, my lady. Are you ready to concoct the transportation potion?"

Easha nodded and shifted her focus to the oak desk positioned to the south of the entrance and asked him to stay seated. Opening the top drawer brimming with writing supplies, Easha pulled out five sheets of parchment, a quill, and a jar of ink before returning to the table with graceful purpose.

"We should compile a list of the ingredients we need for the potion we plan to brew. Would you like to write them down, or read what we need?" The sorceress asked as she placed the materials next to the book.

"Easha, I think it would be best if you took charge of the writing. I'll communicate in your language to guarantee that every detail is accurate." The elf gave her a cheeky wink and a warm smile.

The sorceress dipped her quill into the ink, the tip gliding smoothly across the parchment.

Lagar inhaled deeply, then began.

"We need pollen from a single white daisy, an inch of red tree bark, a feather from a white eagle, ten strands of hair from a white rabbit, six drops of sorcery's blood, and five drops of hummingbird saliva."

He paused, thoughtful. "This potion is intended for just one person. Easha, should we think about increasing the potion's volume? That way, we could have enough to transport both of us to our destination and back."

Easha's expression grew serious. "The potion must be crafted precisely according to the instructions. It's well-known that creating a flawless potion on the first try is quite uncommon. Lundar is set to visit me at dawn tomorrow, and he will be able to check if any daisies are still blooming. I trust he will gather the rabbit fur and a feather from a white eagle. While we wait for him, we can start building the small water house. We will collect the hummingbird saliva after they drink from the water. I will contribute six drops of my own blood."

A hush settled between them, the weight of her words pressing down. At last, Easha rose from her chair, gathering the empty cups from the table as though the small task might steady her thoughts. The kitchen was cool and quiet, the scent of herbs lingering in the air. She opened a wooden drawer beside the sink, her hand hesitating for a heartbeat before closing firmly around the handle of a sharp knife. Returning to the table, she set it down in front of Lagar, her eyes searching his.

"Do you know when to add the blood to the potion, Lagar?"

"Let me take a look." His finger traced the text until he found the section about the blood. He read aloud, "First, mix in the white daisy pollen, red tree bark, white rabbit hairs, and five drops of hummingbird saliva. Snip the tip of the feather into a small piece, then add five drops of sorcery blood. Stir everything well with the feather quill. The potion will require three days to mature." He added, "Just a word of caution: test the potion on an object first, not on yourself."

The two of them bent over the book for a long while, the quiet broken only by the scratch of Easha's quill and the rustle of parchment. The afternoon slipped away unnoticed, shadows lengthening across the cottage floor. By the time Lagar closed the book with a satisfied nod, the light outside had dimmed to a burnished gold. Easha turned her gaze to the window, observing the sun as it sank behind the West Atron Mountains.

"It's astonishing how quickly this day has flown by. Would you care to join me for a meal before we conclude?" The sorceress lightly brushed her fingers over the book's cover.

"I'm not really hungry, thanks. I've been snacking on fruit all day," Lagar replied with a grin.

She chuckled. "I agree; the quantity we devoured during our study session is quite remarkable. Lagar, please make sure your book is safely put away. After we finish the birdhouse, we can delve into the other remedies tomorrow."

Her voice softened as she closed the book with care. "Have a peaceful night, and I'll see you at dawn."

"Same to you, Easha; I'm looking forward to our meeting tomorrow." The elf stood up, tucked the book under his arm, and made his way to his own room. The cottage soon fell into silence, broken only by the crackle of the hearth and the soft rustle of night birds outside. Sleep came quickly, carrying them both into the promise of a new dawn.

• • •

As the initial light of dawn illuminated the Kinnick Mountains, a cool breeze whispered through the northern trees of the Valley of Tonepass.

The sorceress and the elf stirred awake at the same moment and met in the kitchen.

"It looks like we're in perfect harmony, Lagar," she said with a smile, tossing her hair back. After filling the teapot, she placed it on the burner.

"Today, I'll make you a traditional elf brunch, my lady."

"I would love to lend a hand—once I've fed the birds."

"No, this meal is my way of expressing gratitude for your kindness," he replied, grinning as he set his knapsack on the counter.

"That sounds absolutely delightful," the sorceress exclaimed, her eyes sparkling. "I can't recall the last time I experienced something new."

The sharp whistle of the teapot cut through their conversation. After taking it off the heat, Easha opened the cabinet and retrieved two white cups from the lower shelf. The upper rack held a tidy stack of white plates and bowls. She carried the teacups to the kitchen counter by the window, pouring the tea while savoring the beauty of a new day unfolding.

"This tea is for the chef. I'll take mine outside to welcome the dawn. The sunrise never fails to captivate me." After placing Lagar's teacup by the sink, she stepped out of the cottage.

Easha paused to appreciate the crisp morning air as she surveyed her surroundings. Before settling into her pa's old rocking chair, she took a moment to soak in the valley's splendor. Memories of her time spent with her pa came rushing back, recalling the wildlife playing amidst the lush greenery, laughter echoing through the trees. As the sun began to rise, the sorceress marveled at the changing hues of the sky. Colorful butterflies flitted around her, and a wave of nostalgia enveloped her as she thought of Suhzar, her childhood friend. "I know he's safe. I trust that Suhzar and Sirine are out there searching for any signs of darkness," she mused.

Easha cherished the memories of her closest friend. A warm smile lit up her face as she reminisced about their enduring connection, which had withstood the test of time. She felt reassured knowing that zundars shared a lifespan similar to that of elves and herself.

"I'm truly thrilled at the prospect of seeing Suhzar again. I really miss his presence," Easha said, her gaze drifting toward the western foothills as she savored her tea. "I'll finally get to see him when we head to the Middrom Mountains for the wedding celebrations." She gently swayed the chair with her feet, letting the morning settle around her.

• • •

Lagar pulled five items from his knapsack and arranged them meticulously on the work surface. Among them were two jars filled with a distinctive preserve blend. He then laid a tan cotton cloth over the table, unveiling a set of specialized utensils. With swift, practiced motions, Lagar combined the ingredients, creating a smooth, cream-colored pastry.

The elf searched through the kitchen cabinets, eager to find his baking tools. At last, he discovered them hidden away in the third section of the bottom drawer. "Found them!" he called out, triumphantly pulling out two long pans from the stove and placing them next to his special creation on the table.

He sliced the dough into four-inch squares, carefully laying the soft, floury mixture into the pan. With a delicate touch, he pressed his fingers into the center of each square to form a small well, folding the corners upward. Into each hollow, he then added a spoonful of the rich sauce before placing the second pan on top.

"That should do the trick," he said confidently, trusting it would ensure even heat distribution.

After lifting the tartlet tray from the counter, he gingerly transferred it to the oven. He then tidied up the table, sweeping away the remnants of his baking with quiet precision.

Lagar took a moment to inspect the table, making sure everything was in place. He stood up to grab his tea and headed to the door to join the sorceress.

"Are we ready for a meal?" Easha asked, her voice light.

"Not quite yet," Lagar replied, sipping his tea. "But the tarts will be done as soon as I finish my tea."

Their conversation drifted easily, like the morning breeze.

"This valley is absolutely breathtaking," the elf commented, his eyes scanning the horizon.

"I couldn't agree more," she said, her gaze following his. "I feel incredibly fortunate to have grown up here. At both sunrise and sunset, I've seen deer and antelope grazing peacefully at the base of the mountains. A grizzly bear often emerges from the woods to drink from the stream. I look forward to the arrival of the Malar ducks and Crown geese as they soar over the valley. In sixty moons, they will begin their journey south. To your right, you'll see the sunflowers that my pa and I planted together. The seeds I scatter for the birds disappear almost instantly. When the young sparrows take their first flights, their parents bring them to me for feeding. Have you ever tried a sunflower seed?"

"I can't recall ever trying them, so my answer is no."

"I would love for you to come with me." Easha rose and made her way toward the vast field filled with golden flowers. Lagar hesitated briefly before following her to the sunflower patch situated to the north of her garden.

"These are dried seeds." She explained, brushing her fingers gently over the flower heads. "They're ready to eat." A few seeds tumbled into her palm, which she gently cradled with her other hand. "You have to crack the shell to get to the edible part. I've heard some people munch on the shell too, but I prefer to bite through it and savor the nut inside."

The elf listened as he trailed behind the sorceress, intrigued.

He tasted one and nodded. "It's delicious, but it's not quite enough. For a proper snack, I'd need a larger portion. Let's head back inside now." Lagar smiled as he took Easha's hand, worried that his pastries might burn. Together, they walked back to the cottage, hand in hand, the warmth between them as steady as the rising sun.

Back inside, the cottage felt warmer than when they had left it, filled now with the comforting aromas of baked bread and roasted seeds. The faint hiss of the oven reached their ears, a quiet reminder that Lagar's pastries were still baking. He squeezed Easha's hand lightly before releasing it, moving with brisk efficiency toward the kitchen.

"Easha," Lagar said, glancing at her with appreciation as he passed the threshold, "have I told you how wonderful your tea blend is?"

"Thank you," she replied, her smile soft and genuine. "I'm glad you liked it.

While Easha lingered near the doorway, listening to the scrape of chair legs and the rhythmic clink of cutlery being set in place.

When he finally emerged, he swung the door wide with a proud flourish.

The sorceress's eyes widened. In their short absence, Lagar had transformed the space. The table was already beautifully set—plates arranged with care, cutlery gleaming in the morning light, and a neat cloth laid down the center like a makeshift runner. He stepped aside with a little bow and pulled out a chair, gesturing for her to take a seat.

"I'll head to the kitchen with our cups and be back in a moment." The sorceress settled into her seat, listening to the gentle clatter of pots and pans from beyond the doorway. Her imagination stirred, curiosity blooming as she wondered what Lagar might be preparing. The aroma drifting in was unlike anything she'd encountered before—rich, savory, and subtly sweet. Her hunger awakened.

Shortly after, Lagar appeared from the kitchen, skillfully balancing two plates, and set one down in front of her with a proud smile. "This dish is called Canbara," he declared, clearly eager for her reaction.

Easha leaned in and marveled at the golden-brown crust that radiated warmth, while the colorful filling was a sight she had never seen in a meal before.

"You should try it," he encouraged.

She picked up the unfamiliar dish, examined it closely, took a bite, and relished the flavor. Her eyes widened with delight. "This is amazing! I've never tasted anything so perfectly balanced between sweet and salty."

She continued to savor the flavors, each bite more satisfying than the last. When she finally set her fork down, she showered the dish with praise, her compliments flowing freely.

As Lagar stood to clear the table, Easha raised a hand. "No, you prepared a fantastic meal. I'll handle the cleanup."

With a graceful sweep of her hand, the dishes vanished from the table in a shimmer of light.

"You never fail to impress me, my lady. Your talents are truly remarkable." Lagar said, shaking his head with admiration. They walked together into the kitchen, where the dishes had already been cleaned and neatly organized, the space as serene as the morning itself.

34th Chapter

The sky softened into pale gold as night gave way to morning, bathing the treetops in a gentle glow. A cool breeze stirred the leaves, carrying with it the scent of damp soil and blooming herbs. The elf and the sorceress stepped out of the cottage, their hands brushing as they walked side by side. Easha leaned into Lagar's shoulder for a moment, her touch light but familiar, and he responded with a smile that held more affection than words ever could.

"Lagar, what a beautiful morning! I can see storm clouds forming in the east. Do you think we might see some rain?"

"There's a possibility of rain later today," Lagar replied, studying the horizon. "I should start constructing a small birdhouse before the downpour."

"The entrance needs to be just small enough for hummingbirds to fit through." The sorceress noted, her voice thoughtful.

They wandered slowly past the garden fence, the scent of dew-kissed herbs rising around them.

"Easha, I'm confident I'll discover the ideal materials for the birdhouse and create precisely what you envision," Lagar assured her.

"While you gather the wood you require, I'll tend to my garden," she replied, her eyes lingering on his face.

They shared a quiet kiss, soft and unhurried, before parting ways, each drawn to their morning task, yet tethered by the warmth between them.

Lagar stepped into the stone building, carefully moving the firewood to his right. His eyes scanned the pile until he spotted two flat planks, each about six inches long.

"These will work perfectly," he announced, lifting them with care. He then walked over to a bench near the woodpile, setting one plank down beside him and flipping the other to begin his project. Drawing his sharp knife from his pocket, he began his work.

With practiced ease, he bored holes into each corner of the first plank, then repeated the process on the second. Finally, he carved a leaf-shaped opening in the center—just the right size for a hummingbird to pass through. The wood was smooth beneath his fingers, and as he worked, he imagined Easha's delight when she saw it finished. That thought alone made his hands move with even greater care.

His eyes landed on a long stick lying at his feet. Without hesitation, he swiftly chopped it into four pieces, each measuring three inches. Standing tall, he carried the segments to a nearby tree, where he inserted the cut branches into the hollowed-out sections and filled them with sticky sap. He then placed another log across the top as a roof, securing it with quiet precision.

"Once the sap sets, we'll hang it up for the hummingbirds," he said aloud, lifting the birdhouse and heading up the cottage stairs.

The sound of approaching footsteps reached his ears, and he recognized them instantly—Easha.

"Have you figured out how to make a waterhole for the hummingbirds?" she asked, taking a bite of daikon, her presence as effortless as the morning breeze.

Lagar approached, proudly showcasing the birdhouse he had just made.

Easha looked at it in wonder and exclaimed, "How did you finish that so quickly? It's amazing! How long will the drying process take?"

"The sap will solidify swiftly in the sun's warmth, becoming ready for attachment to a branch when the sun reaches its zenith," he explained, his voice tinged with quiet satisfaction. "While we wait for that moment, we can collect the other necessary materials. Where might we locate some red tree bark?"

"I know the perfect place," she replied, extending her hand toward him.

Lagar's mind buzzed with curiosity about her next move, but he chose to keep his questions to himself, trusting her magic as he always had.

With an authoritative tone, she commanded, "AMUCLO."

In an instant, a small fragment of vibrant crimson tree bark shimmered into existence in her palm.

"You're incredible!" His grin grew wider as he watched her enchanting performance. There was admiration in his voice, but also something deeper, an affection that had grown quietly between them, rooted like the trees around their cottage.

Just then, Easha's expression shifted. "Lundar has come. I can hear the sound of his wings."

Before Lagar could respond, the magnificent white eagle descended from the sky, its wings slicing through the air with regal grace. It landed beside Easha, bowing its head slightly in recognition.

With a sense of pride, he remarked, "I see you have a guest."

Easha nodded, her eyes gleaming. "Yes, Lagar and I are delving into potion-making. He's an aspiring mage, and we're learning the art of remedies together. Could you assist us in gathering the needed ingredients?"

"You know I would do anything for you, sorceress," the eagle replied, its voice deep and steady. "What do you require?"

"We need a white feather, some rabbit fur, and a white daisy."

The eagle tilted its head thoughtfully. "Easha, I know the perfect place where the daisies are still in full bloom. Earlier, I had a white-furred rabbit for lunch, and I plan to go back to gather its fur. This morning, while I was chasing the rabbit, I lost a white feather. I'll get what you need, provided the wind hasn't whisked it away. I must leave now, but I'll be back at dawn tomorrow." With that, the eagle spread its wings and soared into the sky, vanishing into the golden light.

As it soared away, the eagle drifted into contemplation about the potion they were brewing.

For a moment, silence settled over the cottage. The eagle's departure left behind a sense of purpose, and perhaps a touch of mystery. Lagar turned to Easha, his expression softening. He reached for her hand and gently guided her to the rocking chairs near the entrance. As they settled in, they watched the sun sink beneath the horizon, fluffy white clouds gathering over the mountains.

"Sorceress, have you ever realized that my most cherished tradition is dancing in the meadow as twilight descends? It brings me immense happiness. My lady, I dream of the day we can dance side by side."

Easha smiled, her fingers still entwined with his. He hesitated, then went on more quietly.

"I also feel a profound connection with animals; perhaps it's a blessing from my elf or mage lineage. I possess some influence over nature; for example, I can call forth floods. Do you know how much longer elves live than humans?"

His gaze lingered on her, tender but searching. "Now, I invite you to share something about yourself, as I've revealed my heart."

Easha's gaze drifted to the horizon, her voice soft with reflection. "There's not much to tell; my mum left this world when I was very young, and all I know is that she was a mage. Like you, Lagar, I share a special affinity with animals. I find joy in the beauty of sunrises and sunsets, mesmerized by the brilliant colors that splash across the sky. My spell casting is a work in progress, a path I'm exploring. I adore wandering through the countryside, discovering its hidden treasures."

Lagar studied her for a moment, sensing the vulnerability beneath her words. Then, with a playful smile, he leaned in. "I couldn't help but notice that you're not wearing your sorceress hat today. Is there a particular reason for that?"

Easha's expression brightened, the shift in tone lifting the mood. "Yes, my hat has a tendency to get blown away when I'm tending to the garden. I used to wear it all the time, but the wind seems to have a talent for whisking it off my head. Now, I only put it on for occasions that truly warrant it."

"What kind of occasions do you consider worthy of wearing it?" he asked, his tone light.

"I wear my hat whenever I make my way to the hidden chamber and back. My journey to uncover its mysteries is ongoing. One day, I will harness its magic and fully comprehend its purpose. The answers I seek are nestled within my white sorcery tome."

She paused, then tilted her head with a teasing smile. "By the way, I noticed you're not in your elf robe either. Is there a reason for that?"

"I've left my robe with Kendar while I figure out where I truly fit in—whether as a male mage or an elf."

With a playful smile, she responded, "I fully support your journey as a male mage."

Their conversation flowed effortlessly, laughter rising between them like sunlight through leaves. The morning unfolded gently, each moment shifted to the next with ease.

As the sorceress looked up, she spotted fluffy white clouds meandering slowly toward the west. Her eyes lit up with sudden realization.

"The bird house should be dry." Easha rushed into the cottage, a sense of urgency emanating from her as she burst into the kitchen.

She grabbed a glass from the cabinet, filled it with crisp spring water, and approached the elf. "Could you hold this for me?" she asked, passing the glass to Lagar before exiting and focusing on the birdhouse.

Lagar followed, careful not to spill a drop, his curiosity piqued. Easha approached the bench to the east of the cottage, where the wooden birdhouse rested. She lifted it with care and carried it to a nearby tree, placing it between two sturdy branches where she knew hummingbirds often gathered to feast.

Lagar watched her secure the house, the glass still in hand. As she stepped back to inspect her placement, he extended the water toward her. The sorceress poured the water into the nearest opening, taking a final glance inside to ensure it was filled with water.

They lingered for a moment, side by side, as hummingbirds began to flit in and out of the newly placed house. The warm afternoon breeze swept through the green valley, rustling the leaves and swaying the branches in a gentle rhythm.

Easha's gaze remained on the birds, but her thoughts shifted. "Before Lundar arrives, let's head inside and get a mixing bowl. We can prepare our potion in the den in case we have guests. No matter the outcome, it must stay a secret."

Lagar nodded and opened the door, letting her step through first. "I'm good with your plan."

"I need to check the pantry," she replied, moving into the kitchen and opening the door to her left, retrieving three satin cloths from the third shelf.

"Could you please hold these for me?" she requested, passing them to the elf before reaching for a cabinet above the sink.

"Lagar," she said, glancing over her shoulder, "which size bowl do we need?"

He considered for a moment, then answered, "A larger bowl is preferable to one that's too small."

She nodded, rising onto her toes to scan the shelf. "You're absolutely right."

"I'll get it for you," he said, extending his strong arms to lift a stack of bowls and set them on the counter.

Easha examined the bowl in her hands. "This is the largest one I have," she remarked, handing the reddish clay bowl to Lagar.

He accepted it and moved to the table, clearing the surface with quiet precision. Then, with deliberate grace, he arranged the satin cloths inside the bowl, layering them like sacred wrappings.

Together, they exited the kitchen and entered the den, where Easha balanced a smaller bowl in her arms. She placed both dishes on the table, aligning them with purpose.

Suddenly, her ears perked. "I can hear Lundar at the door," she called out, rushing to swing the door wide open for her friend. "What a joy to see you!" she exclaimed, welcoming the magnificent eagle.

The great eagle appeared at the threshold, talons gripping a hollow log. Inside lay two of his pristine feathers, a tuft of rabbit fur, and five daisies, their petals bright with living light

"I see you've brought the items I requested," she noted, her gaze softening as she took in the thoughtful arrangement.

"Thank you, Lundar. Your thoughtfulness means the world to me," she added, gently stroking the feathers on his back. "You truly are the best."

The eagle lifted his head, meeting her gaze with unwavering loyalty. "Easha, you know I would do anything for you."

"I am deeply thankful for your presence; you mean the world to me," she said, her eyes drifting over the colorful array of ingredients that Lundar had assembled. "The potion will be quick to whip up. Once it's ready, we can set off for a visit."

But Lundar's tone shifted, softer now. "Actually, Efura is waiting for me by the stream. I'm not really in the mood for magic or potions right now. I should go."

Easha's heart tugged at his words. A small sadness stirred within her—his absence always left the cottage a little emptier—but her smile remained tender. She understood, and that understanding warmed her even as she watched him spread his wings. Easha watched as Lundar soared into the sky, disappearing from view. For a moment, the quiet pressed in, bittersweet and still. She then picked up the log and carried it through the doorway with renewed focus.

"Lagar, I'll be back shortly! I just need to grab the birdhouse!" she called out. Rushing to the tree, she peered inside to check if it still held water. Taking a deep breath, she reached up and lifted the birdhouse from its branch with careful hands.

As she turned back toward the cottage, she saw the elf holding the door wide open for her. "I must be careful not to spill any water," she explained. As she glided past him, a bright smile lit up her face, and she asked, "Are you ready for a new adventure?"

The elf nodded eagerly. "Absolutely, I'm all set," he replied as he gently closed the door behind them.

Inside the cozy and welcoming den, the sorceress and the elf moved in perfect harmony, their steps and gestures mirroring each other with ease. The room glowed with soft light, the air rich with anticipation.

Easha approached the table and delicately placed a white satin cloth over the smallest bowl. With a graceful motion, she poured the shimmering liquid from the birdhouse onto the fabric, her fingers gliding over it, guiding each drop with care.

They both watched intently until the last drop fell into the bowl.

With a flourish, the sorceress lifted the satin cloth, revealing the glistening contents beneath. "It seems we have gathered enough hummingbird saliva to fill three half-walnut shells."

"Easha, I've opened the book. Are you ready? I'll read the instructions and then hand you the ingredients for mixing," Lagar offered, already thumbing through the delicate pages.

"That sounds wonderful," she replied, her excitement palpable.

Taking a deep breath, Lagar recited the first line of the potion and handed her a delicate white daisy.

Easha's dark eyebrows arched in surprise as she accepted the flower, holding it over the bowl. With care, she extracted the pollen from its center, peering into the bowl. "Lagar, this flower doesn't have much pollen."

"The book doesn't specify the size of the flower needed. Next, we require the red tree bark," he replied, presenting her with a small piece. "This could be why potions are so tricky; they often demand a bit of trial and error."

Easha placed the inch-long piece of bark atop the pollen.

"Are you prepared for the hair?" he asked, already reaching for the pouch.

"Yes," she affirmed with a nod.

With a flick of his wrist, ten fine strands of white rabbit fur floated into the bowl. "You know, my lady, the instructions don't indicate the length of the hair. Do you think it's important?"

"I'm not certain, Lagar," she said thoughtfully, gently stirring the three ingredients with a feather quill. The mixture shimmered faintly, catching the light.

"Now we need five drops of hummingbird saliva. How will you measure that?" the elf inquired, leaning closer.

Easha reached for a satin cloth and draped it over the mixing bowl. "This enchanted cloth permits only a single drop of liquid to enter the mixture," she explained.

They watched intently as a single droplet of saliva slipped through the weave and plummeted into the bowl, followed by four more, until the bowl was filled with five shimmering drops.

"It's time for your blood, Easha," he said gently.

She retrieved a tiny blade, placed it alongside the bowl, and gently pricked her finger, letting six drops of crimson fall into the concoction. As she wrapped her finger, the elf skillfully mixed the ingredients, then trimmed the end of a white feather, allowing it to drift into the mixture. They stood mesmerized as the potion morphed into a radiant gold upon mingling with the other components.

Easha met his gaze. "Lagar, we ought to leave the potion in the den to age."

"I agree; it's the safest place," he replied.

After Easha draped a fresh satin cloth over the bowl, they exited the den. She adjusted her robe with her right hand as they walked. "Lagar, we must wait to open the tome until our potion is finished."

"Absolutely, it's time to go outside. Nightfall will come quickly, and we certainly don't want to overlook the sun's farewell." He flashed a mischievous smile. "I'll prepare some tea for us."

Easha mirrored his grin, her excitement radiating. "That's a wonderful suggestion; I'm ready to help."

She trailed behind him into the kitchen. The elf passed her the first tea bag he could find, his fingers brushing softly against her palm. A radiant smile blossomed on Easha's face as their gazes met. His tender touch sent delightful tingles racing through her delicate form.

"The tea kettle is whistling," she remarked, glancing at him. "Could you grab the cups? I left them on the counter."

"Certainly," he replied, retrieving the cups as she poured the steaming tea.

He opened the door and declared, "My lady, it's time for us to step outside."

Easha stepped into the twilight, her robe catching the last golden rays of the sun. The elf trailed behind her, his gaze lingering on the way her silhouette glowed against the fading light. She settled into the rocking chair, and he stood beside her, close enough to feel the warmth radiating from her presence. Together, they admired the stunning sunset, awash in brilliant hues of yellow, orange, and red.

Easha stretched, her fingers brushing against the armrest, and sighed. "Lagar, the potion will be ready by tomorrow. I want to rise early, so I think it's time to call it a night."

He turned to her, his expression tender. "That's a wonderful idea."

He offered his hand, and she accepted it without hesitation. Her fingers curled gently around his, lingering for a moment longer than necessary. He helped her to her feet, and for a heartbeat, they stood close—neither speaking, just sharing the quiet. Then, with a subtle smile, he opened the door once more.

"Thank you, Lagar," she said as she entered the cottage. She paused at the threshold of her bedroom, glancing back at him. "Sleep well; I'll see you in the morning."

His eyes met hers, soft and steady. "Wishing you a restful night as well."

As Easha disappeared into her bedroom, Lagar remained in the doorway for a moment, watching the stars begin to blink into view. The hush of night settled around the cottage, and a refreshing breeze drifted through the front window, carrying with it the scent of lavender and the promise of morning.

In their separate rooms, they lay beneath the same roof, hearts quietly attuned to one another. And though sleep soon claimed them, something unspoken lingered—gentle, golden, and growing.

. . .

As dawn broke, it cast a warm, golden light across the valley, illuminating everything in its path. The cottage glowed softly in the morning hush, its windows catching the first blush of day.

Easha and Lagar, both early risers, gathered in the kitchen, their movements quiet but purposeful.

"Do you think the potion is ready, Easha?" Lagar inquired.

"I'm confident it is," she replied with assurance.

They stepped into the den, side by side, and leaned over the bowl, scrutinizing the creamy white concoction within. A faint shimmer danced across its surface.

"Lagar, we should take this outside to test its effectiveness," Easha suggested, already turning toward the cottage.

Agreeing with a nod, the elf lifted the bowl and followed her out of the cottage.

They approached the nearest tree by the woodpile and set the reddish bowl down on the mossy ground.

"I see you've donned your sorceress hat today," the elf remarked, a playful glint in his eye.

"Indeed, perhaps it will bring me some good fortune," she replied with a smile—just then, a sudden gust of wind whisked the hat off her head.

Easha chuckled, her hair catching the sunlight as she bent to retrieve it. She placed the hat back on with a flourish, then reached into her robe pocket and pulled out a small wooden spoon. Scooping a bit of the potion, she spread it gently across a vibrant green leaf.

"Nothing seems to be happening," she noted, watching the leaf with a furrowed brow.

"Easha, I doubt the leaf is planning to move anywhere," Lagar teased, his grin widening.

They exchanged mischievous glances before erupting into laughter.

Suddenly, a small brown squirrel appeared from the eastern edge of the forest. It sniffed the white mixture on the leaf, hesitated, then devoured it in a single eager bite.

"Lagar, you realize that the squirrel can vanish at will, don't you?"

"Absolutely, that makes perfect sense."

They kept their eyes glued to the squirrel, intrigued, standing close enough that their shoulders brushed.

At once, Easha gasped in disbelief as the front half of the squirrel appeared to dissolve into thin air, leaving only its hind legs scurrying away into the woods. Witnessing an animal escape with only part of its body visible was profoundly disturbing.

"What could have caused such a bizarre phenomenon?" Lagar asked.

"I'm not entirely certain," Easha replied, still staring at the spot where the squirrel had vanished. "It's possible that the tonic rendered it invisible, and that effect might fade soon. I've heard that the components for transportation and invisibility potions are quite alike, though the ratios are significantly different."

She turned to him, her eyes bright with curiosity. "I have no plans today, and I'm eager to explore how these two potions vary. It might shed light on where we went astray."

"I'm free as well, and we should pursue this if we want to improve our potion-making skills."

As they stepped back into the cottage, the morning light trailing behind them, Easha glanced at Lagar thoughtfully.

"Do you ever think about the dragon ghost?" she asked. "Our homes would have been engulfed in darkness without its assistance. Do you think we'll encounter it again?"

"Sometimes, yes," he replied, his tone quiet. "Its purpose remains unclear to me. I sense there's something unresolved that we don't understand. Why do you bring it up?"

"It's just been on my mind. If there's anything we could assist the spirit in finding peace, I would want to help."

Lagar paused, then reached for her hand. "And I would stand by you every step of the way." Lagar softly kissed her cheek before opening the book, wrapping his arm around the sorceress, and browsing through the potion titles. The pages whispered with age, each one a doorway to forgotten knowledge and untold possibility. Outside, the forest held its breath, as if listening. Inside, two potion-makers sat shoulder to shoulder—not just chasing answers, but ready to face whatever magic stirred beyond the veil.

Their fingers lingered on the page marked Healing Tonic, its ink faded but still legible. Easha and Lagar leaned in, their eyes scanning every symbol, every instruction. The recipe etched itself into their minds like a vow. They understood its importance—not just as a potion, but as a lifeline. One day, when darkness rose and lives hung in the balance, this tonic would be their shield. And so, with quiet determination, they began the work.

A month passed. Under the golden gaze of the midday sun, the healing potion was finally complete.

"Lagar, I cannot believe we have finished the potion," Easha whispered, eyes wide with hope. "We must try it to make sure it works. This is our fourth attempt, and I'm sure it's right this time."

"We will ride through the forest as we did before," Lagar replied, already gathering their gear. "I am sure we'll find a hurt or sick animal. If the tonic works, we can heal it on the spot—no need to bring it home and nurse it for days."

"Yes, my love." She took his hand, leaned forward, and kissed him tenderly. With the potion secured, Lagar opened the cottage door, and together they stepped into a calm, sunlit day.

Mounting their horses, the duo rode westward, the sun climbing higher and warming the ground beneath them. Soon, they spotted a lone fawn standing uncertainly in a clearing.

Easha's eye filled with sorrow for the young one. "Where's the mum? The baby is not old enough to be left alone," She asked, scanning the area and listening to any sound that would indicate the adult's location.

"Sorceress," Lagar said, pointing, "Leaves are moving just west of you. We must find out what's making the noise."

They followed the sound, weaving through the underbrush until a sharp bleat pierced the air. Rounding a dense thicket, they found her—the mum deer—lying in a shallow ravine, her leg twisted unnaturally.

"Sorceress, the deer must have fallen in the ravine and broken her leg," Lagar said, crouching beside Easha. "We can see if the potion works. If it does not work, I'll drape the mum over my horse, and you can take the infant."

Easha stepped forward slowly, her voice gentle. "We will not hurt you. We are here to help you." She uncorked the vial and rubbed the shimmering liquid onto the deer's injured leg.

Meanwhile, Lagar walked around the thicket and picked up the baby, carrying him to his mum. By the time he returned, the deer was up and walking around. The elf released the fawn, and the mum nuzzled her baby, and together they turned toward the woods. Before disappearing into the trees, the mum glanced back, her gaze lingering in silent gratitude.

"Well, sorceress—we did it. Our first potion is complete!" Lagar said, beaming. He swept her into his arms and spun her in a joyful circle, laughter spilling into the quiet woods.

For a moment, they simply held each other, letting the weight of their success settle in.

Easha rested her head against his chest, smiling. "It worked. We really did it."

Lagar kissed the top of her head. "We should head home. The forest has seen our triumph—it's time we return and prepare for what comes next."

They mounted their horses, hearts light and spirits high. As they rode home on the windless day, the tree's branches swayed gently, their leaves fluttering in quiet applause. Flowers along the path leaned toward them, as if bowing in reverence. The forest, ancient and wise, was celebrating their achievement with every rustle and whisper.

Side by side, Easha and Lagar rode in silence, the kind that speaks volumes. They knew what they created was not merely a potion; it was a beacon of hope. A testament to the alchemist's unwavering dedication to the art of healing, ready to restore vitality to those in need. It was more than a triumph; it was a promise.

Easha turned to Lagar, her eyes sparkling with excitement. "I can hardly believe our potion actually worked!"

"My dear lady," Lagar replied with a warm smile, "I have complete faith in your abilities. Our future shines brightly ahead of us. Now that we are home, it's time to unwind and conclude our day."

As they dismounted, Lagar wrapped Easha in a gentle embrace, guiding her through the doorway of their cozy cottage. The scent of lavender lingered in the air, mingling with the soft crackle of the hearth. They shared a tender goodnight kiss, arms entwined as they drifted into peaceful slumber.

Above them, the moon cast a silvery glow over the white-and-tan cottage, while the surrounding trees stood silent, embracing the happiness of the night. The forest, once a place of mystery and challenge, now stood as a quiet witness to their journey.

And so, with hearts full and spirits at peace, the sorceress and her companion slept—knowing that healing had begun, not just for the world, but for themselves.

The potion was only the beginning.

The real magic was in the love, the courage, and the quiet promise of tomorrow.